Born in the London borough of Islington, Victor Pemberton is a successful playwright and TV producer, as well as being the author of fourteen highly popular London sagas, all of which are published by Headline. His first novel, *Our Family*, was based on his successful trilogy of radio plays of the same name. Victor has worked with some of the great names in entertainment, including Benny Hill and Dodie Smith, had a longstanding correspondence with Stan Laurel, and scripted and produced many of the BBC's *Doctor Who* series. In recent years he has worked as a producer for Jim Henson and set up his own production company, Saffron, whose first TV documentary won an Emmy Award.

For more fascinating information about Victor Pemberton, don't miss the exciting additional material at the back of this book.

Also by Victor Pemberton

Our Family
Our Street
Our Rose
The Silent War
Nellie's War
My Sister Sarah
Goodnight Amy
Leo's Girl
A Perfect Stranger
Flying With the Angels
The Chandler's Daughter
We'll Sing at Dawn
The Other Side of the Track

A LONG WAY HOME

Victor Pemberton

headline

First published in 2007 by
HEADLINE PUBLISHING GROUP

First published in paperback in 2007 by
HEADLINE PUBLISHING GROUP

4

Cataloguing in Publication Data is available from the British Library

978 0 7553 3456 8

Typeset in Bembo by Palimpsest Book Production Limited,
Grangemouth, Stirlingshire

Printed and bound in Great Britain by
Mackays of Chatham plc, Chatham, Kent

Headline's policy is to use papers that are natural, renewable and recyclable
products and made from wood grown in sustainable forests. The
logging and manufacturing processes are expected to conform to the
environmental regulations of the country of origin.

HEADLINE PUBLISHING GROUP
An Hachette Livre UK Company
338 Euston Road
London NW1 3BH

www.headline.co.uk

For Helen and Geoff Warner,
with thanks for their friendship
and support

At the start of the Second World War, thousands of children were evacuated from London and other main cities across the British Isles. Most of them were welcomed in rural areas with great warmth and kindness. However, not all of them were so lucky.

There is good and bad in all of us.
Unfortunately, the bad part is often
the most difficult to cope with.

Chapter 1

Hannah Adams was convinced that everyone in the world had gone stark raving mad. At any rate, that's how it seemed to her whilst she and her young sister Louie were being shoved and jostled by the hordes of kids outside the primary school in a quiet Holloway back street in North London. As they climbed up the steps into one of the half-dozen coaches that was about to take them to St Pancras station, lumbered down with gas masks in cardboard boxes slung round their shoulders, and identity tags pinned to the lapels of their coats and dresses, the noise was almost unbearable; excited laughter and chatter, mixed with raucous sing-songs and general larking around, pierced the early morning air of a warm September day. And amongst it all, the miserable weeping and wailing of some of the younger kids who didn't want to leave their family nests for the strange unknown pastures of the English countryside. Engulfed all around by the clatter of youngsters who were aged right up to the top form of the school she had attended until just two years before, Hannah was already fed up and irritated with them all. From the first moment she had been told about the school's evacuation plans she just hadn't been able to see why it was necessary for everyone to panic just because some stupid old politicians had declared

1

war on Germany. To a sixteen-year-old Islington girl who had had to give up her first job in Elsie's hairdressing salon in Hornsey Road just to look after her young sister, war was nothing more than a word in a dictionary. After all, old Chamberlain, the Prime Minister, had declared war over two weeks ago now, and so far not one bomb had fallen on Holloway or anywhere else in London. In fact, in all that time she hadn't even seen a single German plane in the sky, so what the hell was everyone going on about? To Hannah, nothing seemed any different from what it had always been, except that food and a whole lot of other things were getting hard to find in the shops, and people kept talking about what would happen when the Germans invaded, as they had already done in other countries around Europe. So why, she kept asking her mum, was it necessary to include *her* with all these kids who were being evacuated as fast as possible away from the potential but highly unlikely bombing of London? After all, she, Hannah, wasn't a kid any more. In fact only that morning she had thought how well her breasts were forming, and how they would no doubt soon be noticed by every Tom, Dick, and Harry who set eyes on her. Not, however, that there were many Tom, Dick, or Harrys left now that they had all been dragged off to fight a war that most of them were too young to really understand. No, as far as she was concerned, the sooner this lousy war came to an end the better. Good riddance to 1939!

'Now look after yer sister,' said their mum, Babs Adams, who was tall and slender, in a tight-fitting floral dress, with permed rust-coloured hair which was piled up high in a great bunch on top of her head, and an unblemished complexion that many a woman her age would die for, a real good-looker for her forty-one years. 'Now remember, darlin', you're goin' ter 'ave ter take on *my* job now. From now on you're not only goin' ter 'ave ter be Louie's big sister, but 'er mum too.'

Hannah bristled; she had always hated being called 'darlin'. Although she had some of her mum's features, such as the same grey eyes, her own hair was more curly, hanging loosely just below her shoulders, and more red in colour, which was why a lot of her mates called her Ginger. 'But I *ain't* 'er mum!' she protested, struggling with Louie to peer down from the coach window. 'An' in any case, why can't *you* come wiv us, like a lot of the uvver mums?'

'Now don't let's go fru all that again, darlin',' replied Babs in her affected pseudo-posh accent. 'Yer know very well I 'ave ter keep the 'ome goin' 'til yer dad gets back.'

'Oh yes?' Hannah sneered dismissively. 'An' when's that s'pposed ter be?'

'When the war's over, darlin',' replied Babs, doing her best to show at least some kind of motherly concern, something which never seemed to come naturally to her. 'Don't worry. It won't be long now. Once we give ol' 'Itler a black eye, yer dad'll soon be 'ome an' we'll all be back tergevver again.'

'Bugger 'Itler!' snapped Hannah, not believing a word her mum had said. In fact she rarely believed *anything* her mum ever said. 'I 'ate 'im.'

'We all do, darlin',' replied Babs uncomfortably, quickly peering over her shoulder to make sure no one had overheard what Hannah had said. 'But do Mama a favour.' She lowered her voice. 'Please don't use words like that. It's so common.'

Louie suddenly started to sob. 'I don't want ter go!' she snivelled, tears streaming down her cheeks. Louie, whose real name was Louise, who some people said looked more like her dad,

3

was nine years old, with naturally curly dark hair and deep blue eyes. But because she was the youngest of the family, her dad had always tended to spoil her, which meant that she only had to grizzle to get what she wanted. 'I want ter stay 'ere wiv *you*, Mum. I ain't scared er no bombs. Please don't send me away!'

Distressed by the child's desperate pleas, Babs reached up for her hands and held on to them. 'Don't worry, Lou-Lou,' she called, her own face crumpling up. 'Mama will come an' see yer, I promise.'

Her mum's language at times sickened Hannah; to her it always seemed so childish. 'That's rich, that is!' she quipped acidly. ''Ow come yer can come an' see us if yer don't even know where we're goin' to? In fact *we* don't even know where we're goin' to!'

'You're goin' somewhere where yer'll boaf be kept safe,' said Babs, with confidence. 'Away from all the bombs when they come.'

'There ain't goin' ter be no bombs!' growled Hannah. 'This is all a waste er time, yer know it is! It said so in the paper only the uvver day.'

'We *hope* it is, Hannah,' said the soft-spoken woman just behind them. Dorothy Hobson was one of the senior teachers at the primary school, quite a large-framed woman, in her late thirties, with short-cropped hair, large grey eyes behind tortoiseshell spectacles, and a warm smile that had endeared her to so many children she had taught over the years. 'But your mother's right. It's best that we all take precautions, just in case.'

'Are *you* comin' wiv us too, Miss Hobson?' asked Louie tearfully.

'No, Louise, my dear,' replied the mild-spoken teacher, giving the child a reassuring smile. 'But some of the other teachers will be with you. If you have any problems they'll never be far away. You'll be in safe hands, I promise you.'

'We would be if *you* came too,' said Hannah, who had always had a strong affection for her former schoolteacher.

Miss Hobson reached up to the window, and took hold of Hannah's hand. 'Don't worry, my dear,' she replied. 'I have every confidence that you'll cope with everything perfectly well. And you can rest assured that I'll be with you in thought – every inch of the way.' She flashed them both a sweet smile. 'Have a safe journey, my dears.'

Hannah felt a huge surge of despair as she watched the school-teacher gradually merge back into the crowd of parents seeing their children off onto the fleet of coaches. All around it was such a frantic, distressing scene, with mums and dads hugging their kids as if it were the last time they would see them, for no one knew how long they would be away, and the kids them-selves gradually realising that, for the first time in their young lives, they were now on their own.

A few minutes later the air was punctured with the slamming of doors as the coach drivers prepared to move off. 'Come on now, boys and girls!' called Mr Jenkins, the headmaster. 'Everyone on board, please!'

The sudden rush of activity caused Louie to burst into tears. 'I don't want to go!' she yelled out loud, utterly distraught and sobbing profusely. 'Please, Mum, *please* don't make me go!'

Babs Adams, struggling to hold back her own tears, reached up and held the child's hand. 'You're goin' on a lovely train ride, Lou-Lou,' she sniffed, 'just like when we all went down ter the seaside at Soufend. D'yer remember?'

Louie could not be calmed; she cried even more.

With the coaches about to move off, Babs quickly babbled some last-minute instructions to Hannah. 'Don't forget I've packed yer fish paste sandwiches in yer 'aversack, an' there's a bottle of Tizer, an' wotever yer do, don't let any of those boys lark around wiv yer gas masks. Yer never know when you're goin' ter need 'em.'

Hannah looked down with complete indifference at her mum. She found it difficult to understand why she still loved her after what she was doing to her and Louie.

'An' don't ferget ter write, Hannah,' Babs demanded. 'I shall worry sick 'til I've 'eard from yer. You too, Lou-Lou. Mama's goin' ter miss yer boaf *so* much!'

The coach drivers started up their engines, and amongst a barrage of farewells, catcalls, whistles, and singing, the fleet of coaches slowly moved off one by one along Roden Street. Hannah stood forlornly at the coach window for a long time, watching the familiar back streets of her beloved Holloway gradually fade into the distance. She felt quite lost and desolate. Neither she nor Louie had ever been away for any length of time before, and they had certainly never been separated from their mum, who, in Hannah's eyes, just didn't really understand how she and Louie felt. As the coach turned the corner into Annette Road, many of the residents were at their front doors and upper bedroom windows waving frantically, calling out friendly words of encouragement to all the kids whose initial elation was gradually turning to bewilderment.

'See yer at Chrissmas, darlin's!'

That was the last Hannah heard from her mum, who had hurried alongside the moving coach for as far as she could before dropping back. For Hannah, they were hollow words, words which were quickly engulfed by a cool morning breeze and the fluttering wings of sparrows panicking to make a quick escape above the grimy chimney pots of those quiet back streets of Holloway.

From early morning, the platforms at St Pancras railway station in north central London had been invaded by a sea of children. The old station with its impressive red-brick Victorian gothic buildings was so overwhelmed with the yells and chatter of excited North London kids that the architect, George Gilbert, must have been turning in his grave. Although the schoolteachers and volunteers from the Ministry of Health were doing their best to maintain some kind of order, some of the young jokers amongst the hordes were doing their best to cause chaos and mayhem. However, a few stern words was enough to keep them in check, and eventually the queues of evacuees, some accompanied by their mums, were filing calmly onto the waiting trains. The incentive to keep discipline, of course, had been a free Milky Way bar each, handed out to every one of the kids as they boarded, a wartime treat beyond their wildest imagination. It was all hectic and unreal, something the station staff had never seen before, made even more incongruous by the background accompaniment of a jolly rendering of 'Oh We Do Like To Be Beside The Seaside' by a vocal group on a gramophone record piped through the station loudspeaker system. There were so many kids, mums, and evacuation officials crowding onto the platforms that it seemed as though every school in Islington was soon going to be empty.

Hannah was having a hard time trying to console young Louie, who had not stopped sobbing and whining ever since she took leave of their mum. Matters were made even worse when they had to share a stuffy compartment with ten other kids of varying ages, amongst whom was nine-year-old Alfie Grieves, a snotty-nosed little ruffian who was in the same class as Louie, and had the reputation of being a real pest to everyone, especially his female classmates. In fact, the train hadn't even left the station platform before Alfie had started his pranks, rolling up Milky Bar wrappers and engaging the other boys in the compartment in a frenzied battle, chucking everything they could lay their hands on at each other. By this time, Hannah was already fed up with it all, fed up that none of them had any idea where they were going or how long it would take to get there; it was like a game of blind man's buff. She flicked a quick look across at Louie who was sitting opposite her, in a window seat facing her own. Louie always seemed to have such a sulky expression, and the freckles on her face looked as though they had been painted on. The trouble was, and always had been, that, being the youngest, Louie had been spoilt by both her dad *and* her mum, so that anything she ever wanted she invariably got, and this was something that Hannah was clearly going to find hard to cope with.

From the back of the train, the guard's whistle suddenly pierced the frantic atmosphere, immediately prompting anxious shouts of *Take care! Don't forget ter write! Brush yer teeth every night!* and *'Ang on to yer gas mask!* Endless calls from parents and relations all along the platform, finally topped by one of the older teachers, a white-haired woman who looked genuinely upset to see the train gradually moving off. 'God speed!' she called out to all the tiny faces trying to squeeze a last glimpse out through their compartment windows. Hannah's only comfort was to close her eyes and pretend that none of this was happening, and that if she could only get to sleep, by the time she woke up she would be back home again in her own bedroom. But when she did wake up, she was not in her own bedroom. The train, nicknamed 'The Children's Express' by the platform staff at St Pancras station, was grunting along the rail track, a slow monotonous chugging sound of wheels making a supreme effort to quell the high spirits of the train's cargo of young passengers, gradually leaving the grime of London town behind, heading out through the northern suburbs of the city. Hannah was suddenly roused by the sound of Louie's niggling voice. 'Wake up, Hannah! Wake up!'

Hannah rubbed her eyes to find Louie tugging at her sleeve. 'What's up?' she asked, startled.

'Alfie Grieves!' Louie whispered in Hannah's ear.

'What about 'im?'

Louie's voice was haughty and indignant. ''E just asked me what's the colour of me knickers!'

Hannah sighed. 'Well tell 'im ter mind 'is own business!'

Louie immediately swung round at Alfie. 'Mind yer own business!' she bellowed.

Everyone looked round with a start. But Alfie just roared with laughter, tucked his feet up on the seat beneath him, closed his eyes, and pretended to go to sleep.

Hannah sighed despondently and tried to go back to sleep herself. But the moment she did so, Louie was tugging at her sleeve again. 'Hannah!' she whispered. 'It smells 'orrible in 'ere! The boys keep blowin' off.'

Irritated, Hannah got up and opened the window. A rush of air filled the compartment, and thick black engine smoke was curling back from the steam engine way up front. Louie briefly put her head out of the window, but the moment she did so she let out a piercing scream.

'Louie!' yelled Hannah, grabbing her sister's dress and yanking her back in. 'Wos up now?'

'Mickey Wilson!' spluttered Louie, wiping her face with the back of her hand. ''E's peein' out the window next door!'

Exasperated, Hannah quickly pulled up the window. With no corridor on the train, and nearly forty-five minutes of a non-stop train journey so far, several such incidents were inevitable, and it was a great relief to all the kids cooped up in the carriages when the train pulled into a small rural railway station. The moment it came to a stop, every compartment door was immediately flung open to allow a desperate flood of young bladders the chance to empty in the nearest lavatory and any available space their owners could find, much to the dismay of the two solitary railway staff on the platform.

By the time the Children's Express got on its way again, most of its passengers, both young and not so young, were feeling the effects of having to get up so early in the morning, and, much to Hannah's relief, were quite prepared to snooze for the rest of the journey. However, as most of the Milky Bars, sandwiches, lemonade and Tizer had long been devoured, the teachers and adults on the train knew only too well that it wouldn't be long before the pangs of young hunger would soon be crying out for something to eat. Not that Hannah cared much about food. She had spent the last half-hour of the journey gazing out of the compartment window, amazed at how quickly the old ramshackle buildings of London town had been replaced by what seemed to be an endless succession of wide open fields, streams, rivers, and small villages, and there were more trees and hedges than she had ever seen in her entire life. It was a strange feeling, a feeling that she was being disconnected from the rest of the world, the only world she had ever really known. And she couldn't help thinking about what she had left behind in that world, such as her friends back in Elsie's hairdressing salon in Hornsey Road. Then she thought about her old school mates, who had gradually drifted away into lives of their own, and her own Grandma and Granddad Adams, who had from the start been against the idea of evacuating Louie and herself. And then, of course, there was her mum. Babs Adams was really never cut out to have kids; she was too much of a loner, too tied up in all the things in life that interested *her*, not what interested her kids, not even Hannah's dad, Len Adams. Babs was a real good-looker, there was no doubt about that, but the only ones who would ever care about that would be men, so when she had a husband of her own, why did she always bother to put on so much make-up every day, and wear short skirts which, in Hannah's mind, were designed for only one purpose: to attract as much attention from men as possible. After all, Babs was only supposed to be a housewife; she didn't even go out to work. And yet, despite all Babs's failings, Hannah *did* love her mum, and would miss her. Somehow, it just didn't make any sense.

Just over half an hour later, the train finally reached what most of the passengers imagined was their final destination, not that anyone knew what that destination was, for wartime emergency regulations were responsible for the removal of signboards showing the actual name of the station. All the passengers from the Children's Express knew was that this was a small rural community which seemed to be in the middle of nowhere, surrounded by green fields and trees, with hardly any sign of habitation but for a few houses scattered here and there.

'First three carriages only, please!' called Mrs Reynolds, a geography teacher who had travelled with the evacuees. 'Follow Mr

Phillips out of the station and get yourselves into a queue two abreast! The rest of you please stay on the train!'

The moment the kids from the first three carriages had swarmed off the train, the tiny platform was filled to overflowing. Surprisingly enough, however, with the exception of the usual mischief-makers such as Alfie Grieves and a few of his giggling girlfriends, the exodus was amazingly calm and orderly.

Outside the front entrance of the station, Hannah, Louie, and the rest of the young evacuees were greeted by a group of local officials and residents, middle-aged ladies in hats and summer dresses, most of them with welcoming smiles. In the background, the train pulled away from the station platform again, taking the rest of the children and adults to their different destinations.

'Welcome to you all!' called one of the women, who was very large and had a ruddy complexion that convinced Hannah she would have a heart attack at any moment. 'My name is Mrs Mullard, and I'm here to take you to our church hall, where you will meet all the kind people who have volunteered to take you into their homes for the duration of this terrible war.'

Hannah groaned, and held on tightly to Louie's hand.

'It's just a few minutes' walk from here,' continued the large lady, 'so I must ask you all to keep closely together, so that we can form a nice, orderly procession. Can you do that for me, please?'

There were a few half-hearted replies of 'Yes, miss' from some of the kids, and a few low raspberries from one or two of the less respectful boys.

'Very well then!' called Mrs Mullard. 'Mothers with small children, please be good enough to follow the main group at the rear. Teachers, please stay with your own pupils. If you have any problems en route, we have all these lovely ladies and gentlemen to assist you.' She indicated her small group of friends from the village, who at that moment seemed quite a motley but well-meaning bunch. All of them were nodding, smiling, waving at the bewildered young crowd lined up in front of the station entrance. 'And so, once again – a hearty welcome to you all. Welcome to Redbourne!'

Louie swung a look at her big sister. 'Redbourne?' she asked, pulling a face. 'Where's that?'

Hannah shrugged. 'A long way from 'ome,' she replied.

The procession moved off at a respectable pace, and with only a smattering of excitement as opposed to the high spirits of the kids when they left St Pancras station. Watching them as they went was the middle-aged stationmaster, Ted Sputter, who also happened to be Redbourne station's ticket collector and porter.

The route of the children's procession took them on a narrow stone bridge over a river, where a posse of ducks and swans took immediate flight for their nearest hiding places, then past what seemed to be a livestock farm, which caused the children to stare in awe and wonder at the sheep and cows grazing in the nearby fields, something many of them had only ever seen in school books or in cowboy films. As they went, a large, rather cross sheepdog came out to greet them with a series of angry barks. Alfie Grieves barked back at him, which resulted in the appearance of three other fierce-looking farm dogs, who clearly did not appreciate Alfie's back-street London humour at all, for they came leaping and snarling at him, and had to be contained by the farmer himself, a rusty-sounding old boy called Percy Bumper.

A few minutes later, the procession approached what was obviously the village of Redbourne, although there were no signposts around to say so. Hannah's eyes took in everything. To her it all looked like a Technicolor picture she'd seen lots of times at the Astoria or Savoy or Gaumont cinema back home, especially when the sun came out and lit up the landscape, and the small cottages where the residents had emerged to greet them, some with friendly waves, others with arms crossed and looks of deep suspicion. As it was a little after midday the air was quite warm, and after ten minutes of walking a lot of the kids and adults found the going quite wearisome, so some of them took off their caps and hats, including Hannah, whose lovely shining red hair immediately glistened in the bright sunlight. The procession was a formidable sight, with more than fifty children and a scattering of mums, led by three jolly village ladies, and followed by two police constables amongst a group of official-looking men, all winding their way along narrow country lanes, which under normal circumstances were obviously used more by bicycles than by the locals' ancient motor vehicles.

As they approached the village, Redbourne seemed to be much larger than everyone had expected, with a mixture of grand stone houses, cottages, and small shops overlooking a large village green, where a horse-drawn cart was making a delivery at the grocer's. By the time they reached the red-bricked church hall, the children's initial high spirits were firmly replaced by looks of intense anxiety, with the dawning realisation that this was not going to be just another lovely day out at the seaside.

As Hannah and Louie filed into the hall with the others, Louie squeezed her big sister's hand so hard that it made Hannah feel quite nervous.

The procession was met inside the hall by a man in a dog

collar, and a flurry of local people who were waiting patiently for the intake of visitors from North London, all of whom would soon be taken into their own families for what everyone hoped would be a temporary adoption.

As soon as everyone was assembled in a suitable formation, the jovial-looking man in the dog collar held up his hands in greeting. 'Welcome, welcome, dear boys and girls!' he called heartily. 'And not, of course, forgetting all you mothers!' He was the only one who chuckled at what he thought was his little joke. 'My name is the Reverend Edward Ripley. I am the vicar of Redbourne Parish Church next door, and I've been given the pleasant task of telling you all how delighted we are to have you in our village. In a few moments, after the initial formalities, you'll be meeting your new foster parents, all the wonderful people who have volunteered to take you into their homes during the terrible times we're living in.'

Hannah looked wary. Formalities? What formalities? She soon found out when she suddenly noticed a long trestle table set up on the stage of the hall, where two women in aprons and summer hats were waiting with metal combs and bowls of antiseptic.

'Please form an orderly queue for lice inspection,' called Mrs Mullard. 'File up onto the stage. Two children at a time. And please remove your caps and hats.'

Lice inspection! Hannah nearly had a fit. Why? Just because they were kids from London did they think that they were dirty or something? No. She and Louie always had a bath and washed their hair regular on Friday evenings, so no one was going to look for lice on *them*.

There was a rumble amongst the other kids, but as most of

them had always had regular lice inspection at school, none of them seemed to care as much as Hannah. So two by two, they filed up onto the stage to bare their heads to the metal combs dipped in antiseptic. But when it was Hannah and Louie's turn, they held back.

'Come along now, my dears,' said Mrs Mullard. 'We must get you all settled as soon as possible.'

Hannah stood her ground. 'We're clean,' she replied firmly.

Mrs Mullard was taken aback. 'It's only a formality, my dear,' she replied sweetly, but awkwardly.

'We wash and barf regular,' insisted Hannah. 'We don't need anyone lookin' at our 'eads.'

Embarrassed, and not sure what to do, Mrs Mullard swung a glance at the vicar, who smiled back at her, indicating that she should let it pass. 'Very well, my dears,' she said. 'Please go back and wait with the others.'

Hannah, triumphant, took Louie's hand, and led her back to the group awaiting selection.

Once the lice inspection had come to an end, the vicar launched into a speech informing them all how the residents were going to choose whom they would take with them. Hannah found it very alarming; she looked at the kids around her, their expressions reflecting their anxiety and bewilderment about what was going to happen to them. She knew many of them, especially those who went to the same school as Louie. What would become of them? Would they ever see their families and homes again? It was such a poignant sight, all those poor little creatures clutching their gas-mask boxes and haversacks round their shoulders, identity tags pinned to their lapels.

The selection process seemed to take forever. Different people stepped forward to inspect the kids and their mothers, stopping briefly to check the identity tags before moving on with a few dismissive words such as *Very nice, dear* or *What a pretty dress*. One or two of the men asked some of the boys questions such as *Do you like football?* or *And what part of London do you come from, young feller?* But what Hannah noticed most of all was how some of the prospective foster-parents looked the young-sters up and down as though they needed a good wash, which after a long journey from London they probably did. Even the kids' mums looked anxious and guilty. To Hannah, the whole thing seemed like the Caledonian cattle market back home in Islington, picking and choosing, numbers and names being called out for local officials to note down at the trestle tables, then one, two, three or more kids being led out of the hall by their new foster-parents, to start whatever strange new life lay ahead of them.

As the hall gradually emptied, Hannah realised that she and Louie would probably be the last of the intake of evacuees to be adopted, especially after her refusal to submit the two of them to the lice inspection. And in any case, she thought a sixteen-year-old girl and her nine-year-old sister wouldn't quite appeal to the locals of this rural community, who seemed to be making their choices by how the children looked. Hannah had no illusions about the way she and her young sister looked; after all, they were only kids from a backstreet in London, and didn't wear the expensive clothes that would obviously make the best impression. However, Hannah was wrong, for just as the last of the evacuees were being whittled down for final selection, the vicar came across with the geography teacher, Mavis Reynolds, together with two local residents, a middle-aged well-dressed man and woman, who greeted them with warm, welcoming smiles.

'Now then, my dears,' said the vicar to Hannah and Louie. 'Don't be downhearted. This could be your lucky day.'

'Hannah, Louise,' said the rather flustered Mrs Reynolds, 'this is Mr and Mrs Bullock. They would like to have a few words with you.'

The middle-aged woman stepped forward and took a quick look at the identification tag on the lapel of Louie's coat. 'Louise,' she said, half to herself, beaming. 'That's a very pretty name. And how old are you, little girl?'

Louie quickly flung her arms round her sister's waist. 'It tells yer on me tag,' she snapped.

The woman's smile stiffened.

Hannah replied for her sister. 'She's nine years old,' she said.

The woman turned to Hannah. She was quite scraggy, but had a pleasant face, although her dark brown eyes were, Hannah thought, just a little too inquisitive for comfort. 'Oh, I see,' she replied. 'I'm so sorry. I do apologise.' Her voice was remarkably articulate, and sounded quite posh to two young sisters from a Holloway back street. 'Forgive me for being so silly, Hannah. That *is* your name, isn't it?'

Hannah nodded.

'And how old are *you*, Hannah,' she asked, without looking at Hannah's identity tag.

'Sixteen,' Hannah replied baldly. 'I'll be seventeen in January.'

'Ah!' The woman beamed, turning to her husband. 'A good age, Sidney.'

The man nodded back. He looked older than his wife, and was quite tubby, and he clearly wore a toupee which was not exactly a good fit. The thing that unsettled Louie, however, was that he wore a black eyepatch over his right eye, which she thought made him look like a pirate.

'This is my husband, Mr Sidney Bullock,' said the woman. 'My name is Mrs Margaret Bullock.' For one subliminal moment, Hannah thought she detected a smirk on the woman's face. But the feeling passed almost immediately. 'So how would you two children like to come home with me and Mr Bullock?'

Hannah turned to her sister. Louie shrugged.

Margaret Bullock smiled at Louie, and with white-gloved hands gently patted the child's head.

'Louise's teacher tells me that Louise is doing very nicely in arithmetic,' said the rather too eager geography mistress. 'Isn't that so, my dear?'

Louie nodded half-heartedly, and continued to hug her sister's waist.

'I'm very pleased to hear that, Louise,' said Margaret Bullock, folding back a dark brown curl of her neatly permed hair. 'It's very important to go through life knowing how to add up. A business cannot thrive without such a skill. Wouldn't you agree, Vicar?'

'Oh – yes, indeed,' agreed the vicar, somewhat flustered.

Maggie then turned her attention back to Hannah. 'And what about you, young lady?' she asked with a fixed smile. 'Are *you* still at school?'

'No,' replied Hannah haughtily. 'I left school when I was fourteen. I went ter work fer Elsie.'

'Elsie?' asked the woman, with raised eyebrows.

'It's a top class ladies' 'airdressin' salon in 'Ornsey Road.'

Once Maggie had taken this in, she beamed. 'Is that so?' she replied. 'Well at least I know who to turn to when I want my hair washed.'

'So what do you think?' the vicar asked the woman and her husband. 'Suitable?'

Margaret and Sidney Bullock turned to look at Hannah and Louie. Their expressions revealed nothing. Then the woman smiled. 'Suitable,' she replied, without further consultation with her husband.

'Excellent!' gushed the vicar. 'Now you can all go home and be one happy family!'

'I'm sure you won't regret your decision, Mrs Bullock,' said the geography teacher, with great relief. She turned to the woman's husband. 'Nor you, Mr Bullock.'

With his one exposed eye, Sidney Bullock acknowledged her with a nod. Louie hugged her sister even tighter.

Margaret Bullock gave both girls a reassuring smile. 'Let me just say something to you, my dears,' she said, putting her arm round Louie's shoulders. 'I know how all this must seem to you. Leaving your family and home must be one of the most terrible things in the world to have to cope with. But I want you to know that Mr Bullock and I will do everything in our power to make you as comfortable as we possibly can. We have no children of our own, and so I promise you that as long as you are with us, we shall treat you as our own family. Isn't that right, Sidney?'

Sidney Bullock grunted with a nod.

'All I ask,' continued Margaret Bullock, 'is that you just look upon us not only as your foster-parents, but also as your friends. You can rest assured that we *shall* love you as if you were our own.'

Hannah's expression gradually changed. After what the woman had said, she was beginning to warm to her, and for one moment she felt quite guilty at the way she had reacted. 'Thank you, miss,' she replied awkwardly.

'Mother,' said Margaret Bullock. 'Please call me Mother.'

Hannah found it difficult to respond to such a request, but she summoned up a smile, and nodded.

'And if you ever have any problems . . .' added Mavis Reynolds.

To her surprise, Margaret Bullock swung a glare at the geography teacher. 'If they're coming to live with *us*,' she said quietly but sharply, 'I see no reason why there should *be* any problems. And if there are, I'm sure Mr Bullock and I are perfectly capable of dealing with them.'

'Quite so,' added the vicar, embarrassed. 'Quite so.'

Mrs Reynolds said not another word.

Margaret Bullock turned back to Louie, and held her hand out to her. 'And so, my dear,' she asked, 'shall we go home?'

Louie, her eyes full and anxious, looked up at her big sister for guidance.

Hannah hesitated just long enough to give Louie a reassuring smile. 'Come on, Louie,' she said. 'Let's go.'

Louie took hold of Margaret Bullock's hand and allowed herself to be led to the entrance door of the old church hall. Hannah followed close behind, leaving Sidney Bullock to complete the formalities of registration with Mrs Reynolds, the vicar, and some of the other officials sitting at one of the trestle tables. As they went, Hannah flicked an anxious look across at the few remaining kids who were still being looked over by prospective foster-parents. Amongst them was Alfie Grieves who looked a sorry sight as he waited nervously for someone to choose *him*.

Once outside, Hannah and Louie got their first real chance to look around at the vast village green. It was certainly a revelation to them, unlike the confined world of back streets back home in Holloway. It was the clean fresh air that Hannah noticed most of all, the feeling that her lungs were able to breathe in the smell of newly mown grass, something she had only ever really experienced in Finsbury Park. Also the peace and tranquillity of country life, of people just walking about at a slow pace instead of the frenzied march of city folk rushing off to work. And the silence, the incredible silence: no hooting of bus and tram horns and motor vehicles, no noise of kids playing football in the streets. For one brief moment, Louie's face lit up as she excitedly pointed out a cluster of brown, speckled, and shining blue and green mallard ducks, all of them bobbing their heads in and out of the surface of the water on the large village pond, now shimmering in the early afternoon sunshine.

Whilst they waited for Sidney Bullock to collect their belongings, Hannah and Louie watched with some fascination as their foster-mother waved to some of the locals she knew, pointing out her two new possessions, as if she had won them in a raffle. Nonetheless, she made a special point of doing her best to make Hannah and Louie feel more at ease by pointing out all the sights of the village, such as the grey-stoned Redbourne Parish Church, the village shop and post office, the small petrol station, and Martha Randle's tea shop, an absolute must for visitors to this quiet corner of north Hertfordshire. Hannah in particular was impressed by all the large period houses that were set around the village green, and felt a sudden surge of anticipation as she imagined what it was going to be like to live in a place as grand as one of those.

Margaret Bullock's floral-patterned dress fluttered in a gradually stiffening breeze, which caused her to hold on to her navy blue straw hat adorned with artificial flowers. 'Don't you worry, my dears,' she said confidently. 'You're going to love living in Redbourne. I can assure you it's a very special place. And your father and I are going to love having you living with us.'

Hannah's moment of reassurance was slightly diminished when she heard Margaret Bullock referring to her husband as their father. As far as Hannah was concerned, she and Louie had only one mum and dad, and that's the way it would always be.

'And as soon as we get home,' continued Maggie, 'I shall put the kettle on, and we can all have a nice cup of tea. Would you like that, Louise?'

Louie shook her head. 'I don't like tea,' she replied sulkily. 'I only like milk.'

Margaret Bullock chuckled. 'Oh, well, you've come to the right place for that,' she replied. 'You shall have a nice glass of cold, fresh milk, straight from one of Mr Bumper's cows.'

Sidney Bullock came out of the hall, loaded down with the girls' two suitcases. The moment he appeared, his wife grabbed hold of Louie's hand, and with an air of quiet exuberance she called, 'Right! Off we go!'

As they made their way to their new home, the two girls experienced such tranquillity that Hannah felt as though she was entering a world she had never known existed. Everyone they passed seemed to be so friendly, so welcoming, exchanging the time of day with the Bullocks, beaming, waving at them as though they were saints. 'We all know each other here,' proclaimed Margaret Bullock. 'We're all good friends. Just you wait and see, they'll soon be *your* friends too.'

Bewildered by everything she saw, Hannah was gradually warming not only to the surroundings, but also to her new foster-parents, who had shown nothing but kindness and consideration since she first set eyes on them at the church hall. And the thought of living in one of those beautiful grand houses was now really beginning to excite her. It would be so different from life back home in Kinloch Street: no more two rooms up and two rooms down, a scullery with hardly enough room to have a wash down, and a boiler to do the laundry that steamed the place out. And then it suddenly occurred to her that there would be a garden at their new place. Yes, of course there would be a garden – this was the country, and there would probably be a garden with a great big lawn and flowers all round, just like the ones she had seen in those magazines that the customers read back in Elsie's hairdressing salon. Yes, the excitement of all the good things awaiting her and Louie was beginning to swell up inside her, and she was now desperate to get home; their sparkling, bright new home. However, once they had wound their way round the edge of the village green they turned off down a narrow terraced street lined on either side by small brick cottages, and her enthusiasm was soon replaced by nagging doubts, which were immediately realised once they had stopped outside a small, narrow-fronted building with a signboard swinging from a rusty iron hook attached high up on the stone wall outside.

'So here we are, my dears!' proclaimed the proud Margaret Bullock, as she pushed open the front door and stood back for the two girls to enter. 'Welcome to your new home!'

Hannah and Louie stared up in bewilderment at the sign-board creaking back and forth in the breeze. The sign read: *The Cock and Crow*.

'You have nothing to worry about now, my dears,' said the girls' new foster-mother. 'From now on, we're going to be one big happy family.'

Chapter 2

It was no wonder the Cock and Crow was so busy. Ever since the evacuees had arrived from the city that morning, the talk was of little else other than who had taken whom and how long it would be necessary for them to stay. However, even though Margaret Bullock was having the time of her life extolling to her customers the virtues of doing her duty for her country, there was no doubt that 'doing her duty' was also good for business, for in the saloon bar of the pub that evening she and her husband Sid were certainly doing a roaring trade. The bar was crammed with local farm workers, all of them sinking their usual pints of bitter and smoking their Woodbines and Player's Weights, all of them in a great state of excitement about the day's activities whilst battling it out in a frenzied game of darts. At the end of the counter, Polly the multicoloured parrot moved restlessly up and down her perch, using her beautifully curved beak and claws to climb up the metal rails of her prison walls, desperately seeking a way to escape the choking fumes of cigarette smoke. 'Shut up!' was her only contribution to the proceedings, especially to any over-imbibed customer who made too much noise.

'Looks like *you've* done well then, Maggs,' called Jack Dabbs above the din. Jack was in his mid-thirties, and worked as a farmhand up at Percy Bumper's place whilst he waited for his call-up, which was expected any day. 'Bit of help come in very useful be'ind the bar, eh?'

Maggie, as she was known to her customers, served him his second pint of bitter, and downed the rest of her own pink gin. 'Come on now, Jack,' she said, folding back one of the curls of her dark permed hair, 'they're only minors. You know Mr Bullock and I would never break the law by using children in a public house.'

Jack grinned. He was always amused by the way Maggie referred to her husband as 'Mr Bullock'. 'Still,' he persisted, teasing her with a sly wink, 'I bet the allowance is goin' ter come in 'andy, eh?'

Maggie stiffened, and gave him one of her glares. 'If you think we're going to get rich on ten and sixpence per child per week,' she replied haughtily, 'then I suggest you and your wife take in a few of your own.'

Jack took his pint and sneaked off sheepishly.

'Well,' added farmer Percy Bumper, 'the coupla boys *we've* taken in, my missus had to practically shave off their hair. She reckoned their 'eads were full er lice.'

'Can't see how that could have happened, Percy,' called Sid Bullock, who was pulling up a draught bitter for another customer at the other end of the counter. 'All the kids had a lice check before they left the church hall. Well' – he exchanged a quick look with Maggie – '*most* of 'em did.'

'That's nothing,' called Will Ferris, who worked as a mechanic at an aircraft factory a few miles outside the village. 'Ron Drayton told me that the young girl he and his ol' woman got don't even have a spare pair of knickers.'

The others guffawed.

Maggie stiffened again. 'With respect, Mr Ferris,' she said prudishly, 'I don't think that's something you should be talking about in public. You can't blame children for the way their parents have brought them up.'

When Hannah was following her new foster-parents through the village, the attic room at the top of a pub wasn't exactly what she had in mind for a bedroom for her and Louie. For a start, even though Hannah was only of average height, the sloping ceiling meant that she had to stoop every time she moved around, and when they had arrived, early in the afternoon, they found that because the window was very little more than a small fanlight they had to turn on the light, which immediately brought a scornful response from their foster-mother who asked them to use the electric light only when absolutely necessary – *to help the war effort* was her excuse. To make matters worse, there was only enough room for two single iron beds, which were crammed up against each wall, and what clothes and personal belongings the two girls had brought with them had to be accommodated in an old broom cupboard on the landing outside their room. On the other hand, it had been a treat for both Hannah and Louie to have a bath in a real bathroom, which was on the landing just below them next door to the Bullocks' own bedroom. Back home in Holloway there had never been such a luxury, and they had either had to use the old tin tub in the scullery, or rely on their weekly visit to Hornsey Road Public Baths. However, the two girls were not happy to have had to share the regulation five inches of lukewarm water, and to have been made to use carbolic soap, and Hannah didn't take too kindly to her foster-mother's saying firmly, *When you've both finished, don't forget to clean out the bath thoroughly with the Dettol disinfectant.*

It was now well after nine in the evening, and Louie, thoroughly miserable and homesick, was already curled up in bed, the bedclothes pulled up tightly round her neck. From downstairs, they could hear quite clearly the laughter coming from the darts match in the saloon bar. 'Is it going to be like this all night?' she snivelled.

'Wot yer talkin' about?' asked Hannah irritably, her voice barely audible, lying on her back in her own bed, staring up dreamily towards the ceiling in the dark.

'That noise downstairs.'

Hannah turned over to face her in the dark. 'Come on now, Lou. Yer know wot it's like in a pub. 'Ow many times 'ave we stood waitin' fer Mum and Dad outside the Eaglet?'

'This ain't like bein' outside the Eaglet,' grumbled Louie. 'It's diff'rent. It's *inside.* It's goin' ter be like this *every* night. I won't ever be able ter sleep.'

'Oh, stop bein' such a cry-baby, Lou,' replied Hannah, determined not to pander to her sister's homesickness. 'Yer'll soon get used to it. This is only the first night.'

'I never wanted ter come an' live in a pub.'

Louie's remark struck home with Hannah. It was true. Waiting outside in the street for their mum and dad was one thing, but actually living above a pub was something quite different.

'Can I come in bed wiv yer, Hann?' asked Louie, close to tears.

'No, Lou!'

'*Pl-ease.*'

'I said no,' insisted Hannah firmly. 'You're a big gel now.'

'Just fer ternight, Hann,' pleaded Louie. 'I'm scared.'

'Scared?' asked Hannah, irritated. 'Scared er wot?'

'I don't like sleepin' in strange places.'

Hannah's bedclothes rustled as she lay on her back again. 'This ain't a strange place, Lou,' she replied. 'From now on it's goin' ter be our 'ome. Yer'll 'ave ter start gettin' used to it. We boaf will.'

There was a moment's silence before Louie spoke again. '*Please*, Hann,' she begged.

Hannah suddenly realised that her sister was standing next to her bed beside her. After a brief moment, she rolled back her bedclothes. 'Come on then,' she sighed. 'But just this once.' She moved over to make room for the child.

Louie hopped into bed and snuggled up beside her. For a moment or so neither girl spoke, until Louie suddenly whispered, 'Hann.'

'Go ter sleep, Lou.'

'I'm 'ungry.'

Hannah sighed again. 'Now don't start that all over,' she snapped irritably. 'You 'ad somefin' ter eat before we come ter bed.'

'That wasn't anyfin' ter eat,' grumbled Louie. 'That was just lettuce an' a tomato. That's wot my friend Josie Higgott gives to 'er pet guinea pig.'

'It was a salad, Lou,' said Hannah. 'That's wot people eat in the country.'

'Wot – all the time?'

'No, not *all* the time, yer twerp!' Hannah sighed. 'But fings're rationed now. They're not easy ter get.'

Louie waited a moment before speaking again. 'That woman and 'er ol' man've got stew fer dinner,' she said. 'Did yer smell it on the stove?'

Hannah was now getting really annoyed with her young sister's whining. 'They're probably savin' some of it fer our dinner termorrer,' she retorted. 'An' listen ter me, Louie – don't call Mrs Bullock *that woman*. It's disrespectful. Just remember, she's lookin' after us now. We've gotta be grateful. So we don't want ter upset 'er.'

'I don't like 'er,' said Louie, without any remorse.

'Why not?'

Louie shrugged in the dark. 'Don't know,' she replied. 'There's somefin' about 'er – the way she looks at yer. An' I don't like that man's eye with the black patch. 'E reminds me of that murder film we saw up the Rink picture 'ouse.'

'Yer mean when you bunked in the back door!'

'I don't like eivver of 'em,' persisted Louie. 'Nobody told us we was goin' ter live over a pub. Mum 'n' Dad always told us kids weren't allowed in pubs.'

'*I'm* not a kid, Lou,' said Hannah firmly.

'No, but *I* am.' Louie turned onto her side and threw her arm across her sister's stomach. 'Nobody told us we was goin' ter live over a pub.'

'Stop grumbling, Lou,' said Hannah. 'Beggars can't be choosers. It was Mum who sent us away, remember. We're lucky to 'ave a roof over our 'eads.'

'Wish it wasn't *this* roof, though.'

Louie's words unsettled Hannah. There was something in what Louie was saying that rang a little too close to what Hannah herself was feeling. Although their new foster-parents *seemed* to be doing all they could for her and Louie, there was something about Maggie Bullock that wasn't quite right. Maybe it was the way she always stared hard at the two sisters when she was talking to them, and the way she and her husband Sid exchanged so many sly glances with each other. But Hannah was also disturbed by little things, such as being asked to put the kettle on when she and Louie had hardly got through the front door when they arrived, and then having no one to help them carry their suitcases up the three flights of narrow, creaking wooden stairs. Of course, all that was nothing *really* unusual, but somehow it niggled.

Fortunately, by the time the darts match had come to an end in the bar downstairs, snuggled up close together, both girls had fallen asleep. It had been a long day.

Hannah woke with a start to find Louie getting out of bed. She didn't know what time it was because it was still dark outside, although a crescent-shaped moon was casting a beam of bright fluorescent light through the fanlight of the tiny attic room. 'Wot yer doin'?' she whispered, as she watched her sister trying to unlatch the door.

'I want ter go ter the lav,' came Louie's reply. 'Will yer come downstairs wiv me? I'm scared er this place in the dark.'

Hannah sighed. 'You're a bloomin' nuisance, Lou,' she returned, getting out of bed.

The door creaked open; hand in hand, the two girls quietly made their way down the narrow, winding staircase. It wasn't easy to see in the pitch dark, so Hannah used her fingers to feel her way down the wooden beams. When they reached the first floor landing, they could hear the sound of snoring coming from the Bullocks' bedroom, but they had no idea which one of them it was coming from. Hannah remembered that the bathroom was right next door to the Bullocks' bedroom, so once she had found the latch she did her best to lift it as quietly as possible. It wasn't easy, but once the door had creaked open she did manage to find the light switch cord inside. However, just as she had let Louie in, the door of the next room suddenly sprang open, and Maggie Bullock was standing right behind them.

'What are you doing?' she asked in a loud whisper.

'Louie wants ter go ter the lav,' replied Hannah, careful to keep her voice low.

'Not here, dear,' said Maggie sweetly, but firmly. 'Your facilities are in the garden outside.'

'Facilities?' asked Hannah, puzzled.

'There's a perfectly good room with toilet and washbasin just near the greenhouse,' said Maggie. 'We've reserved it specially for you two. *This* bathroom is private, dear – just for your father and me.'

'But it's dark outside,' said Louie, without bothering to whisper.

'Ssh!' replied Maggie, putting one finger to her lips. 'You mustn't wake Father. He works very hard, and never sleeps too well. Go on now. There's a torch hanging by the back door in the kitchen. I'll leave the light on until you get downstairs.'

Reluctantly, Hannah took hold of Louie's hand and carefully led her down the rest of the rickety wooden stairs. Before they had reached the ground floor Maggie had turned off the bathroom light.

'I've left two towels and a bar of soap by the sink,' called Maggie in a loud whisper. 'Nightie night. Sleep well!'

Hannah heard the sound of the Bullocks' door closing on the landing upstairs. They were now in the dark again. Fortunately, however, the moon was shining through the front window of the saloon bar, giving the two girls just enough light to find their way into the kitchen behind the counter. The smell of beer and cigarette smoke from the previous evening's darts match was overwhelming, but it was soon replaced by the more pleasant smell of what remained of the Bullocks' stew in a saucepan on the stove. Hannah found the rusty old torch, which was hanging on a hook by the back door. The huge key of the door was still in the lock, so she quickly let them both out.

There was quite a chill in the air outside. Although it was still only early September, there was dew on the grass in the back garden, which looked like a carpet of white snow in the dazzling light of a half-moon. Louie was soon shivering in the cold, and as she and Hannah were only dressed in their flimsy nighties and carpet slippers, she put her arm round Hannah's waist to help keep warm. There was actually very little need to use the torch as there was more than enough light to pick out the greenhouse at the end of the long, wide garden. As they made their way along a neglected lawn, past borders of late-flowering roses and early chrysanthemums, they were suddenly startled by the shrill hoot of an owl from a nearby tree.

Louie immediately came to a halt, and clutched hold of her sister's waist. 'Wot was that?' she gasped.

'It's nuffin',' replied Hannah uncertainly. 'It's only a bird.'

'I ain't 'eard no bird like that back 'ome,' said Louie, shaking with fear.

'This ain't 'ome, Lou,' said Hannah bravely. 'This is the country. Fings're diff'rent out here. Come on. Let's get on wiv it.'

They resumed their journey to the end of the garden. Once they had reached the old greenhouse, with its broken panes and rusting metalwork, they soon found their own so-called 'facilities'. The timber-planked hut alongside was hidden amongst a tall clutch of hollyhocks, which had to be pushed to one side in order to reach the door. As it was in the darkest corner of the garden, the moon was of no help, so Hannah turned on the torch in order to raise the door latch. She shone the beam inside, hoping to find a light switch. However, there seemed to be no such luxury, so she took hold of Louie's hand and gently led her in. It was a sparse place, with nothing more than a cut-out wooden frame over a slops bucket and a washbasin set on an old trestle table. As Maggie Bullock had promised, there were two towels there and a bar of carbolic soap, and there was even a roll of toilet paper, which was at least an improvement on the newspaper they had always had to use back home in Kinloch Street.

'Don't be long,' whispered Hannah, as she ushered Louie towards the slops bucket. 'I'll leave yer the torch.'

'Don't go too far,' pleaded Louie.

'I'll wait for yer right outside. Hurry, Lou!'

Hannah went back outside to wait for her. She was now feeling quite cold, and she shivered in the unfamiliar sharp air of a rural night. In fact there was something quite unsettling about being in surroundings that, at first sight, seemed so alien. However, if she was truthful with herself, going to a lavatory in the back yard came as nothing new to her for it was exactly the same back home. But somehow, *this* was different. At least there was a proper lavatory seat and chain at the small house in Kinloch Street, and there was an electric light switch, but not here, amongst the strange-sounding night birds. She sighed. Louie seemed to be taking forever inside. But whilst she was waiting she had the chance to think about their new foster-parents, and about whether she and Louie really *were* going to be part of one big, happy family, as Maggie Bullock had promised. As she stood there, she thought about all the other kids and their mums who had piled onto that train at St Pancras station, where they were, what they were doing, and whether they were feeling the same way as she and Louie. Leaving home was a terrible thing for *anyone* to have to cope with, especially for kids. It wasn't easy to give up all the familiar things you had been brought up with, leaving mates behind, and all the personal belongings that meant so much. And the smell of the country was so different from the smell of the back streets of Holloway; everything was so clean and spotless, with no sense of people actually living together. The more she thought about these things, the more she realised that it would take time to get used to such changes. After all, nobody wanted to be evacuated, and nobody in their right minds wanted to take strangers into their homes. She and Louie and all the other kids would just have to get used to being the outsiders.

Louie suddenly shrieked out from inside the lavatory hut.

'Lou!' Hannah quickly wrenched open the door, to find her sister pulling up her knickers and weeping profusely. 'What's up?'

'There's a big spider on the wall!' she squealed. 'I 'ate spiders! Yer know I do!'

Hannah suddenly roared with laughter.

'What yer laughin' at?' bellowed Louie. 'It ain't funny, Hann! It ain't funny!'

Hannah, still laughing, threw her arms round her sister and hugged her. 'No, Lou,' she said, trying to comfort the child. 'It ain't funny. But we're in the country now, mate. Come on, let's get back ter bed!'

She turned them round, and led the way back towards the house, unaware that as they disappeared inside, the man with the black eyepatch was watching them from his bedroom window on the first floor upstairs.

* * *

There was a wonderful smell coming from the kitchen. It was so strong that it woke both Hannah and Louie, who leapt out of their beds.

'Bacon 'n' eggs!' proclaimed Hannah jubilantly, rushing to the door. Both girls went out onto the landing and peered excitedly down the narrow staircase. 'Wot did I tell yer, Lou? We ain't 'ad a breakfast like that since we went ter visit Aunt Ada in Camberwell. Come on, mate. Let's get down there!'

It took the two girls just a few minutes to throw on their clothes. Charging down the stairs they made straight for the kitchen where Maggie and Sid Bullock were sitting at a small wooden dining table finishing off their bacon and eggs.

'Ah – there you are, my dears!' said Maggie brightly, dabbing the egg yolk from her lips with a linen table napkin. 'Up bright and early. Early to bed, early to rise! That's what we like to see, don't we, Father?'

Sidney Bullock sipped his tea, and grunted acknowledgement with a nod.

'I bet you're famished, aren't you, my dears?' said Maggie, getting up from the table.

Louie nodded eagerly.

'Well you come with me,' said Maggie. 'Don't let it ever be said that anyone starves in *our* house.'

Hannah and Louie exchanged a look of excited anticipation, and followed her out into the saloon bar. As they went, Hannah cast a quick look back into the kitchen. There was a frying pan there on the stove, but it was empty.

'Here we are, dears,' said Maggie, taking them to one of the wooden pub tables in the corner of the bar. 'Come and tuck in.'

The two girls looked at the table, which had been set with

two plates and knives, two cups, a half-loaf of bread, and a jar of preserve.

'That's my own homemade greengage jam,' said Maggie proudly. 'We have a tree at the end of the garden. It always fruits well, as long as we can get there before the wasps, that is.' She looked at the two girls. 'Come along now, dears, sit yourselves down. You've got a long day ahead of you.'

Louie exchanged a pained look with her sister as they both sat at the table.

'I'm sorry there's no butter,' said Maggie before leaving them. 'But don't worry. We'll get you some margarine as soon as I get your ration books from the committee. Bon appetite!' After her half-hearted attempt to speak French, she quickly disappeared back into the kitchen.

For a moment, the two girls just sat there, staring in disbelief at their 'breakfast', the smell of cigarette smoke and beer lingering in the bar from the previous evening's opening hours.

'Is this all we're goin' ter get?' asked Louie. 'Bread an' jam?'

Hannah was too shocked to speak. Her face was thunderous.

'Did yer see wot *they* was eatin'?' whispered Louie angrily. 'It was eggs 'n' bacon!'

'I *know* wot they was eatin', Lou!' snapped Hannah, getting up to cut a thick slice of bread.

'Then why can't *we* 'ave the same?' insisted Louie. 'I'm starvin'!'

Trying to contain her true feelings, Hannah plonked a slice of bread on Louie's plate. 'We'll 'ave ter make do 'til fings get sorted out,' she said.

'But I don't like bread and jam,' replied Louie, her face crumpling up.

'Well yer'll 'ave ter put up wiv it, won't yer!' snapped Hannah, slapping a piece of bread on her own plate, and sitting down. ''Ow many times do I 'ave ter tell yer, Lou – there's a bleedin' war on!'

'I 'ate the war!' barked Louie tetchily. 'I 'ate this place! I 'ate this smelly ol' place!'

Both girls swung round as Maggie Bullock called from the kitchen doorway. 'There's a nice cup of tea waiting for you when you're ready. And Louise, my dear – I *haven't* forgotten your glass of milk. One of Mr Bumper's cows sent it over for you especially first thing this morning.' She disappeared back into the kitchen again, and closed the door.

'Wot we goin' ter do?' asked Louie gloomily.

'The first thing we're going to do is to eat our breakfast,' replied Hannah, opening the jar of greengage jam and spreading some on Louie's slice of bread. 'Then we'll see wot 'appens. We've only just arrived. It takes a time ter settle in.'

'Why don't we say somefin' ter Mrs Reynolds?' asked Louie. 'She said we could get in touch wiv 'er if we 'ad any problems.'

'Eat!' snapped Hannah irritably.

'Yer know I don't like jam!'

'Then yer'll just 'ave ter get used to it, won't yer!'

Whilst Louie reluctantly ate her bread and jam, Hannah got up and went to the kitchen to collect a cup of tea and Louie's milk. There was no sign of either Maggie Bullock or her husband until she heard the sound of someone in the bathroom on the first floor upstairs. She soon found a cup and poured herself some tea from the pot on the kitchen table, where two greasy plates had been left, waiting to be washed. Then she collected a glass from the old pine dresser and poured milk from a jug on the kitchen table, adding some to her tea. Back in the saloon bar,

Louie was wandering around looking at the photographs on the timbered walls.

'Funny ol' pittures,' said Louie critically. 'Nuffin' but fish.'

'Maybe they like fishin',' replied Hannah, giving Louie the glass of milk.

'We ain't near the sea, are we?'

'No idea,' said Hannah, with a shrug. 'But there's a pond in the village. We saw it on the way in.'

'D'yer fink they 'ave fish 'n' chips 'ere?' asked Louie, with a burst of sudden hope.

'Yer never know.'

Hannah sipped her lukewarm tea, and wandered around the bar, taking in the endless horse brasses hanging on the beams, the snapshot photographs of Sid Bullock proudly displaying fish of varying sizes, surrounded by the same group of male friends. Then there were brass and copper trophies and pewter mugs adorning any shelf that could be crammed into the tiny bar, and a huge stuffed fish in a glass case fixed to the wall over the large inglenook fireplace. Hannah wasn't very impressed with it all, so she quickly passed over most of the prized possessions and went to the front door. To her consternation she found it locked and bolted, with no key in sight. But then she remembered that as it was a pub, the door would be closed until opening hours, which would probably be later that morning. She peered out through the glass in the door; there was hardly any sign of life in the narrow cobbled street outside, which seemed strange to Hannah after living in a community that started its day with people rushing off to catch buses to go to work. As she stood there, her heart was full of foreboding. What with not being allowed to use the inside lavatory during the night, and being given nothing more than bread and jam for breakfast, things had not got off to a good start. But then she remembered that breakfasts back home in Kinloch Street were not much better, usually a boiled egg and bread, and on high days and holidays a bit of bacon *if* they were lucky, so it seemed wrong to expect too much from people who were trying their best to accommodate two strange youngsters who had come from a completely different environment to their own. Nonetheless, there were still nagging doubts in her mind about Maggie Bullock and her strange husband.

'So then, my dear,' asked the voice just behind her. 'What do you think of our little village?'

Hannah swung with a start. 'Oh,' she replied, taken by surprise. 'Looks lovely – *wot* I can see of it.'

'Don't worry, my dear,' continued Maggie, with a beaming smile. 'You'll soon see a great deal of it. I know things may seem a little strange to start with, but – well, I suppose we're all going to have to learn to adjust to – the different circumstances. Your father and I find it strange too, sharing our home with people we've never met before, but we *are* going to do our best to make you as comfortable as we possibly can. If you need anything at any time, all you have to do is to ask.' She then added rather pointedly, 'I'm sure you won't find any need to go bothering your schoolteacher. Never you fear, your father and I will take care of you. Living with us will be like one long holiday.'

Maggie's warm smile again endeared her to Hannah, and she nodded back gratefully. 'Actually,' she said, 'there are a coupla fings I'd like ter ask yer . . .'

To Hannah's surprise, Maggie had already turned away and was heading back towards the kitchen. 'Take your time, my dears,' she called over her shoulder, ignoring what Hannah was about to say. She stopped at the kitchen door, and turned. 'There's plenty of hot water, and not much washing up for you to do. We don't open until noon, so there's absolutely no rush at all.'

Hannah watched in stunned amazement as her foster-mother went up the stairs. She waited until she heard the bedroom door open and close, then turned to look at her sister, who was drinking her milk at the table on the other side of the room. It was several moments before Hannah could take in what she had just heard.

Chapter 3

Hannah's first impressions of Redbourne were, on the whole, pretty favourable. With its picture postcard village green, little cottages, stone houses, and duck pond, it was the essence of peace and tranquillity, a million miles away from the hustle and bustle of poor old 'Smoke', which is what the local people called London town. However, it took a few days to become acclimatised to the people themselves, especially the Bullocks, who although well meaning were showing signs of being a little too demanding. Putting the kettle on for tea as soon as they had arrived on the first day, and washing up not only their own breakfast dishes but also those used by their foster-parents, seemed to Hannah to be just a bit unreasonable even though she was used to doing the chores back home. She was also slightly concerned that before they went out on their first look around the village, Maggie Bullock had asked her to give the saloon bar a quick sweep, as the Bullocks were going to be busy all day checking their beer supplies in the cellar.

Things were slightly better once Hannah had checked Louie into the local school, where Mavis Reynolds was waiting with the headmistress to help the clutch of newcomers resume the lessons they had left off back home. Louie was, of course, not happy to be left behind, but once she had met up with one or two of her old classmates she stopped grizzling and showed signs of settling down. With Louie off her hands, Hannah was able to move around more freely, and the first thing she did was to wander around the village to see if she could get any kind of job.

'Not much chance of that round here, young lady,' said Barney Jessop, who ran the village stores with his daughter Jane. 'Jobs in the villages are always hard to find at the best of times. Most people have to travel down south to Hatfield or St Albans if they want any sort of decent job. Mind you, old Percy Bumper might need some help with his pigs now that two of his lads have been called up.'

Somehow, the thought of cleaning out pigsties didn't quite appeal to Hannah. 'Wot about ladies' 'airdressin'?' she asked hopefully. 'I've bin workin' in an 'igh class salon fer the past two years. I've got a lot of experience.'

Barney laughed. He was a jovial, middle-aged man, who seemed to have a perpetual smile on his face. 'Most er that sort er thing is done by our Jane here,' he replied. 'She does it part time, mostly in the evenings.' He called over his shoulder to his daughter, who was up a stepladder replacing flour on one of the shelves behind the counter. 'Ain't that right, Janey girl?'

'That's right,' called Jane, a good-looking, bright-faced eighteen year old. 'Bit of a dead loss job really, hardly worth the time and trouble. Most of the women round here go into town if they want anything special.'

Hannah sighed despondently. If she wanted to earn money she was going to need a job, so she wanted a job badly.

'I'm surprised Maggie and Sid haven't offered you something,' said Barney, taking off his straw boater to wipe his forehead. 'I heard Sid say they badly need some help, especially during pub hours.'

'Don't be silly, Dad,' called Jane, brushing back a thick strand of dark brown hair which had fallen across one eye. 'You know very well they're not allowed to employ under age. The people round here would shop 'em in no time. In any case, *I* don't think the Bullocks are the sort of people *I'd* want to work for.'

Hannah looked up at her with a surprised start. 'Why's that?' she asked.

'Hush, Janey!' said Barney, scolding his girl. 'I've told yer before, gossip don't do no good fer business.'

Jane shrugged, and shut up like a clam.

'The Bullocks are good folk, young lady,' continued Barney, replacing his straw hat. 'They just prefer to keep themselves to themselves, that's all. Let's face it, there's nothin' wrong with that, is there?'

Hannah smiled half-heartedly. She thanked Barney for his help, and started to leave. As she did so, however, she couldn't help but notice how well stocked the shop was, every shelf filled with many of the things that had disappeared from the shops back home in Holloway.

Once outside, she made her way slowly along one side of the village green, stopping only briefly to peer into shop windows with items on sale that meant absolutely nothing to her – antique furniture, brass and copper, old pots and pans. Then there was what looked like a junk yard where a little old lady in a long black dress and scarf was selling candles and paraffin lamps, and further on was the village post office, a small petrol station, and a butcher's shop with H. TURNBULL above the door, where to her astonishment the marble slabs on show contained rump steaks, legs of pork and lamb, rabbits hanging from hooks waiting to be skinned, and some kind of bird unfamiliar to Hannah, also hanging from hooks with heads slumped over lifelessly to one side. She had always hated looking in butcher's shops, so she quickly moved on towards a baker's called Griffins, where she could see an elderly man and woman inside serving loaves of freshly baked bread, alongside a selection of home-cooked Eccles cakes, a real favourite with Hannah. As she peered through the window, all the customers in the shop turned round to look at her with a mixture of intense curiosity and suspicion.

She crossed the road, and made her way towards the duck pond, where she was greeted with much the same kind of re-action. But it was a lovely morning, so she sat on a weather-worn wooden bench at the side of the pond, and reflected on what she was going to do with her life in such an odd place. Inevitably, her mind returned to her two foster-parents, and the curious remark Barney's daughter had made about them.

'You mustn't take too much notice of Dad.'

Hannah jumped with a start, to find Jane herself, clutching the handlebar of her bicycle, standing just beside her.

'Mind if I join you?'

'Course not,' replied Hannah, moving along the bench to make room for her.

Jane carefully laid her bicycle down on the finely cut grass, then sat beside Hannah. 'Trouble with Dad,' she said, 'is that he's a bit old fashioned. Ever since Mum died of a stroke ten years ago people have been so good to him he doesn't want to upset anyone. Understandable really, I suppose. Bad for business.' She turned to look at Hannah. 'What's your name?'

'Hannah.'

'Think you're going to like living in Redbourne, Hannah?'

Hannah shrugged. 'Dunno,' she replied. 'It's only me first day.'

'It's not so bad here,' said Jane. 'The people are a bit on the cool side, but they mean well. Once they get to know you, you'll get on just fine.'

'But why wouldn't you want to work for the Bullocks?' asked Hannah outright.

Jane hesitated a moment before answering. 'Too many rules and regulations. They used to have a girl there who said that working for them was more like being a slave. Up at all hours, cleaning, scrubbing, waiting on them hand and foot, not getting to bed until last thing at night. And she didn't like being locked in her room every night.'

Hannah did a double-take. 'Locked in 'er room?'

'Apparently that was the reason she gave in her notice. She said there were times when she felt like a prisoner. And the pay wasn't enough to keep a crow alive. Too demanding – that's what she said, especially old Mother Bullock. Poor Chrissie. I liked her.'

'Chrissie?'

Jane turned to look at her. 'That was her name,' she said. 'Lived with her gran over at Brookfields. Her mum and dad are both dead. Soon after she left the Bullocks she joined the Forces. She said she wouldn't want to go through all that again.'

'Go through – *what*?' asked Hannah.

Jane was about to answer when she suddenly caught sight of her father watching her from the door of the village stores. 'Better go,' she said, suddenly getting up. 'I'm supposed to be collecting one or two things for Dad.' She picked up her bicycle and started to wheel it back towards the road. 'Look, Hannah,' she called as she mounted the bicycle, 'if you need company at any time, you know where to find me. You can tell me all about London, and I'll tell you all about Redbourne. OK?'

'OK,' replied Hannah, as she watched Jane get onto her bicycle and disappear along the road skirting the village green. For a few moments she sat just there, watching the ducks dipping their heads in and out of the water, mulling over with some concern what the girl from the village store had told her about her new foster-parents.

Although the Cock and Crow was now open, there were no customers. There was, of course, nothing unusual about that, for most people had to work during the day and midday opening hours were clearly only for people like the old boy Hannah found sitting at a bench table on the street outside, sipping a pint of Guinness whilst watching the world go by. 'So how yer settlin' in, young lady?' he asked, just as Hannah was going into the saloon bar. 'Does our country air agree wiv yer?'

Hannah flicked him a courteous smile. 'Looks like it suits *you* all right, Granddad,' she quipped.

The old boy chuckled. 'Good ol' cockney talk that!' he returned. 'I love it!'

'I ain't a cockney,' said Hannah. 'I come from 'Olloway.'

'Holloway? In't there a prison there or somefin'?'

'We got more than a prison,' replied Hannah. 'We've got a Woolworth's *an'* a Marks an' Sparks. *An'* we've got four pitture 'ouses.'

''Ave yer now?' said the old boy, trying to share her enthusiasm. 'Bet you'll miss all that then. Yer won't find nothin' like that in Redbourne. Still, at least we won't 'ave no bombs 'ere.'

48

That remark rubbed Hannah up the wrong way. It reminded her of the stupid reason why she and Louie were shuffled off out of London: to avoid bombs that, in her mind, would never come. With a polite nod, she left the old boy to his Guinness, and went inside.

Although the saloon bar was empty, she was greeted by a very strange voice: ''Allo. Wot's *your* name?'

Taken by surprise, Hannah caught her first glimpse of the parrot in her cage at the end of the bar counter. She strolled across and peered in at her. ''Allo,' she said. 'Where did *you* come from?'

'Polly stays in the kitchen at night,' said Maggie Bullock, wiping one of the tables on the other side of the bar. 'She doesn't like the smell of beer whilst she's trying to sleep.' She finished what she was doing and came across. 'So. Is our little girl settled in her new school?'

'Can't really tell 'til I see 'er later,' said Hannah. 'I don't fink the new kids're doin' many lessons, just sortin' fings out, gettin' used ter fings.'

Maggie smiled. 'I'm sure. Come into the kitchen, Hannah. I want to talk to you.'

Hannah followed her into the kitchen, where Sid Bullock was reading a newspaper at the table.

'Your father and I were just wondering how we're going to help you to occupy your time,' said Maggie, sitting at the table with her husband. 'Do you have any thoughts about that?'

Hannah shrugged. 'I've bin askin' around about a job.'

'What!' Maggie sat up with a start. Sid put down his newspaper. 'You went looking for a job – *here* in Redbourne? But why?'

'Gotta earn me keep, ain't I?'

'My dear child, we have an allowance for you.'

Hannah crossed her arms uneasily. 'That won't give *me* much pocket money, will it?'

Maggie exchanged an anxious look with her husband. 'But what do you need pocket money for, child?' she asked, agitated. 'You have all your food and accommodation here with us. There's not much else you can spend it on in a place like this.'

Hannah didn't like this. Not only was she being referred to as a child, but she was being treated like one as well. ''Scuse me sayin', Mrs Bullock,' she said defiantly, 'but I ain't a kid. I'm nearly seventeen years old. I 'ave to 'ave money in me own pocket. It's only natural.'

'What about your mother back in London?' asked Sid Bullock. It was practically the first time he had opened his mouth to her since she and Louie had arrived. 'Surely *she's* going to send you something?'

Hannah gritted her teeth. She hated being grilled in such a way. 'My mum ain't flushed, Mr Bullock,' she said. 'My dad's away in the army an' Mum 'as an 'ome ter run. I used ter 'elp out by workin' at the 'airdressers. I can't go around wivout 'avin' me own money. I need ter send some 'ome every week.'

'*This* is your home now, Hannah,' insisted Maggie, sitting up straight-backed in her chair. 'As long as you're in *this* house, as long as *we're* looking after you, I think you'll agree that you *do* have a certain responsibility towards *us*?'

Hannah was now feeling decidedly uncomfortable. 'Wot d'yer mean?' she asked.

'I mean,' replied Maggie, 'that in times of crisis, families always pull together. We all have to do our bit.' She turned to her husband. 'Isn't that so, Father?'

Sid Bullock peered at Hannah with his one eye, and grunted agreement.

'So wot d'yer mean?' asked Hannah, who was resenting having to stand at the side of the table as though she was being interviewed for a new job.

Maggie relaxed a little, and even forced a weak smile. 'It means, my dear, that – as you people in London would say – we all "muck in".'

*

Dear Mum – this is just to let you know that me and Lou are all right though it ain't like home!

Hannah had never been much of a letter-writer, so she certainly hadn't thought she would be using one of the postcards her mum had given her quite so soon. However, once she was alone in her attic room, she did what she had promised, and wrote home.

I'm still not sure where we are. All I know is that we're somewhere in Herts – livin' over a pub!! The people they've put us wiv are a bit funny but I hope we get used to them in time. Will let you know the proper address as soon as I get to know it. Lou is still moanin' all the time but she's all right now she's gone to school. I'll write again. Love Hann.

Hannah blew on the postcard to make it dry quickly, then slid it into the pocket of her dress with her purse. Then she went downstairs again. The saloon bar was still empty and Sid Bullock was passing the time by polishing some glasses. 'Won't be long,' she called. 'Just goin' ter the post office.'

'Know how to get there?'

'Oh, yes,' replied Hannah. 'I saw where it was when I took Lou ter school.'

Sid moved along the counter closer to her. 'Sounds like you're a bit of a fast worker.'

Hannah did a double-take. 'Pardon?'

'You've only been here for five minutes, and you know your way around already.'

Hannah relaxed. 'I've got a good 'ead for direction,' she replied.

'I bet you have,' replied Sid, with a smile. With a wart on the end of his nose, and an unnaturally white complexion, he wasn't a particularly handsome man. But close up, his black eyepatch was a distraction from what Hannah now thought was quite a kindly looking face, very different from when they had first met. 'It must be rough for a girl like you,' he said, 'comin' from a big place like London to a poky little hole in the middle of nowhere.'

Hannah shrugged. 'It ain't so bad,' she said. 'It's worse fer me sister. Lou don't really understand what's goin' on.'

'To tell you the truth, Hannah,' said Sid, 'neither do I. Even before they declared war we were being asked if we could take in evacuees. I'm not sure that's absolutely necessary – well, not yet anyway. I mean, Jerry hasn't dropped any bombs – yet.'

'That's exactly wot *I* said,' replied Hannah, surprised that she was in agreement with her foster-father.

'Still,' said Sid, 'I reckon we shall just have to get used to it, won't we? Your mother's got some funny ways, but she means well. She's always wanted a daughter. Now she's got one.'

Hannah found his change in expression just a little too disconcerting. 'I'll see yer later then,' she said, going to the front door.

'Know how to skin a rabbit, Hannah?'

Hannah swung with a start. This time it was Maggie Bullock calling to her from the kitchen door. 'Pardon?' she asked, taken aback.

'One of our customers hunts rabbits and gives us one every week,' said Maggie, standing there in apron and rubber gloves. 'Skinning is quite easy – when you get used to it. I'll show you how to do it. You *do* like rabbit, don't you?'

'Yer mean – to *eat*?'

'To eat,' replied Maggie, with a mischievous grin. 'It's delicious roasted in the oven – or in a stew. Us people in the sticks love anything cooked straight from the land. It's what God intended. Isn't that so, Hannah?'

Hannah smiled, and turned back to the door.

'Don't be too long, my dear,' called Maggie. 'We're having a little homemade broth for lunch.'

After Hannah had gone, Maggie turned to her husband and gave him a hard, ferocious glare. He ignored her, and returned to the other end of the counter to continue polishing his glasses.

When Hannah reached the village post office, she was delighted to find Mavis Reynolds, the geography teacher, talking to the postmistress at the counter. Although there was very little room to move around, the walls were bulging with wartime posters such as WOMEN WANTED FOR EVACUATION SERVICE: OFFER YOUR SERVICES TO YOUR LOCAL COUNCIL, and CARELESS TALK COSTS LIVES.

'Ah, there you are!' said Mavis, the moment Hannah walked

in. 'This is our young Hannah Adams, one of the girls who used to go to our school back home. Hannah, this is Mrs Beedle.'

''Ow d'yer do,' said Hannah. The postmistress was a woman in her mid-forties, with a lovely fresh face and bright violet-coloured eyes.

'How are you settling in?' asked Mary Beedle from the other side of the counter.

Hannah shrugged. 'Bit too soon ter know,' she answered, with little enthusiasm.

'I know,' replied the postmistress. 'It's going to take time to get used to us, I'm afraid. But I'm sure your new people will take great care of you. By the way, who *are* you with?'

'In the pub,' replied Hannah baldly.

If the expression on the postmistress's face seemed to freeze, she was careful to conceal it. 'Ah,' she said with a courageous smile. 'That will be Mr and Mrs Bullock.'

'How are you and Louise getting on with them, Hannah?' asked the geography teacher.

'I don't know,' replied Hannah. 'I can't quite make them out yet. But the room they've put us in ain't 'ow we fawt it'd be. It's up in the attic. There's 'ardly enuff room ter swing a cat.'

'Think yourself lucky, my dear,' said Mavis wearily. '*I* had to sleep on a put-u-up last night.' She swung a glance at the post-mistress. 'Nobody on the committee seemed to have taken into account that we teachers were travelling with the evacuation groups. Thank goodness they've managed to find room for us over at Thornton.'

'Thornton?' asked Hannah. 'Where's that?'

'About twenty miles and two bus rides from here. Once school is finished here today, Miss Wilson and I are moving up there.'

Hannah suddenly felt a moment of panic. 'You're – yer mean you're movin' out? You *and* Miss Wilson? Boaf of yer?'

'That's right.'

Hannah was flustered. 'But – who's goin' ter look after *us* lot?' she asked.

'There are teachers at the school here, Hannah, good teachers,' said the postmistress. 'I'm sure they'll be able to look after your sister and all her class friends.'

'And there are still one or two mothers in the group to keep an eye on things,' added Mavis, who was middle-aged and had always been one of the more popular teachers back at the school in Holloway. 'It's just a case of getting used to being in a different place.'

Hannah thought that if she heard anyone else voice that sentiment she would yell her head off. For a split second she felt alarm and despair. The thought of being left alone with Louie, without teachers from their own school, without anyone she could turn to in case of trouble, suddenly made her feel very lost and lonely.

'Well, I must be off,' said Mavis. 'I've got a lot to do before I move on.' For a brief moment she caught a glimpse of Hannah's expression. 'You mustn't worry, Hannah, my dear,' she said, putting a comforting arm round the girl's shoulder. 'From what I remember, you're a strong girl, very strong. You'll always know what to do for the best.' She went to the door, calling back, 'In any case, you won't go far wrong whilst you've got Mrs Beedle and her folk around. Believe you me, Hannah, the Quakers are a grand bunch.'

Hannah watched her go, then turned back to the postmistress, who was waiting at the counter for her.

'Can I post that for you, young lady?' said the woman, noticing the postcard Hannah was clutching in her hand.

'Oh – fanks,' Hannah replied. ''Ow much is the stamp?'

'A halfpenny,' replied the postmistress, taking out a stamp from her book, and handing it across the counter to Hannah.

Hannah got out her purse, found a halfpenny coin, and gave it to her. She then stuck the stamp on the postcard. 'Where's the postbox?' she asked.

'I'll take it for you,' replied the woman, with a smile. 'Don't worry, you can trust me.'

'It's only a bit of a note 'ome to Mum,' she said quickly, watching the woman put the postcard straight into the mailbag behind her. 'She made me promise ter write regular.'

'Quite right,' said Mrs Beedle. 'That's what mums are for. It must be terrible for *any* mum to be parted from her children. I know *I* would hate it.'

Hannah just didn't have the heart to respond. 'Fanks very much,' she said, turning to go. She stopped at the door. 'Wot're Quakers?' she asked.

The woman smiled. 'Oh, just a band of people who care about their fellow kith and kin, husbands and wives, brothers and sisters, friends and relations. People who pray for love and peace.'

'Yer mean – like in a church?'

'Something like that,' replied Mrs Beedle. 'But not *quite* the same. You and your sister must come to our Meeting House sometime. It's just behind the post office here. I can assure you – everyone is welcome.'

'I'm sorry,' replied Hannah, standing at the door. 'I don't ever go ter church. Church is only fer old people.'

As she spoke, the front door opened and a handsome teenage boy appeared. 'Sorry,' he said awkwardly, easing his way past her.

'As you can see,' continued the woman with a friendly grin, 'not *all* Quakers are old. This is my son, Samuel. Sam, this is Miss Hannah Adams. She and her sister are new to our village.'

'Hallo, Hannah,' said the boy awkwardly.

''Allo,' returned Hannah, far too casually. 'See yer then.'

'Goodbye, my dear,' replied the woman. 'Come and see us any time.'

Hannah smiled politely, then left the shop. Once outside she moved on as fast as she could without appearing rude. As she went she thought about what the postmistress had said about mums, and people who loved each other. But she dismissed all that with a pinch of salt. As far as she was concerned, whether it was called a church or a Meeting House, none of that was for her. She hadn't been inside a church since she was a small kid, and she certainly had no intention of doing so now. But try as she may, there was one image from the last few minutes that *had* stuck in her mind. Sam Beedle, the son of the postmistress, was just about the best-looking boy she had ever seen, not that she really took that much notice of boys. With his long dark blond hair, bright blue eyes, and awkward smile, he didn't at all seem like the sort of person to be religious. However, by the time she had crossed over to the other side of the village green she had put Sam Beedle firmly out of her mind. She had other things to think of, more important things; how to get a job, how to occupy her mind, how to look after a young sister who was not going to be easy to keep under control. Most of all, she wondered what the hell she was doing in such a place, especially when there was no sign of this war that everyone kept going on about.

But even as these thoughts ran through her mind, she was startled by a sudden roar from the sky above. She came to an abrupt halt, and looked up, just in time to see three fighter planes in formation, skimming the rooftops of the quiet, sleepy village. Alarmed and cowering, she expected everyone to be taking cover, but when she looked out across the village green she was astonished to see that everyone seemed to be going about their business as though nothing had happened.

'Nothing to worry about,' called a voice from nearby. 'It's only the RAF boys from the airfield over at Hatfield.'

Hannah swung around to find Maggie Bullock coming up behind her.

'It happens all the time,' said Maggie. 'They love to scare the wits out of us. Only they don't any more. We're quite used to them now.' She placed her arm round Hannah's shoulder. 'Now come along, dear,' she said, with just a tinge of irritation. 'It's time for lunch. We don't want to keep your father waiting, now do we?'

Chapter 4

The following few weeks proved quite difficult for both Hannah and Louie. Settling into their new way of life and surroundings was bad enough, but living with the Bullocks was turning out to be nothing short of an ordeal. Cleaning and sweeping up after pub closing time was not something that appealed to Hannah, and she only agreed to do it when Maggie Bullock offered her a small wage to cover her pocket money. With no possibility of finding work in the village, Hannah was in no position to bargain, and therefore found herself being treated like a housemaid, cleaning, sweeping, washing endless beer glasses, and generally taking on the job of a lackey. However, Hannah's real worry was Louie. She had always been a bit of a grizzler, but from the very first day at the Cock and Crow absolutely nothing would please her. The worst problem was that she could not find any food that she really liked. Eating locally shot rabbit was, to Louie, nothing short of disgusting, especially as she once had a pet rabbit of her own which she kept in a cage in the back yard in Kinloch Street. But as far as Maggie Bullock was concerned, whatever meal she served up was all the two girls would get, and if Louie didn't like it she would have to lump it. After a while, it became a real battle of wills between the child and her foster-mother, and in early November an ugly exchange between them promised to cause a real crisis. It happened one day when Louie came home from school with the news that, as there had been no sign of enemy bombs in London, a lot of the mates she had been evacuated with were being taken home by their parents. With that in mind, Louie begged her sister to write to their mum and ask her to take them back home too. However, as their mum had so far not replied to any of Hannah's postcards, there seemed very little likelihood that they would be able to make contact with her in the foreseeable future. This angered Louie so much that the moment she sat down in the kitchen to a tea consisting of two slices of Spam and two boiled potatoes, much to the disgust of Maggie Bullock she threw a real tantrum. 'I'm sick of Spam!' she yelled. 'An' I'm sick of bein' shut up in the attic!'

Maggie was outraged. She grabbed hold of Louie's plate and took it away from her. 'When you've found some manners, young lady,' she said quietly but firmly, 'we'll talk about what we can do to address your complaints. In the meantime, I suggest you go to your bedroom, and stay there.'

Hannah was shocked and horrified by Louie's behaviour. 'I'm sorry, Mrs Bullock,' she said, doing her best to cover up for her young sister. 'Lou didn't mean wot she said. The trouble is—'

Before she could offer any explanations, Maggie had dumped Louie's plate on the draining board by the sink, and disappeared out into the back garden.

Hannah immediately got up from the table, and glared at her sister. 'There are times I could murder you!' she growled, rushing outside after Maggie.

It was now dark outside, with no sign of the moon which

was completely trapped behind heavy dark evening clouds. With blackout curtains up at all the windows, Hannah couldn't see a thing, so she remained with her back pressed against the back door. 'Mrs Bullock,' she called softly. 'I'm really sorry about Lou. She's just a kid. She don't know wot she's sayin' 'alf the time.' There was no reply. 'Mrs Bullock? Can yer 'ear me?' She was suddenly startled by the lighting of a cigarette close by.

'What's so wrong with the attic room?' Maggie's face and voice were calm and without anger. 'I've always been under the impression it was very cosy up there.'

For a brief moment, Hannah didn't quite know how to answer. It was the first time she had seen her foster-mother smoking a cigarette. 'There' ain't nuffin' wrong wiv the attic,' she replied quickly. 'It's just Lou, the way she talks. I'm sorry she upset yer.'

'If she's not happy here,' continued Maggie's voice in the dark, 'we could always ask the committee to move her to more suitable accommodation. I'm sure they could find room for one more.'

Realising the implication of that remark, Hannah replied immediately. 'I'd never let Lou go off on 'er own,' she said.

'These days, Hannah,' said Maggie, 'beggars cannot be choosers. Just say the word, and I'll see what I can do.'

'I don't want yer ter fink we ain't grateful,' said Hannah.

'Why should you think that?' asked Maggie.

'Well – the way Lou carries on, all that sort er fing. It's just that she's 'omesick. We boaf are.'

'I thought *this* was supposed to be your home now?'

Hannah didn't quite know how to answer that. With all the chores she had to do every day from the moment she opened her eyes in the morning, the Cock and Crow wasn't exactly *her* idea of home. 'Anyway,' she said, 'we might not be 'ere fer much longer.'

Maggie inhaled on her cigarette, her face momentarily lit up by the soft glow. 'Oh?' she asked.

'Lots er the kids who came wiv us 'ave already gone back 'ome,' said Hannah. 'There ain't no bombs, so most of their mums and dads fink it's a waste er time ter split up the family. I reckon our mum'll be 'ere ter collect us any time now.'

'Is that so?' replied Maggie, who seemed quite unconcerned. 'Nobody has told me anything about that.'

'Oh yes,' replied Hannah confidently. 'As a matter er fact, I'm expectin' a card from Mum any day now.'

For a brief moment, Maggie remained silent. 'It seems you've only been here for five minutes,' she said. 'But I shall find it hard to let you go.'

Hannah was taken aback. 'Let me go?' she asked uneasily. 'Wot d'yer mean?'

'You're a great help to me, my dear,' said Maggie. 'I'm not sure now that I could cope without you. I need you. And so does your father.'

'I don't fink I know wot you're talkin' about,' replied Hannah. 'When Mum comes ter collect us—'

'Your mother won't be coming to collect you,' said Maggie. 'You can be assured of that.'

Now Hannah was really alarmed. 'Wot d'yer mean?' she asked, her voice sounding dead in the lifeless evening air.

'I mean,' replied Maggie, 'that your mother and I have been in touch with each other, and she agrees with me that it would be in *all* our best interests if you stayed here with me and your father. At least – until we know what the situation is going to be like in London.'

Hannah went quite cold. She wasn't aware that she was shaking from head to foot. ''Ow come you've 'eard from our mum, and we 'aven't?' she asked tentatively.

The glow from Maggie's cigarette lit up her face for one last time before she threw it to the ground and stamped on it. 'I think it's time we went back inside, my dear,' she said, opening the back door to allow her face to be flooded with light from inside the kitchen. 'It sounds as though the saloon bar is filling up. Father is going to need you to wash up some glasses.' Without another word, she held the door open for Hannah, who duly went back inside.

A few days later, Louie was invited to a children's Sunday school party in the church hall, which gave Hannah the chance to go to the village shop to talk to Jane Jessop, whom she had made friends with during the previous few weeks. But it was a Sunday and the shop was closed, so as it was a dreary day, with a slow relentless drizzle, she turned back and made her way to the pub. Ever since she had spoken to Maggie Bullock in the back garden, Hannah had been in a restless, anxious mood. *I shall find it hard to let you go.* Those words from her foster-mother were still ringing in her ears; they had kept her awake for hours on end, and then drifted off into disturbing dreams. But the thing that niggled her most of all was the fact that Maggie Bullock had been in touch with their mum. Could it really be true, Hannah asked herself, that Mum had agreed to let her kids stay away from home when so many of the other evacuees were heading back to London? It just didn't seem possible that she would have done such a thing without getting in touch with Hannah and Louie. What was going on? Why *wasn't* her mum answering the postcards she had written? In a few weeks' time it would be Christmas. Before they left Holloway that morning back in September, didn't her mum promise to come and see them at Christmas? What *was* going on?

She was about to cross over to the other side of the village green when she gradually became aware of people singing some kind of hymn, not from the parish church, but from what seemed to be the Quaker Meeting House just behind the post office. By the time she had turned and made her way back, however, the singing had stopped, and when she reached the door of what appeared to be a small timber-framed hall, there was not a sound to be heard coming from inside. Intrigued, she moved round to the side of the hall, and, careful not to be noticed, peered through the window.

Inside the hall, a small gathering of about twenty people were arranged in a square, facing inwards. All of them, men, women, and a few children, sat upright on their stark wooden chairs, most of them with hands resting in their laps. But the most extraordinary thing that Hannah noticed was that everyone sat in complete silence, with hardly a movement, and nearly all of them had peaceful smiles on their faces. Hannah watched them for a few moments, finding it all a bit spooky. But then a middle-aged man started to talk, not in a raised voice like a vicar addressing his congregation in a church, but calmly and quietly, as though he was having a friendly chat with his friends. She put her ear closer to the window to try to hear what he was saying.

'Friends,' said the middle-aged man, 'on this day we think of those who are away from home, those who have been led, against the will of the Lord, into a conflict not of their own making. Will thou join with me in silent prayer, that mothers and fathers and wives and sisters and brothers may one day be reunited with their loved ones?'

There was a barely audible murmur of acceptance from the congregation. Eyes closed as they prayed.

Hannah watched in absolute fascination, until she suddenly caught sight of the postmistress, Mary Beedle, beckoning to her from her chair at the corner of the square. Hannah quickly turned away, and started to hurry off. But just as she did so, Mary's son Samuel came out from the hall, closed the door quietly behind him, and called to her. 'You don't have to run away.'

Hannah stopped and turned, to find the boy calmly walking towards her. 'I'm sorry,' she said, embarrassed and confused. 'I didn't mean ter—'

'There's nothing wrong,' said Samuel, who was seventeen but looked a little older than Hannah. 'There's nothing secret about our meetings. My mother asked me to come and invite you inside.'

Hannah quickly shook her head. 'Oh no!' she replied nervously. 'I couldn't do that. I couldn't do nuffin' like that. I don't know nuffin' about – all that stuff.'

The boy smiled, his bright blue eyes a welcome relief in the grey afternoon light. 'At least it's dry inside,' he said jokily.

Hannah was surprised by the warmth of his greeting. The first time they had met in the post office, he had seemed to be so awkward, so ill-at-ease. 'I'm just on me way back 'ome,' she said. 'I only come ter try an' find Jane.'

'Jane Jessop?' asked Samuel. 'From the shop?'

Hannah nodded.

'Is she your friend?'

Hannah returned a wry smile. 'About the *only* one I 'ave round 'ere.'

'Is it *that* bad?'

'Worse.'

'Want to tell me about it?'

'Why should I?'

'Why not?'

With the drizzle still glistening on her headscarf and topcoat, Hannah felt the only answer she could give was to continue on her way. The boy from the post office was too disconcerting for her. For some reason or other, she found it difficult to stare into his eyes, *those* eyes.

'Don't go,' said Samuel, following her. 'If you're not happy, why not tell me about it?'

'Because yer wouldn't understand,' insisted Hannah, irritated by his persistence.

'Is it something to do with the Bullocks?'

Hannah came to a halt.

The boy joined her. 'We do know about the Bullocks round here, you know.'

Hannah looked at him and warmed to his comforting smile. 'A lot er the kids from London are goin' back 'ome.'

'I know,' replied Samuel. 'I can understand why. We *all* do.'

'The Bullocks don't want me an' my sister ter go,' said Hannah. 'They want us ter stay an' slave away for 'em. Me an' Louie can't bear the place. We just wanna go 'ome. But every time I write ter me mum, she never replies.'

Samuel looked concerned for her. 'Oh, I see,' he replied solemnly.

'The fing that worries me, though,' continued Hannah, walking on, 'is that ol' Ma Bullock 'as bin in touch wiv me mum, an' apparently they've agreed between 'em that we'd be better off stayin' 'ere.' There was now a look of desperation in her eyes. 'I can't believe my mum would do such a fing. I just can't believe it!'

Samuel tried not to show his concern. 'So what are you going to do, Hannah?' he asked.

Hearing the boy call her by her Christian name sent a sudden warm glow through her entire body. Maybe it had something to do with the way he talked, all quiet and calm, not like the rough and tumble of the boys she knew back home. It had never occurred to her until this moment that she didn't like the way she herself spoke. It wasn't the way she was taught back at school by Miss Hobson, who always tried to impress on her pupils the beauty of the English language. Listening to Samuel Beedle brought it all back to her. He spoke so beautifully, his words so clear and easy to understand. 'I wanna go an' talk to Mrs Reynolds,' she replied. 'She used ter be my geography teacher. She come out wiv us from London. She'd know wot ter do. Trouble is,' she turned up her coat collar against the drizzle, 'I don't know 'ow ter get to 'er.'

'What do you mean?' asked Samuel.

'Soon after we got 'ere, she found they 'adn't got any place for 'er ter stay, so she 'ad ter move over to a place called Thornton, wherever that is.'

'Thornton?' asked Samuel. 'I know it well. It's about twenty miles north from here, on the road to Hertford.'

'Is there a bus that goes there?'

'Not really. It's too complicated – you would have to change a couple of times. It'd take forever.'

Hannah sighed. Somehow there was always something to stop her trying to do the things she wanted to do. She was now desperate.

'But if you like, *I* could take you there.'

Hannah looked up with a start. 'Yer could? 'Ow?'

The drizzling rain clouds had virtually cleared by the time Samuel's old Triumph embarked on its twenty-mile journey to Thornton. Hannah had never travelled pillion on a motorcycle before, but within minutes she felt a huge sense of exhilaration as the rush of cold November air battered her face. For Hannah it was an extraordinary journey, for not only was she seeing the tail end of a bleak rural autumn, but she was experiencing it in the company of a young bloke whom she hardly knew at all. With the rationing of petrol now a top wartime priority, they passed very few vehicles on the way, although from time to time they did catch sight of some RAF convoys making their way east, no doubt bound for one of the front line East Anglian fighter stations. The smell of the countryside was unlike anything Hannah had ever known before, so clean and crisp, especially with the roads covered in endless carpets of autumn leaves, all of different shapes and colours, soft hues and dark browns, all wet and glistening in the small beams of sunlight which were struggling to break through the November gloom. Hannah was also struck by the sight of the small hamlets and villages they passed through, most of their inhabitants clearly having surrendered to the Sunday afternoon ritual of a good snooze, but it was always difficult to guess where they were for all the signposts had been removed against the event that enemy parachutists might suddenly descend from the changing skies of rustic England.

Throughout the journey, Samuel said not one word, but as soon as he brought the Triumph to a halt he called over his shoulder: 'This is Thornton.'

''Ow can yer tell?' Hannah called back.

'I was born here,' he replied.

Both of them got off the motorcycle, and while Samuel was putting the machine on its stand Hannah looked around at the rather bleak surroundings. 'Not very big, is it? Who lives in a place like this?'

'People,' replied Samuel, removing his goggles. 'Just ordinary people – like you and me.'

'I wouldn't say *you're* so ordinary, Samuel,' said Hannah cheekily.

'Sam.'

'Due wot?'

'Please call me Sam. Everyone else does.'

Hannah shrugged. 'OK, Sam,' she replied. 'So 'ow do we find Mrs Reynolds?'

'Follow me,' he said. He left the Triumph parked by a horse trough at what seemed to be the end of a tiny village street, and moved off at a brisk pace.

Hannah tagged on behind, but found it quite difficult to keep up with him. The first thing they had to do was climb over an old wooden stile which led into a decidedly muddy field, where the distant sight of what she took to be grazing cattle slightly unnerved Hannah.

'Don't worry,' called Sam, striding off well ahead of her. 'They're only cows. They won't harm you.'

Hannah was not prepared to take his word for it, so she hurried to catch him up. But by the time they reached the old farmhouse on the far side of the field, her shoes were so heavy with mud she could hardly move. 'Where are we?' she asked breathlessly.

'Mr Hatchet's place,' said Sam, once again striding off, seemingly oblivious of Hannah's difficulty in walking. 'He farms cattle and pigs, gave up corn a year or so back. If anyone knows how to find your teacher, he or his mother will.' As he reached the gate leading into the cobbled courtyard he yelled out: 'Mr Hatchet! Anyone at home?' As he spoke, a cream-coloured Labrador came bounding round the corner of the back of the house, and leapt straight up at him. 'Down, boy!' said Sam, vigorously stroking the dog's head. 'Good boy, Houdini! Good boy!'

''Oudini?' gasped Hannah, keeping well out of the dog's path.

'Mrs Hatchet's name for him,' replied Sam, 'because he's always getting out through the fence!'

'Who is it? What d'you want?' An elderly man in duffel coat, flat cap, and wellington boots appeared from the barn on the other side of the courtyard. 'Get down, Houdini!' he yelled at the dog. 'Down, yer stupid lump!'

Sam went to meet him. 'Hallo, Mr Hatchet,' he called. 'It's only me – Sam Beedle.'

'Sam?' He came across to him. 'What *you* doin' here, boy?' He suddenly noticed Hannah holding back nearby, doing her best to avert her nose from the smell of pigs who were grunting and snorting loudly in their pen nearby. 'Who's that yer've got with yer?'

'She's a friend of mine, Mr Hatchet,' explained Sam as they met. Houdini jumped up at him again, and planted his muddy paws firmly on Sam's shoulders. 'We're looking for Mrs Reynolds.'

'Who?' asked the farmer, who was obviously a bit hard of hearing.

'Mrs Reynolds,' Sam repeated more loudly. 'She's from London, staying somewhere in the village. I wondered if you had any idea where we can find her?'

'Yer don't mean that schoolteacher, do yer?'

Both Sam and Hannah turned to see the old chap's mother at the front door of the farmhouse. She was so bent over and lined, she looked as though she was older than time itself. 'Hallo, Mrs Hatchet,' Sam called, doing his best to disentangle himself from Houdini, who was now licking every inch of his face.

'Yer don't mean that schoolteacher woman, do yer?' squawked the old lady again, her parched face peering from behind the door. 'The one that come with those kids down Redbourne?'

'That's the one, Mrs Hatchet,' replied Sam. 'Do you know where she's lodging?'

'She ain't!' replied the old lady. 'Went back ter Lon'n coupla weeks back. She was stayin at Elsie Jackson's place over at Hillwater. Reckoned there was no point in her hangin' on round here when all the kids were headin' back home.'

Sam swung a look at Hannah, who felt as though the ground had collapsed beneath her. 'Oh, I see,' he called. 'Well, thanks for your help, Mrs Hatchet.'

Quite unceremoniously, the old lady slammed the farmhouse door.

'Get off, yer thug!' growled Mr Hatchet, as he lifted Houdini off Sam, and shoved him back on the ground. 'Get out of it!' The dog obeyed immediately, and scuttled off back to where he had come from. 'Sorry about that, boy,' the farmer said, making sure the dog didn't return. 'Stupid mug! He's gettin' old – like me.'

'Thanks for your help, Mr Hatchet,' said Sam, turning to go. 'Sorry to have disturbed you.'

'Don't you an' yer little lady want a cuppa before yer go?' asked the old chap hopefully. 'I'll get the old trout to put the kettle on.'

'No, thanks all the same, Mr Hatchet,' replied Sam with a chuckle. 'Gotta get back before dark. I don't like riding on these wet roads. Too slippery.'

'As yer please,' called the farmer. 'Give my best to yer parents. Tell 'em ter say a couple prayers fer me and the old lady. The way things're goin' on the farm, we're goin' ter need 'em.'

'I will, Mr Hatchet,' Sam called back. 'Thanks for your help.'

The old chap stomped off, leaving Sam and Hannah to make their way back across the field.

'Funny ol' geezer,' said Hannah, who was relieved Sam wasn't racing ahead of her. 'Both of 'em!'

'Not really,' replied Sam. 'Poor man, he's getting old, that's all. He must find it difficult to cope with all the new wartime regulations from the Ministry.'

To Hannah, the journey back across the field seemed to take forever. But despite the lingering smell of pig manure, there was no denying that the air was fresher out here than anything she had ever known in London. When they finally reached the old stile, she felt spoilt when Sam helped her to climb over. She wasn't used to boys having manners; it was a completely new experience for her.

'So what happens now?' Sam asked.

Hannah sighed despondently. 'I don't know,' she returned, as they paused a moment or so. 'If Mrs Reynolds's gone, I don't know *who* ter turn to.'

'You still haven't told me why you're so desperate to get away from Redbourne,' Sam said out of the blue.

Hannah hesitated for a moment, deep in thought. 'I'm scared.'

'Scared?'

'Not just fer meself, but fer Louie too. It's that woman, an' *'im* too. I fawt he were all right at first, but he gives me the creeps the way he moves round the place after closin' hours. I get the feelin' 'e's watchin' me all the time. Oh, I know it's not fair ter fink like that just becos 'e's only got one eye, but I can't 'elp it. I get the shivers down me back every time I see 'im, so shifty, as though 'e's 'idin' somefin'.'

'Perhaps he *is* hiding something,' replied Sam mysteriously. 'Come on. Better get going.'

He led her back to where the motorcycle was parked, leaving her even more concerned and bewildered than before. It was now after four o'clock, and the afternoon light was rapidly thinning to allow the first impatient pangs of night to start swamping the overcast sky. Somewhere nearby they could hear the voice of Bruce Belfrage on someone's wireless, reading what must have been a special wartime news bulletin, something about the Nazis threatening to invade Holland, Belgium and Luxembourg if their demands for collaboration were not met. But Hannah took very little notice, for her mind was too preoccupied with what Sam had just said about her foster-father. 'Wot d'yer mean about ol' Bullock?' she asked warily. '*Wot's* 'e 'idin'?'

Sam put on his leather riding helmet. 'Oh, I don't know, Hannah,' he replied dismissively. 'The Bullocks have had a lot of problems in their time. Most of the village know about it.'

'*I* don't,' replied Hannah, with some trepidation.

'You will – eventually,' said Sam. He flashed her one of those smiles that completely melted her. 'Just don't let them get you down. OK?'

Hannah was not convinced. Whilst Sam was putting on his goggles she climbed back onto the pillion seat. 'D'you like being a Quaker, Sam?' she asked, for no particular reason.

Sam briefly stopped what he was doing. 'It's not a question of us *liking* it, Hannah,' he explained. 'It's a calling from God. It's between Him and us. Why d'you ask?'

Hannah thought for a moment. 'Oh, I don't know,' she said eventually. 'It's just that, when I was lookin' through the window of that hall, it seemed funny ter see all those people sittin' there in a square, not sayin' anyfin'. Who was that man who *did* say somefin' – somefin' about wives an' bruvvers an' sisters?'

'That was my father, Hannah,' Sam replied seriously, getting onto the motorcycle saddle. 'He's a good man. My mother is a good woman.'

'You're lucky,' she replied. 'Wish I could say the same.'

'Not always lucky, Hannah,' said Sam.

'At least you've got religion.'

To her surprise, he swivelled round to look at her. 'Not always, Hannah.'

His strange response took Hannah by surprise. It didn't help that his riding goggles had now deprived her of a look at those beautiful blue eyes.

Chapter 5

Babs Adams didn't get home until after three o'clock in the morning. After far too many gin and tonics she was quite shaky on her feet, for the party she had been to at a pub up in the West End had continued behind closed doors long after opening hours. Fortunately, despite the new wartime regulations, there were still night-time buses to travel on, which was just as well, for Babs was in no condition to take on the long walk back to Kinloch Street, a tiny little terraced street which nestled just behind Charlie Brend's sweetshop in Hornsey Road. By the time she got home she was all in, and after locking the front door behind her, even as she climbed the stairs to her bedroom on the first floor she was already struggling to get her clothes off. But it was late November, and the nights were now getting bitterly cold, so she quickly put her topcoat back on and flopped into bed. However, to her surprise, sleep was elusive, mainly because her mind was still buzzing about the party she had been at that evening, and especially the men she had laughed and joked and drunk with, and in particular one of those blokes, a Norwegian sailor whose rough appearance and hefty muscles brought a smile to her face as she lay in the dark thinking about him. After a few minutes she got up and stumbled over to the electric light switch by the door, but the moment she had turned the light on she realised that her newly installed blackout curtains had not been drawn, so she hurried across to do so. Relieved that Arthur Pilgrim, the local air raid warden, had not been around to see her light flooding the street, she sat down at her dressing table and looked at herself in the mirror there. Despite the fact that her thick red lipstick was smudged and her hair was straggly and unkempt after boisterous fun and games at the party, she quite admired what she saw, so much so that it brought a wry smile to her face. 'You ain't so bad, yer ol' cow, are yer?' she stuttered, her words tumbling out incomprehensibly. Then she picked up her hairbrush, and started to brush her hair, all the while thinking about the Norwegian sailor whom she had reluctantly left behind at a street corner outside the pub. Suddenly, however, her eyes fell on the small framed snapshot on the dressing table in front of her. It was of her husband, Len Adams, a good-looking man in his early forties, smartly dressed in army uniform, with a big come-hither grin on his face. She reached for her Craven A fags, found only one left in the packet. She quickly lit up, inhaled and exhaled lightly, then took another brief look at the snapshot. But simultaneously, amongst the carnage of her precious make-up creams, lipstick, and screwed-up empty fag packets on the dressing table, she suddenly caught a glimpse of something partly concealed beneath a tub of Vick's ointment. She quickly retrieved Hannah's latest postcard, and although by now she could hardly focus through the haze of fag smoke, she started to read it.

Dear Mum — have you received any of my postcards, and if so why haven't you replied? Me and Lou have been worried stiff

*not hearing from you specially as Mrs Bullock told us that she
and you have been writing to each other. Is it true that you
think we're better off living down here than being back home
in Holloway? If it is true then why are all the other mums
taking their kids back home? Please write, Mum, even if it's
only a few words. Don't forget it'll soon be Xmas and you
promised to come and see us, so don't let us down. All for
now. Love from Hannah.*

In her sudden state of alarm, Babs dropped fag ash onto the
postcard; then, getting up from the dressing table, she rushed across
to her calendar on the wall at the side of her bed. The date was
28 November. Christmas was less than a month away. She hurried
back to the dressing table, opened one of the drawers, and dropped
the postcard amongst the others from Hannah that had been left
there, hardly read, over the past two months. Then she went back
to the light switch and turned it off, staggered across to her double
bed in the dark, and huddled up beneath the bedclothes. She lay
there for quite a time before her eyes finally closed, allowing her
sudden flash of panic to fade into the dark winter night.

Hannah got up at the crack of dawn. It wasn't something she
enjoyed doing, but as her first chore of the day was to turn on
the saloon bar lights and clean out the ashes from the fireplace
grate, she much preferred to get it over and done with before
Maggie and Sid Bullock came down for their breakfast soon
after eight o'clock. Once that was done, she drew an enamel
bowl of water from the kitchen tap, poured some carbolic into
it, and set about washing the bar counter and tables. It was only
whilst doing this that she suddenly noticed something that hadn't

caught her attention until now. Dropping her washing cloth back into the bowl, she went across to look at the collection of photographs from Sid Bullock's fishing trips that were hanging in between the timber beams on the wall. One was clearly missing, for there was a clean white space on the wall where it had been on show for some time. Hannah stood there for several moments, staring at the blank space, trying to remember if she had actually seen the photograph and, if so, what exactly what was in it. But as they all looked pretty much the same to her, with Sid Bullock and his friends showing off a catch, she just shrugged her shoulders, collected her bowl, and went back into the kitchen. Whilst she was collecting the dirty dishes from the previous night's meals, she suddenly noticed that the kitchen larder had been left unlocked, for the padlock and key were hanging loosely on the latch. With great excitement, she quietly went to the door of the saloon bar and made sure that she could neither see nor hear any sign of the Bullocks, then returned to open the larder door. She was astonished by what she found inside. Every shelf of the stone larder was packed with provisions: tins of ham, pilchards, baked beans, and even corned beef. There were several packets of sugar, tea, currants and sultanas, two dishes of fresh farm-made butter, a huge homemade fruit cake, a leg of pork, a whole chicken, a string of pork sausages, and a flat covered dish bulging with lamb chops. The sight of it all took Hannah's breath away. How did Maggie Bullock manage to get all this stuff when so much of it was now strictly rationed? Not only that, but why was it that she and Louie were never offered anything like this and only ever got basic leftover food such as stewed rabbit and minced beef and mash? Still recovering from the shock, she was in the act of closing the door when it suddenly occurred to her that there was something else on the top shelf of that larder that she had not fully taken in. She opened the door again, and gazed up at the large floral-designed china barrel marked BISCUITS. The temptation was too great. She quickly collected one of the kitchen chairs from the table, took it to the larder and climbed up on it. When she opened the china barrel she found it crammed with shortbread biscuits. That was it! Throwing caution to the wind, she took one of the biscuits, crammed it into her mouth, and then took another and another, until she had devoured three biscuits. She was about to put the barrel back in its place when she changed her mind, took three more, and shoved them into the pocket of her apron. Now nervous about being caught, she replaced the biscuit barrel on the top shelf, got down off the chair, and closed the larder door. Before returning to the saloon bar, she uncovered Polly's cage, and was greeted with an immediately bright "Allo!"

'Ssh!' said Hannah, putting her finger to her lips. She hurried across to the door, but before she could get there the parrot's shrill voice screeched out at her.

'Mine's a Guinness! Mine's a Guinness!'

Hannah stopped at the door, and called back softly, 'It's too early, Poll! Get back ter bed!'

Redbourne village green was a hive of activity. By the time Hannah got there after taking Louie off to school, a group of about a dozen middle-aged and elderly men, all togged up in their workday clothes with walking sticks and rolled-up umbrellas, were playing out some kind of military-type exercise, lying flat on their stomachs, pretending to fire rifles with their sticks. When Hannah joined the small collection of locals who had turned out to watch, she noticed that amongst the men engaged in the exercises were Barney Jessop, Percy Bumper the farmer, and his farmhand Jack Dabbs. Hannah couldn't believe her eyes. As the goings-on became more disorganised, she found it difficult not to burst out laughing.

'Look a bright bunch, don't they?'

Hannah turned, to find Jane Jessop at her side. 'Wot're they all up to?' she asked.

'They're going to protect us if and when the Germans come,' replied Jane, with a despondent sigh. 'Can you imagine it? If we rely on *this* lot, we'll all end up in Nazi prison camps!'

'Yer mean, they fink we really *could* get invaded?' asked Hannah incredulously.

Jane shrugged. 'It's all because of that man who came over the other day from the town hall in Hertford,' she replied, keeping her voice down. 'He brought some officer from the army with him. The government wants all the men in rural areas who haven't been called up to volunteer for armed home service. They say if the Germans *do* come, there won't be enough troops to protect us.'

The moment she finished speaking, her father, who seemed to be in charge of the exercise, bawled out a command to the men: 'Don't fire 'til you see the whites of their eyes!'

Much to the disgust of some of the village ladies around them, both Hannah and Jane sniggered and moved on.

'Can you believe they've put Dad in charge?' said Jane, wheeling her bicycle.

''As 'e ever been in the army?'

'You must be joking. The most he was ever in was the boy scouts!'

Again the two of them sniggered.

'Still,' continued Jane, 'with the way things are going in Europe now, it's best to be on the safe side, I suppose. Apparently, over the next few months the government wants to get this voluntary home service thing properly organised – uniforms and guns and what have you.'

'Does that mean *all* the men will take part?' asked Hannah. 'Including the vicar?'

Jane giggled.

'What about Sam an' his dad?'

Hannah's question brought Jane to a sudden halt. 'Oh no,' she said. 'That'll never happen.'

Concerned by Jane's sudden change of mood, Hannah asked curiously, 'Why not?'

'Quakers don't take up arms,' Jane replied. 'They're pacifists.'

'Due wot?'

'They're peace-loving people. They don't believe in war. They refuse to fight or kill.'

They were distracted by the sound of Barney Jessop shouting out more commands on the village green. The men suddenly yelled out a battle cry which sent all the ducks on the pond fleeing for their lives.

'I can't imagine *anyone* would really *want* ter kill,' said Hannah, becoming more serious.

'It's not like that, Hannah,' said Jane. 'The Quakers are really against the war, *any* war. They consider it a crime against God to take up any kind of arms against their fellow human beings.'

'So what about Sam?' asked Hannah. 'What 'appens if they call 'im up?'

'He won't go. Or at least, that's what everyone round here thinks. He'll register as a conscientious objector.'

'Come again?'

'He has to do some other kind of compulsory war work, or go to prison.'

'Wot!'

'Oh, don't worry, that won't happen. Sam will probably go and work with the Fire Service in Hertford or something, or at the hospital. It's not that he's a coward or anything – quite the reverse. But the Quakers' beliefs are very strong. They go back a long way in history.' She turned and smiled knowingly at Hannah. 'You must get him to tell you about it some time. Looks like he's taken quite a fancy to you.'

'Git orf!' Hannah laughed dismissively, moving on.

'Well, why not?' asked Jane, following her. 'He's quite a good-looker, and so are you. I reckon you two would get on quite well together.'

'I ain't in the market fer boyfriends, Jane,' Hannah replied over her shoulder. 'Right now I've got too many problems at the Cock and Crow.'

When Hannah got back to the pub, she found Maggie Bullock in the kitchen singing along in a cracked semi-soprano voice to the accompaniment of Sandy McPherson at the organ, on the wireless.

'Ah – there you are, my dear!' called Maggie, above the strains of 'Sweetheart, Sweetheart'. 'Come and sit down. I want to talk to you.'

Hannah's heart sank as she sat at the kitchen table, waiting for her usual morning lecture.

Maggie turned off the wireless, and joined her. 'There we are then,' she said cosily. 'I just want to say how nice and clean the bar is. You've done a good job there, Hannah. Well done!'

Hannah flicked her a grateful, wry smile, only because over Maggie's shoulder she was relieved to see that the padlock on the larder door was now firmly closed.

'In fact,' continued Maggie pleasantly, 'your father and I were both saying how pleased we are at the way you've been pulling your weight around the place. It just shows what you can do when you make the effort.'

Hannah felt quite sick.

'However,' continued Maggie, 'it's time to move on to other things. Bed-making!'

Hannah looked up with a start. 'Due wot?'

'Do you know how to make a bed?'

Hannah hesitated a moment, then shook her head vigorously.

'Ah, my dear,' Maggie wagged her finger, 'then it's time you learnt. Now that we have an extended family around the house, I just do not have the time to make our bed in the mornings. So there's another little job you can take on for me.'

'I've never made a bed in me 'ole life!' protested Hannah.

'Well,' said Maggie, getting up from the table, 'now's the time to try. Follow me!'

Hannah got up from the table, and followed Maggie out of the kitchen and up the stairs. She couldn't believe this was happening to her.

The Bullocks' bedroom was bigger than Hannah had imagined, *much* bigger. The reason seemed to be because two rooms had been knocked into one. But it was certainly a pleasant enough room, with dark timber beams and white distempered walls, and Maggie's choice of miniature paintings was surprisingly pleasing to the eye, with sunsets over the Swiss mountains and golden cornfields together with family portraits. The dressing table was neat and clean: nothing there but a hairbrush and comb, and, to Hannah's horror, a pair of false teeth in a glass of solution. However, her attention was soon focused on the large, double poster bed, which looked a bit of a mess.

'Now then,' announced Maggie with a flourish, 'where shall we start?' She pulled down the eiderdown and sheets, and stood one side of the bed whilst Hannah stood on the opposite side. 'First we straighten the bottom sheet.'

Hannah resentfully copied what Maggie was doing, smoothing the bottom sheet, buffing up the pillows, then straightening and smoothing the top sheet before replacing the blankets and eiderdown. She breathed a sigh of relief when she was finished.

Maggie stood back and looked at what Hannah had done on her side of the bed. 'Oh dear.' She sighed mournfully. 'I'm afraid you'll never make a nurse.'

'I don't want ter *be* a nurse,' Hannah assured her.

'There's a war on, Hannah. We all have to adapt,' said Maggie, adding, 'We all have to make sacrifices, whether it's in the bedroom – or the kitchen.' She went to the door. 'Now why don't I leave you to do some practice? I'm sure someone with your brains will soon make sense of it all.'

Maggie went, and for a moment or so Hannah just stood there, staring furiously at the blasted bed. Then, in a sudden fit of temper, she grabbed hold of all the bedclothes and yanked them off the mattress. As she was struggling to put them back, however, something caught her eye. Protruding from underneath the bed on what appeared to be Sid Bullock's side was a framed photograph. Making sure that no one was at the door, she pulled the photograph out and immediately recognised it as the missing one that had been hanging with the others in the saloon bar. This time she took a long, close look at it. Once again it was of Sid Bullock, complete with fish catch and flanked by his pals, but this time Hannah suddenly saw that there was someone in the group she hadn't noticed until now. It was a young girl, probably a teenager, with a head-scarf, a flashing smile, and overalls. For a moment or so, Hannah stared at the photograph, trying to make some sense of it, trying to work out why the Bullocks had removed it from the wall downstairs. Just as she was doing so, however, she heard a movement from the bathroom next door, so she quickly replaced the photograph where she had found it, and resumed making the bed.

Sid Bullock came in from the bathroom, still wearing his pyjamas. Finding Hannah in the room, he panicked, hurried across to the dressing table, reclaimed his false teeth from the glass there, and quickly shoved them back into his mouth. 'Sorry,' he spluttered, embarrassed. 'Sorry to disturb you!' With that, he scurried straight out of the room again. Bemused, Hannah watched him go. Then she again looked down at the floor beneath the bed where she had just replaced the photograph. Her mind was now working overtime.

During the morning break, Louie and her classmate, Poppy Wilkins, came out into the school playground to play, and drink their free milk together. The two girls had become great pals the moment they had met, for although Poppy was born and brought up in Redbourne, and lived with her mum and Aunt Rosemary there, she and Louie found they had a lot in common, in particu-lar a shared dislike of that terror of the school classroom back home in Holloway, Alfie Grieves. Trouble started the moment Alfie laid eyes on Poppy, for she was a pretty little thing, with laughing grey eyes, a honey-milk complexion, dimples, and a curly top of shining dark blond hair, a combination which, in some of her classmates' eyes, made her the spitting image of the young cinema goddess, Shirley Temple. This was all Alfie needed to know to tease the life out of the poor girl, mocking her every time he passed her in the street with a tuneless rendering of 'On The Good Ship Lollipop'. However, Poppy had found an ally in Louie who, during her time at school back home in Holloway, had given Alfie as good as he gave, calling him 'Mummy's Pet', and telling everyone that he was the worst footballer in the school because he only ever scored goals against his own side. But of late, Alfie had been somewhat subdued and serious, and when he came out into the playground to join the two girls, Louie was surprised to see a huge swelling on his left cheek which was now a vivid dark blue colour.

'Looks like you got what was comin' to yer, Alfie Grieves!' she sniggered, sipping milk through a straw. Poppy sniggered with her.

'It's not funny!' growled Alfie, with a look of thunder. 'I tell yer, that man's got no right ter bash me up. If only I knew who ter go to, I'd report 'im!'

Louie and Poppy exchanged a puzzled look. '*Wot* man?' asked Louie. 'Wot yer talkin' about?'

'That geezer I'm lodged wiv,' replied Alfie, one hand in a pocket, sipping his own milk. 'Fred Winner, the smiff.'

'*Who?*' asked Louie, looking to Poppy for some kind of explanation.

'Mr Winner, the blacksmith,' said Poppy. 'He shoes all the

horses round here. Not a very nice man. Nobody likes him – *nor* his sister.'

'Well, *I* don't like 'im!' barked Alfie. 'It's not the first time 'e's beat me up. The last time I couldn't sleep 'cos me lips were all swollen. I told Miss Thomas about it, but she din't take no notice.'

'Miss Thomas can't do much about things like that,' said Poppy. 'Since you lot all arrived from London, she's had far too much to do to listen to everyone's complaints.'

'So why did 'e bash yer up, Alfie?' asked Louie, who was really quite concerned. 'Wos you bein' cheeky wiv 'im or somefin'?'

'No I was *not*!' snarled Alfie. ''E bashes me up 'cos 'e likes doin' it an' 'cos 'e don't like us folk from Lond'n. An' wot's more 'im an' 'is sister don't give me enuff ter eat.'

'You're not the only one!' said Louie. 'All me and Hann ever get are leftovers. I don't trust the Bullocks. They should never've bin allowed to adopt. If *I* 'ad my way, I'd run off and never come back.'

'Me too!' agreed Alfie. 'I don't get on wiv country people. They ain't a bit like us back in 'Olloway.'

'You shouldn't judge everyone in the village by the way Mr Winner the blacksmith treats you,' said Poppy, finishing the last of her milk, and putting the empty bottle on the trestle table along with all the others. 'And as for the Bullocks,' she added pointedly, 'they've got nothing to boast about, especially after what *he* did to poor Sheila.'

Louie and Alfie exchanged a quizzical look. 'Sheila?' asked Louie.

'Who's she?' asked Alfie, intrigued.

Poppy, revelling in being the centre of attention, straightened up, ready to drop her bombshell. 'The girl who worked for the

Bullocks over at the pub, the one who took over after Chrissie went off and joined the Forces. The one he killed.'

Both Louie and Alfie's eyes widened in horror.

'*Killed?*' gasped Louie, who was absolutely thunderstruck.

Once she had finished clearing up after the lunchtime opening, Hannah went out to the hut in the back garden and did her best to wash off the smell of cigarette smoke and beer that seemed to cling to her so obstinately. Each day she was getting more fed up with her daily chores, and wished that she and Louie could go back where they belonged. As she combed her hair in the tiny mirror over the washbasin, she felt as though she was looking at her mum in the reflection there, so much so that she started talking to her. 'It's not fair, Mum,' she said, with a deep sigh. 'One postcard, just one. At least just ter let us know that you're alive. Just take us away from this place, that's all I ask. I promise we won't be any trouble to yer, an' even if Jerry *does* start droppin' bombs, at least we'll all be tergevver. After all, wherever Dad is 'e 'as ter put up wiv bein' in the front line, so why shouldn't we? I ain't scared, Mum. I want yer ter know that. I ain't scared.' She suddenly swung with a start as she heard Maggie Bullock's voice calling from outside the hut.

'Hannah! Are you in there?'

Hannah called back. 'Just comin'!' She quickly wiped her hands on the towel, and went out.

'Ah, there you are, my dear!' Maggie Bullock was waiting outside like a prison jailer. 'You have a visitor. That young lad from the post office.'

Hannah's eyes widened. 'Sam? *Here?*'

'I hadn't realised you'd formed such a close alliance,' said Maggie tersely. 'If I were you I'd be very careful. From what I hear, Samuel Beedle is not the most reliable person, despite his parents' bizarre religious convictions.'

Hannah ignored what Maggie said and rushed off, leaving her standing alone in the garden. Sam, looking cold and anxious, was waiting in the street outside.

'Sam!' gasped Hannah, relieved to see his friendly face. 'Wot're *you* doin' 'ere?'

'I think you'd better come with me, Hannah,' he said, with urgency. 'We've just heard there's a commotion down at the school. It's about your sister.'

With the nights now drawing in fast, it was getting dark by the time Hannah and Sam reached the gates of the village school. When they got there they found a group of people gathered around. Amongst them was Louie's class pal Poppy.

'What's up?' asked Hannah breathlessly. 'Where's my sister? Wot's 'appened to 'er?'

Louie's new schoolteacher, Helen Thomas, stepped forward to meet her. She was a young woman, wearing a scarf and a warm topcoat, her face racked with anxiety. 'Louise has disappeared,' she said.

Hannah nearly had a fit. '*Disappeared!* Wot yer talkin' about?'

'She went off with Alfie Grieves,' said the schoolteacher. 'As you probably know, that boy really is a bit of a young scoundrel. It seems to have happened soon after the last bell of the afternoon. Usually Louise waits outside until you come to collect her, but after what Poppy told me, well, I just don't know what they're up to. Anyway, I have informed Police Constable Harrington.'

Mrs Mullard was there, her double chin working overtime as

she chewed on her bottom lip. 'Go on, child,' she said to Poppy. 'Tell us what happened.'

'*Nothing* happened,' insisted Poppy, who really couldn't understand what all the fuss was about. 'We were just talking, that's all – about how Alfie gets beaten up by the man he lives with. Then Louie said as how badly *she* gets treated too. She says she hates living at the Cock and Crow.'

'So how come they ran off?' asked Hannah impatiently. 'Where did they go?'

'I don't know,' replied Poppy, who was now getting quite nervous at all the attention she was receiving from everyone. 'But both Louie and Alfie said that they'd like to run away, away from – the people they live with.'

Hannah was shocked. 'Where've they gone to?' she asked quickly, panicking. 'We've got ter find 'em.'

'I don't know!' repeated the girl, close to tears, turning in desperation to her teacher. 'I told them not to do it, Miss. I promise I did!'

'It's all right, Poppy,' replied the teacher, trying to comfort the girl. 'You're not to blame.'

'Listen, mate!' said Hannah, with great urgency, stooping down to talk to the child. ''Ave yer any idea where they could've gone? Any place that you and Louie ever go to tergevver?'

Poppy, snivelling, and hugging her teacher's waist, looked up at her. 'I don't know anywhere,' she replied tearfully. 'Unless they've gone down to the river by Beechers Wood.'

Hannah pressed forward eagerly. 'Where?' she asked.

'I know it!' said Sam urgently. 'I'll get a torch!' He rushed off.

'Why did they do this *now*, Poppy?' pleaded Hannah. 'What made Louie and Alfie suddenly want ter run off like this?'

Poppy was too distraught to answer. She just turned away and held on tight to her teacher.

The beam from Sam's torch darted from one tree to another. Beechers Wood was not the most inviting place on a cold, dark winter's night, and Hannah made quite sure that she did not stray too far away from where Sam was searching.

'Lou!' Hannah shouted over and over again. But the only thing she succeeded in doing was disturbing the wood's bird population who were trying to settle down in their nests for a good night's sleep. 'She's not 'ere, Sam,' she said. 'Lou would never ignore me. If she 'eard me comin' she'd call out ter me. Silly little bugger! Once I get my 'ands on 'er I'll bleedin' frottle 'er!'

'That sort of talk won't help you *or* Louie, Hannah,' replied Sam, searching under every bush he came to. 'Those poor kids must be scared out of their lives. These woods are a dangerous place to be in after dark. Something must have really upset them to have done a thing like this.'

Hannah was beside herself with worry. Despite the anger she was feeling for the anxiety Louie was causing her, she did love her sister, and felt responsible for her safety. If anything were to happen to her, she would never forgive herself.

They made their way through the wet undergrowth, shivering with the approach of an inevitable November frost. At one stage, Hannah was startled by a hare which leapt out from a bush, squealed, and disappeared into the dark, and then again by a bat which took flight from the tree above her and swooped so low that it actually brushed her shoulder. Hannah hated all this. Her heart was racing hard all the time, and all she wanted was to be back home in Kinloch Street in front of the welcoming oven range fire in the back parlour. She was now convinced that country life was not for her.

'We're just coming down to the river,' called Sam, whose torch beam was directed well ahead of them. 'If they're stuck down there, they must be freezing cold.'

In the torchight, Hannah could just see the river through the trees, dark and menacing, but calm and smug, refusing to give up all the secrets it must have encountered over the years. They came to a halt on the river bank. The silence was so eerie, Hannah unconsciously put her arm round Sam's waist. 'Yer don't fink . . . ?'

'Don't jump to conclusions, Hannah,' said Sam. 'If they're hiding, we'll find them. Especially once they start getting hungry.'

Even as he spoke, there was a movement further along the riverside. Sam immediately swung his torch beam round and scanned as much of the area as he could.

'Lou!' yelled Hannah, frantic now. 'Where are yer?'

To their astonishment, there came an immediate reply. 'Hann.' By the sound of Louie's tiny voice, she was shivering with the cold.

Hannah quickly followed Sam as he rushed along the river bank, where his torch beam soon picked out Louie and Alfie, huddled up together beneath the shelter of a huge oak tree.

'Lou!' yelled Hannah, rushing at her sister, and embracing her. 'Wot the bleedin' 'ell d'yer fink you're doin', yer silly cow!' Her language was strong only because of the intense relief she felt at finding the child safe.

Louie immediately started to cry.

'Why, Lou?' asked Hannah. 'Why?'

'We ain't scared!' came Alfie Grieves's firm, confident voice.

'We ain't scared of bein' out 'ere. We much prefer it ter bein' back in *that* place, don't we, Lou?'

'Wot's all this about, Lou?' asked Hannah, quickly wrapping her own coat round the child's shoulders. 'Tell me!'

'Wait, Hannah,' pleaded Sam, giving Alfie a helping hand to get up. 'Let her tell you in her own good time.'

But Louie did answer. 'I don't want ter go back ter that place, Hann,' she sobbed. 'After wot 'appened, after wot that man did, I don't ever want ter go back.'

'Wot yer talking about, Lou?' asked Hannah, now deeply anxious. '*Wot* man?'

'Ol' black eye,' replied Louie, her voice reduced to a scared whisper. ''E killed that gel, an' 'e might do the same to us!'

Hannah held on tight to the child. She felt a cold shiver run down her spine.

Chapter 6

Maggie Bullock was none too pleased when Hannah and Louie returned home an hour after the pub had opened. Fortunately, so far none of the pub's customers had any knowledge of what had happened out at the school that afternoon, which meant that Hannah didn't have too much explaining to do other than to say that Louie and her class had to stay behind to do some extra work with their teacher. But once in the safety of their attic room, Hannah tried to find out more about the reason why her young sister and Alfie Grieves had become so alarmed that they had wanted to run away.

'It's true, Hann,' said Louie, keeping her voice low, perched on the side of her tiny bed with Hannah. 'This gel Sheila used ter work 'ere in the pub. She didn't 'ave no mum an' dad 'cos they died when she was young. When ol' Ma Bullock gave 'er a job, she never stopped workin', 'ardly ever 'ad any time to 'erself.'

'So wot's all this about Bullock killin'' 'er?' asked Hannah sceptically.

'That's wot 'e did, Hann,' replied Louie. 'I'm not lyin', 'onest ter God I'm not. Poppy told me an' Alfie all about it.'

''*Ow* did this gel die?' pressed Hannah. ''Ow did Bullock kill 'er?'

'Poppy don't know exactly how,' continued Louie. 'All she knows is that it 'appened on one of ol' Bullock's fishin' trips on the river.'

Hannah looked at her with a start. 'Fishin' trips?'

'Poppy said that they used ter take this gel along to 'elp with the bait or somefin'. I din't really understand wot that meant. But all the village knew about it.'

For a moment or so, Hannah went quite silent. Going through her head was the photograph that used to hang on the wall in the saloon bar, and she had found tucked under the Bullocks' bed.

'If yer don't believe me,' said Louie, 'yer can ask around.'

Hannah *had* asked around. On the way back from the woods she had asked Sam what he knew about this girl Sheila, but the only reaction she got from him was that they shouldn't talk too much about something that happened some time ago, that Poppy had the reputation of making up stories about nothing. 'I fink we'd better keep quiet about this fer a while, Lou,' she said. 'At least until we know wot it's *really* all about.'

'But I don't feel safe in this place, Hann,' said Louie, her eyes still red from crying on the way back from the woods. 'Every time I come 'ere, I feel ol' black patch 'as got 'is eye on me.'

'Now don't exaggerate, Lou!' replied Hannah firmly. 'We may not like the Bullocks, but they're all we've got at the moment.'

'Why doesn't Mum come an' get us?' Louie's plea was heartfelt and poignant.

'She will, Lou,' Hannah assured her. 'Just give 'er time. We'll probably 'ear from 'er any time now. When she comes an' visits us at Chrissmas, we can tell 'er 'ow we feel, tell 'er that . . .'

'That we want ter go 'ome!'

Hannah sighed. 'Yes, Lou,' she replied forlornly. 'We'll tell 'er that we wanna go 'ome.'

Barney Jessop was known in the village to be a bit of a gossip. If you ever wanted to know anything about anyone, then the person to go to was the old tongue-wagger himself. The village store was a perfect place for this. Most of the local women used the place as a talking shop, where they could swap all the current scandals, such as which married man was sleeping with some other married man's wife, and how disgraceful it was to carry on like that in such a respectable place as Redbourne. That was one of the reasons why Maggie Bullock had called in there. She never liked to be left out when something was going on; tittle-tattle behind her back was the thing that riled her most, as had happened in the saloon bar the previous evening, when one or two of her customers were talking amongst themselves about something that had happened with young Louise after school hours. Unfortunately, when she tried to find out what it was, her regulars had become tight-lipped, more or less suggesting that it was none of their business. Hannah was even less forthcoming. Washing up beer glasses behind the counter and in the kitchen, she would only say that her young sister had had a bit of a tiring day, which was why Hannah had packed her off to bed early. After that, Maggie couldn't get to sleep that night, which meant that her only recourse was to go and plug Barney in the village store.

'Oh, if I were you, Mrs Bullock,' said Barney dismissively, his bushy moustache in bad need of a trim, 'I wouldn't bother your-self too much about that adopted of yours. Sounds ter me like it was no more than a kid's prank.'

Maggie was too wily to be fobbed of with that kind of excuse. *Something* was going on, and she was determined to find out what it was. 'What *kind* of prank, Mr Jessop?' she asked furtively.

'As far as I can make out,' replied Barney, 'it weren't much more than takin' off for an hour or so. Only thing is, it can be a bit dangerous out in those woods in the dark. Yer never know who's lurkin' around. Especially down by that river . . .' He suddenly came to a halt in mid-sentence, and looked up uneasily at Maggie.

'Quite,' said Maggie, without over-reacting. 'Especially for a nine-year-old.'

'Two nine-year-olds,' said Barney inaccurately, but in a helpful spirit. 'She went off with a young lad who come down from London at the same time as your girls.'

'Is that so?' asked Maggie, with concealed curiosity.

'Still, no harm came to 'em,' continued Barney, who had started patting some fresh farm butter into regular-sized packs. 'Good thing that young girl of yours and Sam Beedle got there though. I don't think those two young 'uns would have enjoyed spending the night alone with them foxes lurkin' around. Scared enough as it was, so *I* heard.'

Maggie's ears pricked up. 'Scared?' she asked. 'Scared of what?'

'Good morning, Mrs Bullock.'

Jane Jessop's appearance from the back parlour was deliberately timed to prevent her father from having to answer some awkward questions.

'Good morning, Jane,' Maggie replied curtly, frustrated by having her conversation with Barney interrupted.

'Sorry, Dad,' Jane said briskly, 'but I think we're out of dried peas. Could you just go and check if we need to reorder? The wholesaler's coming this afternoon.'

'Oh, right you are!' said Barney, rushing off into the back room. 'Mornin', Mrs Bullock.'

Maggie was too irritated to reply.

'Sorry to interrupt, Mrs Bullock,' said Jane, smiling sweetly. 'Is there anything I can get you?'

Maggie left the village store, and made her way to the post office. She was none too pleased to be thwarted in her attempt to learn the reason why Louie had run off so suddenly from school the previous evening. Her eyes never left the pavement as she walked. Her mind was concentrating on the problems that were looming with her two new foster-daughters, especially with Louie. It was not only the fact that the child had clearly caused trouble in the village the previous evening, but also those biscuits in her larder . . .

She reached the post office, but didn't go in. From her handbag she took out a stamped envelope. She took one last lingering look at the address she had written on it: *Mrs Adams, 7 Kinloch Street, Holloway, London N.7.* She dropped the letter into the post box in the wall outside the post office, and then went on her way.

With barely a handful of children from London now left in the village, Hannah was becoming increasingly desperate about whom to turn to to express her concerns about the foster-parents she and Louie had been billeted with. Against the government's advice, parents had been turning up every few days to collect their children and take them home, convinced that the scare about bombing raids on London had been a false alarm. However, Hannah's concerns were finally put to rest when Louie's geography teacher, Mavis Reynolds, turned up at the

Cock and Crow in the company of Mrs Mullard from the village evacuation committee. Maggie and Sid Bullock, all smiles and utmost courtesy, were waiting there to greet them, having received prior warning of their visit. However, Hannah was none too pleased when the two visitors were asked to join herself and the Bullocks for tea in the back parlour, an elegantly furnished sitting room which Hannah had never seen before because it was always locked up, and apparently used only on high days and holidays.

'I must say, Margaret,' said the rather ebullient, but breathless, Mrs Mullard. 'This is the first time I knew that you had such beautiful accommodation here in the public house. You and your sister are very lucky to live in such a place, Hannah.'

Maggie Bullock smiled sweetly at Hannah, who sat on an upright chair whilst the two visitors sat side by side on the sofa sipping tea. 'We're very lucky to have Hannah, too,' she replied. 'She's been such a help around the place. I must say, I don't know what we'd do without her now. We've come to think of her as one of our own. Isn't that so, Sidney?'

As usual, Sid Bullock merely nodded, and said nothing.

'What about Hannah's sister?' asked Mavis Reynolds, more perceptively. 'We've just come from talking to her and a few of the other children at the school. I've been told she still seems a little uneasy about settling down here.'

'I know,' said Maggie quickly, making sure that Hannah did not have a chance to say anything before her. 'That poor child. She does miss her home so much. I can well understand how difficult it must have been for her to leave her roots and come to a completely alien environment. But I've assured her mother that we shall never give up trying to make both Louise *and*

Hannah comfortable. It's the least we can do in such difficult circumstances.'

'You've been in touch with their mother?' asked Mrs Reynolds sceptically.

'But of course,' replied Maggie, surprised by her visitor's question. 'We correspond regularly. Sidney and I think it very important to establish a link with the poor mites' home. Mrs Adams has been very helpful in advising us of all the things that are important to Louise and Hannah.'

Hannah felt herself stiffen.

Aware of Hannah's self-imposed silence, Mavis Reynolds put down her empty cup and saucer on the coffee table in front of her. 'What about their accommodation, their food?'

'My dear,' replied Maggie, 'in this house we share what we eat. Times are not as fruitful as they used to be, but we do our best. Isn't that so, Hannah?'

Hannah, aware that she was on show, merely nodded.

'As for their accommodation,' continued Maggie, 'Sidney will be only too happy to take you upstairs to show you their room. It's a little on the small side, but we have never had any complaints when we have rented it out in the past.' She turned to her husband. 'Will you take these ladies upstairs, please, dear?'

'Oh, I'm sure that won't be necessary, Maggie,' said Mrs Mullard immediately, only too conscious that a climb up too many stairs would not help her asthma.

Hannah swung an angry glare at the geography teacher, who to all outward appearances remained impassive and unperturbed.

'I would just like to ask one thing, though,' she said calmly.

Without showing it, Maggie tensed slightly. 'Certainly.'

'The licensing laws. I'm sure you're aware that both Louise

and Hannah are under age. You *do* make sure that they are not around in the bars during opening hours?'

Maggie breathed a sigh of relief, and turned to her husband. 'Sidney?'

Sid Bullock spoke up for the first time. 'I never allow kids in the bars,' he replied adamantly. 'Maggie and I know the law. We'd never do anything to infringe it.'

There was something about the look on the geography teacher's face that showed she didn't quite go along with all that she was hearing.

'I don't believe in under age near alcohol,' continued Sid Bullock. 'I'd never allow it, even if I had kids of my own.' Aware of the insensitive thing he had just said, he put a comforting hand on his wife's arm. Maggie played along with mock sorrow.

'Well, as far as *I'm* concerned,' said Mrs Mullard, 'everything here seems to be quite in order for Hannah and Louise. I don't think we need to detain these good people much longer. Unless,' she turned to the schoolteacher, '*you* have any more questions?'

'Just one,' replied Mavis Reynolds. Again Maggie tensed. 'I wonder if I could have a few moments alone with Hannah?'

Although a little uneasy, Maggie beamed. 'Of course,' she replied, getting up. 'Please take your time.' She led Mrs Mullard to the door. 'We'll be in the kitchen if you need us.' Last to leave was Sid Bullock, who cast a passing, furtive eye at Hannah as he left, closing the door quietly behind him.

Alone with Hannah, Mavis led her away from the door to the bow window, where they both stood looking out. 'So what do you think of Redbourne, Hannah?' the teacher asked, keeping her voice low.

'It's all right fer some,' replied Hannah dourly. 'Yer can't beat 'Olloway.'

'They're somewhat different.'

'Yer can say that again!'

Mavis positioned herself so that she was facing Hannah. 'Why are you and Louise not happy here, Hannah?' she asked directly.

''Ow can yer like a place when you're treated as nuffin' more than a slave?'

Mavis looked at the girl with concern. 'What do you mean?'

'D'yer know wot time I get up every mornin'?' Hannah asked without expecting an answer. 'Soon after six! I get up, I clean out the ashes in the grate, I sweep and wash the floor in the two bars, I do the washin' up in the kitchen, then I wait for that woman ter come in and start givin' me more fings ter do. The latest is makin' their bed. If I knew I was goin' ter be nuffin' more than a skivvie, yer would never 'ave got me 'ere in a million years! I gave up a good job back 'ome ter be wiv Louie, an' none of it makes sense.'

Mavis looked deadly serious. 'Is this true, Hannah?' she asked gravely, meeting the tortured look in Hannah's eyes.

'True?' Hannah looked directly at her former geography teacher. Until this moment she hadn't realised what a handsome woman she was, younger-looking than her fifty or so years, with soft dark eyes, and a well-sculptured face that needed nothing more than a dab of make-up. 'If yer don't believe me, yer should just go upstairs and see wot me an' Lou are sleepin' in. It's nuffin' more than a junk room, 'ardly enuff room ter breave. An' 'ow d'yer fink we feel when we sit down ter bread and marge fer breakfast when we can smell eggs 'n' bacon cookin' in the kitchen, somefin' we *never* get?'

'Did you eat eggs and bacon for breakfast when you lived at home?'

'No, course not, but—'

'Then why should you expect it now?'

The schoolteacher's response was not what Hannah had expected. She had waited in great frustration for this moment, the chance to get off her chest all the things she had been bottling inside her. 'I don't *expect* it,' she replied tersely, 'but if people say they're goin' ter look after yer, then the least they can do is ter give yer a decent place ter put yer 'ead down, an' some decent grub.'

Mavis thought about this for a moment, then sat down on a chair by the window. 'Hannah,' she said. 'I have to tell you that I don't think we have the *right* to expect anything. There's a war on, and in one way or another we all have to make sacrifices.'

Hannah suddenly felt defeated. 'You sound just like *'er*,' she sighed, with irony.

Mavis looked up at her. 'Are you talking about Mrs Bullock?'

'I'm talkin' about *boaf* of 'em.' Hannah sat in a chair directly facing the schoolteacher. Before continuing, she cast a quick, anxious glance at the door. 'Mrs Reynolds, do yer *know* wot kind er people they are? I mean, did anyone check up on 'em before we come 'ere?'

The schoolteacher wasn't quite prepared for that one. 'In the short time at their disposal,' she replied, trying not to be flustered, 'I'm quite sure the authorities did everything in their power to make sure *all* foster-parents were carefully scrutinised.'

'So did they tell you that *our* foster-farver killed someone?'

Surprisingly, the schoolteacher *was* prepared for that one. 'You mustn't believe everything people tell you, Hannah,' she replied. 'Even your sister.'

Hannah shot her an astonished look.

'I talked to Louise just before Mrs Mullard and I came here,' continued Mavis. 'I suppose you're aware that her disappearance after school the other evening caused a great deal of concern and inconvenience.'

'Did Louie tell yer *why* she disappeared?' asked Hannah forcefully.

'Yes, Hannah, she did. Her reason was quite preposterous.'

''Ow can yer say that?' snapped Hannah, running her fingers through her hair with frustration. 'Bullock killed the gel who used ter work 'ere.'

'No, he didn't, Hannah,' replied the schoolteacher firmly. 'Mrs Mullard and I discussed the matter at length. What happened down at the river – was an accident.'

Hannah was completely taken aback. 'Huh?' she gasped.

'I don't know the full details – you'll have to get that from someone else – but it's certainly no secret. Mrs Mullard says that what happened is, and always has been, common knowledge in the village. The girl drowned. It was an accident, Hannah.'

Hannah just couldn't take in what she was hearing. 'But Louie said . . .'

'What your sister told you,' insisted Mavis, 'was nothing more than a silly, dramatic story told to her by one of her school friends.'

'I don't know what's going on down here, Mrs Reynolds,' said Hannah, who was now so troubled and confused that it was making her angry, 'but I 'ate country people. They don't like outsiders, especially from the city. They said they wanted to do their bit, to care for us, but they're nothing like the people *we* come from.'

The schoolteacher would have none of this. 'Now listen to me, Hannah,' she replied calmly. 'Most of the people in this village have done their best for you and the others who came here. How would you or any of the families back in Holloway feel if they were suddenly asked to take in complete strangers, people they have nothing in common with, young people who know nothing about the way city folk live their lives? Yes, I agree with you, not all the foster-parents here have been as welcoming as one would hope, but most of them have tried, they've tried very hard. It's not *their* fault if some of their friends or neighbours do things that are wrong. People are basically the same, Hannah, whether they come from the dirt and grime of towns and cities, or from the green pastures of the countryside. It's wrong of you to be unfair to *everyone*, Hannah – so very unfair.'

For a moment, Hannah remained silent, her head bowed. Then she slowly looked up. 'Just get us 'ome, Mrs Reynolds. This is no place fer me an' my sister. It's our mum we need, our own *real* mum.'

Chapter 7

As each day passed, Hannah was growing more attached to Sam Beedle than she would ever dare admit. Sam was such a kind, caring person that he was the only one who could actually relieve Hannah of the pain of having to remain with the Bullocks. With Christmas now only two weeks away, once she had completed her chores, they spent as much time in each other's company as they possibly could, especially on Sunday afternoons. Their favourite spot was Buller's Hill, which overlooked Redbourne and the surrounding villages, and Sam said was always a marvellous vantage point for watching fireworks on Guy Fawkes night. However, it was a bit of a climb to the summit, and by the time they had negotiated the narrow, craggy path their shoes were quite muddy, and at this time of year the cold winter winds meant that they both had to wrap up warm, Hannah in headscarf and topcoat, and Sam in his duffel coat. This suited them both fine, of course, for once they had reached the old stone bench overlooking the valley the icy winds gave them a perfectly good excuse to snuggle up close together.

On the previous Sunday, Sam had talked a lot about his Quaker upbringing, and why the 'Friends', as his people were known, were so against the idea of taking up arms in a war. It was against the principles of everything they believed in. But on this particular Sunday afternoon, Hannah learnt a great deal more, and not only about what it was to be a Quaker.

'Our one regret,' said Sam, as he and Hannah stared out at the vast barren landscape beneath them, 'was that none of the Friends took in any of the children from London. When we were first asked, we had a meeting about it. There was a lot of heart-searching, a lot of guilt, but the conclusion was that by taking in refugee children from London we would in some way be condoning a war that we don't accept. It's changed since then, of course. Once we'd heard that other Quaker groups around the country were taking in children, we were prepared to follow suit. Unfortunately, by then it was too late.'

Hannah looked up at him, and saw the glow of despair in his eyes. In many ways she found him to be a very solitary, self-contained person, who seemed to be harbouring many anxieties. There was much more she wanted to know about him, like the real reasons why he never mentioned having any friends in the village whom he could talk to as he talked to her. 'Is it true wot they say, Sam?' she asked quite suddenly. 'If they call yer up, will yer refuse ter go?'

Sam turned to her with an agitated start. 'Who told you that, Hannah?' he asked uneasily.

Hannah shrugged. 'Can't remember.'

'Was it Jane?'

'It might've bin. Why? Is it true?'

'If you don't mind,' he replied, 'I don't want to talk about it. I have enough problems with my family about it as it is.'

'Why?'

For a moment, he remained silent, but then he got up and

stared forlornly down into the valley below. Hannah, sensing his disquiet, got up and joined him, gently easing her arm through his. For a few moments they just stood there, the cold breeze chafing their faces, turning them a bright red, and ruffling Sam's short blond hair so much so that he frequently used one hand to calm it down.

'It's ever so flat down there, in't it?' said Hannah. 'This is the first time I knew England was so flat.'

'Not really,' said Sam reflectively. 'Just here and there, that's all. I love this country. It's so full of wonderful things – mountains, rivers, hills, trees and green fields. Just look at it down there, a great patchwork quilt. That's what my mother always calls it. You could almost pick it up and put it on your bed.'

Hannah leant her head against his shoulder. Simultaneously he slipped his arm round her waist.

'But is it worth fighting for?' he went on.

'Wot d'yer mean?' asked Hannah, puzzled.

'I mean that if someone tried to take this all away from me, could I *really* just stand aside and let them?' With his other hand he tried to straighten his hair again, but when it proved imposs-ible he simply gave up. 'You know, ever since I was a kid I've climbed this hill, stood here looking out at all that mass of English countryside. But just lately I've never stopped asking myself what I would do if I saw foreign soldiers come streaming down out of the sky, shooting and killing my people, bombing that quilt so that I didn't know it any more.' He sighed deeply. 'I don't know, Hannah. I just don't know.'

'My dad knew,' said Hannah.

Sam turned to look at her. 'Your dad?'

''E din't 'ave ter go ter war. 'E joined up.' For one brief

moment, she looked up at the sky, which was grey, dull, and foreboding, the clouds rushing past in a great panic to get away. 'Every time 'e took me an' Louie ter the pictures, we used ter see German planes on the newsreels, bombin' all over the place, some er the countries I've 'ardly ever 'eard of. When we come out, 'e was always serious – I mean, at the worst of times Dad was usually good for a laugh. But every time 'e come out the pictures 'e was *always* serious. 'E used ter say that *'e'd* never let the same fing 'appen to *'is* country, to *'is* kids. Personally, I fawt 'e was daft. Especially when 'e suddenly rushed off an' joined up. I mean, when yer fink about it, we've bin at war now fer over two months, an' Jerry 'asn't dared drop any bombs on Lond'n. Ter *my* mind 'e'd never 'ave the nerve.'

Sam, deep in thought, didn't answer.

'Cheer up, mate!' she said buoyantly, changing position so that she could put her arm round *his* waist. 'It might never 'appen. At least we've got Chrismass ter look forward to – that is if our mum turns up.'

'You really hate it here, don't you?' said Sam.

'I 'ate the thought that nearly all the uvver kids've gone back except us,' she replied. 'I 'ate the thought of bein' stuck wiv the Bullocks, the fact nobody seems willing ter wanna talk about that so-called accident.'

Sam turned to her. 'Hannah, listen to me,' he said. 'People don't talk about the Bullocks because what happened two years ago is something that everyone wants to try and forget. It was a painful time, Hannah, not only for the Bullocks, but for the entire village.'

'*Why* was it painful?' pressed Hannah.

Sam hesitated before answering. 'Look,' he said, trying to raise a smile. 'You said yourself we've got Christmas to look forward to. Why don't you think about that rather than trying to dig up something that happened so long ago? It's not relevant any more, Hannah. Believe me, it just isn't relevant.'

'It is ter me,' she replied determinedly.

Sam, aware that he was not getting through to her, made a move to lead her back towards the path.

'In any case,' said Hannah, bringing him to a halt, 'do Quakers celebrate Chrissmas, I mean like the rest of us?'

This actually brought a smile to Sam's face. 'We're all human beings, Hannah,' he said. 'Christmas is just as important to the Friends as it is to everyone else. The only difference is that some of us believe Christmas shouldn't just be tied up to the calendar. It's a "feeling" that takes place in our hearts every day of the year.'

Hannah looked puzzled. 'Say again?'

'We don't think Christmas is necessarily a time to celebrate,' he continued. 'But then, we don't think it's wrong if anyone does want to. But I can tell you that in *our* group, we concentrate on looking to the less fortunate, to make sure that they have enough food to eat, and a warm place to live in. Some Friends I know go to the local hospital and sing carols to the patients. It's just a practical way of showing how much you know what Christmas really means.'

Hannah walked a few paces, then stopped and looked back at him. 'D'yer fink people felt the same way about that gel who died in the river?' she asked pointedly.

Sam stared hard at her, the wind now playing havoc with his hair, his piercing blue eyes gleaming in a rare shaft of sunlight.

★　★　★

Polly the parrot had had a trying day. It was bad enough that the saloon bar had been full of the usual crowd at Sunday lunchtime, but she was still less amused when they all crowded around to mock her and poke their fingers through the bars of her cage. However, divine justice managed to give her the chance to get her own back. She had never liked Jack Dabbs, the farmhand, and at that crucial moment, just as he was putting his ugly drunken face close to the cage, she achieved a first strike, a formidable tweak on Jack's nose with her curved, razor-sharp beak. 'Mine's a Guinness!' she screeched in triumph, but Jack, a trickle of blood on his nose, was in no mood to buy a drink for either Polly or anyone else.

Maggie Bullock was also not in a good mood. It didn't please her that once the bar had closed, Hannah had quickly wiped all the bar tables and washed up the glasses, and then rushed out for the afternoon, no doubt to meet up with her Quaker boyfriend. On top of that, Sid had been irritating her no end all day, first with his constant brooding about what happened to that wretched girl two years before, and then mulling over the visit of the geography teacher and that old busybody from the village evacuation committee, Mrs Mullard. 'I warned you this would happen,' he had said, as he and Maggie had sat down wearily in front of the saloon bar fire, she sipping the remains of her gin and tonic, he with a freshly drawn pint of draught bitter. 'It's a good thing they didn't want to see that room upstairs. You know damned well it's far too small for those two.'

'I do wish you'd stop worrying!' Maggie snapped. 'What the eye doesn't see, the heart doesn't grieve after. In any case, with the allowance we get for them, they're lucky to have a room of their own at all.'

'I still say we should feed them up more.'

Maggie swung him one of her looks. 'What did you say?' she asked.

'We don't give them enough, Maggs,' he replied, his voice low. 'You know we don't. They're young 'uns. They *need* feeding up. They should be eating what *we* eat.'

Maggie had a look of thunder. 'And would you like to tell me where all the food's coming from?' she asked acidly. 'They get breakfast, they get an evening meal. And don't forget that youngest gets a school dinner every day.'

'Every day except weekends.'

Now Maggie was really getting irritable with him. He was talking to her as though *she* was to blame for the nosy way that geography teacher had talked to them before she and Vera had left the pub after their meeting with her and Sid. After all, whose idea was it in the first place to bring two London ruffians into the place? After what had happened to that girl two years ago, it was just inviting trouble. 'It may not have occurred to you, Mr Bullock,' she said caustically, 'but we don't have an inexhaustible supply of food in this house.'

'Don't be ridiculous, Maggs,' retorted Sid. 'Think yourself lucky no one's looked inside that larder.'

'They *have* looked inside it.'

Sid looked up with a start. 'What you talking about?'

'My biscuits,' she murmured tersely. 'I noticed it the other day. There were six of my shortbreads missing. There should have been eighteen. There were only twelve.'

'You keep a count of your biscuits?'

'Well of course I do!' she snapped back. 'It's called good house-keeping, Mr Bullock – not that *you'd* know anything about *that*!'

* * *

In the attic room upstairs, Louie was with Alfie Grieves, who had brought over his collection of cigarette cards, which were spread all over Louie's bed.

'An 'undred an' twenty altergevver!' proclaimed Alfie proudly. 'If I was back at Pakeman Street, I'd win 'ands down.'

Louie sighed. 'If only we was *all* back at Pakeman Street.'

'See this one?' Alfie held up a very colourful card containing a picture of a steam railway engine. 'That's the Flyin' Scotsman. I saw it once up at Finsb'ry Park station. They was showin' it off ter some bigwigs on the platform. Course its real name is *The Royal Scot*. It's ever so posh inside, lovely soft seats, an' on the way people even sit at tables to eat.'

'Bit better than *we* got on the train comin' up 'ere!' grumbled Louie.

Alfie ignored her, and carried on sorting through his cigarette cards. With most of their mates now back in London, the two of them had formed a friendship out of need, rather than choice.

'Alfie?' asked Louie forlornly.

'Wot?'

'Is your dad really comin' ter take yer 'ome next week?'

'I bleedin' 'ope so,' replied Alfie, studying a card with a sleek engine called *The Cornish Riviera*. 'I've 'ad enuff of that bleedin' smiff!'

'Does 'e let yer swear like that all the time?'

'I don't swear.'

'Yes, yer do,' said Louie. 'Yer swear *all* the time.'

'Yeah,' replied Alfie, lining up his cigarette cards in neat rows. 'Well so would you, if yer 'ad ter put up wiv wot *I* 'ave ter.'

'Did yer tell your dad about it?'

'Nah,' replied Alfie dismissively. 'My dad couldn't care a bugger.'

'There yer go again,' said Louie demurely. 'Swearin' again.' She knelt on the floor beside him. 'Alfie,' she asked. 'Would yer do me a favour?'

'Wot?'

After a quick glance at the door, she drew closer. 'Will yer ask your dad ter go an' see our mum?' she whispered. 'Tell 'er wot's goin' on down 'ere?'

Alife looked round at her. 'Wot d'yer mean?'

'Wiv them downstairs. Tell 'im ter tell 'er that we wanna come 'ome.'

'Don't she know that already?'

Louie was getting irritated with him. In fact, to her, Alfie Grieves had always been irritating. That was because he had never had a brain in his head. He was known to be a class dunce, because he could never think about anything more than teasing girls and making himself a nuisance. As she looked at his unscrubbed face, full of freckles, white and clueless, she wished it was someone else sitting beside her right now, someone with a little sense, someone she could talk to, confide in. 'Mum don't know nuffin',' she replied, ''cos if she did, she'd've bin down 'ere in a flash ter take us back.'

Alfie merely shrugged.

'So will yer do it, Alfie?' pleaded Louie. 'Will yer ask yer dad?'

Alfie had no chance to answer before the door was suddenly flung open.

'What's going on in here?' Maggie Bullock, with a look of thunder, was standing over them.

Both kids, scared out of their lives, leapt to their feet.

'Who are *you*?' she growled at Alfie. 'What are you doing in this room?'

Before she could say another thing, Alfie had pushed straight past her and rushed down the stairs.

'Alfie's *my* friend!' yelled Louie, her face racked with anger. 'Yer've got no right ter—'

'Don't you yell at me, young lady!' retorted Maggie angrily, her finger pointing menacingly at the girl. 'This is *my* house. You do as *I* tell you to do, and I am telling you that you are not to have visitors in this room without my permission. Do I make myself clear?'

Louie tried to push past her to get out of the room, but Maggie grabbed hold and held on to her. 'How did he get in?' she demanded. 'How did that boy get into this house?'

'We come fru the gate in the back garden.'

'That is sly, Louise. If you are going to continue to live with your father and me in this house, you will *not* be sly. Do I make myself clear?'

'You an' 'im are *not* my muvver an' farver!' shouted Louie, struggling to free herself from Maggie's grasp. '*My* mum 'n' dad'd kill yer if they knew 'ow yer treat me an' Hann. They don't give us lousy beds ter sleep in, an' nuffin' ter eat but—'

'Biscuits?' asked Maggie, her face stiff and tense. 'They give you – *biscuits*?'

'Wot yer talkin' about?' bellowed Louie, Maggie's arms wrapped in a vice-like grip around her. 'I don't know wot yer talkin' about!'

'Biscuits, Louise,' Maggie replied. 'Those shortbread biscuits you *stole* from my larder.' She released her grip on the child, and pushed her back across the room. 'You're a thief, young lady. What do you think your schoolteacher would say if she knew that our adopted child stole from her foster-parents?'

'I ain't a fief!' wept Louie, her face now crumpled up in tears. 'An' I didn't take your rotten ol' biscuits!'

Maggie slowly moved in on her. 'And what do you think the village evacuation committee will say, Louise,' she said quietly, menacingly, 'when I tell them that you not only steal from my larder, but bring boys up into your bedroom without my permission?'

Louie was shaking her head vigorously. 'I didn't! I didn't!' she sobbed.

Maggie was almost upon the child. 'Nobody likes a liar, Louise – nobody!'

'She *ain't* lyin'!'

Maggie swung with a start to find Hannah rushing into the room. 'It's all right, Lou, it's all right!' She threw her arms round the distraught child, and hugged her. Then she turned with a hateful glare to Maggie. 'Lou din't nick yer rotten biscuits. *I* did! An' d'yer know wot? I'm *glad* I did! It'll teach yer ter keep yer bleedin' larder locked up. Yer never know wot the mice'll take.'

With a look of total contempt, Maggie turned away, and rushed out of the room.

'An' Muvver!' Hannah yelled after her derisively. 'If you ever say a spiteful word ter my sister again, yer'll 'ave *me* ter deal wiv!'

On Monday afternoon, Hannah let her curiosity get the better of her. After the way Maggie Bullock had behaved to Louie the previous afternoon, she was determined to get to the bottom of the so-called accident which resulted in the death of the young girl who had previously worked for the Bullocks. Since no one in the village, including Sam and Jane, was willing to discuss the matter, she decided to at least go down to where the accident had happened.

The river by Beechers Wood was looking decidedly less menacing than on the evening when she and Sam had discovered Louie and Alfie hiding in the undergrowth there. In fact it was looking really quite calm and serene, with the watery sun turning the surface into a smoked-glass mirror, which occasionally rippled in a very gentle breeze. For a few minutes she stood on the river bank staring out to the far side, where the water looked quite shallow, and the muddy bank seemed to slope up to a fairly steep incline. There was no sign of life amongst the tall trees and heavy foliage over there, which made her wonder if anyone ever visited such a bleak and unwelcoming place. To her right, the river seemed to bend off out of sight beyond the further stretch of the woods, and as she stood there Hannah gradually recalled having seen the river from the window of the Children's Express when they passed over a bridge before reaching Redbourne station on that first day. She tried to imagine a boat on the stretch of water out there, struggling against bad weather conditions. But from where she was standing the water seemed to be quite shallow, and she could even see some small silver-coloured fish wriggling in and out of the mud on the river bed. Surely a boat would be in very little danger in such a spot, she asked herself? If a boat capsized, surely its passengers would be able to swim or even wade back to the bank? However, when she turned her gaze to the left, the picture was somewhat different, for the river flowed out into what looked like a very large expanse of water, which, for some reason or another, was more restless than that flowing past the village. She started to move off in the direction of what could have been a lake, and as she did so she gradually became aware of a sound like a constant rush of water, almost like a tap running. A few yards further on she came to a halt, and looked around her. The sound was puzzling her.

'That's the old Beechwood Falls.'

The man's voice close by sent her into a cold panic. But when she turned, she immediately recognised the old boy who seemed to spend the whole of his life sitting at the bench table outside the Cock and Crow.

'It ain't no Niagara,' said the old boy as he approached, 'but it's big enough ter put some life inter the ol' river. Just over there. See it?'

Hannah turned to look where he was pointing. She could just see water rushing down a small incline, and tumbling over stones into the lake.

'This lake,' continued the old chap, 'it ain't real, y'know. The church people dug it out a few 'undred years ago, a man-made lake yer can call it. Apparently they used ter have some nasty droughts down here.' He turned and grinned mischievously at Hannah. 'These days they've got some fancy name fer it – reservoir. 'S all French ter me!'

Hannah felt herself laugh for the first time. The old boy was a real character, a cheeky, perpetual grin on his face, a flock of white hair beneath his battered flat cap, and only three front teeth, which were so yellow they looked as though they had been like that since the day he was born.

'Horatio.'

'Beg pardon?' asked Hannah.

'That's me name,' replied the old fellow, tucking his woollen scarf more snugly into the top of his tatty old sports jacket. 'It was my old dad's idea. He come from Pompey – that's Portsmouth.

Horatio Nelson. He was a big hero with my dad – thought the world of him. He always used ter say that people like Horatio were what ol' England is all about.' He winked and nudged her. 'Not bad fer eighty-seven, am I?'

'Don't believe it!' said Hannah supportively.

'Oh yes!' continued Horatio, straightening up, refusing to lean hard on his walking stick. 'Eighty-seven an' a half ter be exact! I'm proud of bein' Horatio! Though I'm glad I've got both me eyes! Not like poor ol' Sid Bullock.'

Hannah turned back to find him looking mournfully at the lake. 'Did it happen out there, Horatio?' she asked.

'Oh yes,' replied the old boy wistfully. 'Nasty business. Speshully after all him an' Maggie've been through.' As he spoke, a seagull squawked, and skimmed the surface of the lake. 'Ain't you gone yet, mate?' he called. 'Your pals left soon after harvest.'

Hannah pressed him closely. 'What happened, Horatio?' she asked, staring out at the lake.

'Sid's usual fishing beano,' said the old man reflectively. 'They always went out there early on Sunday mornin's. He's a good fisher, y'know. Knows what he's doin', that's for sure. He and the other blokes never come home empty-handed. That day he caught a pike – must've bin nigh on four feet long.' He reached for a dirty old handkerchief in the pocket of his sports jacket, and blew his runny nose. 'Anyway, he had this girl on board with them, young Sheila. She weren't always with 'em; Maggie used ter give her too much ter do on a Sunday, on *every* day really. But when Sid found she was a first-class baiter, he took her out with 'em quite a few times.' For a moment, he stopped talking, and put his handkerchief back into his pocket.

'And then?'

The old boy flicked a quick glance at her, then turned his eyes back to the lake. 'And then – there was some kind of argy-bargy with the others on board.'

'Argy-bargy?'

Horatio hesitated a moment before answering. 'One of the other blokes – he weren't from *our* village – well, as *I* heard it, he tried ter take advantage of young Sheila.'

Hannah clapped her hand to her mouth.

'Apparently, Sid took exception ter this,' continued the old chap, 'and told this other bloke ter cut it out. As far as I can tell, there was a fight, and it ended up with poor old Sid getting the fish hook from this other bloke's line right in his eye. It was terrible, and Sid was in such pain he took it out on that poor girl, so much so that he pushed her in the river. Well, ter cut a long story short, Sheila couldn't swim, and even though two of the other blokes jumped in and tried to reach her, she went down like a lump of rock, right to the bottom. By the time they got her up and back here, it was too late. She was already gone.'

Hannah felt the blood seep from her face. 'Christ almighty!' she gasped.

'Yep,' sighed the old boy, 'terrible, ain't it? I mean, in a way it *was* an accident, weren't it? Sid was in such pain that . . . still, he shouldn't have pushed her in. I mean, that girl was only a kid, no more than seventeen or so. It was a tragedy, a real blinkin' tragedy.' He looked back at Hannah. 'And not only for Sid and the other blokes, but for Maggie too.'

'Why?' asked Hannah with deep foreboding.

'Why?' he asked, surprised she didn't know. 'It can't come easy fer any woman ter lose someone like that, especially when the only thing in life you ever wanted was a daughter and your own baby had died as soon as it was born.'

Chapter 8

Christmas was clearly going to be different this year. In the past Hannah had loved the sheer excitement of it all, the shops back home in Holloway and Seven Sisters Road with all the festive decorations in the windows, and paper chains made by her and Louie in the front parlour. But now there was a war on and everywhere was gloom and despair, especially in Redbourne where there was not only a blackout, which, except on moonlit nights, turned the village green and narrow back streets into difficult places to see and walk in the dark, but a feeling that people weren't as interested in enjoying themselves as they were back in London. However, Hannah's idea of what Christmas in the countryside was going to be like was soon contradicted when, on the morning of Christmas Eve, she turned up with Jane Jessop at the church hall to find a huge Christmas tree covered with small electric lights and different-coloured homemade tree decorations, and the hall itself lavishly adorned with paper chains, holly, mistletoe, twigs and leaves, and ivy painted in different colours, together with a multitude of balloons being blown up amidst enormous fun and excited chatter by the kids from the village school, including Louie, who was clearly having the time of her life.

'Wouldn't think there was a war on, would you?' said Jane, as she and Hannah joined the other villagers to help decorate the stage for the annual Christmas carol concert that evening.

'There must be – somewhere,' replied Hannah tersely. 'Or me an' Lou wouldn't be stuck down 'ere.'

'It can't be that bad, can it?' asked Jane, who was struggling to pin a 'Merry Christmas' cut-out onto the back curtain of the stage.

'Worse,' replied Hannah. 'Ever since I 'ad that barney wiv Ma Bullock about 'er biscuits, she practically don't talk ter me an' Lou.'

'Don't tell me you're sorry about that?'

'I wouldn't be,' replied Hannah, 'but I keep gettin' this feelin' that's she's up ter somefin'.'

Jane stopped what she was doing and looked at her. 'What d'you mean?' she asked, puzzled.

'I dunno *wot* I mean,' said Hannah. 'But the uvver day I saw 'er in the kitchen goin' fru some ration cards, an' those forms she 'as ter fill in fer our allowance.'

'What's wrong with that?' asked Jane, taking a quick look round to make sure that no one could hear them. 'Eventually, everyone is going to have to live with rationing, and if they take in evacuees, there has to be an allowance of some sort.'

'It's not only that,' said Hannah ominously. 'She also wrote anuvver letter.'

'A letter?'

'I knew who it was to,' said Hannah, ''cos I looked at the envelope when she went out inter the back garden. Fer some reason or anuvver, she an' my mum've bin writin' to each uvver. I wouldn't mind so much, but *I've* only 'ad one postcard from

Mum all the time we've bin 'ere, an' she always promised she'd come an' see me an' Lou at Chrismass.'

'Well, it's not Christmas yet, Hannah.' Jane was doing her best to sound reassuring. 'She'll probably turn up tomorrow morning.'

Although Hannah had heard what Jane had said, she knew only too well that the well-intentioned words were just as hollow as her mum's vague promises. For a few moments she stood there on the stage looking around at the excited activities of the kids and the village ladies in the church hall. But no matter how she tried, she couldn't share their enthusiasm for what for her was going to be a lousy couple of days, days of bitterness and recrimination, and all because her mum hadn't the sense or feeling to know that she had sent her two daughters away to a place that they could never come to terms with. Despite the kindness of most of the villagers of Redbourne – and there *were* many kind people amongst them – nothing for her could ever take the place of home, her real and only *home*, a place where for days before Christmas the family would get together and plan what they were going to do: the roast chicken in the oven, then Christmas pudding and mince pies made by her dad's mum, Grandma Adams, and the usual afternoon walk around the streets of Holloway with their dad, who was always still shaky on his feet after spending a couple of hours in the pub with his mate during the morning. But for Hannah, even all that was nothing to compare with the family sing-song in the evening, a time when the usual handful of neighbours in Kinloch Street came in for a booze-up, together with cheese and pickle sandwiches and scraps of leftovers from the Christmas blow-out, including crispy, almost burnt, bubble and squeak. No, no matter how hard they tried, country people, for Hannah, were not like her own kith and kin.

'Can I go an' 'ave tea wiv Poppy, please, Hannah?'

Hannah looked down from the stage to find Louie and her friend Poppy Wilkins calling up to her.

'Poppy wants me ter see the big doll's 'ouse 'er dad's made 'er fer Chrissmass,' continued Louie, who to Hannah's surprise was flushed with excitement. 'She only lives just down the road.'

Hannah looked from one girl to the other. 'I dunno, Lou,' she replied. 'We better ask Ma first. She may not like yer bein' out in the blackout.'

'It *ain't* blackout now!' insisted Louie tetchily. 'An' I don't care *wot* that woman finks. She ain't my mum.'

'It won't be dark for hours yet, Hannah,' said Poppy hastily. 'Dad will take Louie back home.'

Hannah turned to Jane for guidance.

'Louie will be all right, Hannah,' said Jane reassuringly. She smiled. 'It *is* Christmas.'

Hannah looked back at the two girls. She was relieved that Louie was looking so happy, especially as she had been so upset when, during the previous week, Alfie Grieves's mum and dad had taken the boy back home to London. 'A couple of hours, Lou,' she warned. 'If you're not back by pub openin', I'll come an' get yer meself. OK?'

Louie let out a tumultuous 'OK!' before rushing off with Poppy amidst gales of excited laughter. Hannah watched them go apprehensively.

'You mustn't worry about them, Hannah,' said Jane, putting a friendly arm round her friend's shoulder. 'You take too much on yourself, you know.'

'She's my sister, Jane,' replied Hannah, as they both came down the steps from the stage. 'Since our mum don't seem ter care a carrot, it's my place ter keep an eye on 'er. An' as for our so-called adopted muvver, she 'ates the sight of Lou.'

Jane gave her a questioning look. 'You really think that?' she asked sceptically.

'I *know* it!' replied Hannah, avoiding two young village kids who were chasing each other excitedly round the hall. 'Ol' Muvver Bullock still keeps goin' on about 'er biscuits, even though I told 'er it 'ad nuffin' ter do wiv Lou. An' the uvver day, when Lou complained about not 'avin' any soap in the lav, she said if Lou 'ated the place so much, p'rhaps she'd be better off somewhere else.'

'Well,' said Jane, with a sigh, 'there may be some truth in that.'

Hannah came to a halt. 'Wot d'yer mean by that?'

'That in my opinion, the Bullocks should never have been allowed to take in evacuees, especially after – after what happened to Sheila.'

Hannah looked puzzled. 'I thought that was s'pposed to 'ave been an accident?'

'I don't mean the accident,' replied Jane, keeping her voice down. 'I'm talking about the rumours of the way Mrs Bullock treated the girl. Sheila was a bit like you. She often complained that she was treated more like a servant than an adopted daughter.'

Hannah was shocked. 'Adopted?' she asked. 'The Bullocks *adopted* 'er?'

'Not officially,' replied Jane. 'But to all intents and purposes. I think you have to realise that Mrs Bullock is – well, let's say she's quite a complicated person. My dad says she never got over the loss of the baby she had soon after it was born, and that that could be the reason why she acts the way she does.'

Hannah considered this for a moment. 'That don't mean

she 'as ter take it out on me an' Lou.' She lowered her voice. 'Just tell me one fing, Jane,' she said. 'If everyone in the village knew about that accident, why 'ave they all kept so quiet about it?'

Jane hesitated a moment and then replied, 'Hannah, Redbourne is a place where the only thing that upsets our respectability is a baby crying in church. What happened to Sheila is not something we want everyone to know about.'

They moved on and reached the hall entrance, where the vicar was pinning up church notices on the noticeboard. 'Ah, there you are, you two!' he said jovially. 'So what do you think of our lovely decorations, Hannah?'

'Very nice,' replied Hannah, with a strained smile.

The vicar glowed. For a man in his sixties, Hannah thought he looked younger than his age, with hardly a white hair in his head, a healthy white skin, smiling brown eyes, but ears that protruded like one of Snow White's Seven Dwarfs. 'That's the wonderful thing about Redbourne,' he purred. 'Everyone *does* make an effort, not only at Christmas, but throughout the year. It really is so very comforting.' He finished pinning his last notice, then turned to face the two girls. 'Don't forget our Christmas Eve Midnight Service tonight,' he said directly to Hannah. 'It's a wonderful way to see in our Lord's birthday.'

Hannah looked uneasily from Jane back to the vicar. 'Sorry, Vicar,' she answered awkwardly. 'I ain't bin inside a church since my mum's dad died. I ain't really a believer.'

The vicar smiled back benevolently at her. 'My child,' he said, 'you don't have to be a believer to enter God's house. *Everyone* is welcome.'

Hannah smiled back weakly, then started to leave with Jane.

'But at least I hope you'll come to our carol concert tonight?' asked the vicar as they went.

Hannah stopped briefly at the door. 'Don't think Ma – I mean, I don't fink my foster-muvver can spare me fer that,' she replied curtly.

'Oh really?' said the vicar. 'Well, as far as I'm aware, Mrs Bullock is coming to the concert herself. At least, that's what she told me yesterday. I gather her husband is going to hold the fort. After all, there may be a war on but it's still Christmas Eve.'

On the way back to the pub, Hannah had a lot to think about. As she made her way past Griffins the baker's shop, where the queue of villagers waiting for Christmas Day loaves was gradually dwindling, Jane's words kept flashing through her mind: *What happened to Sheila is not something we want everyone to know about.* Yes, it was true, Hannah had to admit, a scandal such as Sheila's death would not be something that a small community like Redbourne would be proud of, and it was perfectly natural that people didn't want to talk about it, especially as that poor girl had been treated so badly by Maggie Bullock. But what of old Ma Bullock herself? After what had happened that day on the river two years before, why would she have wanted to take in another girl to treat badly – and, in fact, why had the evacuation committee given their blessing to such a thing? But then Hannah started thinking about the terrible effect it must have had on Maggie when she had lost the child she had wanted so much. For a few moments, Hannah actually felt sorry for the woman, until she realised that in some bizarre way she was using Hannah as some kind of replacement for the girl she had treated so badly. But that wasn't Hannah's only problem. There was still Louie to think about, and the little hints that were being dropped about its maybe being better if she went somewhere else. What did that mean, Hannah asked herself? Both she and Louie had been adopted by this woman and her husband, and until their mum came down to take them back home where they belonged, there was nothing anyone could do about it.

As she moved slowly past Martha Randle's tea shop, which was already locked up for the holiday weekend, Martha herself poked her head around the front door. 'Merry Christmas, my dear!' called the ebullient elderly lady, whose dazzling white hair was a perfect foil for her neat red and black floral dress.

'Merry Christmas,' Hannah called back. She had liked Martha from the first moment she had met her with Mary and Sam Beedle in the post office a few weeks before, mainly because she was a down-to-earth practical woman who, with her sister Ethel, never stopped cleaning their shop and slaving away serving tea, buttered toast, thinly sliced cucumber sandwiches, and fruit scones to their regular customers.

'It's so cold!' called Martha, shivering, as she scurried back inside to pull down her blackout blinds. 'How I long for the summer days again.'

Hannah smiled, and went on her way. It was indeed bitterly cold, and she was convinced that despite all the forecasts, it was going to be a white Christmas. After all, these days the village green always seemed to be covered in a thick frost, and the resident ducks were becoming increasingly concerned about the real possibility that their habitat pond would soon be frozen over. But Hannah herself was not concerned about the weather. She was not really concerned about the inhabitants of Redbourne either, for as she had passed Mr Turnbull's butcher's shop window there had seemed to be no shortage of Christmas meat there, with turkeys and chickens and geese and pheasants hanging from hooks waiting for their last-minute collection by his regular customers. No, the thing that was on Hannah's mind now was the upcoming carol concert at the church hall that evening, and the fact that Maggie Bullock was going to be in the audience. How come, Hannah asked herself? Old Ma Bullock *never* went out in the evenings, not with the pub opening hours as they were. It was not until she had crossed to the other side of the village green, turned down into the narrow terraced side street, and mooched her way back to the Cock and Crow that she found the answer to that bewildering question.

'Mine's a Guinness! Mine's a Guinness!'

The impact of Polly's strangulated demand, as soon as Hannah entered the saloon bar, was nothing compared to the shock of finding who was sitting with Maggie Bullock, sipping a gin and tonic in front of the fire.

''Allo, darlin'!'

'Mum!' Hannah was so overwhelmed to see her mum again that she rushed straight across and practically threw herself into the woman's arms.

Although embarrassed by her daughter's outburst of affection, Babs Adams rose from her chair to give the girl a hug. 'My darlin' gel!' she gushed. 'Let me look at yer.' She held Hannah at arm's length, and gasped in mock admiration. 'Oh yes!' She beamed. 'I can see country air 'as done wonders for yer.' She turned briefly to Maggie. 'Yer've done a good job 'ere, Mrs Bullock.'

Hannah's excitement was immediately crushed by what her mum had said. It also made her quite sick to see all the make-up she was wearing, the lavish perm beneath a chiffon scarf, and the mock tigerskin coat which Babs had bought in Chapel Market, and Hannah had always hated. 'Mum!' she gasped.

Now it was Maggie Bullock's turn to beam. 'We're lucky to have such a lovely girl to look after.' She quickly corrected herself. '*Two* lovely girls. Where's your sister, Hannah my dear?'

Hannah was so flustered and taken aback she could hardly talk. 'She – she's gone over ter Poppy Wilkins's house for the afternoon.'

'Oh – what a shame,' replied Maggie, with what seemed to be genuine concern. 'She mustn't miss seeing her mother. I'll send Mr Bullock over to collect her.' She got up, and went into the kitchen.

'Wot's she talkin' about?' asked Hannah anxiously, once she and her mum were alone. 'Din't yer get my postcards? Why din't yer write back ter me? Yer *are* goin' ter take us back 'ome, aren't yer?'

Hannah's breathless questions knocked Babs for six. 'Listen ter me, darlin',' she said uneasily, trying to persuade Hannah to sit down with her. 'There's no point in your comin' 'ome when fings are lookin' so dicey.'

'Dicey?' spluttered Hannah, with incomprehension. 'Wot yer talkin' about?'

'The war, my darlin',' replied Babs, trying her best to look serious.

'The war!' snapped Hannah. 'There *ain't* no war! It ain't even started!'

'You're wrong, darlin',' insisted Babs. 'Fings are gettin' bad – *really* bad. D'yer know they shot a German plane down over Margate the uvver day. That's where Auntie Lucie lives.'

'Margate ain't Lond'n!' barked Hannah. 'It's miles away!'

Although Babs had clearly spent some time working out what she wanted to say to Hannah, it was clearly proving more difficult than she expected. 'It ain't like that, Hann,' she said, quickly lighting up a fag. 'The Germans've bin bombin' France an' Belgium. Loads've people've bin killed all over the place – women an' kids – just everyone! It won't be long before they come over an' do the same ter us.'

'My friend Jane said there was somefin' on the wireless about some big German ship that was sunk. She said they wouldn't dare try ter bomb London after that.'

'You can't believe all you hear on the wireless, darlin',' replied Babs. 'D'you know Islin'ton council is goin' ter issue everyone with a free air raid shelter? They're goin' ter put them up in all the back yards – including down Kinloch Street.'

'Mum, there ain't goin' ter be no bombin'!' insisted Hannah, who was now getting desperate.

Maggie returned with Sid Bullock, who was already wearing his overcoat and scarf, and flat checked cap. 'Don't be long, Mr Bullock,' she called, as he left to collect Louie. 'We don't want her to miss seeing her mum before she goes back home.' Hannah swung a horrified look at her mother. 'Why don't you take your mum for a little look around the village?' Maggie went on, turning back to Hannah. 'Let her see for herself what it's *really* like to live in the countryside.'

A few minutes later, Hannah and Babs were doing just that, not because Hannah was interested in taking her mum on a sightseeing tour, but merely because it was clearly the only way she was going to get to talk to her on her own. However, she felt uncomfortable as they walked, mainly because she was so conscious of the way the odd passer-by glanced briefly at the garish way her mum had dressed and made up. With that in mind, she made straight for the bench on the village green where there was very little chance of meeting anyone. However, before they got there, Hannah had decided to tell her mum just what Louie and herself had had to endure ever since they arrived. 'Yer've no idea what kind of people they are,' she said over and over again. 'They're so peculiar, especially that woman.'

'Yer know, I don't fink that's bein' very fair, darlin',' replied Babs, as she and Hannah sat down on the cold wooden bench by the pond. 'Mrs Bullock's been tellin' me 'ow difficult she an' 'er hubby knows it's bin fer the two of yer, leavin' me an' yer 'ome an' everyfin'.'

'She doesn't know anyfin' er the sort!' snapped Hannah. 'All she cares about is gettin' me ter work like a skivvy for 'er fer practically nuffin'!'

'I don't fink you're bein' fair, Hann,' repeated Babs quietly, again lighting up a fag. 'That nice geography teacher told me that whatever Mrs Bullock's failin's, she's really done 'er best ter look after you an' Lou.'

'She's *wot*?' spluttered Hannah. 'Din't yer get *any* of my post-cards? Din't yer see wot me an' Lou 'ave 'ad ter put up with? Why din't yer write back ter me? Why, Mum?'

Babs puffed nervously on her fag. 'Yer know I've never bin much of a letter writer, Hann,' she replied.

'But yer managed ter write to *'er*, din't yer? Ter that woman.'

Babs was taken off guard, and she knew it. 'Mrs Bullock wrote ter me, so it would've bin rude if I 'adn't writ back. She just wanted ter know about little fings, fings that would 'elp ter make you and Lou more comfortable.'

'Such as?'

'Well,' replied Babs, searching desperately for some kind of answer. 'Fings yer like ter eat.'

Hannah couldn't believe what she was hearing. 'Are you jokin', Mum? We've not 'ad anyfin' ter eat wot *we* like since we got 'ere.'

Babs knew that she herself was on the defensive, and she was struggling to get out of it. She quickly tried to change the subject. 'I must say I love those little shops over there,' she said, turning to look at the other side of the village green. 'Bit diff'rent ter dirty ol' Kinloch Street.'

Hannah thought her mum was quite mad. To her, there was nothing wrong with Kinloch Street. She'd sooner be there any day than in the Cock and Crow.

Babs pulled up her coat collar, got up from the bench seat, and went over to the edge of the pond. For a moment she just stood there, looking at her own reflection in the thin layer of ice that was beginning to form. Eventually, Hannah joined her. 'There wouldn't be no point in your comin' 'ome now, Hann,' Babs said. 'Maybe later, but not now.'

'Why not?' asked Hannah.

'Not only 'cos of the bombs,' replied Babs, pulling hard on her fag. 'But 'cos of Gran. She ain't at all well these days.'

'Wot's wrong wiv 'er?'

'Oh – you know,' said Babs, searching all the time for answers. 'She ain't as young as she used ter be. Old people 'ave a lot ter cope wiv.'

'So do young people,' replied Hannah tersely.

For several minutes there remained a silence between them. In the past the two of them had never really talked together very often; Babs never seemed to have the time to do things like that. Nonetheless, there was a great deal going on in both their minds. Hannah was struggling to think how to persuade her mum that she should take her two daughters home with her, and if there *were* any bombs in the coming months, then they should take their chances just like anyone else. But there was something more than motherly love that was plaguing Babs. There was freedom from the responsibility that she had craved to get away from ever since she had first had kids of her own.

On the other side of the village green, the queue outside Mr Turnbull's butcher's shop had finally come to an end, and Hannah could just see the old boy himself, in straw boater and striped white apron, closing up shop for the last time before the real start of the holiday. The post office was already closed, and Hannah wished that Sam was with her at that moment, helping her to deal with a mother who didn't seem to understand anything about her own two daughters.

'Mrs Bullock says you've got a nice boyfriend down here.' Her mum's sudden question broke the awkward silence between them. 'Wot's 'is name?'

''E ain't my boyfriend,' replied Hannah fiercely. ''E's just me friend.' She suddenly thought she had been a bit too churlish. ''Is name's Sam,' she sighed.

'Nice name.'

After another difficult pause Hannah asked, 'When yer goin' back?'

'There's a train at four fifteen.'

Hannah swung her a horrified look. 'Four fifteen?' she gasped. 'That means yer've only got anuvver coupla 'ours.'

Babs turned to her with a look of sheer desperation. 'It's

135

Chrismass, Hann,' she replied. 'Most of the trains stop runnin'
early on Chrismass Eve.'

'Mum . . . !'

The sudden appearance of Louie running across the green
towards her saved Babs the embarrassment of having to make
any more excuses. 'Lou-Lou! My darlin'!'

Hannah watched in absolute despair as Louie leapt straight
up at her mum, smothering her in hugs and kisses.

'Where've yer bin, Mum?' cried Louie, crazed with excitement. 'We've bin waitin' for yer! Where've yer bin?'

'I'm here, Lou-Lou!' replied Babs, smoothing back the child's
hair from her forehead, hugging her tight and kissing her. 'I
promised ter come an' see yer at Chrissmass. Din't I promise?'

Hannah looked away.

'We've 'ad such a lousy time, Mum,' said Louie, repeating
herself over and over. 'They don't give us nearly enuff food, an'
I can't sleep wiv all that noise goin' on downstairs in the pub.'

In the distance, Hannah could see Sid Bullock making his
way back discreetly to the Cock and Crow.

'It's all right, darlin',' said Babs. 'Mama's 'ere. From now on,
everyfin's goin' ter be all right.' She held Louie out so she could
talk to her. 'Fings're goin' ter be diffr'ent. Mrs Bullock 'as told
me all the nice plans she's got for yer.'

Hannah swung her a wary look.

'But we're comin 'ome wiv yer,' replied Louie, whose initial
excitement was beginning to fade. 'That's what yer 'ere for, ain't
it? You're goin' ter take us back 'ome?'

Babs bit her lip anxiously. 'Come an' sit wiv Mama fer a
minute.' She led the child back to the bench seat, where they
sat side by side. 'Fings ain't too good back in 'Olloway, Lou-Lou,'

she murmured indistinguishably. 'Yer wouldn't recognise 'ow fings've changed. They're puttin' in air-raid shelters. Can yer imagine it – an air-raid shelter in our own back yard!'

'Why?' asked Louie directly.

The child's question unnerved Babs. ''Cos of the bombs, Lou-Lou,' she replied. 'They say the Germans could start bombing any day now.'

Louie was not satisfied. 'Then why've all the uvver kids from 'Olloway gone back from 'ere?' she asked firmly.

Babs had no real answer to that, so she quickly had to make up one. 'I dunno, my angel,' she replied. 'Maybe it's 'cos their mums 'n' dads don't care as much fer their little ones' safety as *I* do.'

Hannah felt quick sick, and turned away. There was an upsetting pause whilst the child stared directly into her mum's eyes. She was searching for an answer that in her heart of hearts she already knew. 'Are yer goin' ter stay wiv us fer Chrissmass?'

Babs was taken off guard. 'No, darlin',' she replied. 'I've got ter get back 'ome as soon as I can. Gotta go an' see your poor ol' Gran and Granddad. They've got so many fings wrong wiv 'em now they can hardly move.'

'Are yer goin' ter leave us 'ere, then?'

Again, the child's question unsettled Babs. 'Just fer a while, darlin',' she replied, her insides feeling as though they were about to drop out. 'Just fer a while. But as soon as it's the right time, I promise yer Mama'll be on that train and comin' straight back for yer.'

'When's it goin' ter be *the right time*?' Louie asked.

'Soon, Lou-Lou,' Babs replied brightly. 'Soon.' She leant forward to take the child's hand, but flinched when Louie suddenly pulled away from her. 'But I'll tell yer somefin',' she continued with difficulty. 'Farver Chrismass din't ferget ter bring yer some presents. You'll be really chuffed when yer see 'em. I've left 'em wiv yer foster-muvver.'

Louie stood up. 'She *ain't* my muvver,' she growled angrily, going to stand with Hannah. 'An' neivver are you!' She started to cry, and tucked her head against Hannah's chest.

Hannah wrapped her arm round her sister's shoulder, and looked across at their mum with contempt. 'Don't be late for yer train,' she said, without any feeling. Then she led Louie off slowly back to the Cock and Crow.

Chapter 9

Christmas morning was not exactly what Hannah and Louie had been hoping for. After the brief and traumatic reunion with their mum, Louie had cried herself to sleep, sobbing over and over again that she didn't like either her foster-mother or her own mum. Things had been so bad that, despite Maggie Bullock's scolding remark that it was cruel and unkind to their mother, neither of the two girls went to see their mum off at the railway station. In fact they were so upset that when they woke up on Christmas morning they ignored the presents Babs had brought them, and shoved them under their beds. Fortunately, the Bullocks had decided to close the pub on Christmas Day, mainly because Maggie's cousin Hilda and her French husband, Maurice, were coming to Christmas lunch, to which, Hannah presumed, she and Louie would not be invited. However, when the two girls went downstairs to have their usual meagre breakfast, they received a pleasant surprise.

'Do you like roast turkey?' asked Maggie, who was already stuffing a huge bird for roasting in the kitchen oven. 'This fellow is twelve pounds. Mr Bumper let me have him for a very generous discount.'

'Lou an' I 'ave never eat turkey,' replied Hannah. 'Dad always cooked chicken at Chrismass.'

'Then you're in for a real treat!' proclaimed Maggie, vigorously pushing homemade pork sausage-meat stuffing into the poor gutted turkey. 'When you've tasted *this* fellow, you'll never want chicken again!'

Hannah and Louie exchanged a puzzled, wary look.

'Off you go now, you two!' said Maggie, dumping a large lump of lard into the roasting pan. 'You've got your Christmas breakfast to get through first.' Hannah and Louie were taken aback as she waved them out of the kitchen.

In the saloon bar outside, the girls made their way across to their usual table in the corner. 'Wos all this about?' asked Louie.

Hannah shrugged. But when they reached the table they were even more astonished when they found it neatly laid with two bowls of corn flakes, a boiled egg each, thin slices of well-buttered bread, and two slices of fried Spam fritters. 'Blimey!' gasped Hannah, hardly able to believe her eyes.

'Wos she up to?' asked Louie, staring nervously at the lay-out as though it was probably poisoned.

'I dunno, Lou,' replied Hannah. 'But if Farver Chrismass left this for us, we'd better not waste it. Come on!'

The two girls sat down, and quickly tucked in to what to them was a feast. Whilst they were doing so, they received another surprise when both Maggie and Sid came out from the kitchen, Sid carrying a tray with a glass of milk for Louie, plus three small glasses of a bubbling drink of some kind.

'Merry Christmas, my dears!' said Maggie, with buoyant good cheer.

'Merry Christmas,' added Sid Bullock dourly.

Maggie gave Louie her glass of milk, then passed one of the other glasses to Hannah. 'There we are!' she said with a beaming smile. 'One glass for you, and . . .' she handed another glass to Sid, 'one for you, Mr Bullock . . .' she took the other glass herself, 'and one for Mother.' She then held up her glass. 'Cheers! Merry Christmas, everyone!'

Sid Bullock held up his glass awkwardly. 'Merry Christmas!' he added.

Hannah just stared at the glass in front of her on the table. 'Wot is it?' she asked warily.

'Babycham, my dear,' replied Maggie. 'Don't tell me you've never had it before? It's a lovely drink for special occasions. The bubbles get up your nose and make you feel marvellous. Don't worry, we're not breaking the law. There's only a tiny bit of alcohol in it. Come on now! You too, Louise.'

Hannah picked up her glass, and indicated with a look to Louie to do the same.

'Merry Christmas everyone, especially to our dear young family!'

The two girls watched in astonishment as their foster-parents gulped down a mouthful of the drink. Louie, knowing she was on safe ground, sipped her milk, but Hannah sniffed her drink first before tasting it.

'Good, eh?' Maggie asked. 'Does it make you feel like a grown-up?' Before Hannah had a chance to answer, she rushed off back to the kitchen. 'My bird!' she called out on the way. 'It's going to need at least six hours in the oven.'

For a moment or so, Hannah and Louie, with Sid Bullock still hovering over them, sat in total bewilderment, kicking each other under the table.

'Eat up,' said Sid. 'It's Christmas. Might as well make the most of it.'

Maggie's voice called out from the kitchen. 'No housework today, Hannah! Just make sure you're both back by two o'clock. I don't want to ruin my bird!'

'Mine's a Guinness!' yelled Polly from her cage, no doubt hoping that Maggie was not referring to *her*.

'Wos it all about?' asked Louie, as she and Hannah left the Cock and Crow and made their way up the street.

'Search me,' replied Hannah with her usual shrug. 'Maybe she's seen the light.'

'Seen the light?' asked Louie, puzzled. 'Wot does *that* mean?'

'Maybe it's dawned on 'er that she ain't been treatin' us as she should do.'

Louie was unconvinced. 'I din't like 'er talkin' about *our dear young family*. She ain't *our* family.'

Hannah agreed. And yet, as they picked their way carefully along the frosty, cobbled pavement, she couldn't help dwelling on the uncaring way their own mum had treated them the day before. Was *she* a real family, Hannah asked herself? No contact for weeks on end, a visit for just a couple of hours, and then off she went. Hannah thought about all the other kids who had been evacuated from Holloway at the same time as she and Louie, and wondered what they were doing now, whether their mums and dads were hugging them, giving them their Christmas presents. Surely *that* was what being a family was all about – mums and dads not thinking just about themselves, but about their kids, *wanting* to be with them – and loving them?

As the two girls moved further along the street, they could hear the sound of Christmas carols being sung out heartily by a group of villagers in the cold morning air. When they eventually reached the village green, there they all were, men, women, and children, all togged up snug and warm in their winter clothes, belting out 'Good King Wenceslas' at the top of their voices, accompanied on a small pedal organ by one of the village ladies. For ten o'clock in the morning, they were all in fine voice, so much so that the joyous sound echoed triumphantly round the green, where many of the residents were standing at their front doors joining in. It was a scene that took the two girls, especially Hannah, by surprise, for she had somehow imagined that only people in Holloway celebrated Christmas in such a way. Her spirits were raised even more when she suddenly caught a glimpse of Sam Beedle striding across the green to meet her.

'Merry Chrismass, mate!' she said as he drew near. Her face was beaming.

'Same to you, Hannah,' he returned, pulling down the hood of his duffel coat. 'I hope it'll be a peaceful one for you.'

'I've got me fingers crossed,' she joked.

'You too, Louie,' he said.

Louie's attention, however, was drawn to someone on the far side of the green. Hannah gave her a dig. 'Louie!'

'Oh.' Louie jumped. 'Merry Chrismass.'

'Actually I was just coming to see you,' said Sam. 'I've got an invitation for you both.'

'Invitation?' asked Hannah.

'The Friends have invited you to our meeting. It's starting in just a few minutes.'

Hannah's face dropped. 'Sam,' she said awkwardly. 'Yer know wot I'm like. I don't go ter church or nuffin'.'

'This is *not* church, Hannah,' he replied. 'It's like I told you.

It's just a get-together, a chance for everyone to say how they feel about this day that everyone loves so much.'

Hannah was torn with anguish. She didn't want to hurt his feelings, but at the same time she just couldn't see herself sitting in a hall with everyone's head bowed low in silence. The fact was, whatever people liked to call it, she just didn't believe in religion, especially after the way her mum had behaved. 'It's no good, Sam,' she said, watching his reaction carefully. 'I'd be like a fish out er water.'

Sam smiled. 'You know, Hannah,' he said with a mischievous grin, 'some fish may *like* to be out of water – as long as they can get back in again. I promise you, we won't lock you in. You can leave any time you want.'

Hannah thought hard for a moment. 'But what about Louie?' she asked.

'The invitation is for both of you,' replied Sam. 'But something tells me . . .' he peered over her shoulder to see Poppy and her father just coming along the road, 'she may have other plans for Christmas morning.'

The Friends' Meeting House was filled to overflowing. Even though there were no more than about thirty people present, some of the men had to stand round the sides of the hall whilst the others took their places in chairs set out in the shape of a square. When Hannah arrived with Sam, she was immediately shown to a seat near the back row, where she found herself sitting next to Sam's mother, Mary Beedle, and his father, Joseph Beedle, who was the same narrow-faced man with side whiskers and a beaming expression whom Hannah had seen addressing the Friends on that first day when she peered through the window. 'Merry

Christmas, Mrs Beedle,' Hannah said, as she sat down, but with a friendly smile Mary put her fingers to her lips as a gentle request for silence. Indeed, as Hannah took her place, the only sound that could be heard was the shuffling of the Friends taking their own seats. Then there was a period of silence, when everyone just sat with their hands in their laps, eyes wide open but calm and relaxed. Unnerved by what she felt was a strange atmosphere, Hannah flicked a glance across at Sam for reassurance. From the side of the room where he was standing with two older men and a young teenage boy, Sam gave her one of his lovely, comforting smiles, which immediately calmed her. After several minutes of bewildering silence, Joseph Beedle got up and quietly launched into a few words to those gathered around.

'Friends.' His voice was tinged with a gentle country burr. 'Today, like all days, we celebrate the birth of our Lord Jesus. Today, we celebrate our clear and certain knowledge that nature will soon be experiencing a rebirth after a long, dark winter.' He slowly turned himself round so that he could take in everyone in the room. 'Wilt thou join me in this celebration of our family?'

The response was a soft, unified murmur: 'We shall.'

Joseph sat down, and to add to Hannah's confusion, there followed a few more moments of silence. Then an astonishing thing happened. A young girl, pretty and serene, who looked about the same age as Louie, emerged from a seat at the far corner of the square. In her hands she carried a violin. Everyone watched her in total silence, whilst she went to the empty space in the middle of the square, gathered herself together, placed the violin gently on her left shoulder, raised her bow, and quite effortlessly launched into a haunting rendition of the carol 'Away in a Manger'.

For several minutes, Hannah sat in rapt attention listening to the sweet, mesmerising sound, finding herself strangely moved as she watched the Friends swaying gently back and forth in their chairs to the music. There was no singing, no outward show of emotion, just a quiet, simple display of unity. And when she had finished playing, the young girl returned to her seat surrounded by her family and friends, who all nodded gently with a smile at her contribution.

Hannah couldn't believe it when everyone gradually stood up, and started to file out of the Meeting House.

'Merry Christmas, Friend,' said Mary Beedle at her side. She leant forward and kissed her gently on her cheek.

'Merry Christmas, young Friend,' added Joseph Beedle, her husband, taking Hannah's hand and shaking it vigorously, before joining the others.

'Wot's goin' on?' asked Hannah, bewildered.

'We've said all we have to say,' replied Mary. 'Now it's time to put action to words.'

Utterly confused, Hannah followed Mary to the exit door, where Sam was waiting for her. It did not go unnoticed by her that he and his father did not communicate with each other. As they went, like everyone else, Hannah was offered a small package as a Christmas offering. 'Wot is it?' she asked Mary.

'Coconut ice,' Mary replied. 'It's just a little reminder of the day for us to keep, though with sugar now being rationed, I doubt we'll be able to do this much longer.'

Once outside, Hannah joined Sam and they watched the little group of Friends streaming down the edge of the village green before gradually disappearing into a small turning at the side of Martha Randle's tea shop.

'Wasn't too painful, was it?' asked Sam.

'It was amazin',' replied Hannah, who was still quite numb from the experience. 'The way that gel stood up an' played like that.'

'That's Jenny,' replied Sam. 'Yes, she *is* quite a girl. She has consumption. A couple of years ago we thought she was going to die. But not now.'

Everything she had heard was baffling Hannah, especially remarks like Sam's simple explanation about the child who had played the violin with such assurance.

As they stood there, Mary Beedle approached on the arm of her husband. 'Thank you for coming, Hannah,' she said. 'It was lovely to have you with us.'

'Fanks fer askin' me,' replied Hannah awkwardly.

'Once we've finished at Marjorie's,' said Mary, 'we'll be back in the House to give the children their presents. You're very welcome to join us if you'd like to.'

'Fanks very much, Mrs Beedle,' replied Hannah, 'but I promised me an' Louie'd be back in time fer Chrismass dinner.'

'Ah!' replied Mary. 'I'm happy to hear that. Merry Christmas, my dear.'

'Merry Chrismass,' called Hannah, as she watched Mary and her husband join the others slowly moving off down the road. Then she turned to Sam. 'Where they all off to?' she asked. 'Who's Marjorie?'

'She's the oldest resident in Redbourne,' said Sam. 'Lived in the same house all her life. The thing is, her roof's been leaking, and she's got a few things that need doing in the house, so we're all going down there to do a few repairs.'

'On Chrismass Day?' asked Hannah in astonishment.

Sam grinned at her. 'For the Friends, *every* day's Christmas,' he replied.

The two of them returned to the Meeting House, and Hannah waited whilst Sam locked up. 'Your dad don't say much, do 'e?' she remarked casually.

When Sam turned back to her his face was more restrained than she had seen it all morning. 'At the moment,' he replied uneasily, 'Dad and I are not finding it too easy to say very much to each other.'

Hannah was puzzled. 'Wot d'yer mean?' she asked inquisitively.

Sam shrugged. 'Let's just say that we don't exactly see eye to eye.'

Hannah could tell that he was finding it difficult to talk about him and his dad. 'Yer mean, yer ain't talkin' ter each uvver?'

'That's not the way the Friends think, Hannah,' he said, trying to avoid her look. 'It's just that – well, like I said, we don't exactly agree about – certain things.'

'*Wot* fings?'

'Oh – all sorts of things. The war, the Germans bombing people all over Europe, the way they're trying to destroy Poland. It just gets to me sometimes.' He looked back at her. 'Did you hear they're pouring British troops into France and Belgium?'

Hannah looked quite blank.

'Don't you know what that means, Hannah?' he asked, surprised by her apparent lack of interest. 'It means that any minute now men are going to be called up all over the country.'

'So wot diff'rence does that make ter *you*?' she asked, following him round the back of the Meeting House where he locked the back door. 'I mean, yer can't be called up 'til you're eighteen, and even then someone like *you* couldn't be forced ter go off an' fight.' There was a note of uncertainty in her voice. 'Could yer?'

Sam turned back slowly to look at her. 'I don't know, Hannah,' he replied. 'I honestly don't know. That's something I've got to work out for myself.'

'Well I tell yer,' said Hannah, 'I fer one wouldn't like it if yer *did* go. I mean, I don't see the point. Yer can do much more good round 'ere just lookin' after people.'

'What people, Hannah,' he asked. 'People like *you*, for instance?'

Hannah swung round with a start. She was surprised to find him grinning at her.

Sam stared at her, her lovely rusty red hair flapping in a gentle breeze, her radiant grey-green eyes glistening in the last remains of a watery sun. 'D'you know,' he said, not taking his eyes off her, 'this is the first time I've noticed – you've got freckles.'

Hannah suddenly became very self-conscious, and covered her cheeks with her hands.

'I love freckles,' he said. 'Shows a lot of character.'

Hannah resisted chuckling. She tried to avoid looking into his eyes, but she couldn't stop herself.

'Hannah,' he asked, touching her lips with the tips of his fingers. 'D'you mind if I kiss you?'

Hannah was taken aback. It was the first time anyone had actually asked if they could do anything like that; somehow it seemed so old fashioned. Back home, if any of the boys she knew wanted to do such a thing, they certainly never bothered to ask first, merely gave her a plonker, even if they did get a good slap round the lughole if they tried to go too far. 'If yer want to,' she replied with a casual shrug, even though she couldn't wait for him to do so. 'As long as yer sure the Friends won't object.'

Although he found her remark a bit snide, he grinned back at her. 'Believe it or not,' he replied, 'I *am* human – just like anyone else.' He leant forward, and kissed her lightly on her lips. Then he smoothed back the hair from her face, and kissed her again, his arms tucked snugly round her waist.

Hannah slid her arms round *his* waist, and kissed him back. 'Look!' she exclaimed, suddenly staring up at the sky. 'It's snowin'!'

Sam looked up with her, and as they did so, the first snowflakes came fluttering down onto their faces. Within just a few moments their shoulders were covered with a thin layer of white.

On the way back with Louie to the Cock and Crow, Hannah felt as though she was walking on air. That kiss from Sam, that beautiful kiss – she could hardly believe what had happened to her. It felt so warm and tender, unlike anything she had ever known before, so much so that all the blood in her body seemed to tingle. Of course she knew that this wasn't love. How *could* it be when she had only known Sam for such a short while, she asked herself? Nonetheless, Sam had stirred something inside her that she had never experienced before. He had not kissed her because he *had* to, but because he *wanted* to. And *she* desperately wanted him to kiss *her*. The fact was, someone was actually attracted to her, and it made her feel like a different person. It was the best Christmas present she had ever had.

When she and Louie finally got back to the Cock and Crow, the moment Sid Bullock opened the pub door they were overpowered by the smell of roast turkey. In the kitchen they were met by Maggie Bullock, wearing an apron over her Sunday best dress, basting the huge bird in the roasting pan. 'Don't hang around here!' she barked at the two girls. 'The kitchen today is *my* domain! Mr Bullock! Take them into the sitting room to meet the others.'

Hannah and Louie's eyes were bulging. They could hardly believe that they were being included in the Bullocks' Christmas Day lunch party. Nonetheless, that was what was happening, for Sid Bullock, dutifully obeying his beloved wife, took the two girls into the sitting room to meet the other guests, a man and a woman who were both roughly the same age as the Bullocks themselves.

'Hilda,' said Sid, standing behind the two girls, 'these are our two adopted young ladies. This is Hannah, and this is Louise.'

The girls acknowledged the introduction with some trepidation.

'Ah!' said the woman, who seemed genuinely fascinated to see them. 'We've just been talking about you. I bet your ears have been burning.' Her freshly permed hair was tight with curls, and she had dark grey eyes which to Hannah seemed rather too large for her face. 'I'm cousin Hilda, on your foster-mother's side. You can call me Auntie Hilda. And this is your Uncle Maurice.'

'Hallo, young ladies.'

The two girls turned their attention to the man standing with his back to the fireplace alongside Sid Bullock.

'It's very nice to meet you at last,' he went on, with a friendly smile, and a strong foreign accent. 'I come from France.'

'You mean you came from France a long time ago,' snapped Maggie, as she swept into the room from the kitchen carrying the remains of her glass of gin. 'And you still haven't learnt to speak English properly.'

Hilda glared at her cousin, who sat in an armchair facing her.

'So, *ma chère*,' asked Maurice, ignoring Maggie's snide comments and turning his attention to Hannah, 'what do you think of pretty little Redbourne?'

Hannah was at first hesitant in answering him, mainly because she was so fascinated by his appearance: the thin moustache, sleek dark hair and dark eyes, and a cream-coloured V-neck pullover. 'It's diff'r'ent ter Lond'n,' she replied.

'Ah – London!' he enthused. '*C'est une belle cité!*'

Hannah didn't know what the hell he was saying, but he did bring a smile to her face.

'Go and sit by the window!' said Maggie to the girls, bossily. 'There's plenty of room over there.'

'Don't be silly, Maggs,' said Hilda. 'There's plenty of room *here*.' She smiled at the two girls and patted the empty seat at the side of her on the sofa.

The two girls sat beside cousin Hilda on the sofa.

'So, my dears,' said Hilda. 'Tell us all about yourselves. What part of London d'you come from?

Louie answered immediately. ''Olloway.'

'Holloway?' asked Hilda inquisitively. 'Isn't there a prison there or something?'

'It's a women's prison.' This time it was Sid Bullock who spoke. He was standing with Maurice, his back to the blazing log fire, smoking a cigar. 'The man's prison is just down the road. Pentonville.'

'Oh, how terrible!' gasped Hilda. 'Fancy having two prisons in the same place.' She turned to Hannah. 'Doesn't that scare you, dear?' she asked. 'I mean, what would you do if one of those awful men ever escaped?'

'We never fink about it,' replied Hannah.

'Our Uncle Ernie went ter Pentonville,' said Louie, being deliberately provocative.

'Your uncle?' spluttered Hilda, subconsciously tugging at one of her two drop earrings.

''E got done over fer nickin' a bag er 'orse dung from the mayor's garden.'

Maurice tried to conceal a snigger. 'Your uncle went to prison for stealing horse manure?'

Hannah's attempts to silence her young sister proved futile.

'Not only that,' continued Louie, quite unabashed. 'There were a couple uvver fings as well, weren't there, Hann? An' 'e bashed up this geezer down the pub one day 'cos 'e wasn't payin' up enuff fer the stuff 'e'd nicked.'

Hilda gasped.

Hannah dug her sister in the ribs, whilst Maurice, highly amused to see the horror on his wife's face, turned away to look into the fire.

'Do you think it's wrong to steal, Louise?'

Everyone turned to look at Maggie, who was stern-faced.

'It wasn't quite like Lou said,' said Hannah uneasily.

'I asked your sister a question,' replied Maggie, keeping her attention fixed on the child. 'Louise,' she repeated. 'Do you think it is a right thing to do to steal from someone?'

Louie swung a puzzled look at Hannah for guidance.

'Lou wouldn't steal nuffin' from no one,' said Hannah, firmly answering for her sister. 'Neivver would I.'

'Of course they wouldn't.' Everyone was surprised to hear Sid Bullock entering the conversation. 'I'm sure Hannah and Louise know the difference between right and wrong.'

Maggie's expression showed that she was not convinced. She

decided not to reply. 'I think it's time we had lunch,' she said, getting up.

A few minutes later, everyone was sitting round a table in the small private bar of the pub. Despite the fact that she and Louie had been invited for the very first time to actually eat with their foster-parents, Hannah was decidedly uncomfortable with it all. Maggie's double-edged questions to Louie about stealing had not gone unnoticed by her, especially after the accusations about the so-called theft of Maggie's biscuits from the kitchen larder. But whilst there was good food around to eat, she decided to contain her anger. After all, this *was* Christmas Day, a time of goodwill to all men *and* women, even if the goodwill was not entirely reciprocated. And of course there was always Maurice, who had taken to winking mischievously at Hannah behind Maggie's back, indicating quite clearly that he did not approve of one single thing about his wife's cousin.

Once Maggie had brought out the turkey on a dish and placed it on the table, Sid was given the task of carving it. The two girls watched in total awe; they had never seen a bird that size before, and as Sid transferred each slice onto separate plates, they practically drooled with anticipation. But when it was finally time to eat, it seemed that Maggie, who had clearly not looked forward to sharing her Christmas table with the two girls, couldn't resist picking on them. 'Didn't your parents ever teach you how to hold a knife and fork?' she asked belligerently, once again directing her attention to Louie.

'Wot's wrong wiv it?' asked Hannah.

Maggie held up her own knife and fork, and demonstrated the correct way. 'Like this, Hannah,' she replied, with an unconvincing smile. 'At least, that's the way we do it in Redbourne.'

Aware that this remark had infuriated Hannah, Maurice, who was sitting alongside Louie, turned to the child and took hold of her knife and fork. 'Here,' he said, with a light touch. 'Let me help you.'

Maurice's intervention only just prevented Hannah from an angry outburst, but as she watched the Frenchman showing Louie how to handle her cutlery, she turned a glare towards Maggie, who was busily serving vegetables round the table.

Fortunately, the meal proceeded without further incident, and the taste of some real food helped to dispel the anger both girls had felt earlier. Ironically enough, it was cousin Hilda who quite innocently upset the apple cart again when she tried to engage Hannah in the general conversation about the war. 'I mean, the way things are right now,' she said, mouth full of turkey and pork sausage stuffing, 'you must feel it's all a waste of time giving up your home in London to come and live in a place like Redbourne? Let's face it, you'd never believe there was a war on, would you?'

'Don't speak too soon, Hilda,' said Maurice. 'Remember, Hitler is marching his troops into countries all around Europe. He could start bombing this country at any moment.'

'But 'e won't.'

All eyes turned to Hannah.

'How can you be so sure?' asked Maurice.

''Cos they wouldn've ever taken all our mates back ter Lond'n if they fawt it was goin' ter get bombed.'

Hannah's comments prompted Louie to join the conversation. 'My friend Alfie went back 'ome. 'Is mum said she'd sooner 'e took 'is chances wiv the family back in 'Olloway than 'ung around in a place like this.'

Hannah kicked her sister under the table, whilst the others

just waited for Maggie's reaction. However, for the moment, Maggie said nothing, and merely concentrated on eating her lunch.

'But what about *you*, Louise?' asked Hilda. '*You* wouldn't want to go home if there were bombs dropping, would you?'

'Oh yes I would!' replied Louie. 'I'd much rarver be down Kinloch Street.'

There was a marked silence round the table, until Hannah added quickly, 'What Lou really means is there's no place like 'ome, is there?'

'You're quite right, Louise, my dear.' Once again, everyone turned to look at Maggie. 'The last thing Mr Bullock and I would want to do,' she said, calmly putting down her knife and fork, 'would be to keep you away from a happy home.'

For one lingering moment, Hannah's eyes met Maggie's. It was gradually dawning on her what her foster-mother was thinking, and she feared the worst.

Chapter 10

A few weeks after Christmas, Hannah's fears were justified when Maggie informed her that she had arranged with the evacuation committee for Louie to be moved to alternative accommodation with different foster-parents. Hannah was outraged, not only because her young sister was being moved without prior consultation with her, but also because the two of them were to be separated. The news was broken to her one bitterly cold morning after she had taken Louie off to school and returned to continue her daily cleaning chores at the pub. 'If Lou goes,' she shouted at Maggie, 'then *I* go too!'

'I'm afraid that won't be possible, my dear,' replied Maggie, quite unperturbed by Hannah's outburst. 'Mrs Mullard and the committee agree with me that Louise is a very highly strung child. She has special needs that are obviously not available in this type of establishment. I should have realised it the moment she came here, but I felt sorry for her. Mr Bullock and I wanted to help her.'

'She don't need your 'elp!' snapped Hannah. '*I'm* 'er sister. *I* take care of 'er! That's the only reason I'm 'ere!'

'Yes, I know that, my dear,' replied Maggie calmly, sitting down at the kitchen table to drink her mid-morning cup of tea. 'And that, I'm afraid, is part of the problem.'

Hannah was thunderstruck. 'Wot d'you mean by that?' she growled, standing over Maggie.

Maggie took a sip of hot tea then looked up at her. 'I'm sorry to say that everyone agrees that you are not a good influence on Louise. Your sister needs a calm, steady hand. She relies on you too much, Hannah. She has no time to breathe, to think for herself. Louise is actually quite a sweet, intelligent child – I told Mr Bullock that the first time I met her – but she does need the right kind of people around her.'

'Like *you*, yer mean?'

Maggie stiffened, but refused to let Hannah ruffle her. 'That may be so, my dear,' she replied. 'So maybe we should learn by our mistakes. We can only hope that Louise will prosper in her new environment. We *all* think so.' As Hannah swept off to the door, Maggie called after her: 'Including your mother.'

Hannah came to a dead halt, and swung her a shocked look.

Maggie was smiling sweetly at her. 'Believe me, my dear,' she said, 'a mother does know what's best for her child.'

Wrapped up in her winter coat and headscarf, Hannah hurried as fast as she could across the village green. But it was hard going, for during the previous night there had been a heavy fall of snow, and as the only footwear she had were her everyday shoes, her feet were like ice as they desperately tried to nego-tiate the endless drifts which had covered everything in sight. By the time she had reached the pond, even the ducks were frantically trying to sort out how to reach the surface of the water, which was not only frozen over but covered with several inches of snow.

As luck would have it, Mrs Mullard was at home when Hannah

finally reached the cottage along the back lane where she lived. Puffing and blowing, the poor woman was struggling to clear the downfall of snow that had drifted across her tiny front garden, practically hemming her into the cottage.

'Mrs Mullard!' called Hannah, plodding down the lane to the front gate. 'Can I talk to yer, please? It's urgent!'

Although the woman knew at once why Hannah had come to see her, it at least gave her the opportunity to have a break from clearing snow, and go inside to put the kettle on.

Hannah was too overwrought to think about tea, and she launched immediately into an angry outburst about the committee's giving their permission for Louie to be separated from her and moved to alternative accommodation.

'You mustn't upset yourself, Hannah dear,' said the somewhat dithery old lady, her white hair now a vivid contrast to her blood-red cheeks. 'I can assure you that where your little sister is going she'll be well looked after.'

'I don't *want* 'er looked after by anyone except *me*!' ranted Hannah. 'We've never bin parted since the day she was born. I'm more of a mum ter Louie than our own mum!'

The remark embarrassed Mrs Mullard, who had gone straight into the kitchen to light the gas ring under the kettle on the stove. Once she had done that, she returned to Hannah, who was waiting for her in the small, cosy sitting room. 'Why don't we sit down and talk about this, my dear?' she said, still out of breath from her hectic snow-clearing outside.

'There's nuffin' ter talk *about*!' insisted Hannah angrily. 'Once I tell Lou what's goin' on, she'll do 'er nut!'

'*Please*, my dear,' begged the agitated woman. 'At least sit down for a few minutes.'

Hannah wanted to explode, but she restrained herself, and sat down at the small round polished table.

'Now then,' said Mrs Mullard, trying to deflate the atmosphere. 'Let's try to be realistic about all this. I think you must know that Mr and Mrs Bullock have not been happy about the way your sister has refused to settle down with them.' She raised her hand gently to prevent Hannah from yelling at her again. 'Please let me finish.' She sat back in her chair and dabbed her forehead wearily with her handkerchief. 'This is not an unusual occurrence, you know,' she continued. 'From what I've heard from other parts of the country, many of the evacuees have been found not to be compatible with their new foster-parents. You know, Hannah, it's not an easy task for a committee to judge who and who will not settle down successfully. I'm afraid the outbreak of this war came far too quickly to give us the time to sort things out to everyone's satisfaction.'

Hannah was not to be appeased. 'The Bullocks should never've bin allowed ter take us in,' she replied angrily. 'Espeshully that woman. She's a nutcase.'

'That's not fair, Hannah,' insisted Mrs Mullard. 'Maggie Bullock is a kind and generous woman – once you get to know her.'

'So kind that she accuses us of nickin' from 'er, just because we took a few of 'er lousy biscuits.'

Mrs Mullard sighed, and subconsciously stroked the few white whiskers on her chin. 'Yes, I know,' she said. 'Maggie *is* a very – complicated woman. But, you know, one can hardly blame her after all she's had to go through.'

'Look, Mrs Mullard,' replied Hannah, leaning across the table towards her. 'It's no use takin' it out on me an' Lou just becos' that woman lost 'er baby.'

The old lady shuddered at that remark. 'If you don't mind my saying, Hannah,' she replied uneasily, 'that's a very cruel thing to say – even though it may be true. All I can say is that the Bullocks are not prepared to tolerate any more of your sister's tantrums.' Once again she held up her hand to prevent Hannah from responding. 'No, Hannah, my dear,' she said. 'Don't tell me Louise *doesn't* have tantrums, because I know she *does*. I've seen her once or twice myself in a very ugly mood – at school. In fact, on one occasion, her schoolteacher Miss Thomas had to warn the child that she would be sent home if she didn't stop shouting at people.'

Hannah suddenly looked depressed. Although she would never admit it to anyone, she knew only too well that at times Louie *could* be quite a handful. The trouble was, being the youngest, the child had always been spoilt. Nonetheless, in Hannah's mind, no one had the right to separate the two of them.

'Your mother has been informed about this, Hannah,' Mrs Mullard went on.

Hannah looked up with a start. 'Mum?' she spluttered. 'So Mum really does know me an' Lou are bein' separated?'

'Yes, she does. Apparently, when your mother came to visit you at Christmas, she and Mrs Bullock talked it over. Your mother agreed that it would be in the interests of both you and your sister if Louise was moved to a more compatible family.'

Hannah was so incensed she could hardly bring herself to say anything. The idea that their own mum had been conspiring with the Bullocks to separate her and Louise seemed to her to be almost unbelievable. Right there and then she decided that she would go straight back and write a postcard to her mum, to tell her what she thought of her, to beg her to tell her if what

Mrs Mullard had said was true. 'So,' she said slowly, 'if Lou goes off somewhere else, wot 'appens ter me?'

'Well,' replied the old lady, feeling that she was gradually getting through to the girl, 'I imagine that you will still want to stay around, just to make sure that your sister is being taken care of. In any case, when we talked to Mrs Bullock the other day, she assured us that whatever happened, *you* would still be welcome to be part of their household.'

Hannah nearly had a fit. 'Wot!' she exploded. 'Are you tellin' me you expect me ter 'ang on in the pub?'

'Mrs Bullock is quite prepared to—'

Hannah thumped the table in front of her. 'I don't care a bugger *wot* Mrs Bullock's prepared to do,' she growled, getting up from her chair. 'If Lou goes, *I* go too!'

'Unfortunately, Hannah,' said Mrs Mullard, getting up from the table, 'we would find it very difficult to find alternative accommodation for you. Most of the mothers and children who were evacuated here have now gone home. The villagers are of the opinion that there is no longer a need to offer accommodation to anyone else.'

'Then I'll go 'ome!' snapped Hannah defiantly. 'I'll go back ter 'Olloway where I belong. If my mum finks Lou don't need me any more, then that's fine by me. I'll go 'ome. I'll get away from this place.'

Mrs Mullard looked thoroughly defeated. As Hannah made her way to the door, she called, reluctantly: 'We couldn't allow that, Hannah.'

Hannah stopped dead in her tracks. 'Couldn't allow it?' she asked with incomprehension. '*Who* couldn't allow it?'

'The committee,' replied the old lady stiffly. 'You're under age,

Hannah. That means that until we receive instructions from your mother, you're still our responsibility.'

Redbourne railway station was knee deep in snow. When Hannah got there she found the stationmaster, Ted Sputter, trying to shovel the platform clear single-handed. It seemed an endless task, and to Hannah a fairly useless one, for it seemed as though there were snowdrifts on the railway line at least two feet deep.

'Can't see the ten eighteen getting through today,' said Ted, who was wrapped up in his heavy winter uniform, cap and hood, and wellington boots, with condensation spitting out from his mouth as he talked in the ice-cold wind. 'She's over an hour late as it is. Reckon we'll be getting a cancellation notice from Marks Bell signal box any minute now.'

'Need any 'elp, mate?' asked Hannah, whose shoes and socks were now so wet and her feet so cold, she could no longer feel her toes moving.

'Thank you kindly, young miss,' replied Ted, his nose bright red with the cold, 'but I've done all I can today. And by the looks of you, you could with a good pair of wellies! Come on into the office. I'm just brewing up.'

Hannah followed him into the ticket office, slipping and sliding on the ice along the platform as they went. For Hannah, the warmth coming from the wood stove inside was a godsend, and the first thing she did when Ted opened the stove door was to warm her fingers and try to breathe some life back into them. 'What we could do with,' said the old boy, going straight to the sink to fill his kettle, 'is a nice cuppa cocoa.'

A few minutes later, Hannah was gratefully, clasping both hands round an enamel mug full of piping hot cocoa. 'Sorry to barge in on yer like this,' she said, after burning her lips on the first sip, 'but I need some info on trains.'

'Well, yer've come ter the right place, little lady,' replied Ted, unravelling his woollen scarf and sitting alongside Hannah on a stool in front of the fire. 'We're not exactly St Pancras station out here, but at least Redbourne has a place in the timetables. What can I do for you?'

''Ow often do the trains go ter Lond'n?' she asked. 'I mean, when they're able ter go.'

'Twice a day,' replied Ted, almost parrot-fashion after thirty years on the job. 'The ten eighteen in the mornin', and the six fifty every evenin'. Of course, we get some of the big express trains too, but they don't have a scheduled stop here – pass straight through. They play hell with my petunias in the summer. Covered in soot!'

''Ow much?'

'What's that?' asked Ted, clapping one hand to his left ear. He appeared to be a bit hard of hearing.

Hannah gulped down a mouthful of cocoa. ''Ow much does a ticket cost?' she asked.

'To London, St Pancras?'

'Yes.'

'Single or return?'

'Oh, definitely single,' she replied.

Ted didn't even have to think about his answer. 'Three shillings and threepence,' he replied confidently. 'Mind you, that's a minor's fare. I take it the ticket's for you?'

Hannah nodded. She was clearly shocked. ''Ighway bleedin' robbery!'

'Well, I s'ppose keepin' the fares high is the only way to make sure people don't travel around too much – if you know what I mean?' He drew her attention to the posters on the ticket office wall, one of which said: IS YOUR JOURNEY REALLY NECESSARY? and another showing freight train trucks filled with coke and the legend: FOOD, SHELLS AND FUEL *MUST* COME FIRST. IF YOUR TRAIN IS LATE OR CROWDED – DO YOU MIND?

Hannah looked at the posters and felt deeply depressed, not because of what they said but because she knew that there was no way she was going to be able to pay the fare to London for some time, not until she had managed to save up some of the mingy wage the Bullocks paid her each week for slaving away in the pub. Nonetheless, that was what she would do, was determined to do. Once she had saved up enough, the first thing she would do would be to get on that train straight back home to Holloway, and when she got there she intended to give her mum a real piece of her mind. Her thoughts kept churning over and over at the way her mum had behaved. How *could* she be so cruel? How *could* she agree to Hannah and Louie being separated from each other, in a strange place out in the middle of nowhere? And as for the so-called evacuation committee, she had no time for *them* either. As far as she was concerned they were just a bunch of old fuddy-duddies who treated kids from London as though they were nothing more than numbers in a book. And then a terrible thought suddenly struck her. *Where* were they going to send Louie? In her rage and anger, she had forgotten to ask Mrs Mullard the most important question of all. Didn't anyone think about talking to Louie herself about where they were sending her, about the kind of people who would be taking her in? A cold streak ran down her back. What if Louie's new foster-parents turned out to be like the Bullocks? Suppose they treated her the same way? If she, Hannah, wasn't around to keep an eye on her sister, who could the poor kid turn to? But then her fears turned to anger again. It was true what Mrs Mullard had said about Louie – she *was* a difficult kid. If it hadn't been for her tantrums perhaps none of this would have happened. But then her moment of anger turned back to anxiety. How the hell was she going to cope with Louie when she had to tell her that from now on she was going to have to manage on her own?

'Mind you, you know what I think?'

The stationmaster's voice suddenly snapped Hannah out of her thoughts. 'Beg pardon?' she asked.

'I reckon it's far too early for all you kids ter go running back home to London,' said the old boy glumly, wiping a dewdrop from his nose with the back of the mitten on his hand. 'I mean you've only got to look at the papers each day. Things aren't lookin' good, you know. Oh no.'

'Wot d'yer mean?' asked Hannah, puzzled.

Ted looked up at her. 'Come now, little lady,' he replied with surprise. 'Haven't you been reading them – the papers? Our boys have to go up every day now over the coast. Jerry's ruddy planes keep tryin' to break through all the time now. Thank Gord for the RAF. They got guts, those boys. If it wasn't for them, I don't know *what* we'd do. But I'm telling you, little lady, if Jerry gets a chance, the first place he'll make for is London. And then it'll be *our* turn. Mind you, we'll be waiting for him. Our blokes in the village are training up more an' more each day. They say now old Hore-Belisha's been sacked as War Minister, every village and town in the country's going to mobilise. That means we'll get uniforms, and real guns and ammunition to deal with the invasion.'

'Invasion?' Hannah looked at him with complete astonishment.

'Only a matter of time,' replied the old boy gloomily.

He was suddenly interrupted by the loud sound of a bell clanging on the platform outside, which sent him rushing straight across to the telephone on the wall of the ticket office. Hannah listened to him shouting down the phone as though the person at the other end was deaf. But from what he was saying, there would be no trains passing through Redbourne until the track had been cleared of snow all the way from Hertford to London.

Whilst the old boy was on the phone, Hannah took a passing glance at his crumpled copy of the *Daily Sketch*, which was lying on the table beside her. The ominous headline confirmed what Ted had been saying to her: ENEMY RAIDERS SHOT DOWN. 1940 was still only a few weeks old, but it was already looking decidedly precarious.

On the way back to the Cock and Crow, Hannah was feeling more and more depressed. The idea that not only were she and Louie going to soon be separated, but also that she was going to be left all alone at the mercy of the Bullocks, was deeply troubling her. However, as she wound her way round the village green, where everyone seemed to be out shovelling snow from the front of their shops and houses, her real anxiety was for where and what kind of accommodation Louie was going to be sent to. As she approached the post office she met Mary and Joseph Beedle struggling to clear a large fall of snow that had drifted against the front door, and just nearby, Sam was chiselling away with his shovel at the solid sheet of ice that lay beneath the snow along the pavement.

'Not the sort of day to be out, Hannah,' said Sam's mother, as cheery as ever, her lovely round face flushed red with the cold. 'But at least the Germans won't try anything in *this* weather!'

'I'm not so sure,' called her husband, who was piling snow up in the gutter. 'Just look at that sky. Looks like God's been busy today.' Hannah looked up at the sky, which was a beautiful deep blue, as blue as the favourite dress her mum had once bought her from a roadside stall in Holloway Road when she was a small child. 'Let's just hope that once the sun gets warmer it'll thaw some of this.'

Hannah smiled weakly, and without saying anything started to move off towards Sam.

'Hannah.'

She stopped and turned when Mary called to her.

'I want you to know how happy we are about Louise.'

Hannah was puzzled. 'Sorry?' she asked.

Mary came to her. 'I promise you,' she said, 'she'll have a good home here. Joseph and I are going to do everything in our power to make sure she's comfortable. In fact, only this morning Sam and his father have been getting her room ready. I'm sure she'll be happy there. It's got a lovely view over the fields at the back.'

Hannah was completely taken aback. 'Louie?' she asked in astonishment. 'Comin' ter live 'ere – wiv you?'

Thinking that Hannah was unhappy about it, Mary's lovely smile faded. 'I'm sorry,' she said. 'Didn't you know?'

Hannah shook her head.

'Oh goodness,' said Mary anxiously. 'That's very remiss of the committee. When I left them yesterday, I was given to understand that Mrs Mullard was going to tell you.' She sighed. 'I mustn't blame her, I suppose. She does seem to be getting very absent-minded these days.'

Hannah was still in a daze. 'Comin' ter live wiv *you*? I mean – it's wunnerful, but – why din't no one tell me? I don't understand. I just don't understand.'

'Oh dear,' said Mary, placing her hand gently on Hannah's arm. 'I do hope you approve of the idea?'

'Oh – yes, course I do,' replied Hannah, who found it hard to take it all in. Louie going to live with Sam's family was more than she had ever dared hope for.

'You don't have to worry,' continued Mary, with a slight chuckle. 'We shan't try to convert her or anything.'

Again Hannah was baffled. 'Pardon?'

'To our beliefs,' said Mary. 'That was a condition from the committee which we of course agreed to. Louise will be free to come and go as she pleases. She doesn't even have to come to our meetings, if she doesn't want to.'

'Unless she *does* want to,' added Joseph hopefully, making progress by sheer brute force in clearing the snow from the front door of the post office.

'Anyway,' continued Mary, 'we should have a good talk about things. You must come over and have tea with us some time, then we can sort out what we can do to make your little sister happy.' She gave Hannah a close, reassuring look. 'Please trust us, my dear,' she said, before joining her husband to carry on clearing the snow.

Hannah stood there for a moment or so, trying hard to take everything in. Somehow it was all different now. She knew that Louie was going to be in safe hands, and that suddenly filled her with hope.

'You shouldn't be going around in those shoes.' Hannah swung round to find Sam standing behind her. 'You can tell you're not a country girl,' he said, with a smile that seemed to smother her with affection. 'Come and help me make up the fire in the House.'

She duly followed him into the Meeting House, on the way watching him collect an armful of logs from a pile outside.

'The trouble with a place like this,' he said, as he built up the wood stove, 'is that it soon gets freezing cold. But then, in the summer it's stifling hot.' He turned and looked at Hannah. She was standing there with her hands tucked under her arms trying to warm them up. She was shivering with the cold. He went to her, took one of her hands, and led her to the fire.

Hannah did the same as him, and knelt down on the floor to warm her fingers. The logs he had just put in the stove were already spitting and crackling, but the warmth was so embracing that Hannah gradually felt the life seeping back into her.

'I've missed you,' said Sam. 'D'you realise it's a whole week?'

'Seems longer,' Hannah replied.

They turned and smiled gently at each other. After a quick check that no one could see them through the window, Sam leant forward and softly kissed her lips.

'Louie's coming to live wiv yer.' It was the first thing Hannah said as soon as their lips had parted.

'Yes,' he replied. 'How d'you feel about it?'

'I fink it's – luvly,' she replied. 'I just wish someone 'ad told me.'

Sam shook his head and sighed. 'I knew they wouldn't,' he replied softly. 'Or at least, I guessed as much.'

'Why?'

He sat back on his haunches, and slipped his arm round her. 'You know what it's like with the Bullocks. They're not the easiest people to deal with.'

'You're tellin' me,' she said. 'Everyfin' 'as ter be secret. I just wish I could come an' live 'ere wiv yer too.' Sam pulled her closer to him. 'Why can't I, Sam?'

Sam shrugged. 'Apparently it was part of the agreement,' he said. 'As I told you, when the village asked for volunteers to take in evacuees from London, the Friends thought it'd be condoning a war that they were opposed to. But now they've changed their minds, and when the committee asked Mother and Father to take in Louie, they agreed straight away. Unfortunately, though, the Bullocks didn't want you to go too. I don't know why.'

'*I* do,' said Hannah. 'Maggie Bullock wants a daughter, a daughter she couldn't 'ave. The only trouble is, she don't know the diff 'rence between a daughter an' a servant.'

'Listen, Hannah,' whispered Sam, close to her. 'I overheard Mrs Mullard talking to Mother about you and the Bullocks. She said that once you've stayed with them for a bit longer, the committee will find an excuse for getting you away from them.'

'I'll believe that when I see it,' said Hannah acidly. 'That woman'll never let me go.' She sighed. 'Still, as long as *you're* around, at least I've got someone I can turn to.'

Sam suddenly went silent. After a moment, he gently pulled his arm away from her waist, and got up.

Hannah was taken by surprise, and she looked up at him. 'Wot's up?' she asked anxiously. 'Wot'd I say?'

'Hannah,' he replied awkwardly. 'There's something I've got to tell you.' He hesitated a moment. 'I may be going away.'

Hannah felt a cold chill down her spine. She got up and faced him. 'Wot d'yer mean?' she asked.

'Next month I'm going to be eighteen,' he said. 'By then, I've got to make some decisions, some *important* decisions. It means I might have to go away — not immediately, but sooner rather than later. I can't explain, not until I've worked things out. But I have to do something, Hannah. I can't just go on the way I'm going. My conscience won't let me.'

'Sam,' said Hannah, staring into his eyes, 'I dunno wot you're talkin' about.'

'To be frank, Hannah,' he replied, 'neither do I. All I know is that I can't stay here and hurt my father, my family, the Friends. I've got to do *something*.' He moved closer, took her in his arms, and hugged her. 'You *do* understand, don't you, Hannah?'

Hannah leant her head on his shoulder, and did her best to understand, did her best to take in what he was trying to say to her. Unfortunately, however, all she could see at this moment was that the person she had come to trust most in this world, the person she had come to love, was going to leave her, leave her alone in a strange world that was utterly bewildering to her. As Sam gently cupped her face with his hands and kissed her again, the only words she could hear ringing in her ears were those of the woman she had come to loathe and despise: *I shall find it hard to let you go.*

Chapter 11

It was several days before Louie finally left the Cock and Crow to join her new foster-family at the post office in Redbourne. Greatly to Hannah's surprise, her sister took the news of their separation much better than she had expected, so much so that on the morning of her transfer to the care of Mary and Joseph Beedle, Louie showed more interest in getting away from the Bullocks than any real concern for her big sister's feelings. In fact, on the day that Hannah had reached the ripe old age of seventeen just a couple of weeks before, Louie had forgotten all about it until Hannah opened a birthday card from Babs, which took both of them by surprise. There was no doubt in Hannah's mind that her young sister really was a selfish little girl, who each day was showing signs of growing up to be just like their mum. On the night of her birthday, Hannah lay in bed in the dark, tears streaming down her face, her own sister hadn't even shown enough interest to wish her a happy birthday.

'Wos up?' called Louie from her iron bedstead against the opposite wall. 'You cryin'?'

Hannah took a deep breath to compose herself before replying. 'No,' she answered. 'I'm not cryin'.'

'Sounds like it.'

'Go to sleep, Lou,' said Hannah irritably.

Louie did just that, for from that moment on Hannah never heard another sound from her. As far as Louie was concerned, this had been just another day like any other. But for Hannah, the start of her eighteenth year convinced her that the only person who loved her, who truly cared what happened to her, was herself.

On the morning after Hannah had delivered Louie to her new foster-parents, she returned to the Cock and Crow to find an air letter waiting for her and Louie from their dad. She was thrilled to get it, for, like their mum, Len Adams was no letter-writer, and the fact that he had made the effort was the first real sign that he thought about them at all. However, the letter itself was hard to read, for not only was it heavily censored, with some of the words blacked out, but it looked like a photo which had been squeezed down to half its size. Nonetheless, the moment Maggie Bullock gave it to her, she rushed upstairs, threw herself down onto her bed, and started reading it. There was no date, no address, and no indication where he was.

Hallo mates – how are you then? I got your address from your mum who wrote and told me that your having a real nice time in your new digs and that the folks looking after you are real nice.

As she read that, Hannah felt like puking.

Well you lucky buggers I bet your doing better than your poor old dad. You have no idea how bleedin lousy it is out here in

*(BLACKED OUT). Sometimes at night I cant sleep
thinking what its like back home in those beds of ours. The
only thing though is at least I know you two are safe. It
scares the life out of me and my mates every time we hear
how things could be hotting up in dear old London town. Its
bad enough out here when we are listening to ack-ack guns
over in (BLACKED OUT) but if Jerry started on home
ground I don't know what I'd do. I tell you, I couldn't take it
if anything happened to your mum she means the world to
me.*

Hannah stopped reading for a moment, and wondered if her
mum was feeling the same way about *him*.

*Anyway you two remember to do what your mum tells you.
While I'm away she makes the decisions not me, so if
anything happens to me dont forget what I told you. I dont
know when I'll see you both again but even though its a long
way from here in (BLACKED OUT) to dear old Holloway,
you can bet your life I'm thinking of you. Love from your
dad.*

Hannah put the air letter down, lay on her bed, and closed
her eyes. She was miles away in the place where her dad had
written his letter. With every mention of the place names crossed
out in thick black ink, she had no idea where he was, or even
whether he was still alive. All she knew was that the moment
she held the tiny little letter in her hands, she could feel her
dad's presence. It was all there in those few hard-written words,
a man who cared what was happening to his kids, yes, and to

his wife too, and what he was saying made her start to think that perhaps her mum wasn't really as bad as she thought. Times were difficult, and tough decisions had to be taken. Keeping Hannah and Louie away from home was, under the circumstances, the best thing to do. Things in other countries were not looking good, what with Jerry marching in everywhere, and bombs, and people getting killed. Yes, it *was* true that most people thought that the war hadn't really started yet, not in England anyway, but if and when it did, it was only natural that parents would want their kids to be kept safe. Nonetheless, it *was* difficult to come to terms with living away from home; it seemed to be such a long way away. All she could hope for now was that the rotten lousy war would soon be over, so that she could get away from the Bullocks and get back to the people she knew so much better.

'Hannah! Are you in there?'

Hannah's eyes sprang open as she heard Maggie Bullock tapping on her door. She sat up with a start and perched on the edge of the bed. 'Wot d'yer want?' she called back curtly.

'I'd like to talk to you for a moment,' replied Maggie from the landing outside. 'Can I come in?'

'It's *your* place, not mine.'

The door opened gently. Maggie came in. She wore a sweet, comforting smile. 'Is everything all right in here?' she asked.

Hannah shrugged. 'S'ppose so,' she replied.

'I know how you're feeling,' said Maggie. 'You must be missing Louise. But don't worry. The Beedles are good people. I'm sure they'll take good care of her.'

Hannah was puzzled. For the life of her she couldn't understand why Maggie should want to climb all those stairs just to tell her that the Beedles were going to look after Louie better than she, Maggie, had done. Of course Louie would be taken care of – that was obvious. But now, however, Hannah was more interested in herself. As she watched her so-called foster-mother glancing around the tiny attic room, she wondered what the future held for *her*, the daughter that Maggie Bullock had never had.

'You know,' said Maggie, in a seemingly benevolent mood, 'now that you're on your own, we must try to make you more comfortable. Your father will be coming up shortly to take down Louise's bed. It'll give you so much more room up here. But by the looks of things it's going to need a good old tidy up. Remember, Hannah, cleanliness is next to godliness.'

'I didn't know you was religious,' said Hannah sarcastically.

'Religion isn't only something you find in church, my dear,' replied Maggie, who was looking blandly up at the sky through the fanlight. 'The most important place you'll find it in – is the heart.'

Heart? Hannah thought she wasn't hearing right. Maggie Bullock – with a *heart*?

'Life isn't necessarily about someone else's views,' continued Maggie, who seemed to be miles away. 'It's what you feel *inside* that counts.' She suddenly emerged from her moment of day-dreaming, and turned back to Hannah. Her expression had become more strained. 'I was talking the other day,' she said, 'to Mr Sputter, the stationmaster. He said you'd been asking him about trains to London.'

'That's right.'

Maggie smiled. 'Why is that, my dear?' she asked. 'Are you planning a trip?'

'Maybe,' replied Hannah, who suddenly felt uneasy. 'Yer never know.'

'D'you think that's a wise thing to do?' asked Maggie, arms now folded. 'I mean, have you talked it over with your mother?'

'Not much chance er that, is there?' said Hannah. 'I mean, she don't exactly make much contact with *me*, does she? In any case, it'll be a nice surprise for er.'

Maggie's smile had been replaced by a constrained look of disquiet. 'A train journey costs a lot of money these days,' she pointed out. 'Would you be able to afford the fare?'

'I'll manage.'

'Mr Sputter said the authorities are asking people not to travel by train unless the journey is absolutely necessary.'

Hannah smiled. '*My* journey *is* necessary,' she replied.

At that moment, a pigeon landed on the ledge of the fanlight, and cooed loudly. Maggie quickly shooed him away. 'Nasty smelly things, pigeons,' she said. 'I much prefer tropical birds.'

Hannah resisted the temptation of telling her how she had always hated the idea of locking a bird up in a cage, like Polly downstairs.

'You know, Hannah,' said Maggie, turning round to her. 'I'd like so much to be your friend. There are very few people I can really talk to; that's why I would have loved to have had a daughter. A daughter is someone one can talk to – I mean *really* talk to – someone who knows how a mother feels when she's sad and lonely, someone to share life's problems with. Oh, that's not to say that I can't talk to Mr Bullock – to your father; he's kind and considerate. But he's a man, and a man doesn't really understand how a woman feels deep down inside.'

Hannah was now watching Maggie with intense interest,

realising that in some peculiar way this woman was trying to open up to her.

'Relationships come in different forms, Hannah,' continued Maggie. 'Husband and wife, sister and sister, and – mother and daughter. I may be wrong, but I happen to think that a mother and daughter is the strongest relationship of all. They have the opportunity to form a real bond, a real meeting of minds. D'you understand what I mean, my dear?'

Hannah, still perched on the edge of her bed, remained quite impassive.

'I mean,' explained Maggie, 'that I would like to have a daughter whom I could trust, whom I could confide in. We could be such a formidable team, Hannah.'

Hannah just sat where she was, unable to respond to her.

Maggie sat down beside her. 'Listen to me,' she said softly, placing her arm round Hannah's shoulders. 'From now on, I want us to be a family – you, me, and your father. If you have a problem, I want you to come to me, I want you to talk things over with me, not as an enemy, but as a friend. D'you understand what I'm trying to say, Hannah?'

All Hannah could do was shrug.

'And from now on,' continued Maggie, 'now that there's just the three of us, we're all going to eat together. Would you like that, Hannah, would you?'

'OK,' replied Hannah blandly.

Maggie smiled. For the time being, that was all the response she needed. At least it was a start. To Hannah's distaste, Maggie kissed her gently on her forehead. 'Splendid!' she said, getting up and going to the door. 'Now we *are* making a start.' She was about to go when she suddenly remembered something. 'Oh, by the way,' she said. 'Now that Louise has gone, you've no need to go on using the outside washroom. I'm sure your father will have no objection to your using *our* bathroom. In any case, I don't like the idea of your going out into the back garden in the dark.'

She left, closing the door gently behind her. Hannah immediately got up from her bed, and put her ear to the door, listening to the sound of Maggie going back downstairs. For a moment, she just stood there, dazed and bewildered by all she had just heard. Then, on an impulse, she rushed to the small bedside cabinet between the two single beds, opened the bottom drawer, and took out the small purse her grandmother had bought her for Christmas the year before. She unclipped it, and tipped out the few coins that were in there onto the bed. She quickly sorted through and counted them. One shilling and twopence. Flopping back onto the edge of the bed again, she sighed in despair, for she knew only too well that she still had a very long way to go before she had enough money to buy the ticket for that train journey.

Louie was in her seventh heaven. Her room with the Beedles above the post office was, to her, like a dream come true. Not only did she have her own single bed beneath the window, but the lovely floral-patterned curtains matched the bedspread, which in turn blended in perfectly with the plain, pink-coloured wallpaper. On top of all that, the room was so big it also had a small dressing table, a single wardrobe, and a chest of drawers, all painted white. And the view from the window took her breath away, for it overlooked a vast expanse of fields, which were at this time covered in a thick blanket of snow for as far as the eye could see, a real winter wonderland. Louie couldn't believe her luck, for it was all so different from living up in that attic room in the Cock and Crow with her sister. But best of all, she didn't have to live each day under the constant shadow of the Bullocks, who to her mind spied on her wherever she went. No, if this is what evacuation was like, then maybe being parted from her family and friends back home in Holloway would become more bearable.

On Saturday afternoon, Hannah called in to see how she was getting on, and found her young sister downstairs in the back parlour behind the post office, having tea and homemade jam sponge with Mary and Joseph Beedle. It was a wonderfully cosy affair, with everyone sitting around the wood fire in an old iron grate, with Joseph in charge of toasting crumpets on a long fork, and Louie playing a game of snakes and ladders with Sam Beedle at a small table in front of the bow-shaped window. Mary was knitting a cardigan whilst listening to Uncle Mac reading a story on *Children's Hour* on the wireless, and Hannah flicked through the pages of the popular magazine *Radio Fun*. However, despite the idyllic atmosphere, from the moment she arrived Hannah was aware that Sam and his father seemed to speak very little to each other. Suddenly, the wireless programme was interrupted by the svelte voice of the newsreader Alvar Liddell.

'We apologise to you children for this interruption in your programme, but here is the text of a communiqué just released from the War Office: *Today, in the Saar-Moselle region of France, the British Expeditionary Force came under fire from units of the German artillery corps, which was immediately followed by a small scale offensive from a ground infantry division. Although the offensive was quickly repulsed, British troops suffered some casualties.*'

Sam Beedle immediately looked up grimly from the snakes and ladders board, and as the newsreader continued, his father removed the next crumpet from the toasting fork.

'*The War Minister has therefore issued this statement to reinforce his earlier warning that the call-up of all men of eligible age will need to be expedited, and he urges these young men, together with those volunteers above the age of call-up for national service, to report to their nearest army recruitment office at the earliest possible moment.* That is the end of this special communiqué. We now return listeners to Uncle Mac and *Children's Hour.*'

Mary stopped her knitting, and leant across to switch off the wireless set. As she did so, Sam said something softly to Louie, got up, and left the room. His father put the toasting fork down in the grate, and quietly followed him out. Puzzled, Hannah also got up.

'No, Hannah,' pleaded Mary Beedle, putting down her knitting on the sofa beside her. 'This is something between Sam and his father.'

'But – wot's up?' asked Hannah, suddenly aware of the tension the news bulletin had brought to the room.

'The war, Hannah,' replied Mary, with a deep sigh. 'I'm afraid it's just this terrible war.'

'Is Sam coming back?' asked Louie irritably, coming across to help herself to a ginger biscuit. 'I could've won that game.'

Mary smiled up at her. 'In a few minutes, Louie,' she replied, trying her best not to show the inner torment she was feeling. 'While you're waiting, why don't you go up to your room and get that jigsaw puzzle Uncle Joseph bought for you? I'm sure your sister would love to see it.'

Louie shrugged. 'OK,' she replied airily, rushing out of the room.

Mary waited for her to go, then turned back to Hannah. 'She's a sweet girl,' she said. 'I do hope she'll be happy with us.'

'She will. I can tell,' replied Hannah. 'She's lucky to be here.' She got up from her chair, and went to sit beside Mary. 'Wot's wrong wiv Sam and 'is dad, Mrs Beedle?'

Mary turned to face her. 'Sam is soon going to be eighteen.' She replied with great difficulty, 'He wants to join the army.'

Hannah felt her stomach seize up. It was what she had feared. This was what she had expected ever since Sam had told her that he might be going away.

'His father is, naturally enough, utterly opposed to that,' continued Mary. 'So am I, so are *all* the Friends. It flies in the face of everything we believe in. How can we embrace peace if we let our men go to war to kill other men? And yet . . .' she shook her head sadly, 'if we allow these misguided people to invade our country, where will it all end? It's more than likely that none of us will be allowed the freedom to continue believing in the things we hold so dear. We *know* these people have to be stopped, but at what cost?' She sighed. 'It's such a dilemma for people like us, Hannah; oh, *such* a dilemma.'

'But if Sam stays,' said Hannah, 'if 'e refuses ter go in the army an' fire guns an' fings, wouldn't they let 'im do uvver fings – like some sorta war work at 'ome?'

'Yes,' replied Mary, unconsciously smoothing out the pinafore on her lap. 'He could register as a conscientious objector. My own father did that in the last war. *He* was a man of strong principles too, just like all the Friends. But when he saw how men of all ages on the battlefield were being shot down in cold blood, some of them his own relatives and friends, he took up arms. My mother said the first time he took aim with a rifle and shot a man, he cried openly, like a child. Then he lost his own life at the battle of Ypres. Joseph and I can't bear the thought that the same thing could happen to Sam.'

For a moment or so, Hannah sat there in silence with Mary, both of them staring aimlessly into the fire. Hannah could almost *feel* the torment this poor woman was going through, because she too was feeling the same – or maybe not quite the same, but in a way that told her she couldn't bear it if anything was to happen to Sam. Although she had known Sam for only a short time, she had come to respect and admire and even love him. Nonetheless, in her eyes he was still only a boy. He wasn't like her dad, who was tough and hardy and knew how to mix it with all the blokes down the Eaglet pub in Seven Sisters Road, knew how to line up alongside his mates if they had to go into battle. No, Sam was only a boy. Only fully grown men should have to fight in a war. But then, someone had to stop what Mary called 'misguided' people from taking over the world. After all, sooner or later, boys became men.

After a moment or so, Sam came back into the room. Without saying a word, he went to the fireplace, picked up the toasting fork his father had left unfinished there, and held the crumpet in front of the fire.

'Sam?' Sam looked up to find his mother talking to him. Hannah could see the strained expression on his face. 'Where's your father?'

Sam answered softly. 'He went for a walk.'

Mary got up. 'I'll go and keep him company,' she said.

Hannah watched in sombre admiration as Mary quietly left the room. 'They're lovely people, Sam,' she said, once they were alone.

Sam hesitated before answering her. 'Yes, they are,' he replied at last.

Hannah got up from the sofa, knelt beside him on the rug in front of the fire, gently slipped her arms comfortingly round his waist, and leant her head against his shoulder.

As always, Saturday was a busy night at the Cock and Crow. All the usual regulars were there, including Percy Bumper and his farmhand Jack Dabbs, Will Ferris who worked at the local aircraft factory, and Ron Drayton, reluctantly accompanied by his wife, who sat most of the evening at a table in the saloon bar, glaring at everything her husband was getting up to with his drinking mates. There was, of course, a special reason for the get-together, for Jack Dabbs had finally received his call-up papers, and was leaving for an army barracks near Colchester in Essex early the following morning.

'So they've finally caught up with you, have they, Jack?' Maggie's remark from behind the counter was more a light-hearted statement than a question. 'Your wife's going to miss you.'

'Don't you believe it,' joked Will, who like most of the others was half sozzled, even though they were still only halfway through the evening. 'Once she gets him out the front door, she'll have a queue of fellers waitin' to come in through the back!'

Everyone burst out laughing, everyone that is except Maggie, who turned away and went off to serve a couple of better-class customers in the private bar. However, Sid Bullock *was* amused, and once Maggie had gone he came out from the other side of the counter to join his regulars. 'Must be lousy for the women-folk, though,' he said. 'Not knowin' how long this war's going to last.'

The moment Sid appeared, the mood amongst the group became slightly subdued. It was a sad fact of life that ever since the accident with that girl on the river two years before, the male regulars felt more comfortable in Maggie Bullock's presence than with the guv'nor himself.

'Oh, I don't know,' replied Jack, who still had several farewell pints lined up for him on the counter. 'My missus is taking it all in her stride. Can't do much else really, can she?'

'But ain't she expectin', Jack?' asked Ron Drayton, face flushed with draught bitter, the dog-end of a fag so burnt through that it had nearly reached his lips. 'What she goin' to do when the little one arrives?'

'That's right,' added Percy Bumper, the farmer, who was none too steady on his feet. ''Speshully when 'is dad's not around to help out.'

'Since when do dads *ever* help out?'

All the men glared across at Ron's wife, who was on her third gin and tonic, and was sitting up sternly in her chair, her winter's coat unbuttoned carelessly, and the scarf around her head tied so tightly that only part of her face was visible.

'*I've* never come across one man who was *any* help to his wife,' she boomed out in a far too loud voice. 'In any case, it's a man's job to go out and fight wars, and a woman's job to stay at home and look after the kids.'

Hannah, who had been listening to all this from behind the kitchen door, now entered the saloon bar briefly, carrying a tray of cleanly washed glasses.

'So, Hannah,' called Will. 'What do *you* think about all this? D'you reckon only us men should be the ones to go and fight in the war?'

By now Hannah was used to the men's jibes, and so, as usual, she immediately had an answer for them. 'Funny,' she replied, 'I fawt women are takin' part in this war too, ain't they? In any case, I reckon they'd look far better in their uniforms than some of you lot!'

The men at the counter roared with laughter.

'That a girl, Hann!' bellowed Percy.

'My missus would love to hear that, Hann!' Will laughed, his mouth covered with bitter foam.

'So would all the fellers!' yelled Ron, spluttering all over the place. 'And with *your* looks, gel, I bet they wouldn't mind a lot more!'

This provoked a long outburst of near hysterical laughter, which was suddenly broken by the voice of Sid Bullock booming out at them. 'Cut it out!' Everyone hardly noticed he was shouting at them, so he yelled even louder. 'I said – cut it out – *all* of you!'

Hannah stopped dead in her tracks as the men suddenly became silent.

'This girl's only seventeen years old!' growled Sid, his one eye scanning them all. 'That means she's not only under age to be in this bar looking after *you* lot, but she's also entitled to a bit of respect. So once and for all cut it out!' As the men stared at him in absolute astonishment, he turned to Hannah. 'All right, Hannah,' he said calmly. 'Off you go.'

Hannah took one quick look at the men at the counter, then calmly returned to the kitchen, where, to her surprise, she found Maggie Bullock waiting for her.

'You see,' said Maggie, with a rather superficial smile. 'When you need us, we shall always be there.'

★   ★   ★

187

In bed that night, Hannah lay for hours in the dark thinking about how Sidney Bullock had stood up for her. It was the first time she had realised that he was not just someone who kowtowed to his wife, and seemed to have no views of his own about anything. He had shown something that Hannah had never received before – respect. But then her mind started churning over the things Mary Beedle had said to her, especially about Mary's own father who was also a Friend, but also fought the pain of defiance by going to war, a war that resulted in his own death: *Joseph and I can't bear the thought that the same thing could happen to Sam*. Everything was so strange, so unreal. Whatever she or anyone else thought, men *had* to go to war, they *had* to defend values, *had* to defend their families *and* their country. By the time she fell asleep, Hannah had started to reassess her relationship with the Bullocks. Perhaps they *were* genuine people after all, people who had been deprived of the one thing they had wanted in life. Could they *really* ever become a replacement for her own mum and dad, she wondered? She drifted off gradually, grateful for Sid Bullock's intervention, thankful that he and his wife were treating her like a human being and not as a prisoner. But when she woke up during the night to go to the outside washroom, momentarily forgetting in her sleepy state that she was now allowed to use the Bullocks' bathroom, she went downstairs, but was immediately shocked to find that not only was the back garden door locked, but the key had been removed from its usual place.

In one brief moment of panic, all her fears, all her suspicions returned. With every door in the Cock and Bull now locked, she was no less than a prisoner in a cage – just like Polly the parrot.

Chapter 12

The winter was becoming quite savage, one of the worst recorded for several years. With snowdrifts everywhere, getting around by road and rail was proving to be a hazardous enterprise, and even by foot, crossing a road needed not only extra time, but a great deal of care. Redbourne took its share of the excessive weather conditions. On one night alone, six inches of snow fell on the village, which meant that the locals had a hard time getting to Barney Jessop's shop to collect their weekly rations. Elderly people suffered most: Mrs Mullard fell down on the treacherous ice beneath the snow, fracturing her arm, and Martha Randle's old father suffered frostbite in his fingers whilst trying to thaw out some frozen water pipes in the back yard. And if that wasn't enough, on one of the rare clear days there was an air-raid warning, which meant that as the village had no siren installed, Constable Harrington had to make his way round on foot blowing his police whistle until he nearly swallowed it, and shouting out: 'Take cover! Take cover!' Fortunately, however, his strenuous warnings proved to be unnecessary, for the signal from his headquarters that an enemy bomber was heading for the village from the Hertford area turned out to be a false alarm. Meanwhile, the activities of the Local Defence Volunteers, which was the grand name now given to the mainly elderly village men who were now formed into a more organised home defence unit, were somewhat curtailed. As far as they were concerned, no war should be allowed to take place until the weather had improved.

By the beginning of March, Hannah had had enough of life in the English countryside. It had nothing to do with her relationship with the villagers, who had been the essence of kindness in the way they had accepted her and Louie into their lives; it was the daily drudgery of feeling confined to the Cock and Crow with the Bullocks that had become just more than she could take. She hated the idea that not only was every door of the pub locked each night, but the keys were only accessible to Maggie Bullock herself. Often when she was alone cleaning up the saloon bar at the crack of dawn each morning, she would have a conversation with Polly the parrot, comparing the poor creature's solitary life in a cage with her own miserable existence as a prisoner behind locked doors. And there seemed to be no end to it. Despite the fact that the villagers had been so kind to the evacuees whilst several of them were living in Redbourne, now that most of them had returned home the villagers were not at all keen to take in any more, not even Hannah. However, at least she was now sharing decent meals with her captors, and Sid Bullock had tried very hard to make her attic room more comfortable by removing Louie's bed to give her more space, and even bringing up a small oil heater to help combat the bitterly cold nights, although the stifling fumes of the paraffin were so strong that she had to keep the fanlight window partly open.

Hannah dreaded the moment when there would be a thaw,

for it meant that Sam would be going away from Redbourne, leaving her with no one but her friend Jane Jessop to share her troubles with. Sam's call-up papers had not arrived on his eighteenth birthday as expected, but later, during the last week of February, when travel in and out of Redbourne was virtually impossible. When the thaw did eventually come, there was deep consternation and sadness, not only for Hannah, but also for the Beedles, and everyone in the Quaker community. No one wanted Sam to turn his back on everything he had been brought up to believe in; no one wanted to see him going off to fight in a war that, in the opinion of the Friends, could have been avoided. Nonetheless, after many heartbreaking discussions with his mother and father, Sam decided that his conscience could no longer isolate him from the facts of life. So the moment the thaw set in, with his mother's help Sam packed his bags, and prepared to leave Redbourne for the training camp in Woolwich.

The evening before Sam's departure, he and Hannah went for an evening stroll down by the river in Beechers Wood. Although it was still bitterly cold, there wasn't a cloud in sight, and the face of the man in the big white moon was as clear as if he was standing right next to them. Somehow, in Sam's company, the place didn't seem nearly so menacing to Hannah as on that terrible night when Louie hid out there with Alfie Grieves. As they picked their way carefully into the deepest part of the woods, with no aid from a torch, trees of every shape and size seemed to look down at them with tender love and affection, the tips of their frozen branches reaching down to see the two young lovers safely on their way. At the river bank, the surface water, which had been frozen along the edge for several days, was now flowing freely again, and they lingered for several minutes, arms round each other's waists, illuminated by a flood of radiant white light, staring at their own elongated shadows stretched across the ice-cold water.

'Once yer've gone,' said Hannah gloomily, 'I won't ever want ter come here again. It won't be the same.'

'I think that's a shame.'

'Why?'

Sam leant his head against her. 'Because this is *our* place, Hannah,' he replied softly. 'This is where we shared a great deal together.'

'Yer mean Lou and Alfie gettin' lost in the woods?'

'No,' he replied. 'Before we even found them, we shared our first real moment alone together.'

Hannah suddenly felt a deep sense of despair. She gently eased her head away from his. 'So we'd better make the most of it,' she said, her voice cracking, and not much more than a whisper. 'I don't know wot I'm goin' ter do wivout yer.'

He turned her round to face him. 'I'll tell you what you're going to do, Hannah,' he whispered. 'You're going to learn to have more confidence in yourself.'

Hannah, puzzled, pulled a face. 'Wot d'yer mean?' she asked.

'I mean that you're capable of doing things that you've never even thought about,' he replied. 'Just because you come from some London back street doesn't mean that you're not as good as anyone else. And as a matter of fact, I happen to think that you're *better* than anyone else.'

Although she warmed to what he was saying, she still couldn't quite understand what he was getting at. 'I – I dunno wot yer askin' me ter do,' she replied, flustered.

Sam pulled her close to him, and kissed her lightly on the

tip of her nose. 'All I'm asking you to do, Hannah,' he said, 'is to be yourself, do what comes naturally to you, be proud of who you are and where you come from.'

Hannah hesitated for a moment. 'I could never be like you, Sam,' she said. 'You've come from a good 'ome, wiv a lovely mum an' dad. Yer've 'ad a good education; yer've learnt 'ow ter speak better than me.'

Sam laughed, and held her to him. 'That's not why I love you, Hannah,' he replied. 'I love you for who you are, not for the way you speak.'

Hannah went quiet, and looked up into his eyes.

'Come with me!' he said, suddenly grabbing hold of her hand, and leading her off.

'Where we going?' she asked, astonished by his sudden impulse.

He didn't answer. They stopped alongside a huge elm tree, where he reached into his duffel coat pocket and took out a penknife.

'Wot yer doin'?'

'Watch!'

She did just that, watching him as he carved something into the lower bark of the trunk. At first it was difficult to see what he was up to, but as the bright fluorescent moon continued its slow move across the dark sky, it illuminated the initials Sam was carving into the tree.

'There!' he proclaimed proudly. 'This is just to prove that this is *our* place. So now we'll just have to come back.'

Hannah looked in awe at the initials, H and S, incised in the bark. They were pinpointed with the utmost clarity in the moonlight.

'Do you agree?' he asked her. When she didn't reply, he gently turned her face towards him. There were tears rolling down her cheeks. He smiled tenderly, and with one finger wiped away the tears. 'You see, Hannah,' he said softly, after kissing her passionately, 'tonight is forever.'

When Hannah got back to the Cock and Crow, it was after closing time, and she found that not only had she been locked out, but the place was in darkness. 'Bleedin' cheek!' she growled under her breath. Only one thing for it – she knocked on the saloon bar entrance door, calling out, 'Anyone at 'ome?' There was no reply, so she called again. 'It's cold out 'ere! Are yer goin' ter let me in, or shall I go an' stay at an 'otel?'

Clearly, her humour was not going down well with the Bullocks, for the door remained stubbornly closed. However, just as she was convinced – and indeed beginning to hope – that she had been shut out for good, she heard the key being turned in the latch on the inside.

'Keep your voice down *please*, Hannah,' whispered Sid Bullock, pulling the blackout curtains to one side, and opening the door. 'We don't want complaints from the neighbours.'

Hannah went in, and waited whilst Sid closed and locked the door again. In the moonlight outside she could just see that he was in his pyjamas and dressing gown. 'This *was* s'pposed ter be my evenin' off, y'know!' she spluttered angrily.

'I know, I know!' replied Sid, desperately trying to keep her quiet. 'But we shut up shop over an hour ago. Maggie was whacked out, so we both turned in.'

'That doesn't mean yer 'ad ter lock me out,' snapped Hannah, voice lowered to a whisper. 'I *am* s'pposed ter live 'ere, ain't I?'

'I'm sorry, Hannah,' whispered Sid nervously. 'I'm really sorry.

It was Maggie who . . . I'm really sorry. Just get yourself to bed. I don't want to wake her.'

'It's a bit late for *that*.'

Maggie's voice boomed out from the dark on the other side of the bar.

'Maggs!' Sid swung round. He was completely flustered. 'I – I thought you were upstairs.'

'Go to bed, Mr Bullock,' returned Maggie. All that could be seen of her was a dark shadow, sitting at a table near the dying glow of the log fire.

'When I left you,' pleaded Sid, 'you were fast asleep.'

'I said go to bed, Mr Bullock.' Maggie's response was demanding, but she did have the grace to add, '*Please*, Sidney.'

Sid hesitated for only one brief moment before scuttling off in his carpet slippers upstairs.

A moment after Hannah had heard the bedroom door close, Maggie's voice, quietly tense, called from her seat by the fireplace. 'Come here please, Hannah,' she said. 'I want to talk to you.'

'I'm tired,' snapped Hannah.

'So am I,' came the terse reply. 'But I still want to talk to you.'

Reluctantly, Hannah went across to her, but she was not asked to sit. In the flickering glow from the embers, Maggie's lined face looked red and sinister. She never used very much make-up, but when she did it at least helped to make her look reasonably handsome. But not tonight, not at that moment.

'Yer got no right ter lock me out!' Hannah growled immediately she had reached her. 'Why did yer?'

'The blackout presents a lot of opportunities for rogues and scoundrels to break in.'

'Then why don't yer give me a key?' Hannah demanded. 'Why d'yer treat me like a prisoner?'

Hannah's uncompromising tone was clearly not endearing her to her foster-mother. However, it seemed that Maggie genuinely was trying not to feel offended. 'What have I done wrong, Hannah?' she asked calmly. 'I really thought that you and I were going to be friends.'

'If you want me ter be your friend, then yer don't lock me out in the middle er the night.'

Maggie stiffened, but tried not to rise to what she saw as the girl's lack of gratitude. 'What were you *doing* out so late, Hannah?'

'You *know* wot I was doin'. Sam Beedle leaves fer call-up termorrer mornin'. It was the last chance I 'ad ter see 'im before 'e goes.'

'Does he mean that much to you?'

Hannah was stung by her remark. ''E's my friend,' she replied defiantly.

Maggie hesitated, then got up and came round the table in the dark. 'You may not realise it, Hannah,' she said, 'but as your foster-parents, Mr Bullock and I have a responsibility to care for your well-being. If any harm should come to you, we are the ones who would have to answer to the authorities. I just don't understand why you want to be so independent. Why are you always so cold to me?'

Hannah suddenly felt a sense of guilt. She didn't know why, only that she was aware that her own intense dislike of this woman had built a wall between them. But as she stood there, watching Maggie's silhouette moving silently in the dark, all she could feel was a distance between them, a distance created not by Hannah herself, but by someone who wanted to own her. 'Mrs Bullock,' she said, her tone more conciliatory than she really intended, 'I ain't a kid no more. I'm seventeen years old. I've got a right ter fink an' do fings fer meself. 'Ow can I do that when yer don't even pay me fer all the work I do for yer?'

'Hannah,' replied Maggie, pacing up and down. 'When you first came here I told you that Mr Bullock and I would pay for anything that you and Louise wanted – clothes, food – *anything*. All you had to do was ask.'

'It ain't the same as 'avin money in me pocket.'

Maggie came to an abrupt halt. 'Well of course,' she said with great irritation, 'if that's the only thing that's worrying you—'

'Well as a matter of fact,' snapped Hannah, 'it *is*! 'Ow would *you* feel if yer saw somefin' yer wanted ter get an' yer din't 'ave a penny in yer pocket ter pay fer it?'

Maggie could no longer keep up the pretence of not being irritated by Hannah's attitude. 'And what exactly is it you're so eager to buy, may I ask?' she said, raising her voice for the first time. 'A railway ticket, by any chance?'

Hannah was ready for her. 'Yer never know!' she retorted.

Now Maggie was really exasperated. She quickly turned away, went behind the bar, and started to go upstairs. But as she went she called out angrily, 'Starting from tomorrow, we shall pay you a working salary.' She stopped briefly on the stairs. 'What you do with it will be your concern. Just don't expect Mr Bullock and me to pay for any more of your personal expenses.'

The moment Hannah heard the bedroom door close upstairs, her despair at knowing Sam was leaving first thing in the morning was at least tempered by the knowledge that with money now in her pocket, she would no longer have to rely on her meagre savings to buy that train ticket. ''Olloway,' she called out loud and clear, ''ere I come!'

At number 7 Kinloch Street, Babs Adams was woken by the sound of someone knocking on her front door. She groaned when she looked at the clock and saw that it was only eight o'clock in the morning. Since the kids went away, ten o'clock was more her mark. After a late night out, there seemed no point in getting up early in the morning; a lie-in was now the rule of the house. So who the hell was banging on her door at this time of day, disturbing her beauty sleep? Ever so slowly, she got out of bed, and put on her bright red carpet slippers. By the time she opened the window, the banging on the front door downstairs was getting more impatient. No wonder really, for it was cold enough in the bedroom, so God knows what it was like standing on the front doorstep in a temperature that must have been well below zero.

'Who is it?' she yelled at whoever was on her doorstep. 'Wot d'yer want?'

A young telegram boy, his Post Office bicycle propped up at the kerb, looked up from the doorstep. 'You Mrs Adams?' he called.

'I am!' Babs yelled back.

'Not the famous, the world famous – the one an' only Mrs B. Adams?'

Babs was not amused. 'Wot d'yer want, yer cheeky sod?'

'Got a telegram for yer, missus,' replied the boy.

'Who's it from?'

'I dunno,' called the boy, whose long navy blue scarf was wrapped several times round his neck. 'Probably Cecil B. DeMille offerin' yer a part in his new picture!'

Babs would hear no more. She slammed down the window, put on her ancient candlewick dressing gown, and went down to open the door. 'Yer know,' she said drily, grabbing the telegram from the boy, 'you're so funny, you oughta go on *ITMA*.'

'I know,' the boy whipped back, with a huge grin. 'They asked me, but I turned it down. Not enuff cash for a star like me!'

Babs started to slam the door in his face, but he held it open. 'Sign on the dotted line please, madam.'

Babs signed the receipt on his clipboard, and then slammed the door. She went into the kitchen scullery at the back, on the way studying the brown envelope marked IMPERIAL TELEGRAMS, and for one anxious moment she thought it might be one of those terrible messages that one of her neighbours had had, notifying her that her husband was either dead or missing in action. She sat down at the small wooden table, and quickly ripped open the envelope. Fortunately, the message she read was not quite what she had expected:

PLEASE CALL URGENTLY STOP REDBOURNE 241 STOP
BULLOCK STOP

'Bugger!' she cursed. This was all she needed at this time of the morning. More trouble with the kids!

A short while later, Babs, wrapped up like one of Cecil B. DeMille's Hollywood film stars in a warm dark topcoat with a fur collar, and a bright red headscarf, made her way to the telephone booth at the end of Bovay Place, just round the corner. She cursed again when she had to wait in the freezing cold whilst a doddery old girl spent more than her tuppenceworth on a call that seemed to last forever. Despite Babs's repeatedly tapping on the booth window, the old girl completely ignored her until *she* was ready to end her call. 'Ain't you got nuffin' better ter do than jaw all day on a public phone?' snapped Babs, practically pushing the woman out of the way in her hurry to take over the booth.

'Way *you're* dressed, mate,' quipped the old girl, pulling her scarf snugly round her neck, 'yer've got more ter do wiv yer time than *I* 'ave!' She scuttled off down the road, chuckling to herself, calling: ''Appy 'untin'!'

Babs ignored her, took off her gloves, and got some coins out of her purse. All the way from Kinloch Street she had been dreading the idea of having to spend her hard-earned money on a trunk call to Redbourne. But if the message meant what it said about being urgent, then however much the call was going to cost, it was necessary to make it. After dialling O for the operator and asking for the number, she put the first of her three-penny bits into the coin box, listened impatiently to the ringing tone, and waited.

Maggie answered the telephone behind the counter in the private bar at the Cock and Crow. When she heard Babs's voice at the other end, she quickly looked around to make sure no one could hear her. 'Mrs Adams?' she asked, her mouth so close to the telephone mouthpiece that she could practically have swallowed it. 'I'm glad you called, my dear. I have something to tell you that may be quite disturbing for you.'

The small, silent group of Friends who were gathered on the southbound platform of Redbourne railway station kept as close to Mary and Joseph Beedle as they possibly could. Sam was there with them, one of his two bags strapped over his shoulder, anxiously waiting for Hannah to appear. Unfortunately, the stationmaster Ted Sputter had already informed them that, now that the last remaining snow had been cleared from the line, the ten eighteen to London St Pancras was on time. From time to time he looked across at his mother and father, who were standing side by side, grim-faced. Despite Mary's efforts to smile back at her son, it was proving very difficult indeed, so much so that she found herself having to fight back tears.

When Hannah came running across the station concourse, Sam immediately dropped his second bag and hurried to meet her. Everyone in the small group did their best not to notice as the two young people threw themselves into each other's arms and hugged.

'I thought you wouldn't come,' said Sam. 'I didn't expect you to, but I couldn't bear it if I hadn't seen you before I go.'

Hannah, hanging on to him, was very agitated. 'I couldn't get away,' she said breathlessly. 'She made me clean out the oven in the kitchen before I left. There was no need. She just did it fer spite.'

'It doesn't matter,' replied Sam, giving her one of his reassuring smiles. 'You're here now, that's all that counts.'

Some of the Friends in the group lowered their eyes tactfully as the two youngsters kissed quite openly.

'We haven't got much time now, Hannah,' said Sam. 'I want to tell you something. It's about my mother.'

Hannah looked worried.

'If ever you're in trouble,' he continued, 'I want you to promise me you'll go across and see her. I talked to her about it last night. She said, even though the committee won't let her take in both you *and* Louie, she'll be there to help you whenever you need her. D'you understand what I'm saying, Hannah? Do you?'

Hannah, tears welling up in her eyes, nodded. At that moment, the signal bell sounded on the platform, and almost immediately the ten eighteen could be heard chugging its way from the distance towards the platform.

'Are yer goin' ter write ter me?' Hannah asked tearfully.

'Only if you promise to read my letters!' he replied, teasing her. She punched him playfully on his shoulder, and in the distance the driver of the train sounded his engine horn.

'It's funny, isn't it?' said Sam, without expecting an answer. 'We've only known each other for hardly any time at all, and yet – and yet I don't want to be parted from you for one single minute.' He gently raised her chin with one hand, stared into her tearful eyes, and asked, 'Do you feel the same way too?'

Hannah's face was all crumpled up. 'Wot d'yer fink?' she replied jokingly, with tears streaming down her cheeks. 'I 'ate the sight of yer!'

Sam laughed, hugged and kissed her, and again the Friends averted their eyes.

The old steam train finally reached the platform, but as there appeared to be no passengers for Redbourne not one single carriage door opened. Sam quickly picked up his second bag and, with Hannah still clinging to his arm, made his way to a third-class compartment. Before going on board, he stopped to kiss his mother; then, despite their differences, his father hugged him. After nodding a quick, silent farewell to all the other Friends in the group, he kissed Hannah once more before taking his leave of her. Once on board the train, he opened the carriage window, and peered down at her. 'You know, I have a feeling I'll be back quicker than you think.'

Hannah reached for his hand with both of hers, just one last time. Mr Sputter blew his whistle, and waved a green flag to the train guard who was peering out of the window of the rear carriage. 'All aboard please!' It seemed an eccentric request considering there was no one to get on the train except Sam.

After just a few moments, the train got up steam again, and gradually started rumbling along the railway line on the continuation of its journey to London. As it moved off, neither Hannah nor Sam spoke a word, nor did his mother and father, nor any of the Friends, who watched in absolute silence as Sam started to leave them. But Hannah waved. She waved and waved and let the tears roll down her cheeks as the train engine left behind a thick pall of black smoke, which lay gracefully on the morning air until it gradually disappeared into the clear blue sky.

After the train had gone, each one of the Friends came across to touch the shoulders of both Mary and Joseph before wandering off slowly back to the village in complete silence. For a brief moment, Mary joined Hannah, and gave her a hug. 'Shall I tell you something, my dear?' she whispered into Hannah's ear. 'When Sam was a small boy, he once asked me who painted the sky such a beautiful blue colour? I told him that it was someone very nice who lived high up in the clouds. And d'you know what he replied?'

Hannah, her eyes full of tears, shook her head.

'He said, "Mummy. If this nice person can paint the sky blue, can he help me to grow up to be just like Him?" D'you know something, Hannah? I happen to think that that's exactly what's happened. And that can only be good news for us – and for you.'

Mary put her arm round Hannah's shoulder, and gently led her back to the village.

Chapter 13

A week or so after Sam had been called up, Babs Adams arrived in Redbourne to see Hannah and Louie. Alarmed by the telephone call she had had with Maggie Bullock, Babs's prime concern now was to persuade Hannah not to try to make the journey back home to Holloway. Fortunately she came at a time when the wireless and newspapers were full of reports about the grave situation now prevailing in Europe, with threats by the Nazis not only to invade Belgium, Holland, and Luxembourg, but also to invade the British Isles at the first possible opportunity. Babs discussed all this worrying news with Hannah over a cup of tea and jam scones in Martha Randle's tea shop, away from the ears of Louie, who, by all accounts, was thoroughly enjoying her new life with Mary and Joseph Beedle at the post office. However, Hannah was still not convinced.

'I don't believe a word of it,' she said dismissively. 'They've bin talkin' about an invasion ever since war broke out. Even the old blokes in the Local Defence 'ere 'ave bin trainin' ter deal wiv any German parachute soldiers who might drop in. But most of 'em fink it's all just propaganda. Don't listen ter wot you 'ear on the wireless, Mum.'

Babs, who had hardly touched her jam scone, leaned across

the table and lowered her voice. 'Yer dad finks diff'rently,' she replied ominously.

Hannah stared at her warily. 'Wot d'yer mean?' she asked. ''Ow can yer 'ear fings like that from Dad? Everyfin' 'e writes is blacked out.'

'One of 'is mates on sick leave sent me a letter from 'im,' Babs revealed. 'It wasn't censored, so 'e wrote just wot 'e liked. Dad finks it's only a matter of time before 'Itler lets loose on Lond'n. And when *that* 'appens, yer know wot it means. 'E'll do the same to us as 'e did ter Poland – bomb the 'ell out of us.'

Hannah shook her head. 'It's all scaremongerin', Mum,' she said, after gulping down a mouthful of tea. 'We've got the RAF, ain't we? *They* won't let any German planes get anywhere near us.'

'Mark my words, darlin',' replied Babs, lowering her voice even more. 'I've got it on good authority – it's 'appenin' every day.'

Hannah pulled a face. 'Wot d'yer mean?'

'Apparently, planes're comin' over the seafront in Kent and Essex every day,' said Babs. 'Some of 'em've bin shot down, but they keep on tryin'.'

'Tryin' ter do wot?'

'Get ter Lond'n.'

Again, Hannah leant back in her chair and shook her head disbelievingly.

'Everyone knows all about it back 'ome, Hannah,' insisted Babs. 'They say that people all over the country are gettin' ready ter take in evacuees again.'

'That's rubbish, Mum!' snapped Hannah, who was now getting thoroughly fed up with Babs's feeble reasons as to why Hannah should not attempt to come back home. 'Nobody believes that! All the kids and their mums who were 'ere went back ages ago. Even if there *was* a need, no one would take 'em back again.'

'That's not wot Mrs Bullock says.'

At the mention of Maggie Bullock's name, Hannah looked up with a start. 'Wot *she* got ter do wiv it? 'Ave yer bin talkin' to 'er?'

Babs quickly leant back in her chair, and retrieved from the ashtray the fag she had been smoking. 'I just 'ad a chance to 'ave a few words wiv 'er,' she said uneasily, 'whilst you was outside gettin' the logs. Like everyone else, she's very worried about everyfin' that's goin' on. She says the villagers're on standby for when the bombin' starts in Lond'n.'

Hannah immediately leant across the table to her. 'Mum!' She scowled. 'Do you 'onestly believe *anyfin'* that woman says to yer?'

'I believe she's got your interest at heart, darlin', ' replied Babs. 'An' that's all that matters ter me. All I'm sayin' is that you'd be makin' a big mistake if yer tried ter come 'ome at a time like this.'

'It's a mistake I'm willin' ter make!' retorted Hannah.

'Can I get you some more hot water, my dears?'

Both Hannah and her mum looked up to find Martha Randle hovering over them, waiting to collect their plates.

'Oh, no fank you, ducks,' replied Babs, with a friendly smile, after blowing out smoke that she had been holding in her lungs for too long. 'Luvvely cakes you 'ave 'ere, though. Wish we 'ad somewhere like this back in 'Olloway.'

'Thank you, dear,' replied Martha sweetly, but her expression could not conceal the fact that she didn't really care for the woman. She flicked an admiring smile at Hannah. 'I must say you have a lovely daughter, Mrs Adams. We all think the world of her in the village.'

Hannah tried to return an appreciative smile, but it didn't come easily. As Martha left them to serve two elderly ladies on the other side of the tea shop, Babs leant back across the table to Hannah. 'So,' she said smugly, 'who's my popular little gel then?'

'I want ter go 'ome.'

Hannah's uncompromising attitude completely removed the sickly smile from her mum's face. 'Wait a bit, darlin',' Babs pleaded. 'That's all I ask.'

'Wait fer wot?'

Babs was not prepared for such a sudden, loaded question. She had to hesitate before fumbling for an answer. ''Til we can see wot's goin' ter 'appen,' she replied awkwardly. She was saved from further explanation by Martha, who returned with the bill. 'Fanks, ducks,' she said. Once she and Hannah were alone again, she gave a quick glance at her watch. 'Blimey! I've got ter go an' see Louie before I go. Mustn't miss my train.' She rummaged around in her purse looking for some coins to pay the bill. 'Darlin',' she asked quite shamelessly, 'd'you 'ave any cash on yer by any chance?'

Louie proved more popular with her mum than Hannah had done earlier. After she had gone to meet the child as she came out of school, Babs took her back to the Beedles, who treated her with great courtesy and warmth. The first thing she noticed was how much less spoilt Louie had become, more subdued and content. Although Mary Beedle was obviously delighted that the child had settled down to her new style of life, when Babs turned up at the post office to see her she was really quite distraught at the thought that the child's mother had come to take her back home to London. But by the time Babs had left there was clearly no fear of that, for, unlike her elder sister, Louie now had no wish at all to leave the love and affection she was being given by parents who actually cared about her well-being. By the time she took her leave of Louie, Babs actually felt a sense of great relief that at least she had no need to worry about her younger child wanting to come back home. Hannah was a different story.

Hannah didn't go with her mum to see Louie and the Beedles. After the deeply distressing and traumatic conversation she had had with her mum in Martha Randle's tea shop, the only person she wanted to be with was her friend Jane Jessop. Their usual meeting place was the church hall, where, in the absence of Mrs Mullard, who was still recovering from her fractured arm, Jane had taken over the voluntary fund-raising duties for repairs to the steeple of Redbourne parish church. It was a place where they could talk freely without the constant interruption of customers coming into the village store while Jane was working with her father.

'I've got to go, Jane,' said Hannah, the two of them perched on the edge of the hall stage. 'If I don't get away from the Bullocks, I'll go out of me mind.'

'But are you sure, Hannah?' replied Jane, anxious for her friend. 'I mean, it's one thing getting away from the Bullocks, but if you go back to London, after what you've told me about her, would it be any better living with your mum?'

'No, but at least I'd 'ave me friends round me, people I can talk to and confide in.'

'Don't I fit into that category too?' Jane asked tentatively.

'Oh, Jane,' replied Hannah guiltily, putting her arm round Jane's shoulders, 'of course you do! In fact, since I come 'ere, the only person I could really treat as me friend is you.'

'With the exception of Sam,' Jane reminded her. Hannah sighed. 'Have you heard from him yet?'

Hannah shook her head. 'I don't expect to really,' she said. ''E's got more important fings ter fink of than me.'

'Did you ever tell him about how you're saving up to go back to London?'

Again, Hannah shook her head. ''E was always scared about me goin' back there wiv bombs comin' down. I don't know 'ow many times I told 'im that there won't *be* no bombs. An' even if there are, I'd sooner take me chances there than be stuck in a cage wiv the Bullocks.'

'Hannah, listen to me, please.' Jane drew closer and lowered her voice. 'There's something I overheard when Mr Sputter was talking to my dad in the shop the other day. It was about you.'

Hannah stiffened. 'Me?'

'Hannah,' Jane continued seriously, 'you're going to find it difficult to buy a train ticket if you try to go to London. They're going to stop you.'

'Wot!' Hannah was shocked. 'Wot d'yer mean they're goin' ter stop me. *Who* are?'

'Maggie Bullock. She apparently told Mr Sputter that because you're under age, if you try to buy a ticket and board a train, he has to prevent you from doing so.'

'Wot!' Hannah was so outraged she dropped down from the edge of the stage. 'They *can't* do that! I'm not a kid! I've got rights! They *can't* do it!'

Jane joined her. 'Hannah, they *can* do it, and they *will*. As far as the evacuation committee is concerned, you're still under the protection of your foster-parents. If anything happened to you, *they* would be responsible. If you try to go without the Bullocks' permission, they'd go straight to the police.'

Hannah nearly went berserk. 'This is bleedin' crazy!' she yelled, stomping up and down the hall like a mad thing. 'How can they keep me under their thumb like this? It's not human!' In her rage, she went to the hall door and flung it open. 'I won't let 'em do this ter me, d'yer 'ear! I won't!'

Jane rushed across and held on to her. 'Hannah, listen to me!' Hannah tried to pull away. Jane shook her. 'I said *listen*!'

Hannah calmed down just enough to listen to what Jane was saying.

'Am I your friend, Hannah?' pleaded Jane. '*Am* I?'

Hannah hesitated a moment, then nodded.

'Then if I'm your friend, you must trust me. *Do* you trust me, Hannah?'

Hannah looked at her. It was the first time she had really noticed what a lovely girl Jane was, with her bright hazel-coloured eyes and long auburn hair. She nodded.

'My advice,' said Jane, 'is not to rush into anything. Stay where you are for a few months.'

'A few months!'

'Just until things calm down a little,' continued Jane, keeping her voice low. 'Let the Bullocks think you've given up the idea, and then plan what you want to do. Do you have enough money for the train fare yet?'

'Not yet,' replied Hannah. 'Just a few more weeks. But even when I do, if that stupid stationmaster won't let me get on the train . . .'

'You could always find your way to the next station down the line.'

Hannah stopped talking as the implication set in.

'Mapton is the next station,' continued Jane, keeping her voice low. 'If you get on the train there, nobody would know who you are. After all, you're not a criminal.'

'Sometimes I feel like it.'

Jane, sympathetic and understanding as ever, put her arm round Hannah's waist, and for the next moment or so they just stood in the open doorway with the last of the evening sun drowning them in deep crimson. 'You know, Hannah,' Jane said, 'I'm pretty selfish about all this. The fact is, you're my friend, and I don't *want* you to go. But I wouldn't be your friend if I didn't try to point out all the danger you could be in if you try to be too hasty. One way and another, Maggie Bullock is quite a toughie. You've said yourself she wants to keep you there, and I happen to think that, for one reason or another, she's the sort of person who'll do anything to hold on to you. But – and it is a *big* but – if she finds that you're trying to outwit her, she could make your life hell. D'you understand what I'm saying, Hannah. Do you?'

Hannah sighed, and slowly looked up at her. 'I hate that woman.'

'Yes, I know,' said Jane, trying to comfort her. 'But don't blame just her, Hannah. I hate to have to say this, but your mother is just as bad. If she *really* wanted to have you and Louie home with her, nothing would have stopped her from taking you.'

Several weeks after her mum had come to visit her and Louie, Hannah finally received a letter from Sam. She heard Harry

Dixon the postman pushing mail through the letterbox in the locked front door of the pub early one morning while the Bullocks were still asleep in their bedroom, so Hannah quickly took just her own letter from the rest of the mail lying on the front door rug and went into the kitchen to read it. She washed her hands at the sink and quickly sat down at the kitchen table, and after savouring the neatly written address on one side, and Sam's own army forwarding address on the back, with great excitement she ripped open the envelope and read the letter.

29 April 1940
Somewhere in England

My dearest Hannah,

Here I am again, hoping that you are well and happy in Redbourne, and that you have been enjoying all the letters I have been writing to you.

Hannah froze. What letters? This was the first one.

Things are much the same here, and I have made quite a few friends amongst the chaps I got called up with. I must say it is really strange training with people from all parts of the country, most of them different accents from my own, some of them from the north of England, a Welshman, a Geordie (he's from Newcastle), and guess what? There's even a bloke from Bow in the East End of London – he's a real cockney! (I'm only teasing, promise.) Anyway, they're all very nice, although I don't know whether we'll all still be together when we get posted to wherever they're sending us. (Sorry, even if I knew where that was, I wouldn't be allowed to tell you.) Just wish it

213

*was somewhere near you. You've no idea how I miss you. You
won't believe this, but most nights I lie awake thinking of you.
The only thing is, as I haven't heard from you since I left, I'm
beginning to wonder if you still feel the same way about me?*

Hannah was feeling quite sick. Of course she felt the same
way about him! How could he ever think otherwise? But then,
how would he know if he hadn't heard from her?

*When I write to Mother, I always ask about you. She says
you're well, but that you're still unhappy staying with the
Bullocks. My poor girl. I wish I could be there to cheer you
up. You really don't deserve all you've had to put up with. Oh,
if only I could hear from you! I'm going to write to Mother
today to ask why you're not answering my letters. The last
time I heard from her she said that she hardly ever sees you,
but she knows you have my letters because either she or my
father sorts them out at the post office before Harry delivers
them to you. It's not fair, Hannah! I want to know how you
are, and what's happening to you. It won't be long before I
won't be able to keep in touch with you so easily, so please,
please write to me!*

    *Don't forget our tree, Hannah. Go and pay it a visit some-
time.*

    I love you.

    Sam x

Hannah finished the letter. She was so stunned, she could hardly
believe what Sam had written. *Why* hadn't she heard from him,
she asked herself over and over again? If his letters had been arriving

at the post office, then why wasn't she receiving them? Distraught, she put Sam's letter to her nose and gently smelt it. Suddenly he was there in the room with her. She could feel him at her side.

The kitchen door opened behind her. 'Isn't it time you put the kettle on, young lady?' demanded Maggie as she swept in. As quick as a flash, Hannah hid Sam's letter in her dress pocket.

Maggie went to the kettle and filled it herself. 'You *know* Mr Bullock and I like tea first thing in the morning,' she growled, yawning at the same time. 'I really don't know what we're paying you for, Hannah.'

'There's some post for yer,' said Hannah sourly, getting up from the table.

Maggie stopped dead, and looked across at her. 'What have you done with it?' she asked anxiously.

'Left it for yer, of course,' Hannah replied. 'Ain't that wot yer told me ter do?'

Maggie didn't reply. She just quickly left the room to collect the post.

Whilst she was gone, Hannah uncovered Polly's cage.

''Allo!' came the bright response from the bird.

''Allo, mate,' returned Hannah. 'Bet you slept better than me.'

'Mine's a Guinness!' squawked Polly.

'I know, Pol,' Hannah replied. 'I reckon we could boaf do wiv one.'

'Bills, nothing but bills.' Maggie returned with the morning's post from the front door rug. 'Just wait 'til *you* have to start paying such things. Then you'll know the value of money.'

Hannah started to leave the room. 'Nuffin' from Sam fer me?' she called as she went. She could almost feel the tension as Maggie heard what she had said.

'I think you can forget about that boy,' called Maggie. 'For him, you're just another ship that passes in the night.'

Hannah ignored Maggie's snide comment, and went out into the saloon bar to continue her cleaning. The moment she was alone, she took Sam's letter out of her pocket again, and smelt it. However, she felt so much anger inside that when Maggie came out of the kitchen she felt like going straight across and punching her.

'Oh by the way,' Maggie called as she came across to her. 'Maurice is coming over today to bring some books my cousin Hilda borrowed from me ages ago. He's just joined the French army, can you believe! God help France if the Germans invade!'

Hannah ignored her, got down on her knees, and started to shovel out ash from the grate.

'Hannah,' said Maggie, standing over her. 'Did you hear what I said?'

'I 'eard yer,' growled Hannah tersely, carrying on with her work, refusing to look up at her.

'Then please have the courtesy to respond when I talk to you,' snapped Maggie impatiently. 'Your Uncle Maurice is staying for lunch, so I shall need you to go to Mr Griffin's to get a loaf of bread. Understood?' To her intense irritation, Hannah still didn't reply. 'Hannah!' she snapped. 'Do you understand what I said?'

Hannah turned on her. 'No, I don't understand wot yer said,' she replied, struggling to keep her anger from boiling over. 'In fact, I'm tryin' very 'ard ter understand *anyfin'* yer do.'

Maggie stared hard at her, clearly enraged and concerned by her outburst. But she resisted saying anything more to the girl, turned round, and swept off back to the kitchen.

*   *   *

On her way back from Mr Griffin the baker, Hannah called into the post office to see Mary Beedle. When she got there, she found two other customers being served, so she had to wait a few minutes until Mary was free. Once the other women had gone, Mary asked Joseph to take over at the counter whilst she and Hannah went into the tiny back parlour. Mary was delighted to see Hannah, for it had been some time since they had last met. For a while they talked about Louie and how well she had settled down, and how the child had even taken to coming of her own free will to the Friends' weekly meeting in the House. 'Louie is such a lovely little girl,' said Mary, as she and Hannah sat together on wooden chairs by the small open fire. 'What comforts Joseph and me so much is the way she has adapted to our way of life, the way she no longer complains about everything.'

'Well,' said Hannah jokily, 'it's about time!'

They both laughed. However, Hannah had not come to talk about her younger sister, and when she told Mary about the rather disturbing letter she had received from Sam, Mary was clearly quite shocked.

'But I don't understand,' said the postmistress grimly. 'Over the past few months, I must have given Harry at least a dozen letters for you from Sam. I can assure you he writes more to you than he ever has to us. I never asked you about them because I assumed you were getting them. And in any case, Sam's letters to you were private, just between you and him.'

'Can you remember how he addressed the envelopes?' asked Hannah, who was simmering with anger.

'Well,' replied Mary, who was now quite flummoxed, 'they were all addressed to you, care of Mr and Mrs Bullock. I can't believe Maggie would want to keep Sam's letters from you. She surely knows how much Sam means to you.'

'Oh yeah,' replied Hannah sourly. 'She knows all right. That's why she's always made sure she got up in time to take the letters from Harry when he called on his round. But this time she slipped up, 'cos *I* got there first. I've put up with that woman fer long enuff, but this time she's gone too far!'

Mary was in despair. '*Why*, Hannah?' she sighed. 'Why should Maggie Bullock want to do a thing like this?'

'Yes,' replied Hannah derisively, '*why?* But if I 'ad ter take a guess, I'd say she was jealous.'

'Jealous? Of *Sam*? But she's known him since he was a small boy. As far as I know, whenever they've met they've always been on the best of terms.'

'Maybe,' said Hannah. 'But Sam means more ter me than 'er. That's somefin' she don't like, somefin' she don't *want*. The sooner I get away from that woman the better.'

Mary got up and went to her. 'My dear,' she pleaded, 'do make sure you don't do anything that you might regret. From what Louie has told me, things haven't always been – what shall I say – as they should be back home with your mother.'

'Ha!' Hannah scoffed. 'Yer can say that again! Mum couldn't care less about eivver me nor Lou. She's no better than Maggie Bullock 'erself. They make a fine pair!'

'Hannah, dear one.' Mary stooped down in front of Hannah and gently took hold of her hands. 'There is good and bad in all of us. Unfortunately, the bad part is often the most difficult to cope with.'

Chapter 14

Hannah had no idea how she had managed to get through the summer without going stark raving mad. Oh, she could cope with the boiling temperatures all right, just as she had coped with the bitter cold during the winter, but coping with the Bullocks was something quite different. As time went on, Maggie Bullock had gradually shown just what a tyrant she was. She was obsessed with Hannah, wanting to keep her within her sight for the best part of every day and night, just the way it must have been when that poor girl Sheila had worked there. So why did she put up with it, she kept asking herself? Why did she prolong the agony by not getting on a train back to London even though she now had enough money saved up to buy the ticket? The answer was twofold. First and foremost was Louie, whom she had a duty to remain near until she was absolutely certain that her young sister was completely safe and happy living with the Beedles. But then there was what Jane had said about keeping one step ahead of Margaret Bullock, of making her think that she had won possession of Hannah, so that after a period of time the girl would stop trying to figure out a way of getting back to London. However, Hannah wasn't tired at all, and by the end of August she was more than determined to make the break once and for all. But exactly *how* – and *when*? That was the burning question when, one afternoon, she went up to her attic room to count the number of coins she had saved for that very special train ticket. To her utter consternation, however, when she pulled back the mattress of her bed to recover the purse she had kept hidden there, she found it was gone. After a frenzied search of every nook and cranny of the tiny room, there was no doubt that someone had taken it, and it wasn't hard for her to work out who.

Rushing down the stairs yelling out: 'Where's me bleedin' money!' she made so much commotion that the moment she burst into the kitchen, Polly the parrot fluttered in panic and alarm in her cage, squawking hysterically, feathers scattering, trying desperately to get away from the mad human creature who looked as though she was about to skin her alive. 'Where are you?' yelled Hannah, in a fit of rage. 'Where *is* everybody?'

'Shut up! Shut up!' Polly yelled back.

Hannah came to an abrupt halt. She suddenly remembered that the Bullocks had gone out in their car for the afternoon to talk through the pub accounts with the brewer in Hertford. For a moment or so she was so disoriented with anger that she didn't know what to do next. But she soon recovered her senses, rushed out of the room, and dashed straight up the stairs.

Bursting into the Bullocks' bedroom, she started an immediate search of all the furniture, the dressing table, the bedside cabinets, even beneath the big double mattress on the bed. Utterly frustrated, she turned her attention to the wardrobe, but she found it locked, with no key. Another search, for the wardrobe key, proved fruitless, until she quite casually looked beneath a cushion on the wicker chair. Immediately grabbing it, she went to the wardrobe and opened it without any difficulty at all. Rummaging around all both Maggie and Sid Bullock's clothes hanging inside, she could find no trace of her purse. Cursing out loud, she slammed the wardrobe door, but just as she was about to return the key to its hiding place beneath the cushion she remembered that she hadn't checked the various pairs of shoes on the floor of the wardrobe. Quickly, rechecking, she shook out every shoe, but without success. However, she suddenly noticed that the shoes were resting on top of what looked like a canteen of cutlery. She cast the shoes aside, and lifted out the cutlery box. To her surprise, however, she found that it weighed hardly anything at all, and when she opened it she soon discovered why. To her absolute astonishment, she found not her purse, but a bundle of Sam's letters to her, all tied together with string. For several moments, she just crouched on the floor, slowly removing the string, and scanning through the envelopes, all showing postmarks dating back to within a few days of Sam's departure for call-up. She was so stunned to find them, to know that they even existed, that she just couldn't take in what Maggie Bullock had done. But when she left the room, her mind was made up with what she intended to do about it.

Jane Jessop was waiting for her on the village green. All during the long summer evenings before the pub opened, the two girls had met in their usual place on the bench overlooking the pond, eager to discuss all the things that meant anything to them. But Hannah's news was more than Jane could ever have imagined. 'She kept all Sam's letters?' she asked uncomprehendingly. 'And hid them in her wardrobe?'

'That's not all,' said Hannah. 'She nicked my purse. It wasn't in their bedroom anywhere, but I know it was 'er. It's 'er way of makin' sure I don't get on that train.'

'Hannah, this is terrible! If what you say is true, then Maggie Bullock's a thief.'

'Ter say the least!' growled Hannah. 'I told yer before, that woman's got a screw loose. She wants ter 'ang on ter me. She don't want me ever ter go.'

'It makes no sense, Hannah,' said Jane, shaking her head. 'Wanting a daughter of her own is one thing, but being prepared to go to any lengths and do something like this is – well, I don't know *what* it is.'

Just then, the usual evening gathering of the Local Defence Volunteers, now renamed the Home Guard and led by Jane's father, Barney Jessop, marched in orderly procession, two by two, onto the village green. Smartly kitted out in khaki uniforms and tin helmets, and equipped with rifles and bayonets, they immediately launched into battle exercise, watched by a posse of village children and a smattering of adults. However, despite the noise of their mock manoeuvres, Hannah and Jane hardly noticed them.

'So what are you going to do now, Hannah?' Jane asked nervously, dreading the answer. 'Are you going to tackle the Bullocks about this?'

'You bet I am!' replied Hannah defiantly. 'An' then I'm goin' ter do wot I should've done a long time ago. I'm goin' 'ome!'

'But how can you do that, Hannah?' asked Jane intensely. 'You don't have any money for the train fare. Mind you, I could lend you a little, but—'

'Don't you worry, Jane. If Maggie Bullock finks she's goin' ter 'old on ter me fer as long as she likes, she's got a nasty surprise waitin' for 'er. I don't need no train.'

Jane stared at her in utter astonishment. 'What are you talking about?'

'I've got a good pair er feet, ain't I?'

'You mean – *walk*?' Jane couldn't believe she was hearing right. 'You'd walk all the way – to London?'

'Why not?' asked Hannah confidently.

Jane noticed a pair of village women passing just behind them, so she lowered her voice. 'Have you any idea how far it is from here to London?' she said. 'It must be almost forty miles.'

'If I 'ave ter do it, then I will!' vowed Hannah.

'Don't, Hannah!' pleaded Jane. 'Please don't do it – I beg you. Especially now. Especially after what's happened.'

Hannah was puzzled. 'Wot yer talkin' about?'

Jane hesitated before answering. 'The war, Hannah,' she replied at last. 'The war's really started now. Dad and I heard it on the wireless this morning. They've started to bomb London, Hannah. If you go back there, you'll be putting your life in great danger.'

The Bullocks arrived back from Hertford in their battered old Morris Minor less than an hour before opening time. They were not in the best of moods, for their meeting with the brewery accountants had not been a very amicable one, hardly surprising with the way business at the Cock and Crow had gone down since the start of the war. On top of that, it had been a scorching hot day, with temperatures in the eighties, which left Maggie's dress wet with perspiration, and Sid thoroughly drained after the tense ultimatum he had received from the brewers about the future of the pub.

'Where's that wretched girl?' growled Maggie, the moment she and Sid entered the saloon bar by the front door. 'You see, this is what happens when you let her have a key for a few hours. She's supposed to be looking after the place.' She went behind the counter and yelled up the stairs. 'Hannah! Are you up there?'

'Oh, leave the girl alone, Maggs,' said Sid, who was already unlocking the shorts cabinet at the back of the counter, ready for the first customers. 'For God's sake, she's got to have *some* time to herself.'

Sid's riposte took Maggie by surprise. She wasn't used to her husband's talking so sharply to her, let alone standing up for the girl who had turned out to be a pain in the neck ever since the day she arrived. 'After the way those people in Hertford talked to us,' she said curtly, coming across to him in the bar from the foot of the stairs, 'don't you think we have the right to expect at least *some* degree of efficiency from that girl? I mean, just look at the state of these tables.' She rubbed her fingers over a table that was still wet and sticky from the only customer they had had in during the lunchtime opening hours. 'She hasn't touched them!'

'We have no right to expect *anything* from her, Maggs,' said Sid, hanging up the jacket that he hadn't worn since they left Hertford. 'Hannah's supposed to be our adopted daughter. You don't treat your own kith and kin as servants.'

Maggie couldn't believe what she was hearing. In all the years she and Sid had been married, he had never talked to her like this, never *dared* to talk to her like this. It was intolerable. 'It may have escaped your notice, Mr Bullock,' she retorted caustically, 'that she is *not* our kith and kin – thank God! She's nothing more than a common little urchin from the back streets of London!'

Sid suddenly stopped what he was doing, and turned on her. 'You didn't think that when you first took her on!'

'When *we* took her on, Mr Bullock,' snapped Maggie, rounding on him. 'You wanted someone who could help rid your conscience of the stupid thing you did to that girl three years ago!'

Now Sid was really furious. 'Don't you *dare* say things like that to me!' he barked. 'What happened to Sheila was an accident, and you know it!'

'Do I?' retorted Maggie, eyes blazing. 'Accident or not, you were careless. Irresponsible. Sheila would never have died if you'd behaved like a proper father and looked after her.'

Sid went straight across to her. 'Just exactly *what* do you mean by that?' he asked, seething with anger.

Maggie stared back at him defiantly, eyeball to eyeball. 'You *know* what I mean, Mr Bullock!' she growled, pushing him aside to sweep off into the kitchen.

Sid followed on behind her. 'I can't believe you're talking to me like this,' he said. Maggie ignored him, and went to the sink to fill the kettle. 'Ever since we lost the child,' he said, pursuing her, 'I've done my best to make up to you for what happened. It wasn't *my* fault, Maggs. It wasn't *anyone's* fault. It was an act of God. An act of God, Maggs!'

Maggie turned off the tap, and for one brief moment stood there, kettle still in hand, staring out through the window into the back garden. 'You should never have taken Sheila out in the boat that day,' she said, her voice breaking. 'We lost the only child we could ever have.'

Sid came quietly across to her, a soft tenderness taking over from his anger. He gently turned her round to face him. There were tears streaming down her face. He took the kettle from her and put it down, then pulled her close and hugged her. 'We shouldn't fight, Maggs,' he said, voice low and sympathetic. 'We've been through too much together. So we mustn't take it out on other people. Just remember – what happened to us was an act of God.'

'Was *this* an act er God too?'

Both of them swung round with a start to find Hannah standing at the kitchen door. In her hand she was holding up the bundle of letters Sam had written to her. They watched in stunned silence as she slowly came across to them.

''Ow low can people get?' she asked, glaring intently at them.

Maggie quickly broke away from Sid, and wiped the tears from her eyes with her fingers. 'What are you talking about?' asked Sid, bewildered.

'Ask *'er*,' replied Hannah acidly, watching Maggie as she walked haughtily straight past them.

Sid stared at the letters Hannah was still holding up in her hand. 'What's this all about?' he demanded.

Maggie ignored them both, and hurried straight out into the saloon bar. She was in such disarray that for several moments she didn't know what she was going to do, didn't even know where she was. She went straight across to the bar window, and stared without focus into the street outside. She knew what Hannah was telling Sid in the kitchen. She knew only too well what she had done over these past few months, without telling Sid, without thinking of the consequences if she was ever found out.

After a few moments, Sid came out of the kitchen with Hannah following on behind. 'Is this true, Maggs?' he asked. He came across to her. 'Did you keep these letters from Hannah?'

'I don't know what you're talking about,' replied Maggie airily, using the view through the window as an excuse not to say anything more.

Sid gently turned her round to face him. '*Did* you take those letters from Sam Beedle, Maggs? Did you take them and hide them in our wardrobe upstairs?'

She tried to dismiss what he had asked her, and turned her anger on Hannah. 'So you've been stealing again, have you?' she growled. 'Oh, don't worry, I *know*! I know how you've been rummaging around this house, around our personal possessions.'

Sid was now deeply traumatised. 'Maggs!' he pleaded.

Maggie completely ignored him, and continued to direct her attack on Hannah. 'I should have known!' she spluttered without making any sense at all. 'God knows I should have known that that's how people like you behave in those foul back streets!'

Hannah, aware that Sid Bullock was on her side, refused to rise to Maggie's taunting. 'Did you take my purse?' she asked, in a restrained, subdued voice.

At this, Maggie completely fell apart, as though she had lost all rhyme and reason. 'It's not *your* money, little girl,' she growled, eyes blazing. 'It's what *we've* paid you – Mr Bullock and I. That money we've worked hard for all our lives!'

'Stop this, Maggie!' pleaded Sid, distraught. 'Just stop it!'

'No, I won't stop it, I won't!' Maggie was now positioned as close to Hannah as she could possibly get. 'Don't you see what she's trying to do to us, Mr Bullock? She's trying to drive a wedge between us. I won't let her do it, d'you hear. I won't let her!'

'You're exactly wot I always fawt you were,' replied Hannah, staring at Maggie in sheer disbelief. 'No wonder yer never 'ad no kid of yer own!'

Maggie's eyes suddenly widened, and without a moment's thought she raised her hand and slapped Hannah's face hard.

'Maggs!' yelled Sid, grabbing hold of his wife's arms from behind.

Hannah reeled back, but instead of retaliating, she just let Sid Bullock restrain his half-deranged wife. Then she calmly composed herself, went to the front door, and left.

Louie was still on her school holidays, but Hannah knew where to find her, for she and her friend Poppy always spent a lot of their free time playing basketball and other games with some of the other village children on the school playing field.

When Hannah got there soon after her bust-up with Maggie Bullock at the pub, she found Louie in high spirits, laughing and giggling and rushing around madly with the other kids, which meant that she was none too happy to have to stop and talk to her big sister, whom she rarely saw anyway these days. And when Hannah told her why she had come to see her, after the way Louie had settled in so well with the Beedles, her response was no less than Hannah had expected.

'Go ter London?' gasped Louie, with complete astonishment. 'Yer must be mad, Hann! Wot do I wanna go *there* for? It's much better *'ere.*'

'But it's yer 'ome, Lou,' Hannah reminded her. 'All yer friends're there. Remember all the times we've dreamed about goin' back ter 'Olloway — Seven Sisters Road, 'Ornsey Road, Finsbury Park, Kinloch Street.'

'I 'ate Kinloch Street.'

Louie's blunt remark completely shook her big sister. ''Ow can yer 'ate it, Lou? Yer was born there. That's where Mum is.'

'I know,' replied Louie uncompromisingly. 'But I've got a better mum where I am now.'

After she had left Louie, Hannah took a brief look back at her, resuming the game of tag she was playing with the other kids, laughing and joining in with them as though she had lived in the village all her life. It was a strange feeling saying farewell to someone who had meant so much to her. Although Louie had always been a handful over the years, selfish to the core, not caring a hoot for anyone but herself, she was still of the same flesh and blood as Hannah; there was a bond between them that no one could ever replace, not even the Friends.

Hannah wanted to go to take leave of Jane, but she felt that if she did that, Jane would again do her utmost to stop her from undertaking something that would be not only challenging, but dangerous. So when she caught a distant glimpse of her best friend working in the village shop as she passed by, she reluctantly kept out of sight, and moved on to her final important destination before embarking on her great, perilous adventure.

Beechers Wood was bathed in the ravishing gold of a typical harvest sunset. It was a wonderful time of day, when all the wildlife was busily preparing to get ready for bed, the tall elm and oak trees looked as though they were already deep in slumber, and the gradual approach of a deep crimson sunset was beginning to reflect the change on the surface of the calm, free-flowing river.

As she slowly picked her way through the undergrowth, Hannah felt no fear. Ever since her last visit there with Sam, the trees had embraced her, as if assuring her that she was now perfectly safe in their neck of the woods. Even the rabbits and big buck hares weren't afraid of her; they just gambolled through the grass quite merrily, making her feel as though their home was her home too. At the river's edge, she stopped briefly to watch a fox ease its way cautiously in and out of the foliage on the opposite bank, stopping only briefly to take a drink of cool water from one of the puddles left over from a downpour a few nights earlier. For several moments, Hannah just stood there staring in awe at all the magic laid out before her, tilting her face up towards the changing colour of the sun, which caressed her flamelike hair and transformed it into a burning fire all its own. For the first time that day, she felt nothing but calm, and peace. And she knew why, for Sam's presence was all around her, in the grass, in the water, in the air, and in her own heart. Oh, how she missed him, missed that comforting smile, the blue eyes and straw-coloured hair, and his constant reassurance that life really was worth living. But then she felt a weight in her mind that kept telling her that she would never see Sam again, and that hurt, *really* hurt.

She moved on to her last stop – the tree, *their* tree. As she looked at the initials carved on the bark there, H and S, she could hear his words echoing in the trees right above her: *This is just to prove that this is* our *place. So now we'll just have to come back.* But could she believe him, she pondered, as she stood there alone in the approaching twilight? Could she really believe that she and Sam would one day come back and claim these woods as their own? Could she really believe those final parting words, *Tonight is forever*? Only time would tell.

The Bullocks were sound sleepers. Most nights, after they had turned in after a busy time in the pub, they went straight to bed, both of them snoring within minutes. This was fortunate for Hannah, for it meant that she didn't have to wait too long to put her carefully planned operation into progress.

At about eleven thirty that night, Hannah collected from under the bed the one travelling bag she was taking with her. She had already decided that she wouldn't, couldn't, take too much with her, only the bare essentials for the journey such as a change of underclothes, which had been bought for her by Maggie Bullock soon after she and Louie had been 'adopted', together with a flannel, soap, and a hand towel. Fortunately she still had the cardigan her grandma had knitted for her the year before, for although it was still summer the evenings were beginning to feel just a little bit like autumn. The one clever thing she had done over the past few weeks was to stow away bags of potato crisps and small packets of cheese biscuits, which the Bullocks always kept on show under a glass case on the counter. As she tucked them all into her travelling bag, she could almost hear Maggie Bullock accusing her of stealing, but Hannah reckoned that after all the free work she'd done in the pub since she first arrived, the least she was entitled to were a few rotten old bags of crisps. Her one real concern, however, was the lack of money. Thanks to Maggie Bullock's nicking her purse she had nothing in her pocket but the odd tips she had received from some of the pub's customers who felt sorry for her. But if one shilling and a penny farthing was not going to take her very far, at least it would be enough to get her on the road, maybe buy some bread or a cake or something when she got really hungry. Hannah's great asset was her ability to use money wisely – 'good housekeeping', her granddad had called it. In any case, as soon as she got back home to

Holloway, the first place she would go to was Elsie's hair-dressing salon in Hornsey Road where she used to work. The one person she could rely on to give her a job was Elsie, a real pal if ever there was one. After she had put on her head-scarf and cardigan and picked up her torch and travelling bag, she took one last look around the claustrophobic attic cell she had had to endure for so long. 'Good riddance!' she whispered. Then she switched off the light, and quietly opened the door. Satisfied that the coast was clear, she picked her way cautiously down one stair at a time.

As she passed the Bullocks' bedroom door, she paused a moment, just to check that she could hear their snores. As always, it was an odd experience. So many nights she had gone down to their bathroom and heard those snores, nervous that when she pulled the lavatory chain she would wake them up. Fortunately, however, that disaster had not so far ever occurred, and as she moved off down the last flight of stairs, she hoped that this would not be the first time.

Once she was in the kitchen, she knew that this was going to be the hardest part of her escape. As Maggie had stubbornly kept the key to the back garden door hidden, Hannah had had to devise an alternative way to get out of the place. By the light of her torch, she went to one of the two drawers in the kitchen table, and took out a screwdriver that she knew Sid Bullock always kept there for emergencies. As this was one of those emergencies, she quickly got to work on the lock of the garden door. As she expected, each screw was as tight and rusty as hell, so she went to the gas oven and dipped her finger in the fat left over from the roast pork Maggie had cooked that day in the baking tin there. Using an old trick taught to her once by her dad, who numbered carpentry amongst his many odd jobs, with her fingers she smeared the pork fat onto each one of the screws on the brass plate covering the door lock, and left it for a moment to soak in. Then came the hard part. Once again she got to work on the first screw, but it remained as stubborn as anything. Cursing under her breath she used every bit of strength in her hands to get some movement into the rotten thing. Just as she was going to give up, the screw moved, only a fraction at first, but slowly, gradually, it capitulated to her willpower. The other screws, realising they were no match for this girl, budged much more easily – either that or she had gained in strength in just a few minutes. But she received a shock when the brass plate, released abruptly by the final screw, suddenly came loose and clattered to the tiled floor, Hannah dropped to her knees in horror, convinced that this was the moment when her carefully arranged plan was going to fall in on her. All she could do now was to wait in the dark, and do something that she had not done in a long time – pray. As she did so, there was a whimpering sound from Polly beneath the cover on her cage. 'Ssh, Pol!' she whispered. 'I'll be wiv yer in a sec!'

After several minutes, Hannah realised that the falling lock plate had not disturbed the sleeping beauties upstairs, so she stood up again, and got to work on the door latch. Remembering another of her dad's devices, she slipped the screwdriver into the latch as far as she could, and started searching for the one small lever that would open it. In the dark, using only the light of the torch propped up on the sink beside her, she pushed and twisted that screwdriver deep into the lock, a task accompanied by whispered language that most people would only expect to hear from a fishmonger down at Billingsgate Market. But then – hey presto! The latch suddenly flipped back, and the door opened immediately. Breathing as hard and fast as her lungs would allow, she pulled it back, and took in her first taste of the sweet night air outside. She hesitated not a moment more. Leaving the screwdriver on the floor, she quickly collected her bag and put it outside. But before she left, she had one more thing to do, one very important thing, something she had wanted to do ever since the first day she had arrived. Going to Polly's cage, she removed the cover, and directed the beam of her torch straight at the beautifully coloured bird who seemed quite bewildered at being woken up so ungracefully from her sleep. 'Come on, gel!' whispered Hannah, picking up the cage, and carrying it out into the garden, and placing it on the ground. Then came the moment she had been waiting for. She opened the cage door. 'It's all yours, Pol,' she whispered. 'Don't ferget yer old friend!' To her bewilderment, however, the bird remained quite static, its large grey eyes reflecting the light from Hannah's torch. 'Well wot yer waitin' for, yer silly ol' bag?' Polly refused to budge, and despite Hannah's desperate attempts to show her the way out through the cage door, the bird remained stubbornly fixed by her claws to the perch. Finally, Hannah gave up. 'All right, mate,' she said. ''Ave it *your* way!' Reluctantly she closed the door, picked up the cage, and carried it back into the kitchen. Before she covered it up again, she took one last look at those two grey eyes staring at her. 'I know, mate,' she whispered. 'It ain't easy leavin' wot yer used to.'

A few moments later, Hannah was on her way, out into the dark of a late summer night at the start of a long journey that was fraught with danger. But at least she was free, free from the clutches of a woman who had lost not only her way in life, but also the chance of gaining the daughter she would now never have.

Chapter 15

Hannah hadn't the faintest idea where she was. It was bad enough that the night was dark and bleak, but the blackout across the countryside made it almost impossible to see where she was going, and on top of that all signposts had been either obliterated or simply removed and taken away, presumably to confuse the Germans if and when they decided to invade. Hannah's only real guide was the railway line, so the first thing she did after leaving the Cock and Crow was to make straight for Redbourne railway station, from where she could follow the track all the way south to London. Unfortunately, however, it wasn't as easy as that, for the trains did not go in a straight line all the way, but followed the lie of the land which from time to time had to divert across bridges and through tunnels, or avoid any difficult terrain such as steep hills or inaccessible villages. All this meant that the journey would take longer, and, unfortunately, Hannah found this out to her cost. After the first few hours she felt that she had got nowhere, and despite using her torch for practically every step she took, there were no clues anywhere to help her. By around three in the morning, her legs were feeling like heavy weights, and she was so tired that all she wanted to do was to find somewhere sheltered to put her head down. Fortunately, she eventually found such a place, a disused workmen's hut just behind what seemed to be a huge flour mill. However, the prospect of spending the rest of the night in such a place unnerved her, and she slept very little. By that time also she had devoured two bags of crisps and one packet of cheese biscuits, and was almost halfway through a bottle of Tizer, which meant that, at the pace she was going, it was not going to be easy for her to get through the entire journey without at least some substantial food and drink.

As soon as the sun rose, Hannah woke up and immediately realised that if she was going to make faster progress, most of her journey would have to take place in daylight. After collecting her things together, and taking a last swig of Tizer from the bottle, she left the hut and went outside. To her utter astonishment, she found herself surrounded by people in white coats and caps, all of them presumably manual workers from the flour mill. 'Wot place *is* this then, mate?' she asked one of the girls, who was munching sandwiches, perched on a brick wall with some of her work friends.

'Where've you been then?' replied the girl cheekily, showing off to her mates who all giggled. 'Locked up in a dog's kennel all night?'

'Somefin' like that,' replied Hannah, who was feeling the pangs of hunger as she watched the girls tucking into their sandwich boxes. 'Wos the name of this place?'

'Why d'yer want ter know?' asked one of the other girls. 'Ain't you ever bin ter Letty before?'

Hannah pulled a puzzled face. 'Where?'

'Letty Green,' replied the girl. 'Gateway to Hollywood!' All the girls roared with laughter.

'Are we very far from the railway line?' asked Hannah, ignoring their teasing.

'Railway line?' asked another girl, who actually looked quite sorry for Hannah. 'Where d'you come from, dear?'

'Redbourne,' she replied. 'D'yer know it at all?'

'Somewhere up near Hertford, isn't it?' asked another girl. 'How d'you get here? By bus?'

'Don't be so daft, Jess,' said the first girl who had spoken, and now had jam all over her lips. 'You won't get a bus from Redbourne to here. Well, not that *I* know of.'

'D'you know Redbourne?' Hannah asked eagerly.

'Not really,' replied the girl. 'I went there once with my boyfriend before 'e got called up. Bit quiet up there as I remember.'

'So where's the nearest railway station?' Hannah asked.

All the girls exchanged puzzled glances. They were now all feeling a bit suspicious of this complete stranger who had suddenly turned up out of nowhere.

'Miles away,' said the most concerned of the girls. 'You need a bus to get there – *if* and when one ever appears. Where you making for then?'

'Lond'n.'

'Your best bet would be Hatfield for that,' said another girl. 'You *will* need a bus for that, though. But at least it's on the main line to King's Cross.'

''Ow long would it take to walk?'

Once again the girls exchanged a wary look. 'Are you jokin'?' asked one of them.

A bell sounded from the mill, and the girls immediately hurried off. However, the concerned one remained behind for a moment. 'You're not from round here, are you?'

Hannah shook her head.

'Are you lost?'

Hannah thought carefully before answering. 'I – I ran away from 'ome,' she replied awkwardly.

'Oh, I see,' said the girl, with an understanding smile. 'Been out all night?'

Again Hannah nodded.

'Where d'you sleep?'

Hannah indicated the disused workmen's hut.

'You must be feeling all in,' said the girl. 'You look terrible!' They both chuckled. 'Well, I don't know anything about you, or what you want to do, but if you're trying to get to London, you're taking the wrong route. You're only about five or six miles from Redbourne. To get south you should take the A road, about a mile away, on the other side of the village – well, it's not really a village, it's just a cluster of houses. Then make your way across country, until you reach this big main junction. Once you get there, anyone will tell you how to get to the station. There's a good connection from there – provided they don't bomb the line again further down.'

Hannah stiffened. 'Bomb it?' she asked.

'Jerry's bombed the line a couple of times now. Hasn't stopped the trains running, though – well, not so far. But it's touch and go these days. If you're going to London, do be careful. They say there's a real blitz going on there, bombs and fires and a lot of ordinary people getting killed. I'm just glad I live in the country. I'd better get going.' She started to move off, but briefly turned back. 'Oh, I wonder if you could finish off these sandwiches for me? Mum always makes me far too many.' She thrust a newspaper-wrapped bundle at Hannah.

Hannah took the sandwiches gratefully. 'Fanks a lot,' she said, then called to the girl as she went: 'Wot kind of flour do they make 'ere?'

The girl called back over her shoulder. 'Flour! It's not flour we make, it's ammunitions. Safe journey!'

Hannah watched the girl disappear back into the factory, then, hungrily, she quietly tucked into the Spam sandwiches.

A few minutes later, she was on the road again, heading off cross-country in a desperate attempt to find the main line railway track. But after what the girl had told her, she was gradually becoming apprehensive about what she would be finding on her long journey home.

It was nearly midday by the time Hannah reached the big road junction the girl at the factory had talked about. The road itself seemed to stretch for miles, and passed what looked like some kind of airfield in the distance, from where there was a deafening sound of what Hannah thought must be plane engines constantly revving up. As she moved laboriously along the endless main road, an old Tiger Moth biplane looped the loop above the fields, before disappearing back to the airfield.

Although it was still quite warm, it was beginning to cloud over, and the moment she started to follow the road south alongside the track itself a slight drizzle began, which meant that intermittently she had to take cover wherever she could. Nonetheless she did eventually manage to find her way to the red-bricked railway station at Hatfield, and after spending a few coppers of her paltry one shilling and a penny farthing on a sardine fish cake and a cup of tea at a stall in the station entrance she was caught in a sudden torrential downpour, so she found a wooden bench seat inside near the ticket office, and sheltered there. Without realising it she fell asleep, and she only woke up when a train came rumbling to a halt along the platform.

'You for King's Cross, little lady?'

Rubbing her eyes wearily, Hannah found a station porter standing over her. 'Er, no,' she replied.

'Well, if you want the down line you'll have to go over the bridge,' said the porter, hurrying off to attend to the passengers getting on and off the waiting train.

'Is it far to walk to London from here?' Hannah called after him as he went.

Before he disappeared onto the platform, the porter stopped and called back: 'Wot? You round the bend or somefin'?'

Hannah shrugged, picked up her travelling bag from the bench, and started to move off. As she did so, however, a police car, bell clanging uncontrollably, raced up past her. In a sudden fit of panic, she immediately backed into the station entrance again, and kept out of sight. The thought that Maggie Bullock might have notified the police about her disappearance sent a chill down her spine, and she decided that from that moment on she had to be careful about whom she talked to on the journey; the implications of the police's catching up with her were too terrible to contemplate. Once the coast was clear, she left Hatfield station, and resumed her long trek south. Just then, however, the train left the platform, and as it rumbled off and gathered speed on its journey to London, with every breath in her body she cursed Maggie Bullock for nicking her purse.

By nightfall she had only reached the outskirts of London. Her estimate of getting home within thirty-six hours now seemed a fanciful dream, and as she found herself still wandering through open countryside she began to wonder whether she would even reach Kinloch Street within a week, especially now that she could feel blisters forming underneath her toes. However, when she reached a place called Barnet, her spirits were slightly raised when she saw a number 609 trolley bus coming up the high street, and purring to a halt at a terminus on top of a hill. To her, this was like a breath of fresh air, for many a time she had seen the 609 trolley stop outside the Marlborough cinema back home in Holloway. Suddenly she was engulfed by a wave of excitement which sent her hurrying across the road to the bus whilst it was manoeuvring its precarious turnaround.

'Nag's 'Ead?' she yelled at the conductor, who was smoking a fag on the platform.

'Nah, mate!' he called back. 'We're done fer tonight. No way we're goin' back into all that!'

'All wot?'

The bus conductor nodded down towards the hill. 'That!' he repeated.

When Hannah looked down Barnet Hill, the whole distant skyline was like Guy Fawkes' night. Not only were there what seemed to her to be thunderflashes bursting across the sky, but there was the glow of massive fires everywhere.

'Looks like the city's gettin' it again ternight,' said the conductor. 'When we come fru about an hour ago, we 'ad ter be diverted around Farringdon. The 'ole place is burnin' like a bleedin' inferno. This is the third night they've done us down on this route. Poor buggers – must be goin' down like ninepins. They'll be busy round the 'ospitals, that's fer sure!'

Almost as he spoke, the air was fractured with the terrible

wailing of an air-raid siren. It was a sound Hannah hadn't heard since the day war broke out, when it had turned out to be a false alarm. 'Wot's goin' on?' she asked, whilst the few people on the streets started to rush off frantically.

'If I was you,' called the bus conductor as he and his driver left their vehicle, 'I'd get under cover. Sounds like Jerry's on 'is way over to pay *us* a visit.'

Hannah watched the two men go, but had no idea what action she should take herself. Nervous about the situation she was finding herself in, she merely started walking at a quick pace down the hill, but she had gone no farther than the entrance to the London Underground tube station when the air was shattered by the deafening roar of fighter planes zooming in and out of the clouds overhead. As Hannah rushed for cover into the tube entrance, there followed several bursts of machine-gun fire, which sounded like an aerial dogfight, although the night was much too dark to be able to see what precisely was going on. However, a few moments later a barrage of ack-ack guns echoed out from somewhere in the distance, and the station entrance shook with the vibration.

'I knew they'd get this far sooner or later,' said a middle-aged, well-dressed woman who was sheltering with Hannah close to the ticket office. 'There seem to be waves of them just coming in as fast as our boys can catch up with them. God knows how those poor devils are coping down in London.'

After ten minutes or so, the barrage of artillery fire subsided, and the aerial dogfight appeared to have moved on. But when Hannah and the woman came out of the tube entrance, they were shocked to see that the fires over London were more intense than ever.

'Must be the East End again,' said the woman. 'They seem to be taking the brunt of it. Islington too.'

Hannah swung with a horrified start. 'Islin'ton?' she gasped.

'Islington, Archway, Holloway, Finsbury Park,' continued the woman solemnly. 'When I was down there the other day, it was a real mess. Especially around the Nag's Head. There were fires all along Seven Sisters Road.' She turned to Hannah. 'D'you know the area at all?'

Hannah was almost too shaken to answer, but she did. 'Oh yeah,' she replied faintly. 'I know it well.'

'I must be off,' said the woman, hurrying away up the hill. 'My husband will wonder what has happened to me. If I were you, young lady, I wouldn't hang around here for too long.'

Hannah remained where she was for several minutes, staring out at the flickering red glow along the distant horizon above her beloved home town. From that very first day, when the Prime Minister Mr Chamberlain had declared that Britain was at war with Germany, it was a sight Hannah had firmly believed she would never see. If this was war, then she wanted no part of it.

By midnight, after following the route of the 609 trolley bus, she managed to reach Finchley. It had been a long, hard slog in the pitch dark of the blackout to get even this far, and she was thoroughly worn out, suffering the most awful pain in her legs and feet. On the way it had been odd to notice how even the traffic lights had been covered over in such a way that whatever colour they changed to could only just be seen through thin slits, and it was chilling to see fire engines and ambulances racing past her, all headed towards the most badly hit areas of outer London. When she came to the Gaumont cinema, everything there seemed to be a world away from the ugliness of war, with its bright coloured posters advertising forthcoming pictures such as a musical called *Down Argentine Way*, with Betty Grable and Carmen Miranda, and an Arabian Nights fantasy called *The Thief of Bagdad* with Sabu. Now thoroughly exhausted and aching all over, Hannah sat down on one of the steps outside the plush cinema, and looked in her purse to see if she had enough money to buy something to eat in the all-night workmen's café just across the road. But to her dismay, she found that she only had four pennies and a farthing left, which would not have got her very far if she had tried to board that trolley bus up at Barnet. She leaned her head back wearily against the wall, and closed her eyes. With all the noise of distant gunfire and the clanging bells of emergency vehicles rushing back and forth, it was clear that she wasn't going to be able to get any sleep, so she just used whatever time she had before sunrise to think about all she had experienced during the day, and cast her mind back to the Cock and Crow, wondering whether the Bullocks were running round in circles talking to Constable Harrington, Mrs Mullard, and the evacuation committee about where that London street urchin had run off to. She also recalled with great affection her friendship with Jane, and how, if it hadn't been for her kindness and advice, she would never have been able to get through that terrible long summer. But her main concern was still for Louie. What would she make of all the fuss her big sister had stirred up by getting out of the back door of the Cock and Crow in the middle of the night? And how would the Beedles react to what Hannah had done? Would they feel ashamed that Hannah had deserted her little sister just because of her own selfish need to go back home to Holloway? Sam, of course, was always there in her mind; in fact he had never left it. She had read all the letters he had sent her so many times that she could almost remember each word, each sentence, off by heart. But where was he now? Both Hannah and the Beedles knew that it was only a matter of time before Sam would be taking his place on the battlefield somewhere, allowing his conscience to defy the beliefs he had been brought up with all his life. Oh, where was he now, Hannah kept asking herself over and over again? She didn't even know if he was dead or alive.

'Miss?'

Hannah's eyes sprang open to find a torch beam dazzling her. Oh God! It's the police! They've caught up with me!

'You all right, then?' The voice behind the torch was firm, but not severe. 'Not the place for a young 'un like you to rough it out.'

Hannah's first alarm was quickly dispelled when she saw the letters painted in black on the man's white helmet: ARP.

'No, I'm OK, mate, fank yer,' said Hannah, quickly getting up. 'I was just on me way 'ome. Bin out all day – visitin' – visitin' me gran,' she stuttered. 'Must've nodded off.'

'She all right, Bert?' Another man joined them. He was dressed in a khaki Home Guards uniform.

'Nodded off,' replied Bert. 'She's OK.'

'Better get on 'ome then,' said Hannah, brushing down her dress, and pulling her cardigan snugly around her. 'Don't want Mum ter fink I'm up ter no good.' Both men laughed. ''Night then!' Hannah reached down onto the step for her travelling bag. To her horror, it had gone. 'Christ!' she gasped.

'Wos up?' asked the Home Guard.

'Me bag!' spluttered Hannah. 'Someone's nicked me bag!'

The two men exchanged a puzzled glance. '*Wot* bag?' asked Bert the ARP man.

'Me luggage! It was *'ere* – it was 'ere beside me.'

'You sure?' asked Home Guard.

'Er course I'm sure!' growled Hannah, half out of her mind with worry. 'I've got all me clothes in there, an' me money!'

The men exchanged another look, this time one of despair. 'That's the trouble,' said Bert. 'These buggers on the loot. Got no scruples! It 'appens all the time these days.'

'That's war for yer, mate,' added Home Guard. 'Come on now, little lady. Why don't yer go across the road and get yerself a nice cuppa?'

'Wot wiv – air?' As soon as she had snapped at them, she regretted it. 'I'm sorry, but me purse was in that bag.'

'Well, if we can't buy a little lady in distress a cuppa ter calm 'er down,' said Bert, 'we ain't worth much, are we? Come on then!'

As he spoke, the air-raid siren sounded the all-clear.

The cup of tea from the workmen's café certainly helped, but it didn't stop Hannah from feeling that her whole world had crumbled in on her. However, despite their kindness, she declined the two men's offer to call over one of the flatties to look into the loss of her travelling bag, and quickly made off as fast as she could in the direction of Highgate. Even though it was getting light very quickly, she had no sooner gone a couple of miles down the main road than the air-raid siren sounded again. It threw her into a spin, for she didn't know what to do or where to go, especially when, within a few minutes, all hell broke loose in the skies again. With no travelling bag now to slow her down, and despite the fact that she was dead on her feet and aching in every part of her body, she decided to make as much progress as quickly as she could, feeling that the sooner she got home the better chance she would have. For now, food seemed totally unimportant, although she was still very thirsty.

Shells were soon exploding all over the sky, and with jagged pieces of shrapnel tinkling down onto the pavements all around her she had no alternative but to take shelter in an underground ladies' public lavatory. To her astonishment, she found more than a dozen women crammed in down there, one or two of them in ATS uniforms, and others who had been caught in the air raid on their way to work. The atmosphere was foul and acrid, but as one of the women said stoically, 'Beggars can't be choosers.' But at least Hannah was able to get a drink of fresh water from a tap over one of the sinks, which helped to put some life back into her.

Whilst she was crammed in there, the women chattered about nothing but the war, and in particular the various places that had received direct 'hits' during the night. One young girl, who was putting on her lipstick at a cracked mirror over the sink, was quite lurid in describing what her fireman boyfriend had told her about an oil bomb raid on Docklands the night before, how people were running around in pain covered in burning oil. A middle-aged woman crammed up against the lavatory door just behind Hannah cursed Hitler and Goering with some pretty choice language, and hoped the RAF would do the same to them sooner or later. When an explosion from a bomb nearby shook the ceiling, from inside one of the cubicles an elderly lady, on the lavatory seat only because there was nowhere else to sit down, called out nervously, 'How long are we going to have to stay down here?'

'Don't worry, Gran,' said one of the ATS girls. 'Ten minutes an' we can all get home.'

But it wasn't just ten minutes. It was nearly three hours, and by the time the women emerged from their underground nightmare, the sun was shining brightly, and those who had jobs to go to scuttled off to the nearest bus stop or tube station. Hannah was the last to leave. The first thing she noticed was the debris strewn over the pavements, mainly broken roof tiles blown off by the powerful blast of bombs in the distance. There was also smashed window glass everywhere, and as she moved down the road she had to be very careful to avoid the jagged pieces of shrapnel that littered the pavements and front gardens, and were causing havoc among impatient motorists who had been held up by the air raid for so long.

By late afternoon, Hannah's laboured progress had only managed to get her as far as the northern edge of Highgate Woods. Here she found pandemonium, as two houses on one side of the street had apparently taken a direct hit, and with fires still burning the emergency services were using Alsatian tracker dogs to sniff out victims who were still buried beneath the debris. Worse was to come, for no sooner had Hannah got to the top of Archway Road than the air-raid siren sounded yet again, and she found herself quite literally sprinting down the hill beneath the towering Archway bridge, heading straight into the tube station. Only just in time, for once again the heavens seemed to open up, with what sounded like an armada of enemy aircraft engines droning menacingly across the sky, and a cacophony of ack-ack barrage gunfire, followed immediately by rapid-firing pom-pom guns mounted on trucks, adding to the deafening chaos from the streets nearby. Hannah was overwhelmed by it all. The thought of enduring one air raid was enough, but three in one day was quite unbelievable. As she stood waiting with the crowds of other people sheltering there, she started to have very real fears about the safety of her mum. With all she could see and hear right now, she felt sure that Holloway must be right in the thick of the raid, and she only hoped that her mum was being sensible and taking shelter somewhere safe. Hannah was sick with worry, and became even more so when she caught a glimpse of a newsvendor's billboard just inside the station entrance which read: BLITZ COMES TO LONDON.

A few minutes later, everyone sheltering in the tube entrance was directed down onto the platforms below, where several hundred people were either sprawled out or propped up against the sloping tiled walls, trying their best to put a brave face on what was clearly going to be a regular terrifying ordeal that they were just going to have to live with. As all tube trains had come to a complete stop during the air raid, the power had been cut on the electric rails down on the track, and young people had recklessly climbed down from the platform to sit there. Hannah, now thoroughly worn out by the hazards of her long journey, tried to remain by the bottom of the stairs, hoping to make a quick getaway as soon as the all-clear sounded. However, reports coming from the station staff and emergency services in the road up above suggested that the air raid now taking place up top was pretty severe, and there was no way of forecasting how long it would last. To pass the time away, a group of sailors who had become stranded in the station started up a sing-song, which at least raised everyone's spirits enough to get them all to join in a rousing chorus of 'We're Going To Hang Out The Washing

On The Siegfried Line', which drew gales of laughter and rude comments from everyone crammed along the platforms.

Tired and exhausted, Hannah had no idea how long she had been sitting on that bottom step. All she knew was that it was frustrating to be stuck there when she was now only a stone's throw from home in Holloway. So near and yet so far, she kept telling herself. Before setting out on her long journey from Redbourne, she never imagined how much she would be longing to see her mum again, and then and there she vowed to do everything in her power to show more love and understanding to her.

After a while, she got talking to a happy-go-lucky couple named Betty and Phil, both of whom were about the same age as herself, and worked in the Woolworth's store in Holloway Road, close to the Nag's Head.

'We wouldn't be stuck down here in this dump if it hadn't been our day off!' said Betty, who had rather a posh speaking voice. 'The thing is it's our last day together. Phil has been called up. He's off to do officer training in the RAF. We wanted to go to the Electric Palace to see a flick – you know, that cinema just down Holloway Road.' She turned to give her boyfriend a mischievous grin. 'That's where we first met, wasn't it?'

'Well – something like that,' replied Phil, returning her grin.

'*Rebecca*,' said Betty, dreamily. 'It was such a wonderful film, even though we only saw half of it. Have you seen it, by any chance?'

'Nah,' replied Hannah. 'Don't get much chance ter go ter the pittures.'

'Oh, but you should see *this* one, shouldn't she, Phil?' said Betty. 'It's so romantic. I adore films about people in love. Mind you, it *is* a bit creepy. But that's Alfred Hitchcock for you.'

'Well, at least you had someone to hold on to,' added Phil, slipping his arm round Betty's waist and kissing her lightly on the cheek.

'Do *you* have a boyfriend, Hannah?' Betty asked.

'Me?' replied Hannah mournfully. 'Yeah – I s'ppose I do really.'

'Well take my advice and hang on to him,' said Betty, turning a loving gaze up at Phil. 'This damned war's now turning pretty nasty. We have to live for today. Isn't that so, darling?'

Phil hugged her tightly.

By the time Hannah left the tube station, she felt as though she had been sheltering underground all day. Already the evening was drawing close to night again.

Walking down Upper Holloway Road was a strange experience for Hannah. It was not the first time she had been there, for when they were kids she and Louie were often taken by their dad for a ride on the top of a tram right up to the Archway and back, one of the regular treats she had never forgotten. But it was different now. It was the smell she noticed most of all, the smell of burning timbers and the thick black smoke that was spiralling right up into the rapidly darkening evening sky. Further along, on the approach to the Royal Northern Hospital and the Empire Picture House, the emergency services were spread right the way across the main road, trying desperately hard to deal with the carnage that had been inflicted by a bomb on the opposite side of the road to the hospital; and in one of the side streets fires were still raging from a clutch of Molotov cocktail incendiary bombs that had come crashing down from a passing raider, sending out a lethal spray of dazzling white phosphorescent sparks. Everywhere windows had been blown out of their frames, leaving curtains to dangle out helplessly, parked vehicles covered with debris, and broken glass spread erratically all over the place. The closer she got to the Nag's Head and Kinloch Street just a short distance ahead, the more Hannah worried about her mum, wondering whether she had managed to survive the carnage that she had warned Hannah about so many times. Once she had passed the restaurant at Beales' Corner, exhausted as she was, she practically ran all the way to the junction with Hornsey Road. But just as she got there, once again the air-raid siren wailed out from the nearby police station, which meant that whatever happened she had to get home as fast as her feet and legs would carry her. But it wasn't easy, for every street was now blacked out, and the only light available was coming from the torch beams of people rushing off to the nearest shelters.

By the time she had reached Charlie Brend's sweet shop in Hornsey Road, she was practically home and dry, for Kinloch Street was now just round the corner behind the shop. However, she had hardly reached the front door when the air was once again filled with the sound of ack-ack gunfire and the roar of raider bombers overhead. She made a beeline for the spare front door key, which was always tied to a piece of string hanging through the letterbox. Once she had retrieved it, she opened the front door without any effort at all, and once inside she slammed the door behind her, and shouted out: 'Mum! Are yer there? It's me! I'm 'ome . . . !'

There was no reply, and this made Hannah even more nervous, especially as the house was in pitch darkness, blackout curtains up everywhere, but no lights on. As she knew where the back scullery was by heart, she had no difficulty in finding her way there and switching on the light. There was still no sign of her mum. She went to the foot of the stairs, and shouted up: 'Mum! Where the 'ell are yer?' With still no reply, she rushed straight up the stairs and into her mum's bedroom, which was in darkness. Now Hannah was really worried. Going downstairs again, she looked around to see if there was any clue as to where her mum might have gone. With her hunger and thirst now taking a real hold on her, she went back into the scullery and found a half-loaf of bread, immediately cut a thick slice, smeared it with margarine from the greased wrapper on the table, and wolfed it down without coming up for breath. Then she found a fresh bottle of milk in the store cupboard alongside the stone copper, pulled off the metal cap, and drank half the bottle straight down. She wiped her mouth, and looked around. Where the hell was Babs? Thank God the place was intact, but where *was* her mum? The question was still burning when she switched off the light, and took a casual glance through the window into the tiny back yard outside. What took her completely by surprise was the fact that there was hardly any yard to be seen, for it had been dug up to accommodate a peculiar-looking hut made of what looked like aluminium or stainless steel. She could hardly believe her eyes, for when she and Louie had left the previous year there was certainly nothing like that in their back yard. Intensely curious, she went to the back door, and to her surprise she found it unlocked.

Outside, all hell had broken loose in the sky above, and so, with the dark constantly being fractured by the incessant bursts of shell fire, she picked her way to what looked like the entrance to the steel hut, which seemed to be set slightly below ground level. She slowly went down the concrete steps that had been erected there, and immediately saw a thick chink of light coming from behind a blackout curtain draped across the entrance. She waited a moment, listening at the curtain, but there seemed to be no sound coming from down below, so with one swift movement she pulled back the drape.

To her horror, in the dim light of a paraffin lamp, Hannah saw two naked figures suddenly sit bolt upright on a single bunk bed.

Chapter 16

Hannah and her mum were sitting opposite each other at the scullery table. For several moments they had not said a word to each other. It was after eleven o'clock at night and still dark outside, but although the all-clear had not sounded all that remained to be heard was the rumble of ack-ack gunfire in the far distance. To Babs's intense embarrassment, her male visitor had left within minutes of Hannah's peering through the blackout curtain of the Anderson air-raid shelter.

''Ow could yer do such a fing, Mum?' Hannah said, breaking the silence. ''Ow could yer do such a fing – ter *Dad*?'

'Yer dad's bin away a long time, Hann,' replied Babs, drawing nervously on a fag. 'You're too young to understand that a woman needs – company.'

'Company!' Hannah shot an angry look across at her. 'Is that why yer sent me an' Lou away – becos' yer wanted – *company*?'

'It's not the same, Hann,' Babs replied defensively, closing her dressing gown snugly round her neck. 'You an' Lou can't take the place of yer dad.'

'Yer can say *that* again!' retorted Hannah.

Babs was irritated. 'It's not *my* fault that 'e went away!' she snapped.

256

'It's not *'is* fault eivver!' replied Hannah angrily. 'In case yer've forgotten, Mum, there's a war on!'

'Now you listen ter me, Hannah,' said Babs, after exhaling a mouthful of fag smoke. 'I don't 'ave ter answer ter you. I don't 'ave ter answer ter you fer *anyfin'*. Nobody told me you was comin' 'ome. Nobody asked my permission ter let yer come 'ome! First fing this mornin' I'm goin' ter phone that bleedin' woman an' give 'er a piece er my mind. I do 'ave some rights, yer know!'

'*Rights*, Mum?' returned Hannah, staring at her in disbelief. 'You 'ave rights, do yer, ter send me an' Lou off ter some nutcase in the country, just so that you can 'ave a fling wiv some chinless wonder?'

Babs thumped the table. 'Don't you say fings like that, d'you 'ear!' she growled, standing up. 'Don't you ever say fings like that ter me. I'm still yer muvver, yer know. You 'ave no idea about the way life is. You're a minor, Hann! Don't you ever ferget that!'

Hannah refused to be put down. However, she was too sad and upset to engage in a blazing row. 'I'm seventeen years old, Mum,' she replied calmly. 'In a few months from now I'll be eighteen. If I don't know about life now, when will I?'

On the defensive, Babs slowly sat down again. This time she tried to be more reasonable. 'I – I know 'ow yer feel, darlin',' she said, with difficulty. 'I know – 'ow all this must look ter you. But yer've got ter believe me – it ain't wot yer fink. I've bin stuck 'ere on me own month in an' month out, waitin' fer yer dad ter come 'ome, fed up wiv 'avin' no one ter talk to.'

'Didn't look ter me like it was talk you was interested in,' replied Hannah acidly.

Babs stiffened again. She was not prepared for this. In the

space of just a few minutes, her entire life had been turned upside down. And it was all that woman's fault, that stupid woman who promised to let her know if Hannah tried to get on a train to London. Just look at the mess she had got her into now.

How was she ever going to convince Hannah that it was only a one-night fling, when she herself knew that it wasn't? There was no doubt that this was the end of the line for her, the end of her freedom. 'Hannah,' she said, sitting down again and reaching out to take hold of Hannah's hand. 'Let's be sensible about this. Let's try an' be'ave like sensible adults. You say yer *walked* all this way. Well that's marvellous, darlin' – wonderful! Mum's very proud of yer. But now you're 'ere, yer must've seen wot it's like – it's like a livin' 'ell. So don't yer fink I was right ter send my two babies away from all this? I told yer it was bound ter 'appen one day. Din't I tell yer?'

Hannah, eyes lowered, pulled her hand away. 'Yes, Mum,' she answered quietly. 'Yer did tell us. But wot yer didn't tell us was that yer preferred uvver people's company ter me an' Lou.'

'That's not true, darlin',' replied Babs, trying her old tactic of looking as though she wanted to cry. 'When you an' Lou went off, I 'ardly got a wink er sleep every night. I don't fink you know wot it's like for a muvver ter 'ave ter part wiv 'er kids. It's like cuttin' that cord when you're first born.'

Hannah turned her face away. She found it difficult to listen to this stuff.

'Look, Hann,' said Babs, who was getting desperate. 'I'll try to make it up to yer – I promise, I *will* try. You're me daughter, an' I only want ter do wotever makes you 'appy. But it's not goin' ter be easy, my baby. If these air raids go on the way they're goin', I don't know wot we're goin' ter do.'

'I know wot *I'm* goin ter do, Mum,' said Hannah, getting up from her chair. 'I need some sleep. I need time ter fink fings over.'

Babs got up at the same time. She watched Hannah go to the door with deep foreboding. 'Sleep as late as yer want, darlin',' she said. 'When yer come down in the mornin', I'll make yer a nice breakfast.'

Hannah turned at the door. 'It's funny,' she replied. 'The last fing I'm interested in right now is breakfast. I've got far too much on me mind.' She left the room, and for a moment or so stood outside in the passage in the dark, trying to take in what had happened, trying to make any sense at all of what her mum had been saying to her. She summoned up enough energy to go upstairs, but after that mammoth walk from Redbourne her body was so racked with pain that she could hardly move. For one so young, climbing those stairs one by one was an immense effort, a real test of mind over matter.

When she opened her bedroom door on the one and only landing in the house, she couldn't see a thing in the dark, so she limped her way to the window and closed the blackout curtains that her mum or someone had put up there. She turned on the light. The room was more or less the same as she and Lou had left it on that never-to-be-forgotten early morning just over a year ago. A year! Was it really so long? For Hannah, it hardly seemed possible. So much had happened in that time, so much had brought her into an adult world that she didn't care for at all. She quickly got out of her clothes, went to the chest of drawers and took out a clean flannelette nightie. By then her mind was so battered she could hardly stand up, so she switched off the light and jumped into the small double bed that she had always shared with her young sister. She groaned, for her body was aching all over. But despite her excessive weariness, she just lay there in the dark, unable to sleep, unable to think about anything other than what she had seen in the air-raid shelter in the back yard when she got home a few hours ago. It was so horrifying, so unreal. But then she thought about her dad. She thought about what he would do if he knew what his wife had been getting up to. Would he beat her up, bash the living daylights out of her, or would he just walk out of the door and vow never to set eyes on her again? It was a question that stayed with her until her eyes felt so heavy that she thought she must be ill or something. But she wasn't ill. It was merely that tears were trying to force their way out of her eyes and down her cheeks. She was unhappy, desperately unhappy. She wanted her dad. She wanted him to hug her and say, *It's all right, Hann. We'll sort it all out*. But would he, *could* he? That was a question she would never be able to answer until she wrote to let him know all the rotten things her mum had been getting up to behind his back.

It took Hannah several days to get on her feet again, and even when she did, nothing was the same. Thanks to what her mum had done, the home she had left a year ago, that tiny little two up two down terraced house in an equally tiny street just behind Charlie Brend's sweet shop, was no longer the home she had always thought it was. Needless to say, for the first day or so, her mum had done everything in her power to show Hannah that what she had come home to that night was just a passing phase, and she wanted to make it up to Hannah as best she could. But there was no 'best' that could ever make any difference to the way Hannah now felt about her mum; none of the breakfasts or attempts at cooking decent meals for her meant a damned thing. What haunted Hannah most of all was the feeling, the certain knowledge, that her mum had deceived her dad, and no excuses in the world could ever disguise the fact.

In her desperation to stay out of her mum's way, as soon as she felt strong enough to get out again, Hannah took a stroll around her old stamping grounds, the streets around Holloway that she had dreamt about all the time she had been in Redbourne. Although she knew all the old haunts like the back of her hand, she just wanted to reacquaint herself with them, to touch them with her hand, just to know that they were still there, all the shops like Hicks the greengrocer's, Stagnells the baker, Woods the furniture people, Liptons, Sainsbury's, even Mr Dorner, the butcher in Hornsey Road, who sold the best hot saveloys and pease pudding in the neighbourhood, but had apparently received a lot of nasty remarks from people just because he happened to be German, regardless of the fact that he had run his popular shop in Hornsey Road for over twenty-five years. Hannah couldn't resist having a quick stroll around the picture houses in the area, the Gaumont, the now closed Empire, and the Marlborough, all of them in Holloway Road, and also the spanking new Savoy cinema just next door to the Jones Bros department store, which had only opened earlier in the year, just a few months before the first air raids. What amazed Hannah most of all, however, was that even though there were terrible signs of bomb damage in many of the streets and roads she knew so well, great gaps where houses and shops had just disappeared to be replaced by huge piles of rubble, everyone seemed to be going about their business as though nothing had happened.

Where windows had caved in, they were replaced by scrawled notices such as BUSINESS AS USUAL or WINNIE'S THE MAN!, some of which were accompanied by a picture of the new Prime Minister Winston Churchill, who had replaced the sad, ailing Neville Chamberlain, who had been forced to resign just a few months before. This then was the home Hannah had come back to, the people she knew so well; people who, although bruised and shocked, were prepared to take anything that Hitler could throw at them, despite her mum's ominous warning that *the worst was yet ter come*.

Hannah, however, was now in urgent need of someone to talk to, someone with whom she could share all the horror of the past months, who would give her some advice about what to do about her mum. The first person who immediately came to mind was her former boss, Elsie Manners. When Hannah left school she had gone straight to work at Elsie's 'high class' hairdressing salon in Hornsey Road, where she learnt the trade she had come to know and love so well. During that time, Elsie, who was nearly twice Hannah's age, had nonetheless become her best friend. She was like an elder sister who knew how to keep both her customers and her staff happy; to make everyone believe that they were the most important people in the world. Many a time Elsie, who was a real cockney, born within the sound of Bow Bells, had warned Hannah about being too tied to her mum's apron strings. *She likes a bit er life, that one!* she would say on the side on more than one occasion, whilst giving one of her regulars a perm, a rinse, or a blow dry. *Take my advice, love, keep out of 'er way an' let 'er get on wiv it!* Elsie knew what she was talking about all right. She not only had one of the best dyed blonde bouffants Hannah had ever seen, but she could see right through people too. Yes, Elsie was the one to go to. Once she had given Hannah back her old job then everything would be all right again.

Elsie's salon was situated in Hornsey Road, quite close to the junction with Seven Sisters Road. As there wasn't much competition around, despite the difficult war conditions she did a roaring trade, mostly with young and middle-aged women who didn't want the bother of washing their own hair or doing their own styling with curlers. But, of course, if the truth were known, most of her customers always loved a good old chinwag, and where better to go than to Elsie's?

When Hannah got there, she found two women with their heads under the driers, reading the morning copies of the *Daily Sketch* and the *News Chronicle*. Elsie always insisted on having good reading for her customers; it made for such interesting topics for conversation.

'Hann!' she yelled out, as Hannah walked through the front door of the shop. The two of them hugged each other as though there was no tomorrow, which these days might be only too true. 'Yer look marvellous. Wunnerful. Don't she, ladies?'

The women under driers looked up casually from their newspapers, and nodded with a smile.

'Yer look much more grown up since I last saw yer,' enthused Elsie, looking her up and down. The woman waiting for her hair to be cut in one of the two chairs was doing her best not to look impatient. ''Ow was it then? 'Ow did all that country air suit yer? Where did they send yer to, anyway?'

When Hannah finally managed to get a word in edgeways, she said in a low voice, 'It was too bleedin' awful, Else. I'll tell yer about it some time . . .' she looked around to make sure that she wasn't overhead, then whispered, '*and* about me mum too.'

'Huh!' scoffed Elsie dismissively, refusing to lower her own voice. 'Yer can't tell me *anyfin'* about that one that I don't already know! Don't tell me you're back wiv 'er again?'

Hannah nodded.

'Yer poor little sod!' Elsie was never one to mince her words. 'You should find a nice boyfriend of yer own, an' dump 'er. I said that to yer the last time I saw yer. D'yer remember I told yer?'

Hannah, embarrassed, looked from one customer to another for any sign of a reaction. Then she nodded back. 'Else,' she pleaded, 'I need some 'elp.'

'Come on, Hann,' replied Elsie, returning to her customer in the chair. 'You know *me*. Anyfin' yer want, just ask.'

'Can we talk in private – just fer a minute?'

'All right wiv you, Sylvie?'

''As ter be, don't it,' replied the elderly customer, who actually had very little hair left for Elsie to curl.

Elsie patted her on the head, and led Hannah to a padded bench seat over by the window. 'Wos up?' she asked.

Hannah sat down beside her. 'Else,' she asked hopefully, 'can I come back?'

Elsie was taken by surprise. 'Come back?' she repeated.

''Ave me ol' job again. I can't tell yer 'ow I miss it. Yer know 'ow I 'ated it when Mum sent me off wiv Louie. I 'aven't done anyfin' like it since I left 'ere – just slavin' away in a pub like a bleedin' servant.'

Elsie was clearly not prepared for this. She sat there with a painful expression.

'If yer want,' continued Hannah, 'you can put me on shampoos. There's no need for me ter get back on cutting or stylin' fer a bit – well, not unless yer want me to.'

'Hannah . . .'

Now that she was actually back in the salon again, Hannah was so enthused, she just rambled on excitedly. 'When I was lyin' in bed at night at this dump I was in, I used to dream about all the marvellous times I used ter 'ave 'ere. I don't fink you realise 'ow much I learnt from you, Else. You must be one of the best stylists in the 'ole of London . . .'

'Hann,' said Elsie, trying hard to get a word in. 'Please listen ter me.'

'Yer don't 'ave ter pay me so much,' continued Hannah, hardly coming up for breath. 'Oh, no, it wouldn't be fair. I mean, I've bin out of practice fer some time. I'd 'ave ter train up again – I do realise that. In any case . . .'

'Hannah!' Elsie's firm intervention visibly shook Hannah. 'I'm sorry,' she said with immense difficulty, 'but I can't take yer back.'

Hannah felt as though she had been hit by a thunderbolt. 'W-wot d'yer mean?' she asked anxiously.

Elsie smiled comfortingly at her. She was actually quite a striking woman, with strong features, beautiful brown eyes that were just a little too heavily made up, and a mole on her chin that had been touched up with mascara. 'I can't take you on, Hann, becos fings ain't wot they used ter be 'ere. Since the bombs started, a lot er people've gone away, moved out ter somewhere safe. I've lost no end of my customers like that. I've also lost one or two in that bomb up Tufnell Park. D'yer remember Agnes Reed, that woman who used ter work in Manor Gardens library? Well, she copped 'er lot in a fire at 'er place up near 'Ighbury.

They say it was covered in incendiary fings or wotever. Oh, Hann, yer've no idea wot a nice woman she was . . .'

'*Why* can't I come back, Else?'

Elsie found Hannah's pathetic plea heartbreaking, and could hardly bear to look the poor girl in the eyes.

'There's only you 'ere,' continued Hannah, with fading hope. 'Yer can't manage all these customers on yer own.'

Elsie raised her head to look at her. There was real anguish in her eyes. 'Hann,' she replied softly, 'I'm not *on* me own.' She drew Hannah's attention to a young girl, much the same age as Hannah, who was just coming out from the back room, carrying cups of tea on a tray for the two women under the driers.

Hannah looked as though she wanted the ground to open up beneath her.

'She's bin with me for nearly five months now,' said Elsie. 'She's still a bit raw, but she's learnin' fast, an' she's really a very nice gel.'

Hannah immediately got up from the bench.

'Not as nice as you though, Hann,' said Elsie, getting up at the same time. 'I mean it. There's no one I've 'ad workin' for me that's bin anywhere near as good and clever as you. You're one in a million, Hann – believe me.'

Hannah tried to smile bravely, but it wasn't easy. 'It's all right, Else,' she said. 'I understand. I'm really sorry I bothered yer.'

'Bothered me?' spluttered Elsie, with incomprehension. 'You're me pal,' ain't yer, me mate? I told yer before, I'd do anyfin' for yer – *anyfin'*.'

'Yes, I know,' replied Hannah, trying desperately hard to put a brave face on it. 'Don't worry, Else, you don't owe me nuffin'.' She went to the door, and opened it. 'Anyway, it was nice seein' yer again. 'Bye!'

Elsie rushed after her into the street. 'Hann!' she called anxiously. 'Come an' see me again – any time yer like. Will yer promise me?'

'Fanks, Else,' said Hannah. 'I'll see yer some time.'

Without turning round to look, she knew that Elsie was watching her go. It was only when she turned the corner into Seven Sisters Road that she suddenly quickened her pace, and never stopped until she reached the bicycle shop on the corner of Thane Villas. She stayed there for several minutes taking stock, trying to work out why she had ever imagined that a job, *any* job, should still be waiting for her when she had been away for such a long time. But there was no denying that Elsie's refusal had hurt her deeply. It made her realise that nobody – absolutely nobody – owed her a favour. And she didn't owe them one either.

Hannah met her former schoolteacher, Dorothy Hobson, quite by accident. Most of the children who had been evacuated at the start of the war had been brought home by their parents after only a few weeks, mainly because there had seemed to be no sign of the bombing campaign against the big cities, especially London, that had been thought to be a real possibility. But now that that possibility had become a reality, mainly because of the fall of France and the invasion of other countries, the 'six-day evacuation', as it had been called a few weeks before, had sent children and their mothers hurrying back to the safety of the countryside, away from the horrors of the London blitz which had finally dispelled the idea of a 'phoney war'. But there were still kids around who, to their parents' despair, had refused to budge, and for that reason Dorothy Hobson had stayed in the thick of things to help give those kids some basic education, which she carried out either in the front or back parlours of their own homes, or even, during air raids, down in their Anderson shelters. Hannah caught up with her just as she was coming out of a house in Arthur Road, where she had been giving an English lesson to three of the younger children who had remained behind. Although Dorothy was absolutely thrilled to see Hannah again, she was shocked to see her looking so pale and dejected, and as she had some time to spare she took her for a cup of tea in the Lyon's tea shop in Holloway Road. They sat there for nearly an hour whilst Dorothy listened to Hannah pouring her heart out about her time away on evacuation, the long walk home, and the terrible thing she saw when she found her mum with a strange man down in the air-raid shelter.

'Oh, Hannah,' sighed Dorothy, with one of her warm sympathetic smiles, 'my heart breaks for you. You're such a good, honest girl. You shouldn't have had to go through all this. If only I'd known.'

'Yer couldn't er done anyfin', Miss,' replied Hannah, who was still reeling from the shock of being turned down for a job with Elsie. 'I know now Mum 'ad 'er own reasons fer wantin' me an' Lou out er the way. It 'ad nuffin' ter do wiv wantin' us ter keep safe when the bombs come.'

Dorothy shook her head. 'You know, Hannah,' she replied, 'I don't think that's entirely true. I've known your mother a long time. I know she has a lot of failings, but I really do think that what she did, she did for the best.'

'Sleepin' wiv uvver men ain't fer the best,' replied Hannah, who from time to time looked as though she would burst into tears. 'When the cat's away, Mum sure knows 'ow ter play.'

Dorothy briefly took off her tortoiseshell spectacles, put them down on the table in front of her, and looked across at Hannah. She had nothing but the deepest sympathy for the poor girl. The question was, with all that Dorothy knew about Hannah's parents, how was she going to be able to help the girl without actually telling her the truth? 'I know how you feel, my dear,' she said, 'but the only thing you can do is to think of this as your mother's weakness, because that's what it is, you know. It was bound to happen. The moment this wretched war broke out and the menfolk had to go off to fight, it was a lot to expect their wives to stay at home without them for long periods at a time. Your mum is not the only person I know who's had this problem. I'm only grateful I never got married myself. I'm sure it would have happened to me too.'

Hannah shook her head. That was something she would never believe of someone like her former schoolteacher. If there was anyone in Holloway that she could still trust, it was practical, down-to-earth Miss Hobson. 'Never,' she replied.

'You're wrong, Hannah,' said Dorothy, whose short-cropped hair made her pretty face look larger than it actually was. 'War does extraordinary things to people. It plays havoc with their lives.'

Hannah held her cup in both hands, and sipped her tea. 'I wouldn't've minded so much, but Mum 'as lied ter me so much. While I was down there livin' in that pub, I wrote 'er so many postcards, and yet she only ever wrote ter me once. An' yet, all the time, she was in touch wiv that – terrible woman. I got the feelin' that they were in it tergevver. They *wanted* me ter be kept prisoner. Yer know wot *I* fink, Miss? I fink boaf of 'em are off their chump.'

Dorothy half smiled. 'I see you haven't been studying much of the English I taught you!' That brought a smile even to Hannah's face. 'The point is,' continued Dorothy, serious again, 'what are you going to do with yourself now?'

Hannah shrugged. 'I s'ppose now Elsie can't take me on again, I'll 'ave ter find a job, but Gord knows 'ow or where.'

'Have you tried talking it over with your mum?'

Hannah gave a dismissive shake of the head. 'Mum's got too many uvver fings on 'er mind,' she replied. 'No. I'm on me own, I know that.'

'No you're not, Hannah,' insisted Dorothy. She squared up her large frame and leant across the table towards her. '*I'm* here. I'll *always* be here. Please remember that. The only thing is, you must try to be positive about all this, have some idea about how you intend to cope with things.'

'Don't worry,' replied Hannah firmly. 'I know the first fing I'm goin' ter do. I'm goin' ter write ter Dad, an' tell 'im wot Mum's bin gettin' up to.'

Dorothy stiffened, and sank back into her chair. She shook her head slowly. 'No, Hannah,' she replied with a look of deep foreboding. 'If you don't mind my saying so, I don't think that's a very good idea. I don't think it's a good idea at all.'

Hannah was puzzled. 'Why not?'

Dorothy leant forward again, and lowered her voice. 'Hannah,' she pleaded. 'Remember what happened at Dunkirk? Remember what happened to all those poor men who survived, who struggled to stay alive just so that they could get home to see their wives and families again?' She paused just long enough to let the waitress pass by their table carrying a tray for customers nearby. 'When did you last hear from your father?'

Hannah shrugged. 'Months ago.'

'Do you know where he is at this moment?'

''E never tells yer,' replied Hannah. 'The army wouldn't let 'im.'

'Then he could be anywhere,' said Dorothy, keeping her voice low. 'Each day his life could be in danger. For all you know, he may even have been at Dunkirk or in North Africa or somewhere even more dangerous.'

Hannah looked puzzled. She wasn't quite sure what Dorothy was getting at.

'What I'm asking, Hannah, my dear,' Dorothy continued with deadly seriousness, 'is if your poor father *is* right in the middle of a battlefield somewhere, how d'you think he's going to feel if he receives a letter from you, telling him that his wife is being – unfaithful to him? Is it the right thing to do at this time, Hannah, this *very* time?'

Hannah was unable to reply. For several moments she just sat there, staring at the tea in her cup, weighing up the pros and cons of what her former teacher had just said, knowing in her heart of hearts that it was true, that it would be cruel to ask her dad to cope with something like this on top of all he was having to go through at the present time. Finally, she slowly shook her head.

'Keep it to yourself, Hannah,' said Dorothy awkwardly. 'I know it's not easy coping with a situation like this, especially under the circumstances.'

Hannah looked up with a start. 'Circumstances?' she asked, puzzled. '*Wot* circumstances?'

Dorothy's sudden withdrawn expression showed that she had said rather more than she intended to. 'All you're having to go through,' she replied vaguely. 'Look, let's keep in touch.' She reached into her handbag, and took out a small notebook and a pencil. 'This is where I live.' She quickly scrawled her address on one of the pages, ripped it out of the book, and gave it to Hannah. 'Whenever you feel like talking, whenever you feel low, just come along and see me. I live with my sister, Tilda. You'd like her. She's far more understanding than me. We could all talk things over together. Would you like to do that, Hannah?'

Hannah looked at the piece of paper, and smiled gratefully. 'Fanks.'

'But just remember,' said Dorothy, leaning forward to her again, 'whatever you do, don't do it without thinking first. There are so many – complications – in your parents' marriage, Hannah. I know. I know only too well. All I'm saying is, don't be hasty. Just get yourself on your feet again, find a decent job, and try to put this whole thing behind you. It's the only way, Hannah. Believe me – it's the only way.'

she replied vaguely. 'Look, let's keep in touch.' She
to her handbag, and took out a small notebook and
This is where I live.' She quickly scrawled her address
the pages, ripped it out of the book, and gave it to
Whenever you feel like talking, whenever you feel low,
along and see me. I live with my sister, Tilda. You'd
e's far more understanding than me. We could all talk
together. Would you like to do that, Hannah?'
looked at the piece of paper, and smiled gratefully.

st remember,' said Dorothy, leaning forward to her
ever you do, don't do it without thinking first. There
– complications – in your parents' marriage, Hannah.
now only too well. All I'm saying is, don't be hasty.
urself on your feet again, find a decent job, and try
whole thing behind you. It's the only way, Hannah.
– it's the only way.'

Dorothy briefly took off her tortoiseshell spectacles, put them
down on the table in front of her, and looked across at Hannah.
She had nothing but the deepest sympathy for the poor girl. The
question was, with all that Dorothy knew about Hannah's parents,
how was she going to be able to help the girl without actually
telling her the truth? 'I know how you feel, my dear,' she said,
'but the only thing you can do is to think of this as your mother's
weakness, because that's what it is, you know. It was bound to
happen. The moment this wretched war broke out and the
menfolk had to go off to fight, it was a lot to expect their wives
to stay at home without them for long periods at a time. Your
mum is not the only person I know who's had this problem.
I'm only grateful I never got married myself. I'm sure it would
have happened to me too.'

Hannah shook her head. That was something she would never
believe of someone like her former schoolteacher. If there was
anyone in Holloway that she could still trust, it was practical,
down-to-earth Miss Hobson. 'Never,' she replied.

'You're wrong, Hannah,' said Dorothy, whose short-cropped
hair made her pretty face look larger than it actually was. 'War
does extraordinary things to people. It plays havoc with their
lives.'

Hannah held her cup in both hands, and sipped her tea. 'I
wouldn't've minded so much, but Mum 'as lied ter me so much.
While I was down there livin' in that pub, I wrote 'er so many
postcards, and yet she only ever wrote ter me once. An' yet, all
the time, she was in touch wiv that – terrible woman. I got the
feelin' that they were in it tergevver. They *wanted* me ter be kept
prisoner. Yer know wot *I* fink, Miss? I fink boaf of 'em are off
their chump.'

Dorothy half smiled. 'I see you haven't been studying much of the English I taught you!' That brought a smile even to Hannah's face. 'The point is,' continued Dorothy, serious again, 'what are you going to do with yourself now?'

Hannah shrugged. 'I s'ppose now Elsie can't take me on again, I'll 'ave ter find a job, but Gord knows 'ow or where.'

'Have you tried talking it over with your mum?'

Hannah gave a dismissive shake of the head. 'Mum's got too many uvver fings on 'er mind,' she replied. 'No. I'm on me own, I know that.'

'No you're not, Hannah,' insisted Dorothy. She squared up her large frame and leant across the table towards her. '*I'm* here. I'll *always* be here. Please remember that. The only thing is, you must try to be positive about all this, have some idea about how you intend to cope with things.'

'Don't worry,' replied Hannah firmly. 'I know the first fing I'm goin' ter do. I'm goin' ter write ter Dad, an' tell 'im wot Mum's bin gettin' up to.'

Dorothy stiffened, and sank back into her chair. She shook her head slowly. 'No, Hannah,' she replied with a look of deep foreboding. 'If you don't mind my saying so, I don't think that's a very good idea. I don't think it's a good idea at all.'

Hannah was puzzled. 'Why not?'

Dorothy leant forward again, and lowered her voice. 'Hannah,' she pleaded. 'Remember what happened at Dunkirk? Remember what happened to all those poor men who survived, who struggled to stay alive just so that they could get home to see their wives and families again?' She paused just long enough to let the waitress pass by their table carrying a tray for customers nearby. 'When did you last hear from your father?'

Hannah shrugged. 'Months ago.'

'Do you know where he is at this

''E never tells yer,' replied Hanna 'im.'

'Then he could be anywhere,' said low. 'Each day his life could be in d may even have been at Dunkirk or where even more dangerous.'

Hannah looked puzzled. She was was getting at.

'What I'm asking, Hannah, my de deadly seriousness, 'is if your poor of a battlefield somewhere, how d' if he receives a letter from you, telli – unfaithful to him? Is it the rig Hannah, this *very* time?'

Hannah was unable to reply. Fo there, staring at the tea in her c cons of what her former teacher heart of hearts that it was true, th dad to cope with something like to go through at the present tir head.

'Keep it to yourself, Hannah it's not easy coping with a si the circumstances.'

Hannah looked up with puzzled. '*Wot* circumstances?

Dorothy's sudden withdr said rather more than she

through,' reached a pencil. on one o Hannah. just come like her. S things ove

Hannah 'Fanks.'

'But ju again, 'wh are so mar I know. I Just get y to put this Believe m

Chapter 17

By late September, the London blitz had been raging for almost a month, with the air-raid sirens sounding constantly, during daylight hours as well as at night. The German onslaught on the capital was not only on military targets and the Thames-side ports in the East End, but took its toll also on the civilian population, with houses, shops, and familiar buildings reduced to rubble, with an alarming number of casualties everywhere.

Hannah slept through all the mayhem around her, refusing to join her mum each night in the Anderson air-raid shelter in the back yard, which for Hannah had become a symbol of something that she was doing her best to forget. For Babs's part, she was trying to be as discreet about her secret lifestyle as she possibly could, making quite sure that whatever casual relationships she was making were kept out of the critical gaze of her elder daughter. Even so, contact between the two was at an all time low. As far as Hannah was concerned, she only wanted to see her mum when it was absolutely essential, so for the time being at least she was prepared to heed the advice of Miss Hobson and not write to her dad about what had been going on behind his back. Her main priority now was to try to find a job, and take her life in a direction that would help her to stand on her own two feet. That opportunity eventually came when she applied for a position as a counter sales assistant at Woolworth's department store in the Holloway Road. The pay wasn't exactly marvellous, but at least it gave Hannah a chance to have some money in her pocket and to go out with some of the friends she soon made at the store. One of those friends turned out to be Betty Pilkington, the girl she had casually met with her boyfriend Phil whilst sheltering down the Archway tube. Although Betty was from what was thought of as a higher-class family who lived up in posh Canonbury Square, Hannah admired the way Betty had done her own thing and taken a job which others would have deemed below her station in life. It was one of the reasons why Hannah got on so well with her. But life as a shop girl soon proved to be quite demanding for Hannah, especially as the constant day and night air raids, which had already caused a great deal of damage and loss of life in the area, were still forcing both staff and customers to make frequently for the nearest shelters. It was during one of those raids that, whilst the staff were taking cover in Woolworth's own air-raid shelter, Hannah was horrified to catch a glimpse of the man she had seen briefly with her mum in the Anderson shelter on that fateful night.

'That's Tom Barker,' said Betty, seated on a bench seat alongside Hannah, looking across at the middle-aged man in suit and tie whom Hannah had pointed out. He was smoking a cigarette and laughing and joking with some of the girls at the far end of the shelter. 'He's a manager in Admin upstairs. I can't bear the man – always so full of himself. I think he imagines he's God's gift to the female sex. Well not me, I can tell you! He's only here because he was turned down for the army – bad eyesight or something – or so he says.' She leant closer to whisper.

'Rumour has it he bribed someone in the War Office to avoid call-up. Dreadful man! God knows what his poor wife must see in him.'

Hannah looked up with a start. 'Wife?' she asked, shocked. 'Yer mean – he's married?'

'I suppose you could say that,' replied Betty, retying the ribbon that was holding her long hair together behind her head. 'He's slept with so many people in this store, I doubt he even remembers that he *is* married.' She turned to look at Hannah, and was worried when she saw that her friend had turned as white as a sheet. 'Duckie,' she asked, 'are you all right?'

'I – I'm OK,' replied Hannah, who suddenly felt quite disoriented. 'Don't like being stuck down in these places, that's all.'

'I know,' replied Betty. 'Ditto!'

At that moment, there was a loud explosion outside, which brought screams from some of the girls, and tiny flakes of plaster fluttering down from the ceiling above them.

'No alarm!' boomed the man Hannah despised so much. 'Keep yer knickers on, girls!' Some of the girls, who found him funny, roared with laughter. Others ignored him.

'Ugh! Horrible man!' spluttered Betty with utter disdain, standing up to brush the plaster off her shop uniform. 'I wish someone would stuff something in his mouth – preferably a fist!'

As soon as the all-clear siren had sounded, everyone emerged from the shelter and returned to the store upstairs. Whilst Betty returned to her own counter in haberdashery, Hannah waited around for a moment or so to watch the smooth Mr Barker emerge from the shelter in the company of a couple of admiring counter girls. There was no doubt that he clearly had something that the girls liked, but at that precise moment Hannah couldn't understand exactly what it was. In fact, with his receding hair-line, smarmy schoolboy looks and a large wart on the side of his nose, she was at a loss to know what anyone saw in him – especially her mum.

Hannah's worst fears were realised when she arrived home after work to find a police car, surrounded by neighbours, parked outside the house. Her first inclination was to take fright and run, but she suddenly heard her mum calling to her. 'Hannah! Come quick!'

Reluctantly, Hannah turned round and made her way through the small group of curious neighbours. Once she was inside the house, Babs closed the door quickly and took her into the front parlour, where two special constables, one male, one female, were waiting for her.

'This is me elder daughter,' said Babs, behaving like a hostess at a smart dinner party. 'Hannah, these gentlemen – I mean, these constables – want ter talk to yer about your runnin' away from your foster-parents.'

'I didn't run,' snapped Hannah sourly. 'I walked.'

Babs gave the two constables a *Yer see, wot did I tell yer* type of look.

The man left his female colleague to ask most of the questions. 'Hannah,' she said gently, 'what made you walk out on them like that?'

'I 'ate 'em,' Hannah replied bluntly.

'Why?'

''Cos they're bleedin' nutcases, that's why.'

Babs, who had sat down, shuddered with embarrassment. 'Language, darlin',' she said.

'In what way were they "nutcases", Hannah?' asked the middle-aged female constable, who had soft features and a warm expression, something Hannah had never recognised in a flatfoot before. 'Did they ill-treat you in any way?'

Hannah stood looking into the empty fireplace. 'Don't know wot yer mean by "ill-treat",' she replied evasively.

The female constable nodded to her colleague, who was scribbling in a notebook. 'I mean,' she continued, 'did either Mr or Mrs Bullock ever assault – hit – you?'

Hannah wanted to answer immediately. If being slapped hard around the face by that woman was what was called 'assault', then that's what it was. However, she came from a pretty rough family, so getting a whack around the lughole was nothing new to her. 'Nuffin' that I remember', she replied reluctantly.

'So why did you want to walk out like that?' asked the younger, male constable, speaking for the first time.

''Cos I didn't like bein' locked up in a prison!' Again her answer was firm and to the point.

'A prison?' asked the male constable.

'Well – that's wot it felt like,' replied Hannah, who suddenly pulled off her headscarf in frustration. ''Ow would *you* like ter be shut in whenever they felt like it, not even bein' allowed ter go out wivout permission?'

'But they did feed you?' asked the female constable.

'Oh, they fed me all right,' agreed Hannah, 'if yer call left-overs a good meal.' The two constables flicked a quick glance at each other. 'And Gord 'elp yer if they ever caught yer 'elpin' yerself ter their precious bleedin' biscuits, or pourin' yerself one lousy ginger beer. That silly cow treated me as though I was a bank robber or somefin'. She used ter say she'd always wanted a daughter, but she treated me like a lump er dog's, so wot she'd do wiv the real fing . . .' She shook her head slowly. 'You don't know. Yer just don't know.'

'Did you ever complain to anyone about all this?' asked the female constable.

'Complain?' asked Hannah haughtily. 'Complain ter who, may I ask?'

The female constable shrugged. 'The police station, the evacuation committee in the village?'

Hannah scoffed with a laugh. 'The so-called evacuation committee weren't interested in complaints,' she replied sarcastically. 'They 'ad an excuse fer *everyfin'*.'

The female constable turned to Babs. 'And what about you, Mrs Adams?' she asked. 'Were you aware how unhappy Hannah was?'

'No, I wasn't,' replied Babs quite blatantly. 'If I had bin of course, I'd have brought her back immediately.'

Hannah turned and glared incredulously at her mum, hardly able to believe what she had just heard her say.

'So you weren't in contact with Hannah's foster-parents?'

'Not really,' replied Babs. 'Just the occasional telephone call ter check on 'ow my babies were gettin' on. The Bullocks never gave me any 'int that anyfin' like this was goin' on.'

'She didn't even know that me an' my sister Louie 'ad bin separated, did yer, Mum?' Hannah's sharp-tongued question completely flummoxed Babs, who quickly looked around for her packet of fags.

'Is this true, Mrs Adams?' asked the male constable.

''Onest ter God,' replied Babs, desperately searching for an answer, ''alf the time I never knew *wot* was going on down there.'

'Don't you think it was your responsibility to find out?' asked the female constable wryly.

'There was so much goin' on up 'ere,' she replied defensively. 'Yer've no idea 'ow upsettin' it's bin fer me since my 'ubby was called up.'

The two constables exchanged a knowing look. 'The point is,' said the woman, 'after the concern caused by Hannah's disappearance, the evacuation committee in Redbourne have asked the Ministry of Health to look into the matter, and that's why we're here now.'

'What they want to know is,' said the male constable, still scribbling, 'where do you go from here?'

Babs looked up with a start, realising that it was she who was being asked the question. 'Go?' she asked with a dither. 'W-wot d'yer mean?'

'Mrs Adams,' said the woman. 'With the situation in London as it now is, do you want Hannah to remain at home, or do you want her to return to her foster-parents?'

'No!' objected Hannah, angrily.

Now Babs was really flustered. On one hand she had the law asking her an awkward question, and on the other, Hannah was in danger of revealing far too much about the real reason why she had sent her kids away. 'I really don't know,' she replied evasively. 'Of course it is terribly dangerous round 'ere now, all these air raids an' bombs an' everyfin' – I mean it really would be better if Hannah was away from it all, nice an' safe in the country . . .'

'No!' Hannah yelled again. 'If yer try ter send me back ter that place, I'll do the same fing all over again!'

'But as yer can see, Hannah's a big gel now,' said Babs, quickly responding to Hannah's threats. 'If she wants ter take the chance an' stay behind wiv me, then I'll do me best . . .'

'Mrs Adams,' said the man. 'Your daughter may be a big girl now, but at the moment she is still under age, and therefore still *your* responsibility.'

'Mrs Adams,' said his female colleague, with a warning smile, 'if you *can't* promise to look after Hannah, to keep her here with you safely at home, then I'm afraid we shall just have to go back to the authorities and tell them that you're not carrying out your legal responsibilities.'

Babs suddenly sprang to her feet. 'I've told yer!' she growled angrily. 'I'll do wot I can. Wot more d'yer expect!'

The two constables exchanged a quick nod of agreement. 'Very well, madam,' said the man, sternly, closing his notebook and replacing it in the top pocket of his uniform. 'We'll convey your message back to the authorities. If you have any more problems in this connection, please get in touch with our special young persons' unit at the police station just up Hornsey Road. Do you understand what I'm saying, Mrs Adams?'

Babs nodded reluctantly.

As they left, the female constable stopped briefly to say a last comforting word to Hannah. 'Give your mother a chance, Hannah,' she said. 'These are dangerous and difficult times.'

Her male colleague followed her out. As he went he pointed a warning finger at Hannah. 'You behave yourself now.'

After she had heard the front door close, Babs quickly knelt on the tatty old sofa in front of the window and peered out through the lace curtains. With the neighbours still watching in awed fascination, the two police constables got back into their car and drove off.

Hannah left the room, but when she was halfway up the stairs her mum came out of the parlour to call up to her. 'I 'ope you're satisfied?' she yelled, her voice high and shrill. 'That's the first time I've ever had a flatfoot inside this house!'

Hannah carried on up the stairs, and without coming to a halt, called back calmly over her shoulder, 'Is it really? Well never mind, mum. You'll just 'ave ter make do wiv Mr Barker, won't yer?'

The following morning the heavens opened, and it rained so much that the drains in the gutters outside Woolworth's store were finding it difficult to cope with the sudden rush of water. Holloway Road was awash with people struggling to keep up their umbrellas in the high wind, and every time a bus passed by some poor souls on the pavement were getting drenched by thoughtless drivers. But the rain was welcome, for with it came heavy grey clouds which at least gave the bomb-weary residents a respite from endless day and night air raids.

Hannah arrived at the store just before nine o'clock, entering through the back entrance in Enkel Street. The moment she got inside out of the rain, she went straight to the staff locker room to take off her topcoat and headscarf. As there was now a shortage of material to provide uniforms for all the staff, she had to be content with serving at the hardware counter wearing her own clothes, which today happened to be a simple grey dress which matched the colour of the sky outside.

'Your friend Casanova just turned up,' said Betty, when she came across to say hallo to Hannah at her counter.

'Who?'

'Who d'you think?' asked Betty, surprised that Hannah didn't know whom she was referring to. 'Mr Heartthrob himself, of course – from Admin upstairs.'

Hannah's face dropped. 'Oh,' she groaned, '*him.*'

'I can't tell you how awful he looks!' giggled Betty, lowering her voice. 'God knows who was the poor unlucky soul he spent last night with. You know what they say – "a cat on the tiles never looks the same after the night before!"' Both girls laughed.

'What I don't understand is,' said Hannah, 'if 'e's married, 'ow come 'e manages ter stay out at night?'

'Search me,' replied Betty, who was doing her best to tidy her damp hair after making a rush for cover in the rain. 'You'd have to go next door and ask his long-suffering wife about *that.*'

Hannah looked at her with a start. 'Next door?'

'Yes,' replied Betty quite casually. 'She works in Selby's in women's underwear. I've never seen her myself, but apparently she's quite a nice woman – if somewhat stupid. How on earth did she ever get mixed up with a creep like that?'

Just then, the store's entrance doors were opened and the usual handful of customers who had been waiting patiently under cover outside for the nine o'clock opening immediately rushed straight in.

'Here they come!' said Betty, quickly scurrying off to her own counter. 'Just to get out of the rain! Bet you they don't buy a thing!'

As it happened, once the rain had stopped it did turn out to be a busy morning, and for some reason or another there was quite a rush on the hardware counter. As Hannah was a fairly new girl on the job, she found it all a bit difficult to handle. Shovels and brooms seemed to be the hot sell, which since people were constantly having to clear up after bomb blast damage, was quite understandable, but apparently there was also a rush on Lifebuoy soap and Persil powder, after a rumour had gone around that there would soon be a great shortage of such items.

By lunchtime, Hannah was only too ready for the dried egg omelette, boiled potatoes, and tinned peas which she got for threepence in the staff canteen, and which was certainly better than some of the shoddy food her mum served up at home. It also gave her the chance to have a break in the company of Betty and some of the other girls, who spent a lot of time talking about their boyfriends who had been called up. At the end of the meal, however, all Hannah wanted to do was to get the day over, for once Saturday afternoon was behind her, at least she had a day off to look forward to.

In the ladies' washroom, Hannah splashed cold water over her face in an effort to prepare herself for what looked like being a heavy last few hours of the working weekend. She looked at herself in the mirror above the basin, and hated what she saw. In her view she looked tired and really dowdy, and she told herself that it was no wonder she didn't have someone like Betty's boyfriend Phil, or indeed anyone else, to make a fuss of her. As she stood there, staring into the mirror, she could see a variety of people reflected there, all of them trying to say something to her, to warn her, to scold her, and, in the case of Sam, to love her. People like Maggie Bullock were there, fading in and out of the reflection like a wicked witch, that familiar expression telling Hannah how lucky she was to have a decent roof over her head, and foster-parents like her and Mr Bullock. Then there was Louie, mischievous Lou who was lucky to have fallen flat on her feet in a wonderful new home with Mary and Joseph Beedle, but whom Hannah missed so much. Jane was there too, dear, caring Jane Jessop, who knew more about the Bullocks than she ever admitted, but had been a tower of strength to Hannah during that terrible year in Redbourne. But surprisingly enough, the one person who really *did* bring a warm smile to Hannah's face was Horatio, the old boy who seemed to spend most of his time sitting at the bench table outside the Cock and Crow. She could see him in the mirror now, pint of bitter in hand, a mischievous grin on his craggy old face, and his great flock of white hair hanging down from beneath his battered flat cap. *My old dad always used ter say that people like Horatio Nelson were what ol' England is all about.* She could hear him saying it now, as though it really *was* him who was grinning down at her from that mirror, his front teeth so yellow they looked as though they had been like that since the day he was born. Hannah smiled. Horatio. How she loved that name. But Horatio what? She never did know his surname. Oh well, she sighed, what did it matter? He was real, and that's all that was important to her. However, whilst she kept on staring into the mirror to see who else from those days at Redbourne would appear, a face gradually emerged that she didn't recognise. Unconsciously, she found herself leaning in closer and closer to the mirror, so that the face became clearer and quite suddenly clearly defined. With a look of sheer horror, she identified the face: it was the face of the man she had glimpsed in the Anderson shelter that night. She swung round with a horrified start to find herself looking straight into the piercing eyes of Tom Barker.

'Hallo, little lady,' he said smoothly, menacingly. 'Nice ter see yer again.'

Panicking, Hannah pushed him aside and rushed straight for the door, but in a flash he was ahead of her, and pulled the latch closed.

'Yer've got no right ter be in 'ere!' growled Hannah. But when she attempted to shout out, he immediately clasped his hand over her mouth.

'Now you listen ter me, little lady,' he said, talking close to her face, blocking her efforts to reply. 'You an' your mum've got ter come ter some agreement about me.'

Hannah was repulsed by his looks, the piercing dark brown eyes with the heavy bags beneath them, and the wart, that terrible black wart on the side of his nose. And she hated the strong smell of whisky on his breath.

'Apparently, your mum don't want ter see me no more,' he continued. 'It's all your fault, little lady. If you 'adn't barged in on us like that the uvver night, fings wouldn't've bin like they are. But as it so 'appens, I *like* your mum. In fact, I like 'er a lot, an' I wanna go on seein' 'er – right?'

Hannah struggled to free herself from the hand still clamped hard over her mouth.

'Take it easy now, just take it easy,' he said calmly. 'Now then, if I take my hand away, are you goin' to promise not ter do anyfin' stupid?'

Hannah still struggled.

'It's up ter you, Hannah,' he said. 'That *is* yer name, in't it? At least, that's wot I read in your file up in Personnel. Shall we talk or shall we not?'

Hannah felt a cold chill run down her spine, but she finally agreed, and stopped struggling. The man took his hand away. 'There we are then. That's much better – yes?'

'If they catch yer in 'ere,' growled Hannah, 'they'll 'ave yer guts fer garters!' She tried to back away from him, but he had her pinned against the wall by the door.

'Now look,' he said, trying to remain calm and reasonable. 'A little bird told me that you'd bin askin' questions about me. Now I don't like *anyone* doin' fings like that. Do I make myself clear, little lady – do I?'

Hannah refused to reply.

'Yer see,' he continued regardless, 'I'm a happily married man. I love my wife very much. And I love my job too. But from time ter time, I'm entitled to a bit er private life of me own. D'yer get my meanin' – Hannah?'

Hannah glared at him. 'If anyone tries ter get in 'ere . . .' she warned him.

'Don't you worry about fings like that,' he replied quickly, with a grin. 'I've already taken care er that. Just you listen, and take in wot I'm sayin'. OK? 'Cos if yer don't, I 'ave ter tell yer that fings could get out of 'and for you, workin' in this place. I've got a lot er contacts in this store, yer know, a lot er mates who wouldn't mind doing me a favour any time I like.' He leaned close to her again. 'Now I tell yer again. Wot goes on between yer mum an' me is nuffin' ter do wiv you – right? If I ever 'ear you talkin' about me an' 'er ter anyone – *anyone* – even yer mates out there – especially yer mates out there – you won't last five more minutes in this job. An' wot's more, when yer get kicked out you won't get the kind of references you'd like. D'you understand wot I'm sayin', little lady – do yer?'

Hannah continued to glare at him in absolute silence.

'Good!' said the man. 'Then we appear to understand each other perfectly. So the next time I pay your mum a visit, I don't expect you ter be around. OK?'

Hannah turned her face away.

The man grinned, quietly opened the door, and peered out

to find the coast clear. 'Be seein' yer then,' he called back in a low voice. 'Don't work too hard!'

'Oh – Mr Barker!' He was surprised to hear her call his name. 'Just one fing. Wot makes yer fink that you're Mum's *only* visitor?'

The man's face crumpled, but before he could respond someone approached along the corridor outside, so he quickly disappeared in the opposite direction.

After a few minutes, Hannah left the ladies' washroom, and made a shaky return to her counter in the shop. On the way she felt quite sick, so she turned off towards the entrance doors, and slipped outside to get some fresh air. It was raining heavily again, but as she stood there, trying to pull herself together, all she could think of was what she had just had to go through a few minutes before. She didn't know whether to feel hate or anger, only that if she had had a gun in her hand when that man talked to her, she would have shot him stone dead. For several minutes she stood out there, the rain seeping out of a broken drainpipe above the shop entrance dripping down and splashing her. But it didn't matter. Nothing mattered. She was too numb to think about anything other than what she was going to do now, what she could possibly do about this night-mare situation for which her mum was entirely responsible. Oh, if only her dad were home, if only Miss Hobson had not pleaded with her not to write to him, not to tell him what was going on. But she *needed* him. If ever there was a time when she needed her dad then it was now, right *now*! What could she do, she kept asking herself over and over again? Whom could she turn to to sort out this terrible mess for her? She wanted to cry, but the tears wouldn't come. She was so upset that she didn't even notice the man who was standing nearby, absolutely sopping wet in the rain which was pouring down onto his army greatcoat and uniform hat. Hannah didn't take in that the young man was smiling at her until gradually, through the torrential downpour, she saw that he was holding out his arms to her. Suddenly, her heart missed a beat. Under her breath she uttered just one word: *Sam!* The two of them gradually started to move towards each other, slowly at first, until they both broke into a trot.

'Sam!' yelled Hannah, now at the top of her voice. 'Sam . . . !'

She leapt into his arms, and he kissed her for so long and so passionately that neither of them was aware that the rain was now absolutely drenching them.

Chapter 18

Hannah had never been to Hampstead Heath before. When she was young she used to hear tales of wonderful fair-grounds that were held there on Bank Holidays, but because her mum and dad had always thought Hampstead a bit too posh for people like them, she and Louie had never been taken there. Today for Hannah, however, Hampstead was the most wonderful place in the whole wide world, because Sam was home on forty-eight hours' leave, and the two of them were together for the first time since he had been called up nearly seven months ago. It was Sunday morning, and they had climbed right to the top of the hill, where there were the most spectacular views of London far away in the distance, with St Paul's Cathedral clearly visible against the bright blue skyline, together with what were once fine city buildings, many of which had now been reduced to rubble by the brutal air power of the German Luftwaffe. But for these few golden moments at least, the only real sign that there was a war on were the dozens of silver barrage balloons that were dotted around the clear blue sky, their umbilical cables allowing the giant defensive creatures to twist, turn, and bounce up and down gently in a cool late September breeze.

Perched on the only bench on top of the hill, Hannah sat

with her arm round Sam's waist, he with his arm round hers, their heads resting against each other. She was so proud of him, so proud to see him wearing the khaki uniform of the Royal Fusiliers, especially the two stripes he had pinned to the left arm of his tunic. Hannah knew only too well the sacrifice he had made by breaking his lifelong allegiance to the Quakers and following his own conscience at a time when so many young men around the country had answered the call to arms, the call to defend their country.

'I can't tell you how strange it was,' said Sam. 'All my life I've had my own bedroom, until quite suddenly I'm sharing an army billet with eleven other blokes, all of them from different parts of the country, different walks of life, one or two of them so distressed that they actually cried themselves to sleep at night. At first, most of us were quite suspicious of each other, as though we were from a different planet or something, but gradually, once we sat around talking to each other, it was as though we'd known each other all our lives. You know, Hannah, I honestly believe that, whatever happens, me and the blokes will always remain good friends.'

'But wot about yer mum an' dad? I mean, you're only 'ome fer forty-eight 'ours. Wot're they goin' ter say when they know yer've bin ter see me and not them?'

Sam thought about this for a moment. 'As a matter of fact,' he replied, turning to look at her, 'I think they'll understand. I think they know what I feel for you.'

Hannah snuggled up to him. 'Yer mum did write ter me, yer know. It was such a lovely letter – all about Louie, an' 'ow she seems ter absolutely love livin' wiv all your people. Apparently, she even goes to the meetings. I'd love ter go an' see 'er sometime –

not walkin', though.' They both laughed. 'Fing is,' she continued, 'if I went back ter the village, it'd all come back ter me. The thought of seein' that pub again, an' the Bullocks. I don't fink I could ever fergive that woman fer wot she did, keepin' all your letters from me.'

'Well,' said Sam, 'at least you got them in the end.'

'It's not just that, Sam,' she said. 'There was somefin' really nasty about the way she kept in touch wiv my mum. It was as though they boaf 'ad their own reasons fer not wantin' me ter come 'ome. It wasn't 'til I got back that I knew why.' She turned and looked at him. 'Sam, there are a lot of fings I don't know about my mum.'

Sam was puzzled. 'What d'you mean?'

'I dunno. It was just somefin' Miss Hobson said ter me. She used ter be my schoolteacher, one of the nicest people yer could ever wish ter know. She's known my mum an' dad fer years – on and off, that is. I just get the feelin' that she knows somefin' about Mum, somefin' she don't want ter tell me about.'

'Such as?'

'If I knew, I'd know 'ow ter deal wiv it – or at least, I 'ope I would. Trouble is, deep down inside I still love Mum. I don't know why, but I do. Somewhere in 'er life she seems to 'ave got lost.'

'So where does that leave *me*?' asked Sam.

Hannah did a double-take. 'Wot d'yer mean?' she asked, taken by surprise by his question.

'I mean,' he continued, 'if and when I ever get the chance to meet her, will she take to me?'

'Don't be daft, Sam!' she snapped. 'I don't care a twopence 'a'penny if she don't!'

'*I* do.'

'Why?'

'Because I wouldn't want you to brush her under the carpet whilst I'm around,' he replied with conviction. 'You must remember, Hannah, I come from a loving family background. Good relations are important to me.'

'They're important ter me too. But it's like I told yer, Mum ain't the easiest person ter get on with. It's just that I can't bear this feelin' that I'm bein' kept in the dark about somefin'.'

'Are you going to stay on living at home?'

'Wot else can I do? Unless I join up wiv you in the army!'

'I wouldn't want that, Hannah,' he said. 'I wouldn't wish that on my worst enemy.' To her surprise, he got up and strolled across to the brim of the hill to look out aimlessly at the view.

Hannah got up and joined him. 'Wos wrong, Sam?' she asked tenderly. 'Wot is it?'

'I'm being posted, Hannah.'

Hannah suddenly felt quite cold. 'Wot does that mean?' she asked anxiously.

'It means that this leave could be the last time I see you for some time.'

Hannah felt herself seize up inside. 'Where they goin' ter send yer?'

'You know better than to ask that,' he replied gently. 'Even if I knew myself, I couldn't tell you. All I know is that it won't be a posting in *this* country.'

At that moment, a solitary air-raid siren wailed out from the distance, almost immediately joined by another, and then another, until the air was filled with the now familiar warnings from all over London.

'We should go,' said Sam, putting his arm round Hannah to lead her off.

'No,' she said. 'I ain't scared. They won't wanna come up 'ere. Let's just stay an' watch the show.'

It was several minutes before the first action took place. The droning sound of what seemed like a fleet of enemy raiders approached from the south-east to their left, but even before they arrived over London the air was cracked by the sound of what was obviously going to be a massive ack-ack defence barrage, and it was not long before shells and tracer bullets were sending out small puffs of white smoke into the sky, narrowly targeted to avoid bringing down one of the barrage balloons.

'Oh my God!' said Sam, as the first wave of bombers came into view, defying all the flack that was being thrown up at them, and scattering into position in and out and above the balloons. The ground defences were soon bolstered by a small group of RAF fighter planes, who immediately zoomed in straight at the raiders, machine guns blazing, taking them out like skittles in a bowling alley. The sky was soon a patchwork of white vapour trails mixed with bright red bursts of fire and thick black smoke which exploded from one raider after another as it plunged to the ground in flames. 'Come on, Hannah!' Sam shouted, trying to drag her away. 'We've got to get out of here!'

'No, Sam – wait!'

Once the raiders had broken through to the city, the bombing started, followed within a moment or so by huge explosions and fires bursting out on the ground. Then came a fierce aerial dogfight in and out of the barrage balloons in which the home-based fighters made one attack after another on the enemy aircraft. Several of the barrage balloons were shot at by the German machine gunners, causing huge explosions, and sending them fluttering in flames to the ground. It was an astonishing spectacle which both horrified and mesmerised Hannah. It was too much for Sam, who virtually had to drag Hannah away. However, just as they started to run back down the hill, a stray enemy raider fighter swooped low over them and opened fire.

'Down, Hannah!' yelled Sam.

Both of them threw themselves down onto their stomachs. As a rapid fire of machine-gun bullets ripped into the grass alongside them, they both rolled over and over into the undergrowth. Only when they emerged a few minutes later did they see that the enemy fighter aircraft was on fire, and within seconds it crashed further down on the other side of the heath.

Sam hugged Hannah tightly as they lay there, waiting to be quite sure that the danger had passed. 'That convinces me,' he said, holding on to her. 'Your mother was right. It was madness for you to come back to all this. Hannah, I want you to go back to Redbourne.'

'Sam!' Hannah was horrified.

'You can stay with Mother and Father at the post office,' he continued, clearly shaken by what had just happened. 'I know they'll look after you. I can talk to them. You'll be near your sister again . . .'

'No!' insisted Hannah defiantly, pulling herself away and standing up. 'I'll never go back to that place – *never*!'

Sam got up as well. 'But it's too dangerous for you here, Hannah,' he replied, visibly upset. 'I'll never rest if I know this is going on around you all the time.'

'Look, Sam,' she tried to explain, 'everyone's in the same boat. We've just got ter get through it as best we can. I'd sooner take me chances out here than go back to a place where I just don't fit in.'

'Isn't it better to stay alive?'

Hannah looked at him, looked at those beautiful blue eyes that were now so racked with tension. 'Shall I tell you something, Sam?' she asked tenderly, trying to calm him. 'I ain't scared er no bombs. As long as I've got *you*, that's all I care about. An' in any case, I'm far more worried about wot's goin' on at 'ome. Until I know fer sure, I'm tellin' yer – I won't budge.'

Dorothy Hobson hadn't called on the Adams family for some years. There seemed to be no point, for the last time she and Babs Adams had really talked, their conversation had been tense and acrimonious. But Dorothy wanted to see Hannah. She knew the turmoil the girl was going through, and she felt it her duty to keep in touch no matter how difficult it was to be in contact with the girl's mother again.

'She ain't 'ome,' said Babs at her street door in Kinloch Street. She was on edge the moment she saw Hannah's former schoolteacher standing there. 'She's gone off wiv 'er boyfriend.'

'Boyfriend?' Dorothy's face lit up. 'The boy from Redbourne? He's here?'

'As far as I know he's on leave 'til termorrer.'

'Oh – that's wonderful!' Dorothy's face lit up even more at the news. 'It'll make so much difference to Hannah.'

'D'yer want ter come in an' wait for 'er?' asked Babs.

Dorothy was taken by surprise. 'Oh, I don't think so, Mrs

Adams. But thank you for asking me. If you could just tell her that I called.'

'Right you are then,' replied Babs, about to close the door.

'On second thoughts . . .' said Dorothy, changing her mind. Babs opened the door again. 'Could you *really* spare me a few minutes? I promise I won't stay long.'

Babs hesitated just a moment, then opened the door for Dorothy to enter.

Sam seemed to have been more unnerved by the incident on top of the hill on Hampstead Heath than Hannah, who had quite clearly taken it all in her stride. He wasn't worried for himself, of course, but for the danger Hannah was in, and what might happen to her after he went away the following morning. On the top of the bus going back home to Holloway, Sam expressed his fears in the strongest way he could. 'It's not only the bombs, Hannah,' he warned. 'It's only a matter of time now before Hitler tries an invasion. He's been blasting out about it in every speech he's made over the last month or so. He won't be satisfied until he and his foul storm troopers are marching triumphantly behind a military band down the Mall.'

'It won't 'appen,' replied Hannah confidently. 'It won't *ever* 'appen – and d'yer know why? Becos people like us won't *let* it! Yer've only got ter listen to ol' Churchill. 'E ain't a fool, yer know. 'E reckons we've all got enuff guts ter see this fru.'

'Bravado, Hannah!' snapped Sam, in a rare display of irritation. 'I admire Mr Churchill, and I love *you*, but all this talk of guts and standing up to the German storm troopers is nothing but bravado. When the invasion comes, *everyone* is going to be in real danger. What Hitler has done in other countries has been really brutal. How can the likes of the Home Guard resist that kind of force with shovels and pitchforks?'

'Yer know, it's funny, Sam. I know 'ow you was brought up an' all that, but I've never fawt of you as a defeatist.'

'I'm not being a defeatist, Hannah!' insisted Sam. 'I'm a realist.'

'So wot der we do – just sit down an' open the door for 'em?'

'I think all women and children ought to be evacuated to safety,' he replied. 'Wars should be fought by men, not women.'

Hannah scoffed. 'That's so old fashioned, Sam,' she replied jokily. 'Women 'ave got as much part ter play in this war as men. As soon as I'm eighteen next year, *I'm* goin' ter join up meself.'

Sam swung a horrified look at her. 'You – what?'

'Wos wrong wiv that?' replied Hannah, surprised by his re-action. 'Let's face it, it's better than 'angin' round sellin' shovels and broomsticks in Woolworf's!'

Conscious that their conversation was proving quite riveting to an old lady sitting in the seat just in front of them, Sam moved his head closer to Hannah and lowered his voice. 'I would *hate* it, Hannah,' he insisted. 'It's one thing for men to take up arms, but the idea of women in uniform is absolutely appalling.'

Hannah remained stubbornly tight-lipped.

'But that's not the real reason, is it?' he asked.

She turned to him. 'Wot d'yer mean?'

'The war isn't the reason why you want to join up. It's because of what's going on at home.'

Hannah went silent. Sam had touched a raw nerve.

'What happened, Hannah?' he pressed. 'What's happened in your family that's giving you so much pain?'

Hannah hesitated, then spoke. 'It's somefin' ter do wiv *me*,' she replied solemnly. 'That's all I can tell yer, Sam. All I know is 'ow I 'eard Mum an' Dad gettin' at each uvver one night. I was only a kid at the time, no more than five or six I reckon. I 'eard this screamin' match goin' on downstairs, so I come out of my bedroom, sat down on the stairs, and listened. I couldn't 'ear everyfin' they said, but it was definitely about me – exactly *wot* I've never known ter this day. It was all such a jumble, so nasty an' – oh, I dunno – so personal.'

'About *you*?'

'As far as I could make out,' she replied, 'about boaf me an' Dad. Anyway, I more or less forgot about it all this time – until Miss Hobson said somefin' that made me fink . . .'

Sam waited for her to continue.

'I don't know, Sam,' she said at last, with a sigh. 'I just don't know. But wotever it is, sooner or later somebody's got ter tell me.'

It had been a long time since Dorothy Hobson had sat in the front parlour in Kinloch Street. She had never set foot in the Adams' house since that day many years ago, that eventful, extraordinary day. However, the parlour itself hadn't changed a bit since the last time she had seen it. The faded, peeling wallpaper was still the same, the blue velvet sofa and two matching armchairs, which had been bought second-hand in the furniture shop just round the corner, were just as worn as ever, and the spring protruding from the side of the sofa still hadn't been repaired. But what Dorothy noticed most of all was the musty smell, which for her, with her weak lungs, gave the room such a stifling atmosphere that there were moments when she could hardly breathe, and as she sat there on that sofa talking to Babs in one of the armchairs, she just wished the woman would get up and open the window. But she persevered, for she had important matters to discuss with Hannah and Louie's mother. 'I'm sorry, Mrs Adams,' she said, with great dignity, 'but I still think it's a great mistake not to have told Hannah, especially now that she's old enough to understand.'

'I disagree,' replied Babs, who had made matters worse by lighting up a fag. 'Hann may seem old enough ter you, but ter me she's got a chip on 'er shoulder the size of a football. I mean, just look at 'er, up an' runnin' off from 'er foster-parents wivout even a by yer leave. Yer've no idea 'ow 'umili-atin' it was fer me when those flatfoots walked through that door. Fer all *she* cared I could've bin chucked in prison fer wot she done.'

Dorothy hated the way Babs Adams talked. To an English language teacher it sounded so fractured, so lazy, so offensive to the ear. 'As a matter of fact, Mrs Adams, I happen to think that Hannah is quite an intelligent girl.'

'Wiv a mind of 'er own.'

'Is that such a bad thing?'

'It is when somebody else 'as ter take the can back!'

'You know,' continued Dorothy, 'when I talked to Hannah about what happened during her evacuation, I can't help feeling that it was a mistake to send her to those particular people. I saw Mavis Reynolds, our geography teacher, a few days ago, and she said that if Hannah had been allowed to go to the people whom Louise is living with now, none of this would have happened. But I have to say, surely you must admire what she did, walking on her own all that way from Hertfordshire to London. It shows great spirit.'

'Yeah, it does,' replied Babs flippantly. 'Fer someone as stubborn as 'er!'

Dorothy knew that it wasn't going to be easy to get through to Babs. From the first moment she had set eyes on the woman, even before that disastrous evening, she had disliked her. 'The point is, Mrs Adams,' she said, 'what are we going to do about Hannah?'

'*We?*' As usual, Babs was taking umbrage at every word Dorothy spoke. 'Where do *you* come into this?' she asked sarcastically.

'I've known Hannah a long time,' replied Dorothy, refusing to be provoked. 'I don't want her to be hurt.'

'Yer didn't fink about that, did yer – that night wiv Len?'

Dorothy found Babs's remark deeply offensive. 'You know very well,' she said, trying to recover her composure, 'that all that was completely out of my control. I never wanted it to happen, and I certainly didn't encourage it. And in any case, you know very well that the way your husband behaved was – quite simply – an act of defiance.'

'Defiance?'

'Against you, Mrs Adams,' said Dorothy plainly. 'Against you for what you'd done over the years.'

It took a brief moment for Babs to take this in, but when she did, she calmly got up, and threw her fag end into the fire grate. 'You fink yer know, don't yer?' she said quietly. Then she turned to look straight at Dorothy. 'Nice, sweet, innocent schoolteacher, loved by all the kids at school, butter wouldn't melt in yer mouf. But they ain't *your* kids, Miss 'Obson. And neivver are *my* kids. You don't know wot it's like ter live wiv a man who don't care a skew-whiff about yer. You don't know wot it's like ter know that the man you're sleepin' wiv every night loves somebody else, and can't get 'er out of 'is rotten mind.' She slowly went across to stare Dorothy straight in the eyes. 'So wot am I expected ter do, schoolteacher?' Embarrassed, Dorothy started to get up. 'No!' insisted Babs, pushing her back down again. 'I've listened ter you, now *you* can listen ter me. Wot 'appened 'ere that night, before my very eyes, before I even 'ad a chance ter know wot was goin' on, well I tell yer – it's stuck wiv me – *'ere*,' she thumped her chest with the palm of her hand, 'right *'ere*, ev'ry day, ev'ry bleedin' night of my life. OK, OK, so you 'ad nuffin' ter do wiv it, it was all Len an' nuffin' but Len, but you liked it, din't yer? All those fings 'e said about you, yer liked it. And d'yer know why? Becos yer knew that yer was goin' ter end up a spinster, an' ol' grey-'aired spinster, who was never goin' ter know wot it's like ter 'ave wot any uvver woman could 'ave!'

Dorothy had had quite enough. She got up and stormed off out of the room. Before she had reached the front door, however, Babs called out to her. 'Wot's wrong, Miss 'Obson? Gettin' too close ter the bone for yer?'

Dorothy suddenly swung round from the front door and responded to her. 'And what about you, Mrs Adams?' she asked, without raising her voice. 'How much love have *you* ever shown your husband? How many times have you seen him go off to work in the morning, making him feel really sad about having to leave you for the day, so that the only thing he can think of during that day is how happy he'll be when he sees you again that evening? A man is like a child, Mrs Adams. He needs love, care, and protection. He needs to feel wanted. Can you honestly say you've given him all that?'

'I gave 'im kids, din't I?' growled Babs.

'Yes, Mrs Adams,' replied Dorothy, quite calmly. 'If only they could have been his own.'

Without saying another word, she quietly opened the door and left.

Chapter 19

Charlie Brend's sweet shop in Hornsey Road was nothing less than an institution. When the kids came out of school every afternoon, there was no question of going straight home before crossing the road to down one of his lemon or raspberry sherbet drinks. Although they seemed to take forever to make, with soda gas bubbling up in huge glass bowls, they were always worth the wait. And at a penny a glass, they were a real pinch. When Hannah was still at school, she and Louie would never think of passing the shop without stopping for one of Charlie's 'specials', and for old times' sake that was what she was doing today. However, business there wasn't too good these days, especially now that so many of the kids had been evacuated for the second time. Nonetheless, despite the bomb blast that had blown out the front window of his shop, those glass bowls had somehow managed to survive.

'So, Charlie,' said Hannah, slurping down her penny lemon sherbet drink, 'wot yer goin' ter do when Jerry comes in fer one of these?'

Charlie laughed, something he didn't do very often, for his well-worn old face always seemed to be scowling. 'Bit er cyanide fer that lot in the mix should do the job!'

Hannah chuckled. She had always had a lot of time for Charlie, for apart from his legendary soft drinks, he was the eyes and ears of the neighbourhood. 'I 'ope yer wouldn't do the same fer any of *our* boys?' she said.

'Chance'd be a fine fing,' he replied, wiping the glass bowls with a clean cloth. 'They've called up most er the lads that used to come in 'ere regular. Includin' yer dad. 'Ave yer 'eard from 'im lately?'

Hannah felt a sudden wave of despair. 'Not fer some time,' she replied. 'S'ppose 'e's forgotten all about us.'

'Ha!' retorted Charlie. 'Fat chance er that, specially you – apple of 'is eye!'

'Come off it, Charlie!'

'It's true, I'm tellin' yer.'

'Can I 'ave an 'alfpenny liquorice stick please, Charlie?' A small, snotty-nosed boy had burst into the shop holding up a halfpenny coin, and rushed straight up to the counter.

'Wait yer turn, young man!' snapped Charlie. 'Can't yer see I'm talkin' ter the lady?'

The boy glared at Hannah.

'Wot yer talkin' about, Charlie?' asked Hannah, sipping the rest of her drink. 'Dad's favourite's always bin Louie.'

'Don't you believe it!' replied Charlie, wiping his hands on the clean cloth. 'When Len Adams was in 'ere a coupla months ago, 'e never stopped talkin' about yer – said if 'e'd've bin 'ome at the time, 'e'd never've sent you pair off fer no evacuation.'

Hannah nearly choked on her glass of lemon sherbet. 'Wot yer talkin' about?' she asked. 'Dad ain't bin 'ome since he got called up a year ago.'

'Then 'e's got a bleedin' double.'

'Can I 'ave my liquorice stick?' demanded the small boy impatiently.

Charlie swung an angry glare at him over the counter. 'Ain't yer ol' man ever tawt you no manners, Nick Fiddick?' he growled, turning round to take a liquorice stick out of a glass jar on the shelf behind him. 'One er these days, if you don't learn some manners, I'm goin' ter separate you from yer breff!' He snatched the halfpenny from the boy, and handed over the liquorice stick. The boy rushed out of the shop, blowing Charlie a raspberry as he went.

'Dad come in 'ere – a coupla months ago?' spluttered Hannah. 'Are yer sure?'

'Listen, me gel,' said Charlie, leaning towards her over the top of the glass bulbs. 'I've known your dad since he was the same age as that little sod who was in 'ere just now. So if I don't know who I was talkin' to, then I'm really goin' round the bend. The only diff'rence now is that Len Adams wears an army uniform.'

Hannah was really taken aback. ''Ow long was 'e home?'

Charlie shrugged. ''Aven't the faintest,' he replied. ''E only ever come in 'ere once, ter buy a packet er Woodbines an' 'ave a good ol' chinwag. Sounds like 'e'd 'ad a pretty rough time of it at Dunkirk, though.'

Hannah's eyes widened. 'Dunkirk?' she gasped. ''E was at Dunkirk?'

'Nearly copped 'is lot by all accounts,' replied Charlie gravely. ''Is arm was still in a sling from a shrapnel wound. Don't your mum tell yer nuffin'?'

Hannah left Charlie's shop in a daze. Although home was less than a minute or so away, she made a deliberate detour via Tollington Road, just so that she could take in all that Charlie had just told her. So her mum had lied when she told her and Louie that their dad was all for their being evacuated? And why hadn't she told them that their dad had been home on leave instead of that lie about not hearing a word from him since he'd been called up? And then she remembered what her dad had written to her on that airmail letter whilst she was staying with the Bullocks up at Redbourne: *I got your address from your mum who wrote and told me that your having a real nice time in your new digs and that the folks looking after you are real nice . . .* That lie from her mum really hurt. *I couldn't take it if anything happened to your mum she means the world to me . . .* Hannah squirmed when she thought about seeing her mum in the Anderson that night. *Anyway you two remember to do what your mum tells you. While I'm away she makes the decisions not me . . . I dont know when I'll see you both again . . .*

Lies, lies, and all for what? Hannah finally plucked up the courage to go home.

Kinloch Street was already plunged into darkness, for it was way past blackout time, which meant that if the Luftwaffe were going to follow the same pattern by raiding London soon after dark, then the air-raid siren would be wailing out any minute now.

Once inside the front passage, Hannah made sure she had pulled the blackout curtain back over the door before switching on the light. She did the same in the back parlour and scullery. She wasn't surprised that her mum was nowhere around. Over the past few nights she was well aware that Babs had taken to spending the evenings out and about, but as what her mum now did made very little difference to her Hannah never even bothered to ask her where she'd been. After a while, however, her curiosity began to get the better of her. After the night she had caught her mum down in the Anderson shelter with Tom Barker, she had vowed that no matter how bad the air-raids got, she would never set foot inside the place, which was the reason she had spent so many nights sheltering in the cupboard under the stairs. But over the past day or so she had become strangely obsessed by the thought of the Anderson, to the extent that she couldn't get the place out of her mind. So now she took the torch hanging on a hook by the scullery back door, and went outside into the back yard. It was an odd feeling to be out there, for as the torch beam picked out the Anderson shelter, dug deep into the ground, memories came flooding back of how it used to be before the war, when she, Louie, and their dad used to play all kinds of games in the tiny space there, games which always seemed to scare off every back yard moggie that strayed over the wall. The shelter was a real monstrosity, with its curved corrugated steel roof and earth piled all over the top of it. Hannah hated it. As she flashed the torch beam over the outside of the monster, all she could think was that whoever invented it should be made to sleep in it himself. She moved closer to the steps leading down into the shelter and paused for a moment, memories of that fateful night thumping away in her mind, still not quite sure that she was doing the right thing. Finally, however, she plucked up enough courage to pull back the heavy blackout curtain. The moment she flashed her torch beam down there, she was completely shocked by what she saw. The shelter was flooded with water right up to the bottom step of the entrance.

'Satisfied now?'

Hannah jumped so much at hearing her mum's voice suddenly just behind her that she dropped the torch down into the flooded shelter. 'Mum!' she gasped.

'Pretty, in't it?' replied Babs, in the dark. 'When they dug this place out they didn't tell us we'd be livin' in the middle of a pond! So wot der they do? They give us a bleedin' stirrup pump ter get rid er the water! If they fink *I'm* goin' ter—'

''Ow long 'as it bin like this?'

'Can't remember,' replied Babs, going back to the house. 'Since all that rain the uvver week.'

'So where've yer bin sleepin' every night?' called Hannah as she followed her inside.

'Where d'yer fink?' replied Babs, in the scullery. 'Round the public shelter end of Arthur Road. Don't turn on that light 'til yer pull the curtain.'

Hannah came into the scullery, drew the blackout curtain over the door, closed it, and switched on the light. '*You've* bin goin' round the public shelter?'

'Yer don't fink I'm goin' ter stay in this place in the middle of a bleedin' air raid, do yer? *You* may be stupid, but *I* ain't!'

As Hannah watched her mum light up a fag, she suddenly felt a wave of guilt. All these past nights she had thought that Babs had been off having a fling somewhere, when all the time she was doing the same as everyone else – taking cover. Nonetheless, there were a lot of questions she wanted answering, but she waited until her mum had lit her fag. 'Why didn't yer tell me Dad came home a coupla months ago?'

Although she did her best not to show it, Babs was visibly taken aback. 'Wot makes yer fink that?' was the only answer she could draw on at such short notice.

'Charlie said Dad came in the shop,' said Hannah. ''Is arm was in a sling from Dunkirk.'

'Charlie Brend!' growled Babs, pulling up the collar of her

fake leopardskin coat. 'Such a bleedin' ol' woman that one – never stops 'is gossip!'

'Is it true, Mum?'

Babs quickly realised that it wasn't going to be easy to wriggle out of this one. ''E only come for a coupla days.' She shrugged. 'One day in, next day out. 'E 'ad ter get back ter 'ospital down the barracks somewhere.'

'Why din't yer write an' tell me an' Lou?' demanded Hannah.

''Cos 'e didn't want me to,' replied Babs, cool and calmly, burying one of her hands deep inside her coat pocket. ''E said yer'd only worry, espeshully if yer'd 'eard about Dunkirk.'

'Well of course I 'eard about Dunkirk!' snapped Hannah. '*Everyone* knew about what'd 'appened at Dunkirk! It was a bleedin' bloodbarf!'

'So now yer know.' Babs started to collect the things together that she would be taking to the public shelter for the night.

'No, Mum!' insisted Hannah forcibly. 'I *don't* know. I 'aven't 'ad any news from Dad since that airmail letter 'e sent ages ago. If I'd known 'e'd got injured, I'd've worried meself sick! An' so would Lou!'

'So then 'e was right not ter tell yer, wasn't 'e?' retorted Babs, struggling to tie up the lightweight mattress she was taking with her. 'An' in any case, I don't know wot yer goin' on about. By all accounts 'e's perfectly OK now, got 'is arm out er the sling, an' probably gone off back ter duty somewhere.'

'Mum!' said Hannah, unable to comprehend the way Babs was playing it all down. ''Ow can yer talk like this? 'E *is* my dad, yer know. I do 'appen ter love 'im.'

Babs suddenly slammed the mattress down on the stone floor, and turned on her. 'Now look 'ere, you!' she spluttered angrily.

'Don't you get on your 'igh 'orse wiv me! When yer dad come 'ome, all 'e wanted ter do was rest. 'E din't want no fuss, 'e din't want me nor you nor Lou runnin' around gettin' all worked up just 'cos 'e'd got 'is arm in a sling!'

'Mum . . .' Hannah tried to protest.

'No, Hannah!' snapped Babs, overriding her. 'Now you listen ter me! I don't 'ave ter answer ter you fer every single fing I do. You 'eard wot that flatfoot said. In the eyes of the law yer still a minor, Hann. While yer dad's away, *I* make the decisions for yer, *I'm* the one who knows wot's best for yer. Now if yer dad tells me that 'e doesn't want yer to know somefin', then as far as I'm concerned – so be it! You say 'e's yer dad, an' that yer love 'im. Well, it may not 'ave occurred to yer that I'm 'is wife, an' it's just possible that *I* love 'im too!'

'Sounds like it, Mum,' replied Hannah sourly, 'don't it?'

Babs was just on the verge of going for her when the air-raid siren wailed out. 'If yer take my tip,' she said, quickly fluttering around to pick up her mattress and carrying bag, 'yer'll get round ter the shelter wiv me.' She went to the door. 'I don't fink yer dad would like ter know that we'd boaf bin blown ter pieces!'

In utter disbelief, Hannah watched her go, the front door slamming behind her as she went. For a few minutes she just stood there in a daze, trying to work out in her mind what kind of uncaring mum she had; what kind of person it was that was such a bundle of tightly kept secrets. But it wasn't very long before the nightly aerial bombardment outside started to shake the very foundations of the small house, so she slowly went out into the passage and took up her usual nightly position in the cupboard beneath the stairs.

* * *

Dorothy Hobson lived with her elder sister Tilda in a pleasant red-bricked terraced Edwardian house, set on four floors in Coniston Road, Muswell Hill. This leafy area of North London had long been a favourite of the middle classes, not only because of its wonderful views of the majestic Alexandra Palace on top of the hill in Alexandra Park, but because of the fresh, invigorating air that set it apart from the stifling atmosphere of Central London. To get there, Hannah had to take a single-decker bus from behind the tube station at Finsbury Park, something she had never done before, and there were times during the journey when she became quite nervous at the steep climb the bus had to make before it reached its ultimate destination at Muswell Hill Broadway. Nonetheless, it was a journey that she felt she now had to make, for Miss Hobson was about the only person she could turn to for the kind of advice she needed to unravel the secrets within her family.

'My dear!' exclaimed Dorothy, the moment she opened her front door to find Hannah there. 'What an absolutely wonderful surprise!'

'I'm really sorry ter trouble yer, Miss 'Obson,' she said, hesitating on the doorstep, 'but I remember yer gave me yer address an' . . .'

'Come in, Hannah! Come in!' said Dorothy, opening the door wide to let Hannah in. 'You need no excuses to visit me whatsoever!'

Hannah followed her through the hall into the spacious sitting room at the front of the house.

'Tilda!' called the schoolteacher, with modest excitement. 'Look who's here! We've got a visitor!'

The woman who stood up to greet them had a lovely crop

of dark brown hair, streaked with grey, and tied in a bun behind her head, and tiny metal-rimmed spectacles that seemed to slightly enlarge her equally tiny eyes.

'Tilda, this is Hannah Adams,' said Dorothy, bubbling with delight. 'One of my girls from the school.'

'Ah!' said Tilda with an engaging smile, holding out her hand to Hannah. 'We know all about *this* young lady, don't we? Hallo, my dear. I'm Dorothy's sister.'

''Allo, Miss,' replied Hannah, shyly shaking hands. 'Look, I didn't mean ter barge in on yer like this. I could always come back some uvver time?'

'Nonsense!' replied Dorothy. 'Tilda and I were just about to have a cup of tea. We always have a cup of tea about this time on a Sunday afternoon, don't we, dear?'

'Always!' repeated Tilda.

Dorothy bustled around, patting a cushion on the armchair where she wanted Hannah to sit. 'You have a nice little chat with Tilda whilst I go and put the kettle on.'

'No, that's my job!' said Tilda, going to the door. 'You leave that to me. I'm sure you two have a lot to talk about. Back in a jiff!'

Once her sister had left the room, Dorothy's welcome took on a more serious note. 'So, Hannah,' she asked tenderly, sitting down opposite her. 'How are things? How's the job going at Woolworth's?'

'It's OK,' replied Hannah, with little enthusiasm. 'At least I've got money in me pocket, an' I do get one Saturday afternoon off in four.'

'That's nice. And what else?' asked Dorothy pointedly. 'What's been happening?'

'I wish I knew, Miss,' Hannah replied. 'There're so many fings I wish I knew about. So many fings that people're keepin' from me.'

Dorothy's smile faded.

'Did *you* know that my dad came 'ome on leave a coupla months ago?'

It took Dorothy a moment to take this in. 'No,' she replied. 'I didn't know that, Hannah.'

'Mum kept it from me,' continued Hannah. 'Gord knows why. An' when I ask 'er why she din't tell, she comes up wiv all kinds er fancy stories. D'yer know, I've only ever 'ad one letter from 'im since the day 'e was called up. Fer all I know 'e's written a lot more than Mum's told me. It's as though she wants ter keep 'im away from boaf me *an'* Louie.'

Dorothy sighed. 'Have you – talked this over with her?'

'Mum doesn't know 'ow ter talk fings over,' replied Hannah tersely. 'When she talks, you listen. That's 'ow she is.'

Dorothy lowered her head.

'I just need someone ter talk to,' continued Hannah. 'Someone ter tell me wot's bin goin' on all this time that I don't know about.' She hesitated for a moment. 'The last time I saw yer, you said if ever I wanted ter talk fings over, I could come an' see you.'

'I'm glad you did, Hannah.'

'Yer see,' continued Hannah, 'I know you told me not ter write ter Dad ter tell 'im about Mum . . .'

Dorothy was suddenly alarmed. 'You didn't, did you?' she asked tensely. 'You didn't write to him?'

Hannah shook her head. 'No, I didn't,' she replied. 'Because I think wot you said was probably right. The only fing is – the only fing that worried me after you an' me talked – was wot you said about 'ow yer knew 'ow difficult it was fer me tryin' ter cope wiv a situation like this, especially under the circumstances. I never really understood wot yer meant, an' it's preyed on me mind ever since. Wot *did* yer mean, Miss Hobson?'

Dorothy was suddenly riddled with guilt and apprehension. She got up from her seat, and went to look out of the window. 'If I told you, Hannah,' she said in the most strained voice, 'I'd be betraying everything I know about your mother and father.' She turned to look back at her. 'D'you think I would be right to do that, Hannah?'

Hannah thought about this for a moment. 'Works boaf ways, don't it?' she suggested. 'I mean, if somefin' ain't right between Mum 'n' Dad, don't yer fink I 'ave the *right* ter know about it?'

'Yes, you do, Hannah.' Dorothy came back and sat opposite her again. 'But I was only your schoolteacher. It's your parents' responsibility to tell you – what one day they will *have* to tell you.'

'That day won't ever come, Miss,' Hannah assured her. 'If you don't tell me – no one will.'

Alexandra Park was virtually deserted. With the October nights now drawing in fast, it was no place to be after dark, especially with night-time air raids now such a part of London life. Nonetheless, as Hannah and her former schoolteacher strolled slowly up the hill, Alexandra Palace looked quite magnificent up on top there, bathed in the deep hues of a full-blooded sunset. When they felt they had walked and talked enough, Hannah and Dorothy found the nearest wooden bench, and sat there for a few minutes. On the way, Dorothy had told Hannah everything she knew about how her fellow teachers at the school had felt about the way Babs Adams had bundled Hannah and Louie off to the countryside only to satisfy her own need for freedom. However, the real reason Dorothy had suggested those few minutes alone in the park with Hannah was to get out of her system the secret she had kept for so long, even from her own sister. 'Here,' she said, taking a small photo snapshot out of her handbag.

Hannah took the photo from her, and stared at it. 'It's Dad,' she said, surprised.

'Yes,' admitted Dorothy, watching tensely for Hannah's reactions. 'It was taken a few years before the war, when you were quite young.'

Hannah was quite taken aback. 'Where d'yer get it from?' she asked.

Dorothy took a deep breath. 'He gave it to me.'

Hannah stared straight into her schoolteacher's eyes, which were now reflecting the last rays of the sun. 'Dad gave *you* 'is picture?' she asked.

'He gave me a lot of pictures, Hannah,' replied Dorothy, with great anguish. 'They used to arrive from time to time at the school, in plain white envelopes. Look at the back.'

Hannah turned over the photo, and gasped. Scrawled there were the words: *I won't ever give up. L.*

Hannah was truly shocked. 'You – an' *Dad*?' she asked.

'No, Hannah,' replied Dorothy, taking back the photo and looking at it. 'Just him – not me. From the first time I met him, when he came one day to collect you and Louise at the school gates, he became – for want of a better word – infatuated with me. From that moment on, I got photos with things like this on the back. Then you may remember yourself that he took it upon himself to collect you and Louise more and more often. I tried to stop him from doing so, but he just wouldn't give up. On one occasion, he followed me all the way to the bus stop at Finsbury Park. He told me that he wanted to see me, for us to go out together, to have a drink in a pub, or that he'd even take me to a good meal somewhere. I just couldn't believe that he was doing such a thing, a married man with two children.'

Hannah was dazed. 'Did yer tell 'im that?' she asked.

'With all my heart and soul, Hannah,' she pleaded. 'You've got to believe me.'

Hannah got up, put her hands in her coat pocket, and stared up unseeingly at the sun just casting the last rays of sunset across the glass dome of the palace. 'Did Mum know about this?'

'Not right away,' replied Dorothy, putting the photo back into her handbag. 'Not until I told her.'

Hannah swung with a start. 'You *told* Mum?'

'It was the only thing I could do. If I hadn't . . . well, I'm afraid it would have gone on forever behind her back. But it wasn't easy. When I went to see her at your house, she didn't believe a word I said. She called me all sorts of horrible names.' She got up from the bench, and moved alongside Hannah, both of them now staring up at the magical sunset. 'Then when your father came home and found me there, everything became so unreal . . . it haunts me to this day.'

Hannah turned to look at her.

'He said he loved me,' said Dorothy. 'He said he wanted to leave your mother, and come to live with me.'

Hannah was utterly devastated.

Dorothy turned to look at her. 'I told your mother that it was all fantasy,' she insisted. 'I told her that nothing in the whole wide world would ever persuade me to have a relationship with another woman's husband, that everything your father was doing was of *his* making, and not mine. Unfortunately, your mother didn't believe me. She called both me and your father terrible names, and shouted at him about things – things that I'd never heard before.'

'Wot fings?' asked Hannah.

At this point, Dorothy virtually seized up. She had said enough, and could say no more. 'About you, Hannah. About you – *and* Louise.'

Hannah gave her a pleading look. There were tears in her eyes.

'No, Hannah,' said Dorothy, herself distressed by the trauma of all she had just revealed. 'I can't tell you any more. I've told you all this because that's what you wanted, because I happen to think that you're now old enough, and adult enough, to cope with it. But the rest is up to your mother. All I can say is that everything I've told you is the absolute truth.'

'Then can I ask yer just one question, please?'

Hannah's frankness took Dorothy by surprise. 'Of course,' she replied.

Hannah paused for just a moment, then asked shrewdly: 'D'yer love my dad, Miss 'Obson?'

Dorothy, standing there bathed in the crimson sunset, felt as though her whole body had caught fire. 'Hannah,' she replied, 'that's a question I would never dare to answer.'

Chapter 20

Thank God for half-day closing! That's how Hannah and Betty felt when, on the following Thursday afternoon, they both made a quick exit through the back doors of Woolworth's in Enkel Street. Betty was in a particularly buoyant mood because Phil was coming home on forty-eight hours' leave from the Royal Air Force, where he had just finished an amazingly quick officer cadet training course.

'He reckons he'll get his wings in no time at all,' said Betty, as she hastily took her leave of Hannah to catch her bus in Seven Sisters Road. 'They're churning out pilots quicker than they can keep up with making the planes for them. But at least I've got him for forty-eight hours – forty-eight glorious hours!'

Hannah watched her friend rushing off in a plethora of excitement, thrilled that at least someone's relationship was blooming so happily, which is more than she could say for her and Sam. Still no word from him, even though he had been gone now for several weeks. It was so depressing, not knowing where he had been posted to, or even if he was alive or dead. The only thing she *was* sure of, however, was that, no matter what, Sam would be faithful to her – his personal beliefs were as firm as a rock, and he would never desert her. She only wished the same could be said about her mum and dad's relationship.

As she strolled along Roden Street, the first thing she saw was the school building at the far end, the school she had gone to from the age of four until she left at fourteen. But ever since her visit to Dorothy Hobson up at her home in Muswell Hill, the sight of the red-bricked school had taken on a new significance for Hannah. How could her mum and dad have really loved each other after what the schoolteacher had told her, she asked herself over and over again? Ever since that afternoon up at Alexandra Park, Hannah's mind had been haunted by the image of her dad waiting outside the school gates in the hope of meeting up with the woman he was obsessed with. And if that wasn't bad enough, what was it Miss Hobson had said about Hannah's mum having to be the one to tell her something about her and Louie? *What* did she have to tell her? By the time she got back home to Kinloch Street, Hannah decided that she could wait no longer. If she was going to get these family secrets out of the way once and forever, now was the time to do it.

However, the moment she opened the front door, she sensed that something rather odd was going on, and when she went into the front parlour, she soon found out why.

'Hallo, Hannah.'

Maggie Bullock remained seated on the sofa as Hannah walked in.

Hannah was thunderstruck.

'Isn't this nice?' said Babs, who had laid out her best china teaset for her visitor. 'Mrs Bullock has come all the way down just ter see 'ow you're gettin' on.' She turned to Maggie. 'It's so good er yer, considerin' 'ow dangerous it is in Lond'n these days.'

Maggie nodded graciously. 'And how *are* you getting on, my dear?' she asked Hannah.

Hannah wanted to turn and go straight out, but Maggie continued talking. 'We miss you, Hannah,' she said. 'Mr Bullock was only saying the other day how he missed your bright, cheery face around the place. We were so very sad when you . . . oh, well, that's in the past. At least you're safe and well, so thank God for that.'

'Where're yer manners, Hann?' asked Babs. 'Come an' sit down an' talk ter Mrs Bullock, thank 'er fer comin' down all this way ter see yer.' She picked up the tea tray. 'I'm goin' off ter put the kettle on. This pot needs topping up.' She called from the door as she went. 'We've 'ad such a luvvely chinwag before yer came.'

After Babs had left the room, Hannah remained standing. 'Wot d'yer *really* come 'ere for?' she asked sourly.

Maggie's expression changed immediately. 'You're a very clever girl, Hannah,' she replied. 'Getting out of the back door like that must have taken a lot of ingenuity. It took Mr Bullock quite a time to put that latch together again. How on earth did you do it?'

'You din't come 'ere ter ask me about yer back door.'

Maggie smiled. 'No, Hannah,' she admitted, with her customary smile. 'I came to apologise.'

Hannah eyed her suspiciously. 'Oh yes?' she asked disbelievingly.

'When Mr Bullock and I first took you in for adoption,' said Maggie, 'I was still reeling from an unhappy period of my life that I found difficult to cope with. I'd always desperately wanted a daughter of my own, someone I could sit and talk to, especially as I grew older. But when I lost my baby, and was told that I could never have another one, I felt as though my whole world had come to an end. The evacuation scheme gave me the chance to start all over again. I could look for a daughter to adopt, even if it was only for the duration of the war.' She paused, and looked with pleading eyes up at Hannah. 'As far as *I* was concerned, Hannah,' she said poignantly, '*you* were that daughter.'

'So,' asked Hannah, 'is that why yer treated me like a servant?'

Maggie got up from the sofa, and stood looking out through the lace curtains at the window. 'You know, my dear,' she said, 'I've made quite a lot of mistakes in my life, but treating you the way I did was probably the worst mistake of all. Ever since you ran away, I've deeply regretted it. Don't ask me why I did it – that's something I'll never know. But something inside me wanted to keep you, to hold on to you, and not to share you with anyone else.'

'Ter take control of me, yer mean?'

Maggie flinched, but didn't turn round. 'I know it was painful for you, Hannah,' she said, 'but it was painful for me too. It's a real battle inside to know that you're doing something so wrong, so awful, and yet there is nothing you can do to stop yourself from doing it. But I must tell you this . . .' She slowly turned round to face Hannah. 'I swear to God that I never ever meant you any harm.'

Hannah thought carefully before answering. 'And what about the gel who come before me?' she asked tersely. 'The gel who people in the village 'ardly ever saw, the gel who ended up in a grave in the churchyard? Did yer never mean '*er* any 'arm neivver?'

Maggie was visibly stung. 'Sheila . . . poor Sheila,' she said with growing emotion. 'She didn't deserve to die. She was as harmless as a field mouse.'

'People kill mice, don't they?'

Hannah's cryptic comment wounded Maggie, so she leant her hands on the back of the sofa. 'Did you know that we had to leave the Cock and Crow?'

Hannah was totally taken aback. 'Leave the pub?' she asked incredulously. 'Wot yer talkin' about?'

'Shortly after you left,' continued Maggie, 'we had a visit from the people at the brewery. They said the figures weren't adding up – adding up, that is, to *their* advantage. They spent nearly three hours looking over the place from top to bottom – the list of criticisms they came up with was as long as my arm. And that was it, really. Our lease was terminated, and we were – as you would probably say – kicked out. Kicked out after twenty-five years service, can you believe? Twenty-five years of *good* service to our customers, even if we didn't always come up to their expectations as the perfect pub landlords.'

'So – wot 'appens now?' asked Hannah, who found it difficult to believe what Maggie was saying.

'Oh – we've moved on,' replied Maggie. 'Still in the pub business, but not in Redbourne. We've gone to East Anglia, Norfolk, a small village near a place called Swaffham. A different location, a different brewer – hopefully a less demanding brewer.'

It took Hannah a few moments to take this in, so she sat down on an armchair. 'So wot's all this got ter do wiv me?'

Maggie moved round from behind the sofa, and went to her. 'We want you back, Hannah,' she said.

Hannah swung an astonished look at her. 'Are yer mad or somefin'?'

'No, I'm not, my dear,' replied Maggie. 'But what I *would* like to do is try to make things up to you, try to convince you that I'm really more worthy than I've shown so far.' She sat down on the sofa facing Hannah again. 'I've already spoken to your mother about it, and she thinks it's a grand idea. We both think it's far too dangerous for you to stay in London the way things are. Mr Bullock has asked me to tell you that we've kept a most beautiful bedroom for you in the new pub – it's much bigger than that poky little attic room you had to put up with before. You would so love it, Hannah. Even as I speak he's painting it up so that you wouldn't be able to resist it.'

'That's where you're wrong,' replied Hannah, getting up quickly. 'I *can* resist comin' ter live wiv you again, an' I *will*. What do you take me for, Mrs Bullock? D'yer really fink, after all I went fru wiv you, that I believe one single fing yer say?'

'I don't ask you to believe me, Hannah,' replied Maggie. 'All I ask is that you give me another chance to prove that I *can* be a mother to you, even if it's only a foster-mother.'

At that moment, Babs came back into the room, carrying the replenished teapot. 'Did you tell Hannah, Mrs Bullock,' she said buoyantly, ''ow wot a good time Louie's 'aving wiv her Quaker friends down the post office? Apparently, she absolutely loves her new mum. I must say I'm beginnin' ter get quite jealous.' She looked up to find Hannah and Maggie staring at each other. 'Ooh – sorry,' she said hopefully. ''Ave I interrupted somefin' important?'

'No, Mrs Adams,' said Maggie. 'Hannah and I were just having a little talk about . . . our new circumstances.'

'Oh, I see,' said Babs. 'Well, I must say, Hann, this pub up in Norfolk sounds a luvvely place ter go to. At least yer wouldn't 'ave ter live under the stairs every night!'

'I'm not goin' ter no pub in Norfolk,' replied Hannah sourly. '*This* is me 'ome. *This* is where I stay!'

Babs swung a despairing look at Maggie, who slowly shook her head.

'Well, d'you know what I think we should do?' said Maggie, trying to put a good face on things. 'I think we should leave Hannah to sleep on it. Maybe by the morning, she'll have other thoughts on the matter. I'm going back on the train later this afternoon, but perhaps you could telephone me tomorrow? You can always reverse the charge. You already have my new telephone number and address, Mrs Adams, don't you?'

Babs looked a bit sheepish. 'We certainly will call yer,' she replied eagerly, 'won't we, Hann?' She looked embarrassed when Hannah refused to reply. 'Well, at least let's sit down an' 'ave a nice cuppa tea ter drown our sorrows!' Her pathetic little joke did little to lighten the atmosphere.

'If you'll excuse me,' said Maggie awkwardly, 'I don't want to be late for my train. Goodbye, Hannah.' She tried to shake hands with her, but Hannah turned away. 'Goodbye, Mrs Adams. Thank you for the tea.'

'You're welcome, I'm sure,' replied Babs, throwing a quick glare at Hannah, whom she would clearly love to have murdered right there and then. 'It was so nice to see you again.' She followed Maggie out into the passage, leaving Hannah alone in the parlour. After talking for a moment or so on the front doorstep, she shut the front door and stomped back into the parlour. 'You stupid little cow!' she yelled at Hannah. 'Yer 'aven't got a brain in yer 'ead!'

Hannah completely ignored her, and rushed straight out into the passage and into the street, where she just caught a glimpse of Maggie about to disappear round the corner into Hornsey Road. 'Mrs Bullock!' she called. Maggie turned with a start to find Hannah rushing towards her.

Hannah was breathless, but calm. 'I just wanted ter say,' she said, 'I – I 'ope yer get on well in your new place. Please say 'allo ter Mr Bullock for me.'

Maggie's face lit up, and tears suddenly welled in her eyes as Hannah offered her hand to shake. She responded by suddenly throwing her arms round Hannah, and hugging her. 'Forgive me,' she said, her voice cracking. Before Hannah could say another word, she hurried off, disappearing round the corner into the peace and quiet of a half-day closing in Hornsey Road.

The following few weeks seemed to fly by. The blitz continued with ferocious day and night attacks on London, with what appeared to be no end in sight. In October, the home of the BBC at Broadcasting House was badly damaged whilst the news was being read by Bruce Belfrage, who was reported in the newspapers as having been 'outraged' by the audacity of the attack, but mercifully survived it. Many other parts of the British Isles suffered too, and on one Saturday morning in the middle of November, Hannah and the other girls at Woolworth's gathered around a wireless set on the electrical counter to listen grim-faced to the voice of the BBC newsreader Joseph Macleod, as he read out an account of the savage aerial onslaught on the city of Coventry, which had apparently caused massive death and destruction. However, there was pandemonium when one of the girls tuned in to hear the voice of the British traitor known as Lord Haw-Haw, as he revelled in his account of the 'glorious' German air force who had dealt a mortal blow to the English city in the Midlands, dropping thirty thousand fire bombs within just a few hours.

'Pity *you* weren't there too, yer ol' bugger!'

All the other girls yelled out their agreement as one of them ranted at the wireless as though the hated traitor was right there with them at the electrical counter. All of them quickly dispersed, however, when Tom Barker, who had recently been promoted to junior store manager, was seen approaching from the Admin office.

'Anuvver mothers' meetin', I see!' he remarked as the girls hastily returned to their own counters.

Hannah ignored him and started to hurry off.

'Now don't forget what I said,' Betty called mischievously as she went. 'It won't be long now.'

Hannah gave her a thumb's up sign and smiled back, before continuing on to the hardware counter.

'Oh, Miss Adams!' called Barker. 'Can I have a word wiv you, please?'

Hannah came to a reluctant halt, and waited for him to come up to her.

''Aven't seen much of yer mum just lately,' he said, with a wry smile. 'Come ter think of it, I 'ain't seen 'er in quite a while.'

Hannah started to walk away.

'That wouldn't 'ave anyfin' ter do wiv you by any chance, would it?'

Hannah stopped dead, and swung round on him. 'Look, Mr Barker,' she snapped acidly, 'it ain't of any interest ter me wot you get up to in yer spare time. But if yer wanna know wot *I* fink, well now – I can tell yer that these days my mum seems ter 'ave quite a lot of uvver interests ter occupy 'er time.'

Barker's face took on a look of thunder.

'In fact,' continued Hannah, 'I'd say she's never bin so busy at night in 'er whole life!' She turned round and walked off.

'I 'ope you remember wot I said to yer that day?' said Barker, pursuing her as discreetly as he possibly could without drawing attention. 'I 'ave quite a lot er influence in this place now. One word from me an' it's goodbye ter you, mate.'

Once again Hannah came to a halt, and slowly turned round. 'An' wot makes yer fink, Mr Barker,' she said with a huge smirk, 'that you'll still be around ter say goodbye ter me or anyone else?'

Barker's air of confidence became taut. 'Wot're you talkin' about?'

'Just that any minute now,' Hannah continued defiantly, 'you'll be receiving a little letter in the post marked OHMS, a letter from 'Is Majesty the King's War Office, *requesting* your presence at your nearest Army Recruitment Centre. The only fing is, they won't be takin' no fer an answer this time. In uvver words, you're about ter be called up – mate!'

'Silly bleedin' little cow!' he growled angrily. 'Yer don't know nuffin', do yer? Yer don't know that I'm exempt from military duty.' He lowered his voice to a whisper. 'I've got contacts in 'igh places!'

She leant so close towards him that their noses were almost touching. 'Well, I'm afraid they ain't 'igh enuff,' she retorted, with a triumphant grin. 'Sadly, Mr Barker, we're goin' ter 'ave ter say bye-bye to yer. From what I've 'eard from *my* contact, everyone upstairs knows all about it, *everyone*.' She shook her head slowly. 'An' so does your missus, I'm afraid. In fact that's not *all* she knows.'

Barker looked as though he had been hit by a thunderbolt. 'You – lyin' little . . . !'

'I'm sorry yer fink that, Mr Barker,' said Hannah, first taking a look across to where Betty was watching them, and then to the senior member of the Admin staff who was also watching them from the door of the office behind the main cash desk. 'Anyway, yer won't ferget ter come an' say goodbye to us all before yer go, will yer?'

As she went, Hannah resisted the temptation to turn round and see Barker's reaction. But she did just catch a glimpse of the senior store manager signalling Barker to come back to the office. For Hannah it was a wonderful moment. Ever since Barker had cornered her in the ladies' room, it had been an ordeal having to come into work each day. If it hadn't been for Betty, whose father knew someone who knew someone who could talk to the right people at the War Office about cancelling Barker's exemption from call-up, he would have gone on trying to blackmail her for ever more. The one person she felt sorry for was Barker's wife. How much did she really know about him, Hannah wondered, and if and when she did find out what he'd been up to, how would the poor woman cope with it? Hard as he had tried to dodge call-up, it seemed to be the obvious way out for Barker. As far as Hannah was concerned, that sort of man deserved every bit of retribution that was coming to him. And come to that, her mum deserved the same for encouraging him in the first place.

Babs Adams had finally given up her attempts to persuade Hannah to leave the dangers of the London Blitz, and go to live with the Bullocks in Norfolk. There seemed no point, for Hannah was not only determined in her ways, but also totally unperturbed by the horrific air raids that were taking place without stop night after night and day after day. With the threat of an imminent invasion the main talking point in every pub, office, factory, and home, the emphasis now was how to cope with what Prime Minister Winston Churchill called *these indiscriminate attacks*. Now that the Anderson shelter in the back garden was completely unusable owing to the constant flooding, Babs had virtually taken up residence in the public air-raid shelter in Arthur Road, which was not only a soulless experience night after night but, in view of the criticism being levelled at brick-built shelters, also a risky one. On the other hand, Hannah felt safe and secure in her cupboard under the stairs, where most nights during the air raids she wrote letters to Sam by torchlight. In fact, her one big comfort was to read over and over again the letters he had written to her, with their wonderful descriptions of the men he was fighting with, their fears, depressions, and homesickness, but also their immense good humour. It was hard for Hannah to love someone who couldn't be with her, and there were times when she almost gave up hope of ever rekindling the passionate closeness she had experienced for so short a time with Sam. However, as she squatted on that tiny bed, straining her eyes in the dim light, writing to Sam *was* like being with him, and she constantly hoped that he would be feeling the same way about her when *he* wrote, too.

By the end of November, Hannah was beginning to feel guilty about not having gone to visit her young sister Louie, who was still living with Sam's parents in Redbourne. But the fact was that even though the Bullocks had left the Cock and Crow and were now living in Norfolk, Hannah felt no enthusiasm at the thought of seeing the place again. In any case, there seemed no point, for Louie was sublimely happy living with her foster-parents at the post office where, judging by her letters, the Quaker way of living was giving her a real purpose in life. Visiting her just at the moment seemed to Hannah to be an unnecessary intrusion which could just possibly unsettle the child. But there was also more on Hannah's mind, and that was her real concern for her mum. Not only was Babs looking tired and worn out, but she seemed to be spending more and more time at home. During the months following Hannah's mammoth walk home from Hertfordshire, she and her mum had had very little to say to one another, and when they did speak, it was usually only because they had to. Hannah hated the way their relationship had deteriorated since the start of the war. Her mum's lies about men and just about everything she ever did had put a severe strain on the love Hannah had always felt for her, especially the way she had just bundled her and Louie off to the country for her own personal reasons. But now, when she looked at Babs's face, it seemed to be so full of despair, so lost and without hope. Of course, after the life she had led after Hannah's dad had been called up, it was inevitable that disillusion would set in sooner or later, but nonetheless Hannah still had a deep-rooted affection for her, and it distressed her to see this marked deterioration. It didn't help that letters from Len had virtually dried up; not one had been received for several months, which left both Hannah and Babs not knowing whether he was alive or dead. But then, Hannah couldn't help wondering how much her mum really cared whether Len was alive or not. *You say 'e's yer dad, an' that yer love 'im. Well, it may not 'ave occurred to yer that I'm 'is wife, an' it's just possible that I love 'im too!* Her mum's words during that terrible row never ceased to prey on Hannah's mind. *Did* Babs Adams really love her husband, and if she did, what had happened during her relationship with him that they had tried so desperately to keep from their two daughters?

The air-raid siren had only just sounded when Hannah came in from work. The first place she made for was the scullery, where she smelt her teatime meal being kept warm as usual in the oven. When she got the plate out, she was delighted to see that it was sausages and baked beans, one of her favourites, and so, knowing that her mum had already left for the public shelter to claim her nightly place, she sat down at the scullery table to tuck in to her meal. As she ate, it occurred to her that it was the first time she had consciously considered that her mum had taken the trouble to prepare a meal for her, and that she, Hannah, had always taken this for granted. She felt a gradual wave of guilt, and by the time she had finished the last of the baked beans she had made a conscious decision to thank her mum as soon as she saw her the next morning.

After switching off the light in the scullery, she went out into the passage, and made her way upstairs, but just as she was going into her own bedroom she noticed that there was a light seeping out from beneath the door of her mum's. Thinking that Babs had forgotten to switch off her light, Hannah went in. To her surprise, she found her mum sitting in her leopardskin coat in front of the gas fire, staring absently into the flickering glow. 'Mum!' she said, with some surprise. 'Wot're yer doin' 'ere? Why ain't yer round the shelter?'

'No rush,' replied Babs, with very little energy.

'Din't yer 'ear the siren?' said Hannah, going to her. 'They'll be over soon. Don't yer fink yer ought ter be on yer way?'

Babs looked up at her. 'No rush,' she repeated. Her eyes seemed quite lifeless.

'Is anyfin' wrong?' asked Hannah apprehensively. 'You OK?'

'As much as I'll ever be,' replied Babs.

By now, Hannah was really concerned. She had never seen her mum like this before, with no make-up, her hair not even combed through. 'The bangers and beans were lovely,' she said brightly. 'Fanks fer doin' 'em.'

'I ain't bin the best er muvvers ter you an' Lou, 'ave I?'

The question came like a thunderbolt to Hannah. 'Depends wot yer mean,' she replied with a shrug.

Babs's eyes were again transfixed on the gas wicks. 'Like bein' a mum, a *real* mum,' she said. 'Someone yer can rely on ter tell yer the truth.'

Hannah crouched on the floor at her side. 'Wot d'yer mean?'

Babs turned towards her. 'Am I a stranger ter you, Hannah?' she asked oddly.

Only at that moment did Hannah realise that Babs had been drinking. ''Ow can you be a stranger when I'm yer own daughter?'

Babs's face crumpled up. 'No,' she replied, slowly shaking her head. 'That's not the way I planned it, but that's wot 'appened.'

Hannah was beginning to feel confused and nervous. 'Mum, I don't know wot you're talkin' about.'

'No,' said Babs. There were smudges beneath her eyes where her mascara had run. ''Ow *can* yer know, when yer've never bin told.'

Hannah felt her whole body flush. This was the moment she had been waiting for, the moment that Miss Hobson had prepared her for some weeks before: *. . . I happen to think that you're now* *old enough, and adult enough, to cope with it. But the rest is up to your mother . . .*

'Told *wot*, Mum?' asked Hannah gently. 'Wot 'ave I never bin told?'

Babs raised her hand, and slowly reached out with her fingers to outline Hannah's features. It was clear to see that her thinking was impaired by whatever it was she had been drinking. 'I – I – never wanted ter 'urt 'im,' she said, stumbling over her words. 'Yer dad . . . 'e's a good man. 'E's always bin a good man. I never deserved 'im.'

Hannah lowered her voice almost to a whisper. 'Mum,' she said, 'wot're yer trying ter tell me?'

'People used ter say 'ow much Louie looked like 'im,' continued Babs, now rambling freely. 'They said you looked like *me*.' She shook her head. 'I couldn't tell 'em.' She stared straight into Hannah's eyes. ''Ow could I *ever* tell 'em, Hann? 'Ow *could* I?'

Hannah took hold of her mum's hand, and held on to it.

'When I told yer dad,' continued Babs, tears now beginning to well up in her eyes, ''e wouldn't believe me, 'e just wouldn't believe me. 'E said I was makin' it all up becos . . . becos I fawt 'e din't *want* kids. But 'e did, Hann. 'E wanted 'em more than anyfin' else in the whole wide world.' Her voice was now beginning to crack, her face crumpling up. Then she slowly shook her head. 'But it was no good. I told 'im boaf times – it was no bleedin' good. It wasn't possible, it just wasn't possible. Even when the doctor told 'im, 'e still wouldn't believe it – it was just not possible . . .' She suddenly dissolved into tears.

Hannah felt her whole body seize up. Until this moment, she never thought the day would come when she would see her mother like this, so distressed, confused, so vulnerable. This really was, at last, the moment of truth. For Hannah, it was also an extraordinary moment when she found herself cradling her mum's weeping face against her chest. 'Wot couldn't 'e believe, Mum?' she asked softly, holding her tight.

Babs slowly looked up, tears streaming down her face. 'Yer don't belong to 'im, Hann,' she uttered almost incomprehensibly. 'You nor Lou. Yer don't belong ter 'im. 'E thinks yer do, but yer don't.'

At that moment, the house shook from top to bottom as the first barrage of ack-ack artillery opened up on the night's first approach of enemy aircraft.

'We 'ave ter go, Mum!' said Hannah, gently easing them both up onto their feet. 'Come on now! We 'ave ter go!'

A few minutes later, lugging Babs's mattress over her shoulder, trying to balance her mum's belongings with one hand, and doing her best to keep Babs on her feet with the other, Hannah struggled to guide them the short distance across the road to the public air-raid shelter. But it was an appalling journey, with the sky lit up by searchlights and ack-ack shells bursting in and out of the barrage balloons, and the anger of artillery fire so deafening that Hannah thought her eardrums would burst under the strain. When they finally got to the shelter, they found that one of the neighbours had very kindly kept Babs's usual place in the corner free, so after quickly spreading the narrow mattress on the cold stone floor, Hannah carefully eased her mum down onto it. It was an advantage that the only light available came from a flickering oil lamp high up on a ledge, which helped to avoid too much attention being drawn to the condition Babs was in. Eventually, however, the two of them managed to settle down together on the mattress, both of them leaning against the bleak brick wall, with Hannah cradling her mum in her arms, until she finally dozed off.

As they lay there, clasped in each other's arms, Hannah closed her eyes and tried to make sense of the things her mum had been telling her. It was a chilling, despairing thought that she and Louie did not belong to the dad they had known and loved all their lives. With her eyes still closed, Hannah felt a lump in her throat, and tears struggling to break loose. All she could see in her mind's eye were moments throughout her life when she and Louie were together with their dad, laughing, joking, playing games with him, listening to him telling them simple fairy tales as he put them to bed, a proud dad, a proud, loving man.

She was still awake when the savage air raid finally came to an end, the noise of the huge guns replaced by the frenzied sound of fire engines, ambulances, and police cars rushing from one bombed site to another. By the time the first light of a new day started to filter through the blackout curtains over the entrance, Hannah, still propped up against the wall, arm round her mum's shoulders, opened her eyes without having had more than a few minutes' sleep. This had been a night she would remember for the rest of her life, a night when she woke up to find that the world was suddenly a very different place.

Chapter 21

Four years later

The journey to Redbourne was much the same. The only difference was that the trains were now departing from King's Cross station rather than St Pancras, as they had done during that short period of the evacuation at the start of the war. With her mind now awash with memories, Hannah peered out through the anti-blast gauze on the carriage window and watched the countryside flashing by, just as it had done nearly five years before. Today, however, there were no kids to share the carriage with, no Louie moaning and groaning about Alfie Grieves teasing her, no foul smells from the other kids who were desperate to get to lavatories. Now there were only one strict-looking middle-aged man in a bowler hat reading a copy of the *Daily Telegraph*, an elderly lady with an equally elderly white poodle, and a certain young army sergeant as her fellow passengers. But this was not the only thing that was different. Hannah was no longer a child herself, she was a young woman, who within the last few months had officially come of age. Today, she was more firm, more confident than she had ever been. After all the trauma of living with the Bullocks, followed by that long walk back home, and the desperate efforts each day to survive the horrors of the London Blitz, during the past four years everything had changed for Hannah. Now she made her own decisions, for, in the continued absence of the man she had always thought of as her natural dad, she herself had become the breadwinner of the family, which up until now had consisted only of her and her mum. However, during the past few days there had been a distinct and wonderful change in direction for Hannah, and the man who was responsible for that change was Sam Beedle, the young soldier now sitting next to her, his arm clasped round her shoulder. 'Not far to go now,' he said. 'We've just passed over the old bridge. Ten minutes at the most.'

As he spoke, the train began to lose speed. 'Nervous?' he asked.

Hannah snuggled up to him. 'You've no idea.'

'I think I have,' he replied reassuringly.

'All the times I've been to see Lou down here,' said Hannah, 'I've kept it all back from your mum an' dad, even though I've wanted to shout it out loud!'

Sam chuckled. 'Well, you'll soon be able to. Although I bet they'll be so shocked by how different you are they'll hardly recognise you.'

She grinned mischievously. 'You mean becos I talk more posh than I used to?'

'It's got nothing to do with the way you talk, Hannah,' he replied. 'It's the fact that you've become so assured and confident. Let's face it, you've grown up.'

'I suppose you could say the same about you,' replied Hannah. 'Yer can't stay young forever.' She snuggled up even closer to him. 'Still, it's a funny feeling knowing that you're somebody else's child, yet not being able to tell the only dad you've ever known that it's *him* me an' Lou love, no matter who or where our so-called *real* dad is lurking around.'

'Well, I'd say it must have taken a lot of courage for your mum to tell you about it all,' said Sam, holding her tight. 'How did Louie take the news when you came up here to tell her?'

'Louie?' Hannah broke into a huge grin. 'My little sister couldn't care two penny ha'pennies *who* her real parents are. The last time I saw her a year ago, she was too happy living with *your* mum and dad, and joining in with their Quaker Friends and all the other kids in the village, to be bothered about us. It was really amazin'. If you think *I've* changed, just wait 'til you see *her*.'

When the train drew in to the northbound platform at Redbourne, only one or two passengers got off the train. But Ted Sputter the stationmaster was there to greet Hannah and Sam. 'Crikey!' he exclaimed, the moment he set eyes on Hannah. 'You've grown since I last saw you! One minute you're a young girl, the next you're like a spring flower!'

Both Hannah and Sam roared with laughter at the compliment. 'You should've been a writer, Mr Sputter,' said Hannah.

'Writer? *Me?*' replied Ted dismissively. 'I spend too much time on me feet all day to do daft things like that!' Once he had seen off the train with his green flag and whistle, he turned to Sam. 'As for you, young man,' he said sombrely, 'I tip my hat to yer. I heard you was in the thick of it at Salerno. I bet the poor old Fifth Army took quite a few casualties on those beaches, din't they?'

Sam was uneasy, and tried to move on with Hannah. 'We'll be on our way then, Mr Sputter,' he said. 'Nice to see you again.'

'You could take the 'orse and buggy, if yer like,' called Ted, as he followed them out through the station entrance. 'That's about all we've got left after we lost the old taxi.'

'No thanks,' Sam called back over his shoulder. 'We could do with the walk.'

'Don't blame yer!' called Ted, determined to have the last word. 'At least it's safer up 'ere than wiv those ruddy ol' doodle-bugs up in London!'

Sam waited until they were well out of range of the station before he spoke again. 'He's right, you know. I don't like you staying at home with those damned flying bombs blowing the place up all over again. It was bad enough during the Blitz, but with those things you can't even see them until they're right on top of you.'

'There's no need for you to worry, Sam,' replied Hannah, tucking her arm round his waist as they walked. 'Jerry did his best to knock us out in Holloway, but he didn't get away with it then, and he won't get away with it now. The Allies are in France. It's only a matter of time before it'll all be over.'

'I wish I had your confidence, Hannah,' replied Sam. 'But a lot of people could still die before we see the back of Hitler.'

They walked on beneath the glare of a hot June sun. It had been over a year since Hannah had last come to visit her sister Louie, and yet everything, as always, seemed exactly the same, even the ducks who were squabbling for scraps on the village pond. Before they moved on across the green towards the post office, Sam suddenly drew them to a halt. 'What is it, Sam?' asked Hannah anxiously.

'Oh, nothing,' he replied dreamily, taking in the view. 'It's all so special, isn't it? I mean, just look at the colour of everything, so green, so fresh. When I was a kid, I often used to sit on that bench by the pond and imagine I was a figure in a landscape picture, especially when I wore my red pullover. Red is such a vibrant colour, isn't it? It sticks out so wonderfully in any picture.' His reflective mood changed as quickly as it had come. 'It's funny, but you know I thought about it soon after we came wading ashore from our landing craft at Salerno. I spent the first half-hour lying flat on my face trying to avoid German machine guns, but every so often I managed to sneak a glimpse of the Italian countryside inland. The trees were so different from ours here, just as green, but somehow – in a different kind of way.' He turned to look at her. 'I can't really explain it,' he said.

'You don't have to.'

They were suddenly interrupted by Louie, who came rushing across the green to meet them. 'Hannah! Sam!' she yelled out excitedly.

Both of them called back just as excitedly. 'Lou!'

The moment she reached them, Louie threw herself straight at Sam and hugged him round the waist. 'Sam!' she gasped.

'Hey, just a minute!' growled Hannah light-heartedly. 'He's *my* feller – not yours!' Sam laughed.

'We're all waitin' to see you!' gabbled Louie, practically dragging them off. Like Hannah, her fractured English had somewhat mellowed over the past few years. 'Yer mum's made a lovely fruit cake for yer – no currants though – she knows yer don't like them, and anyway we don't 'ave enough ration coupons.'

Sam allowed her to slip her arm through his. Just like Hannah had said, Louie *had* changed. The last time he had seen her she was still a child; now she was a teenager, a dazzling young girl with dark naturally curly hair that hung down lazily over her shoulders, and, like Sam himself, ravishing blue eyes that just seemed to sparkle in the sunlight. Sam was astonished by the transformation, and was convinced that one day Louie would become a beautiful young woman. But, as far as he was concerned, not nearly as beautiful as his very own Hannah.

After listening to Louie's excited chatter all the way across the village green, they eventually came within close sight of the post office, where a group of people, including Sam's mother and father and some of the Friends, were waiting to greet them. The reunion was quietly emotional, but dignified. Very few words were spoken, but the atmosphere was charged with relief that, after nearly two years of absence, Sam was at last home safe and sound.

Sam hugged his mother, leaning his head gently on her shoulder. 'We never gave up hope,' said Mary, allowing herself just those few words of faith. She then turned to Hannah, with a loving, welcoming smile. 'It's a wonderful treat to have two birds returning to the nest at the same time,' she said, adding prophetically, 'even if it's only for just one moment in time.'

After Sam's father had offered a silent prayer of thanks, Mary served up a delicious vegetarian lunch. It wasn't often that she had the chance to do something that she liked doing so much, but having Sam and Hannah sitting down to eat with her, Joseph, and Louie, was certainly worth every minute of her effort. 'Fortunately,' she said, ladling some hot cauliflower, onion, and tomato stew onto Hannah's plate, 'we don't have to rely on the food ration to eat. Everything we get is from our plot at the back.'

'It's marvellous, Hann,' said Louie, with great enthusiasm. 'I 'elped Dad dig up the potatoes, didn't I?'

Joseph Beedle raised his heavy eyebrows and cast a benevolent smile back at her. Hannah loved to hear her young sister so happy, but still found it strange to hear her talking of him as her 'dad'.

Sam was happy, too, not just to be tucking into his mother's home cooking again, but also to be sharing the lunch table in the back parlour with Hannah.

'So, Hannah,' said Mary, 'I hear things are looking up for you at Woolworth's. What's all this I hear about your becoming a store supervisor there?'

Hannah reacted uneasily. 'Oh, it doesn't mean all that much, Mrs Beedle,' she replied. 'But I've been there some time now, and the extra money does help a lot. Although I must say, if it hadn't been for my mum's being so poorly, I'd have joined up in the ATS, or at least volunteered for work in the emergency services.'

'I'm so sorry to hear about your mother,' said Mary, speaking quickly to cover what Hannah had just said, while Sam watched carefully for his father's reaction. 'What seems to be the trouble?'

Hannah was reluctant to talk about her mum. Ever since that night in the air-raid shelter nearly four years ago, a weariness, a disillusionment with the way life was going for her, had been proving just too much for Babs to cope with. On top of that came the nightly air raids, the constant bombing, the loss of people she had known so well over the years, and above all the struggle to come to terms with what she had had to tell Hannah about her dad — it had just worn her down. 'Oh — she gets these nasty headaches and bouts of tummy trouble,' was all Hannah was prepared to say.

'You should try to get her out of London,' said Mary. 'The country air would do her so much good. Don't you think so, Joseph?'

What his wife had just said seemed to go straight past Joseph, for without looking up he addressed himself directly to Sam. 'Have you taken life since you left us, son?'

The question came like a bolt out of the blue for everyone around the table. 'Joseph – please don't,' Mary begged.

Sam looked at his father, and quietly answered his question. 'Yes, Father,' he replied. 'There were many men who lost their lives, on *all* sides.'

Joseph flicked his eyes up from his plate. 'Did you see them as they died?'

'The enemy is evil, Father.'

'There's a part of God in everybody,' said Joseph firmly. 'God works through people.'

'We don't kill for the sake of killing, sir. Evil *has* to be stopped wherever it comes from.'

There followed several moments of silence. Everyone, even young Louie, realised that the conflict that had plagued both Sam and his father before he went off to fight in the war was never likely to be settled. Only Hannah broke the tension.

'Mr and Mrs Beedle,' she said, quite suddenly and openly, 'Sam an' I would like to get married.'

Both Sam and Louie, completely taken aback by Hannah's forthrightness, looked to their father for his reaction. To their surprise Joseph exchanged a knowing smile with his wife. 'Well now, young lady,' he replied. 'There's an interesting thought.' After a split second's silence, everyone laughed. Even Joseph chuckled.

Hannah looked surprised. 'Does that mean it's OK?' she asked.

'No,' said Joseph. 'But it doesn't mean that it's not. Sam. What do *you* say about this?'

'The same as Hannah, Father,' he replied, totally bewildered. 'That is, if you and Mother will give us your blessing.'

'The blessing comes from God, son,' replied Joseph, 'not your mother and me. But I imagine this news is not entirely unexpected, so I think I can say . . .' he exchanged another gentle smile with his wife, 'that we'll be very happy to see you both standing before Him to make your declaration.'

Louie was first to leap up excitedly and hug her sister. 'Hann!' she yelped. Then she did the same to Sam. 'Oh, Sam! You're going to be my relation!' Again everyone laughed, as Sam reached across to clasp Hannah's hand.

'However,' said Joseph, sounding very official indeed. All eyes turned towards him. 'There *are*, of course,' he continued, looking back and forth between Hannah and Sam, 'several questions that will have to be taken into consideration before you proceed any further. That is – if you intend to marry into the faith of our Society?'

Sam looked to Hannah to answer for them. 'We'd both like that, Mr Beedle,' she said.

Joseph was beaming, something he rarely did. 'Then before you make your application to our registering officer we have a lot of things to sort out. The Friends will have to give their approval to a union between one of our own and a non-member.'

'That would have to be at the next meeting in two weeks' time,' said Mary, struggling to contain her own excitement. 'But you could probably have the ceremony in the House before the end of the summer.'

Sam again exchanged a look with Hannah. 'Well, that would be fine by both of us, but I'm afraid we can't get married as quickly as that.' Mary's enthusiasm was suddenly deflated. 'You see,' continued Sam, 'I have to report back for duty the day after tomorrow. The way things are at the moment, I have no idea when I'll be back.'

A sudden silence descended on the room. Everyone seemed to be staring into the remaining food on their plates.

'Then if war comes first,' announced Joseph solemnly, 'God's work will have to wait.'

'Father,' said Sam quickly, 'I can assure you that Hannah and I want to wait for as little time as possible. We love each other very much, and we're dedicated to spending the rest of our lives together.'

Mary's face crumpled momentarily. Joseph hesitated before replying. 'That's settled then,' he said. 'As soon as we've finished lunch, Sam, you and I will have a talk.'

'Yes, Father,' Sam replied formally.

Once lunch was over and Sam and his father had left the room, Louie rushed off to her own bedroom to sort out all the things she wanted to show Hannah that she had made on her own over the past few months. Once the washing up was done, this left Hannah and Mary free to go out into the back garden, where they stopped at the gate to stare out at a vast meadow which was a sea of yellow cowslips, a sight which thrilled Hannah for she had never seen anything like it in her life before. 'In America they call them marsh marigolds,' Mary said. 'I have a cousin over there who wrote to me once about how people in her village always referred to them as their *English Friends*. It's a lovely thought, isn't it?'

Hannah sighed. 'Quakers are such lovely people,' she said. 'I envy you all.'

Mary immediately turned to her. 'Oh, don't envy us for

anything, Hannah,' she replied. 'On the face of it we're ordinary people, just like anyone else. We just happen to have our own special beliefs that go back a long way. But we have our disagreements too – yes, and we can lose our temper just like anyone else, although we do make strenuous efforts to keep *that* under control.' They both chuckled. 'I'm very proud that you and Sam love each other so much,' Mary went on. 'Sam is such a good, honest boy, so different from when he was young.'

Hannah swung her a surprised look.

'Oh yes,' said Mary with a smile. 'In fact at times he was quite a little tartar, always displeasing his father. As a matter of fact, if you don't mind my saying, he's always been independent, just like you. He has views that not all the Friends share. I remember once – I suppose he was about eight or nine years old at the time – he badly wanted to have a dog, but his father said that, much as we all love animals, there wasn't enough room in the post office here to keep one. A few days later, after he'd been out roaming around the village, he came back cradling a kitten in his arms. He said its mother had been knocked down, and he wanted to look after it. So what could we say? Cornelius – that's what he called the little thing – stayed with us until he eventually died at a ripe old age. When Sam wants his way, he gets it. He's never changed.'

Hannah loved listening to Mary. She was somehow the perfect mother, who never seemed to get flustered over anything. For her part, Mary had come to love both Hannah and Louie. But as she watched Hannah, breathing in the fresh meadow air, vibrant shoulder-length red hair shining in the early afternoon sun, she felt a surge of sympathy for all she had been told about the two girls' own parents, and the trauma they had gone through trying to survive so much falsehood and deceit.

'Have you heard from your father yet?'

Mary's question seemed to come out of the blue, and seemed to cast a passing shadow over the sea of yellow. Hannah shook her head. 'It's been a long time,' she replied. 'I've written to him so many times now. I can only think that my mum's told him what she told me, and now he can't face up to Louie an' me. I don't even know whether we'll ever see him again.'

Mary put a comforting arm round Hannah's waist.

'The thing is,' continued Hannah, 'I want him to know that what happened makes no difference to me. After all, he's the only dad I've ever known, an' I love him.'

'What about your mum?'

'I love her too,' replied Hannah. 'What she did, I honestly think she did fer the best. Poor Mum.'

'She's lucky to have a daughter like you,' said Mary.

Hannah shook her head. 'No,' she replied. 'Over the years, I've been very unkind to her. I've never tried to understand how difficult it's been for her to bring up kids. I think I'll always regret it.'

'Well,' said Mary encouragingly, 'let's hope you and Sam will bring some new hope to her life. Bring her down to see us sometime. We'll do everything we can to make her happy.'

Hannah responded with a grateful look, but her attention was all the time focused on Sam and his father, strolling lazily out in the middle of the meadow, deep in serious conversation. 'How much longer will they be, d'you think?'

'Oh, who knows?' replied Mary. 'They have an awful lot to talk about.'

Hannah didn't really hear what Sam and his father had been talking about until later, when she and Sam were wandering around the green, stopping every so often to exchange a few words with some of the villagers who came out to greet them.

'It was nothing really,' said Sam. 'As you know, Father's very dedicated to our faith. He likes to do everything by the book. He was merely asking if, when you eventually go before the Friends, will you be able to say that you're in sympathy with the nature of the Quaker marriage ceremony. We also have to get letters of recommendation from two other members, not that that'll be any problem.'

'Is that all?' asked Hannah, not altogether sure that Sam was telling her everything.

'More or less,' replied Sam, with a shrug.

'So he didn't ask anything about my mother,' she asked shrewdly, 'the type of woman she is?'

'Don't be silly, Hannah,' he replied dismissively, only too aware that Hannah was no fool. 'You're not responsible for your parents' actions.'

'No,' she replied, 'but I can't ignore them either. An' neither can your dad.'

They came to a halt before they reached the village store, where they knew Barney Jessop was waiting to greet them. 'You know, Hannah,' said Sam, 'I've always had a pretty up and down relationship with my father, but this much I can tell you: regardless of how ashamed you may feel about what your mother did, he urged me to show her – and you – as much love as I possibly can. He told me quite clearly that he would never stop praying for all of us.'

Hannah felt a sudden pang of emotion. Somehow, whenever she had been in Joseph Beedle's company over the past few years, she had always felt as though he disapproved of her. But after what Sam had just told her, she was beginning to see her future father-in-law in a new light.

'Bless my cotton socks!' exclaimed Barney Jessop triumphantly, as he came out of the village store to greet them. 'Just look at you two young things! The young lady and her sergeant!'

Both Hannah and Sam laughed, as they shook hands energetically with him. 'And what about *you*, Mr Jessop?' returned Hannah. 'Yer 'aven't aged a bit since the first day I saw you.'

'Ah!' chuckled Barney. 'Flattery will get you everywhere! Come on in!'

They followed him into the shop where two other customers, who had just been served, quickly finished their chinwag, greeted Sam as though he was a hero, and left the store.

'So how are things, Mr Jessop?' asked Sam. 'Looks like you've still got plenty of business.'

'Bit sluggish,' replied Barney, taking off his straw boater to wipe the sweat off his forehead. 'But that's the war for yer. Martha Randle at the café was saying the same thing, and so was Henry Turnbull down the butcher's – it's a struggle to put goods on the shelves, and that's a fact. Mind you, it's not easy being without Jane since she went and joined the WRNS.'

'I know,' said Hannah. 'Even though we keep in contact, I do miss her. Does she write to you very often?'

'Oh my goodness yes,' replied Barney, back behind his counter again. 'That's the trouble. My Jane never *stops* writin'. It's not fair, I tell you. She knows her poor ol' dad doesn't have the time to write back.'

'But you must be very proud of her,' suggested Sam. 'And I bet she looks wonderful in her WRNS uniform.'

'Oh, yes, she does that all right. Take a look at her.' He turned round, took a snapshot of Jane in uniform from the shelf behind him, and gave it to them to look at. 'Though Heaven only knows why she chose to go in the Navy. The only water we've got round here is in the village pond!'

Hannah looked forlornly at the snapshot. 'I still envy her,' she said sadly, handing it back. 'If it wasn't for . . . Yes, I do envy her.'

'Yes, well she thinks the world of you, young Hannah,' said Barney, blowing his nose loudly on his handkerchief. 'Calls you the best friend she ever had.' The compliment brought an affectionate smile to Hannah's face. 'She always said it was a miracle what you did, walking all that way back to London. And it was! You got real guts and that's no mistake. Don't know how you stuck it, livin' over that pub with the Bullocks.'

'Has anyone heard from them at all?' Hannah asked. 'I haven't seen Mrs Bullock since she came to visit me and my mum in London nearly four years ago.'

Barney looked up at her with a start. 'Maggie?' he asked, surprised. 'Maggie Bullock? You mean you don't know what happened to her?'

Hannah exchanged a swift, puzzled glance with Sam. 'No,' she replied. 'What?'

'Died,' replied Barney gloomily. 'Apparently she had something nasty lurking inside her stomach for years. It wasn't 'til she and Sid moved up to Norfolk that they found out what it was. Seems she'd had quite a bit of pain for years. Sid wrote to old Griffin in the baker's about it. A peaceful end, though. She's buried up in the church graveyard there. Don't know what's happened to Sid.' He shook his head. 'He was always a bit of a rum one, that.'

The news of Maggie Bullock's death didn't really sink in for

Hannah until later, when she and Sam found themselves wandering off towards the tiny cobbled street where the Cock and Crow was still discreetly wedged between all the other terraced houses. For a few minutes they stood outside looking up and down the façade of the building, and Hannah felt a wave of mixed emotions as her eyes finally rested on the front window of the saloon bar. 'It all seems like a dream,' she said. 'I half expect Maggie Bullock to come out an' ask me where the hell I've been all day. I never thought I'd ever be sorry to know she's not around any more.' She sighed. 'If only she could have had a daughter of her own, things could have been so diff'rent for her.'

From inside, they could hear the sound of the regulars enjoying a raucous game of darts in the bar. 'Would you like to go in?' asked Sam, his arm round her shoulder.

'No. It's not the same, is it?'

They went off arm in arm, but in her mind Hannah was sure she could still hear the demanding squawk of *Mine's a Guinness!*

Chapter 22

Babs Adams had also changed. Ever since the great weariness had taken over, she had spent much of her time either sleeping in bed, or sitting propped up in a chair in the back parlour listening to the wireless. Gone were the days when she was out each night, picking up men friends at random and bringing them back to the house in Kinloch Street. Now she was content to spend as much time as she could with Hannah, just longing for the moment when Hannah got home from work each evening, occasionally cooking a meal for her, but usually doing as little as she possibly could. Dr Ferguson from across the road was convinced that the main problem with Babs was psychological; he put it all down to stress and chronic depression. But Babs didn't agree one bit with the old fool's diagnosis; as far as she was concerned, she was a very sick person, with probably little time left to live. Hannah, of course, ridiculed this idea, and was always arguing that people these days were far more likely to die from a V1 buzz bomb than any stress-related disease. However, for the past week or so, Babs's one great joy had been to see Hannah walking out with Sam. Despite the painful things she had had to tell her daughter nearly four years before, she had never seen Hannah looking so happy. However, Louie was a different story, and when Hannah and Sam got back from their weekend visit to Sam's parents in Redbourne, she was more or less prepared for the news Hannah brought her.

'Louie wants to stay there,' Hannah said, with some difficulty. 'She says she much prefers the country to living in London.'

'Oh well,' replied Babs philosophically, smoking her usual evening fag on a chair out in the back yard, 'I don't blame 'er. I mean – wot's she got 'ere in *this* dump?'

'Mum!' snapped Hannah firmly. 'You mustn't say things like that! This isn't a dump – it's our home. *I'm* not ashamed of it!'

Babs shook her head. 'No, Hann,' she replied, almost as if she was apologising, 'this ain't a place ter bring up two gels in, a poky little two up two down, not when yer could be breevin' in some *real* fresh country air. This place was fine when me an' Len first rented it before you was boaf born, but not now. We've outgrown it, Hann. I don't blame Lou, I don't blame 'er at all.' She looked up affectionately at her daughter. 'I don't blame you neivver. The sooner you an' Sam get out an' find yer own place in the country, the better chance yer'll 'ave ter get on.'

'I'm not goin' ter move out, Mum,' said Hannah, sitting on the chair by her side. 'Sam an' I can't get married 'til he leaves the army for good, an' in any case I love London, it's my town. And you're my mum – don't you ever forget that.' She suddenly halted, and swung a look up at the sky. 'Listen!'

For a moment or so there was a tense silence between them, until gradually, from the distance, there came the now familiar droning sound of an approaching V1 flying bomb.

'Oh, bleedin 'ell!' griped Babs. 'Not anuvver one!'

'Quick, Mum!' barked Hannah, leaping up from her chair. 'Under the stairs!'

'No!' Babs stayed where she was. 'I wanna see it! I wanna see wot the sod looks like!'

'Mum, it's dangerous!'

'No!' insisted Babs, getting up from her chair, eyes turned firmly towards the sky. 'I ain't scared of no bleedin' plane wiv its arse on fire!'

With Babs refusing to budge, Hannah put her arm round her, and held her close. Both of them watched and waited, eyes staring up tensely at the evening sky, where the sun was still high, drowning the back yards of Kinloch Street in a bright golden sunlight. The droning sound of the pilotless enemy plane drew closer and closer, but as yet it was still not visible, until quite suddenly there it was, streaking over the rooftops from the direction of Finsbury Park, tail blazing with flames, the dreaded throbbing sound of its engines piercing the air, just waiting to cut out.

Babs glared at the machine with sheer hate. 'Yer sod!' she growled angrily. Almost as she spoke, just as the plane was passing right overhead, its engines cut out.

'Oh, Christ!' yelled Hannah, grabbing hold of her mum and dragging her into the scullery doorway. For what seemed like an eternity, they stood there paralysed by the silence, just waiting for what was to come. There was a swishing sound, followed by a deafening explosion, and the sound of glass shattering in the near distance. Simultaneously, Hannah and her mum were practically blown off their feet, falling to their knees on the scullery doormat. They stayed like that for several moments, clutching each other for protection. Only when they were sure that it was all over did Hannah finally speak: 'That was too close for comfort,' she said breathlessly.

'Sounded like 'Olloway Road, up Archway somewhere.'

As she spoke, the same thing happened all over again. The distant approach of another V1 caused them to swing their attention up to the sky.

'Inside, Mum!'

This time, Babs allowed herself to be dragged into the house, where they immediately rushed for cover under the stairs. Overhead, the droning sound of the flying bomb approached closer and closer.

'They don't give up, do they?' As the two women squeezed themselves into the cupboard under the stairs, covering their ears from what was to come, Babs's voice could hardly be heard above the sound of the plane's engines above. This time, however, they did not cut out until the lethal machine had passed right over into the distance. But then came the silence, followed by a further massive explosion. When it was over, Hannah and Babs breathed a sigh of relief.

'We can't go on like this, Mum,' said Hannah, helping her up and out into the passage. 'Now they've got these things, they're not going to stop. We've got to find somewhere safe for you to go.'

Babs laughed dismissively. 'I ain't goin' ter spend ev'ry day an' night in that bleedin' public shelter!'

'You don't have to do that,' insisted Hannah. 'Why don't you go and stay with Gran and Grandad out in Edmonton?'

'Ha!' scoffed Babs. 'Can't yer just see their faces when yer suggest me goin' ter live wiv 'em!'

Hannah sighed with exasperation. 'Well, we've got to do something, Mum!' she said. 'I'm not going to have you here in the house with all this going on. It's going to get worse before it gets better. When Sam comes over from the barracks tomorrow, I'm going to get him to help me pump out the water from the Anderson.'

'Bleedin' Anderson!' sniffed Babs. 'Waste er time!'

'Mum!' yelled Hannah, losing her temper. 'We've got to do *something*! It's too dangerous here!'

Babs turned to look at her. In those few subliminal moments, she realised how much she loved Hannah, how much she had probably *always* loved her. She stretched out her arms and drew the girl close to her. 'Anyfin' yer say, Hann,' she said, with gentle affection. 'Anyfin' yer say.'

Tilda Hobson swept up the glass from the shattered window into the kerb in front of the house. Muswell Hill, like Hampstead and St John's Wood, had had yet another day of V1 flying bombs crashing down into the area. Nobody quite understood why this part of north-west London had been singled out, unless something had been going seriously wrong with the Germans' own calculations.

'I don't know why these devils keep picking on us!' said a thoroughly irritated Tilda, who had spent the previous night taking cover under her bed on the first floor. 'I would have thought Downing Street or the Houses of Parliament would have been more their mark.'

'Well it's just as well it isn't,' called Dorothy, who was standing on the ground-floor sitting room windowsill, trying to salvage what was left of the ripped lace curtains. 'We need Mr Churchill. Without him we'd have no one to get us through this war.' As she spoke, a fire engine went racing past up towards Muswell Hill.

'Thank goodness they didn't get Alexandra Palace,' said Tilda. 'I'd hate to see *that* succumb to a damned doodlebug!'

'Don't speak too soon!'

'Miss Hobson!'

Both women turned with a start to see Hannah and Sam hurrying up the road towards them.

'Hannah, my dear!' called Dorothy, her face lighting up to see her former pupil again after several months. 'What are you doing up here?'

'We heard what happened was near you, so we came straight up,' said Hannah, breathless after a steep climb up the hill from the bus stop. 'Are you both all right?'

'Perfectly all right!' insisted Tilda defiantly. 'It'll take more than a few broken windows to get *us* down!'

Dorothy was more sceptical. 'I'm afraid the Broadway had a nasty hit. They say there have been quite a few casualties.'

'What can we do to help?' called Sam, who had changed into his civilian clothes for his last day before returning to duty.

'Oh, Sam, that's very kind of you,' replied Tilda, who had taken quite a girlish liking to him on the previous occasions Hannah had brought him up to the house. 'I think we can manage now. Come on inside. I'll put the kettle on.' She stopped what she was doing and scurried off into the house.

'What about you, Miss Hobson?' asked Sam, going into the front garden. 'What are you going to do about that window?'

'Oh, I shall get someone to board it up as soon as there's anyone available,' she replied.

'Well *I'm* available!' said Sam immediately, rolling up his shirt sleeves. 'D'you have anything around the place I can use?'

Dorothy was impressed by his instant offer of help. 'Well, yes.

You'll find some plyboard in the back garden. We had it left over after the last time the windows were blown in. Tilda will show you where it is.'

'Be right with you!'

Dorothy and Hannah watched him rush off into the house. 'What a treasure that boy is!' said Dorothy. 'And so very nice.'

'I know,' purred Hannah. 'I'm lucky ter have him.'

'It cuts both ways, you know,' said Dorothy, coming out from the front garden to join Hannah on the pavement. 'It seems to me you two are absolutely made for each other.'

'Sam's a very special person,' replied Hannah. 'I s'ppose it's because of how he was brought up.'

'Perhaps,' agreed Dorothy. 'There are Quakers who live in a house just down the bottom of this road. They'd help anyone who's in trouble. But it seems to me Sam's not just nice, he's also practical.'

Hannah laughed. 'Don't say that 'til *after* he's finished your window!'

Dorothy fetched the broom Tilda had left in the kerb, and swept the coping stone so that she and Hannah could perch there. 'It's all so terrible, isn't it?' she said with a sigh, her eyes scanning the broken windows and fallen chimney pots right the way along the road. 'After D-Day I thought it would only be a matter of time before it was all over.'

'Oh, it won't be long now,' said Hannah, distressed to see so many of the neighbours piling up rubble outside their houses. 'Once the RAF have sorted out the places where these things are coming from, it'll soon be all over.'

For a moment or so, both of them sat there in silence. They were taking in more than just the activity going on along the road. Each was reflecting in her own individual way all that had taken place over these past few years.

'How's your mum coping with all this?' asked Dorothy.

'I think everything that's happened is getting her down,' replied Hannah. 'I don't know what it is, but she seems to have just . . . given up.'

Dorothy turned to look at her. 'In what way?' she asked anxiously.

Hannah waited a brief moment before answering. 'This morning, just as we were having a bit of breakfast, she asked me if she should sign any papers about Louie.'

'Papers?'

'She thinks Sam's mum and dad should . . . adopt her.'

Dorothy went silent for a moment. 'Oh I see,' she replied eventually. 'How do you feel about that?'

'At first I thought it was a mad idea,' replied Hannah. 'I mean, Louie's her own daughter, my sister. She belongs with us. But then Mum made me stop an' think. She asked if it would be right for her to stand in the way of both her daughters having a better life. She said there was never going to be any way that she could look after Louie, and if she was happy where she was, it'd be wicked to take her away.' Although she found it difficult to talk about all this, she carried on. 'I talked to Sam about it. He said his parents love Louie as though she was their own, and if Mum isn't well enough to take care of her any more, then they would be only too proud to bring her into the family — permanently.' She faltered a moment before continuing. 'I don't know *what* to think, Miss Hobson,' she said, agonising.

Before answering, Dorothy thought carefully for a moment. 'You know, Hannah,' she said, 'I think your mother is a very shrewd and loving woman. With all the difficulties I had with her and your father, I never thought of her in such a way. But during this last year or so, when I've been to call on her, I could see how much she was trying to be the kind of mother that she had never been before. I suppose we women have the right to change, not only physically, but in the way we think. Your mum has been on her own long enough to do that, to think about all the things she's done wrong, to work out how she could put them right. Allowing another woman and her husband to adopt Louie won't be to lose her. *You* know that, Hannah, and so does your mother. My feeling, for what it's worth, is that you should go along with your mother, and allow Louie to continue the new life that she knows and loves.'

A short while later, Sam had been recruited by Hannah to bale out the flood water from the Anderson shelter, and when she got home from work he was still down inside the shelter and had more or less completed the job – or so he thought. 'May I never see another stirrup pump as long as I live!' he ranted. 'Every time I think I've got to the bottom of this damned hole, it starts filling up all over again! Whoever designed this contraption ought to be—'

'Watch it now, sergeant!' Hannah teased. 'Just remember where you come from.'

Sam chuckled with her, but threw down the stirrup pump. 'Well,' he said, rubbing the sweat from his forehead. 'Just come and look for yourself.'

Hannah went to the entrance and looked down inside the shelter. The water was quickly seeping up through the sides of the concrete floor, and within just a few minutes had already covered the feet of Sam's wellington boots. 'Ugh!' Hannah groaned. 'There's no way Mum's going to sleep down *here* tonight.'

'Not *any* night!' warned Sam.

Hannah held out her hand to help him climb up out of the water. 'But we've got to do something, Sam,' she said. 'They were saying at work today that the Germans are going to send over masses more doodlebugs. It's not safe for Mum to stay in the house.'

'It's not safe for *either* of you to stay in the house,' he said, once he'd reached the top of the steps. 'Why don't you both just pack up your things and go and stay with my parents?'

'Don't be silly, Sam,' she replied. 'I can't just give up my job like that. And in any case, Mum's far too unwell to leave London. I mean just look at her. This time of day, and she's still fast asleep up in bed.'

Even as Hannah spoke, the sound of party music came from the back parlour.

'Doesn't sound like she's *that* tired,' Sam replied jokily.

Hannah rushed inside the house, leaving Sam to take off his boots. She stopped dead at the back parlour door, hardly able to believe what she was seeing. To a gramophone record of 'Knees Up Mother Brown' being played on the old wind-up in the corner, Babs was performing a raucous rendering of the song, whilst doing her own frenzied 'knees up'. Hannah watched her mum's antics in silent awe, astonished not only by her sudden rush of energy, but also by her appearance, which found her transformed from her dowdy old dressing gown, which she seemed to wear each and every day, to a lovely green summer dress that complemented her rust-coloured hair, a small cocky straw hat, and the high-heel patent leather shoes that Hannah had not seen her wear for years. But even more extraordinary was that she had returned to wearing make-up, only this time not tarty as before, but discreet, with just a suggestion of lipstick and no mascara. Sam came in and stood there watching her, wide-eyed. As the gramophone gradually wound down, she suddenly grabbed hold of him and tried to get him to join in the 'knees up'. Fortunately, however, he was saved by the music, which came to an end.

'Wonderful!' exclaimed Babs, taking the needle arm off the record, replacing it on its rest, then flopping onto a chair exhausted. 'Just like the good old days!'

'Am I seeing things?' Hannah asked her incredulously. 'Aren't you supposed to be ill or something?'

'Ill?' returned Babs, roaring with laughter. 'Wot d'yer take me for? It's about time I enjoyed meself.'

'You're right about that, Mum,' replied Hannah. 'You look wonderful but – what's it all in aid of?'

'In aid of?' Babs asked, leaping up from her chair again. 'Do I 'ave ter 'ave an excuse ter enjoy meself?' She went straight to the gramophone, took the previous record off the turntable, and replaced it with another. 'As a matter of fact, I'm going out for a night on the town.'

Hannah exchanged an anxious glance with Sam.

'Oh, don't worry!' said Babs, with a chuckle. 'It's nuffin' like that. It's only me an' Gloria goin' to a black market meal up the Archway.' She lowered her voice. 'Steak an' mash!'

'Gloria?' asked Hannah. 'That woman on the corner of Caedmon Road?'

'That's 'er,' replied Babs proudly. 'She's bin my friend fer years. She's bin comin' in ter see me while you've bin off at work.'

At first Hannah looked worried, but she relaxed when she realised that the woman her mum was going out with was a leading light in the Emmanuel Parish Church in Hornsey Road.

'Are you sure you're going to be safe, Mrs Adams?' asked Sam. 'Is there somewhere you can shelter if there are any more flying bombs over again tonight?'

Babs smiled at him affectionately. 'Safe as 'ouses,' she replied. 'So don't you two start worryin' about me. I need a break. I need ter start pulling meself tergevver. Gloria's a good sort. Yer can bet yer life *she* won't let me go astray.' She looked at Hannah. 'Not that I want to,' she said tenderly, before suddenly becoming all bright and lively again. 'But before I go,' she said, hurriedly winding up the gramophone, 'I just want us all ter 'ear this.'

Hannah exchanged a puzzled look with Sam. 'What is it?' she asked.

'You'll soon know,' replied Babs mischievously. She put on the record. It was a lovely rendering of the old ballad 'Always', sung by Deanna Durbin. 'Remember?' she asked.

Hannah's face lit up. It was the first song her mum had taught both her and Louie when they were kids. Babs joined in with the words of the song, and almost immediately Hannah went to her mum, put an arm round her waist, and joined in with her, while Sam watched the two of them in awed astonishment and admiration.

The number of doodlebugs that fell on north London that evening far exceeded anyone's imaginings. It was bad enough that Hannah had to say farewell to Sam, who was leaving for duty first thing the following morning, but knowing that her mum was out in the middle of all the mayhem was giving her a great deal of anxiety. From ten o'clock onwards she spent a great deal of her time taking shelter in the old cupboard beneath the stairs, but the later it got the more concerned she became that her mum might not have been able to find a public shelter near enough to wherever it was that she and her friend Gloria had gone for their illicit meal.

Shortly before midnight, a loud explosion came from the direction of Camden Road, which was no more than five minutes' walk from Kinloch Street. Almost immediately, all hell broke loose as the emergency services swung into action, fracturing the night air with the frenzied clanging of bells and horns. Hannah crawled out on all fours from the cupboard under the stairs to find that all the plaster from the passage ceiling had come down, which meant that she had to tread carefully in her carpet slippers. Amazingly enough, all the lights in the house seemed to work, at least on the ground floor, but she turned them all off when she made her way to the front door. Fortunately, she was still in her day clothes which meant that she could leave the house to see how extensive the damage had been. In the street outside, it seemed that the entire neighbourhood had turned out to see what had been going on; everyone was speculating on the rough location of this latest doodlebug explosion, and doing their best to assess the damage to their own homes.

'Anyone seen my mum?' Hannah called wildly as she made her way into Hornsey Road. The reaction was negative. No one had seen Babs Adams all evening.

In Hornsey Road, Charlie Brend, still in his pyjamas, was clearing up the shattered glass from his shop window. 'When this is all over,' he half joked, 'I think I'll get a job as a carpenter. I could earn a fortune!'

Hannah left him, and wandered in a daze down towards Seven Sisters Road. There, she was greeted with scenes of utter chaos, with people rushing back and forth as fast as they could, many of them totally disoriented. She had no idea in which direction she was headed. All she remembered her mum saying was that she and Gloria were going for a meal up somewhere near the Archway. Wearing only her ragged old carpet slippers, she picked her way carefully along the main road, doing her best to avoid the broken glass that was scattered all over the pavements. Alarm bells were piercing the frenzied scene, waiting to be switched off by the shop owners, many of whom lived some distance away. 'Have you seen a woman with red hair?' was the question she asked practically every person she passed, only to receive the same negative response. 'On a night like this, mate,' replied one shopkeeper, 'I'm bleedin' colour blind!'

By the time Hannah reached the Nag's Head, she was desperate. Wandering aimlessly to the other side of the main Holloway Road, narrowly missing speeding police cars and fire engines, she managed to get as far as the Gaumont cinema, now blacked out in complete darkness after the last evening performance. Every inch of the way her eyes scanned the road ahead of her. But it was an impossible task, for everyone was out on the pavements trying to clear away the rubble resulting from the blast of the explosion, wherever it had taken place little more than ten minutes before.

'There's another one!' The voice of the man who shouted out so loudly echoed in the night air.

'Down!' called a woman's shrill voice from the other side of the road. 'Doodlebug! Get down!'

Everything came to a sudden halt – cars, a fire engine, two

ambulances – and when their engines were turned off their clamour was replaced by the unmistakable droning sound of a flying bomb. She caught her first glimpse of the fiery light from its tail when it was a long way off in the direction of Highgate. But then she also caught a glimpse of something else in the distance that sent a cold chill down her spine. It was the figure of a woman in a neat summer dress and cocky straw hat, hurrying down Holloway Road, heading straight for where Hannah was lying flat on her stomach. 'Oh, Christ!' she said to herself, before leaping to her feet. 'Mum!' she shouted. 'Down, Mum! Down!' As she spoke she heard the spine-tingling silence as the flying bomb engine suddenly cut out.

'Mum . . . !'

'Hann!' The moment Babs caught sight of her daughter waving frantically at her, she broke into a laboured trot in her favourite high-heeled patent shoes.

In the awful silence that followed the cut out of the doodlebug's engines, the only sounds that could be heard were of people everywhere shouting to Hannah and her mum to 'Get down!' But there was still a long gap between the the two women, and before they could get any closer the sinister shape of the monster machine suddenly dived from the sky and headed straight for the buildings close to where Babs was still running.

'Mum . . . down!' shouted Hannah hysterically, her voice echoing in the ugly few seconds of silence. 'Mum . . . !'

'Hann . . . !'

The explosion that followed immediately dwarfed Babs, over-whelming her in a huge shower of rubble, and simultaneously sending a rush of deadly hot air straight at Hannah, completely knocking her off her feet. She lay there for nearly twenty minutes before she could be rescued, but it was almost daylight before she managed to open her eyes. As she lay in the hospital bed, all she could hear ringing in her ears were the words of the song that her mum had loved so much: *I'll be loving you – always . . .*

Chapter 23

In January the following year, British and American troops were gradually advancing on the German occupying forces in Belgium. Both Field Marshal Montgomery and General Eisenhower were optimistic about the prospects, forecasting that within a few weeks the Allies would be crossing over the River Rhine and into German territory, after which they both predicted an early end to the war in Europe. This was all good news for Hannah, for it meant that it would not be too long now before Sam came home for good. The last time she had seen him was at her mum's funeral in November, one of the most distressing and traumatic times of her life, in which he had shown her the most wonderful love and support.

Hannah had been completely devastated by her mum's death in the doodlebug explosion. She blamed herself for what had happened, telling everyone that she should never have allowed her mum to go out at a time when the V1 attacks were at a peak. To make matters worse, when Hannah had checked with Gloria, the friend her mum had said she was going out to have a meal with, Gloria had told her that she knew nothing about such an arrangement. Nonetheless, Hannah was convinced that her mum had not gone back to her old ways, for when she checked with the most likely restaurants up the Archway she was told in one that a woman answering her mum's description *had* in fact met up with another woman for a meal earlier in the evening, but had left soon after her. All this had haunted Hannah. Who was this other woman she met up with, she asked herself over and over again, and why had her mum lied about going out with her friend Gloria?

Mercifully, Hannah's own injuries had been superficial, and she had only had to remain in hospital for one night. However, the mystery of her mum's last hours remained, and she would not rest until she knew the identity of that other woman.

Since her mum's death, Hannah's one great salvation had been her job at Woolworth's, where all the girls and Admin staff had rallied round, offering her all kinds of moral comfort, some of them asking her to go out for the evening with them, others offering advice about going to live out in the country with Sam's family. But kind as they were, she made it quite clear that until Sam came out of the army she would remain in the same house where she was born almost twenty-two years before, in Kinloch Street. Sadly, her friend Betty Pilkington had left her job at the store nearly two years before, following the death of her boyfriend Phil, whose Hurricane fighter plane had been shot down in a dogfight over the English Channel, and this left Hannah with no one with whom she could really share the same kind of confidence and trust. Betty had been a tower of support to Hannah, especially during the dreadful time when Tom Barker had tried to bully and intimidate her, and she felt that, nice as the new staff were, there was no one there who could ever replace Betty's friendship and good humour. However, things started to look up again when she arrived back home from work one evening to find the shadowy figure of someone standing on her doorstep in the pitch dark. 'Hallo – who's there?' she called warily.

'Hannah?' returned a woman's voice. 'Is that you?'

Hannah quickly directed her torch beam onto the face of the young woman, who was in naval uniform. 'Jane!'

'Oh, Hannah!' The two girls threw themselves into each other's arms, and hugged.

'Blimey, Jane!' Hannah stuttered excitedly. 'I can hardly believe it's you! Oh, God, it's wonderful, wonderful! Come in, come on in!'

A few minutes later the two girls were sitting together at the back parlour table, sipping tea, chatting wildly as if there was no tomorrow.

'Oh, Jane,' sighed Hannah, 'I can't tell you how I've missed you. Getting your letters was such a relief. I didn't know what WRNS really do, whether they go on ships with all the sailors, and if you did, would you be in danger?'

Jane chuckled. Although she had filled out a little, she still had that lovely cheeky smile which had endeared her so much to Hannah when they first met. 'Most of us don't really go on ships, Hannah,' she replied. 'They leave the girls to do all the paperwork. I think they're frightened about what might happen if we were out at sea with the lads!'

It was Hannah's turn to chuckle.

'But it'll change one of these days,' said Jane.

'*Everything* changes,' said Hannah sombrely.

Jane reached across and placed her hand over Hannah's. 'Father told me about your mum,' she said sympathetically. 'I'm so very sorry.'

Hannah shrugged. 'I don't know why,' she replied, 'but I always felt something like that would happen to her one day. The only thing is, when it *did* eventually happen, she was just getting on top of things, just about to enjoy life again. I sometimes wonder what He thinks He's doing up there.' She flicked her eyes briefly up at the ceiling. 'He doesn't seem to have any mercy.'

'I bet that's not what your feller thinks,' Jane reminded her.

'Sam was brought up differently from me,' replied Hannah. 'He has more endurance, more faith.'

'Yes,' said Jane, reflectively. 'It's a funny old thing about faith, isn't it? When the *Royal Oak* was torpedoed by that U-boat at the beginning of the war, and then after that the *Hood*, when I thought about all those boys and men going down with their ships, I thought to myself, how can I possibly believe that there's still *anyone* up there who can help us? But the fact is, Hannah, we *have* to, because if we don't, there's nothing left.'

For one brief moment Hannah took in her friend's words, but then she suddenly got up from the table. 'We're getting morbid!' she proclaimed. 'How about a drink?'

'A drink?' replied Jane, astonished. 'Don't tell me *you've* taken to the hard stuff too!'

'I have!' returned Hannah, going to the small dresser at one side of the room. 'I'm a big girl now!'

'And why not!' agreed Jane.

'What'll it be?' asked Hannah, with a flourish, opening a lower cupboard. 'Anything you like.'

'Rum!'

Hannah looked up with a start. 'Rum?' she asked, astonished.

'I *am* in the Navy, you know,' replied Jane firmly. 'Me and the fellers drink it all the time.'

'Good God!' joked Hannah, sorting through the bottles in

the cupboard. 'The next thing you'll be telling me is you smoke fags too.'

'Ah!' replied Jane, reaching into her uniform jacket pocket. 'I'm glad you reminded me!'

Hannah laughed. 'Well, there's no rum,' she said. 'But there's some gin, and a little bit of whisky left over from Mum's funeral.'

Jane smiled affectionately at her, and lit up her Player's cigarette. 'Gin will do fine.'

After doing the honours, Hannah took Jane into the front parlour. As there was no fire in the grate the room was bitterly cold, but they remained there just long enough for Hannah to show Jane the framed photos of her mum, her dad, Louie, and her grandparents. 'We used to be quite a family,' said Hannah, her voice tinged with some regret. 'Or at least I *thought* we were. It's amazing how things are never quite what they seem, isn't it?'

'In what way?'

Hannah lingered over a framed snapshot of her dad. 'Well, one minute you think you belong to someone, and the next you don't. But what really hurts is that the person you once loved turns out to be such a coward, and just runs away from everything.'

'You still haven't heard from him?'

Hannah shook her head. 'He didn't even get in contact with me when Mum was killed.'

'Perhaps he didn't know?'

Hannah shook her head. 'I notified the army. They assured me they'd get in touch with him right away.'

'Strange,' said Jane, with a sigh. 'I wonder why?'

'Well, after what went on all those years ago, I suppose I can hardly blame him.'

Jane took a slow, despondent look around the room. 'You know, Hannah,' she said eventually, 'you should think about getting away from all this. Oh, I don't mean that there's anything wrong with the place, but you're too surrounded by the past, memories that are going to be with you day and night. Isn't there somewhere you could stay until Sam gets demobbed?'

'Miss Hobson asked me to go and live with her and her sister,' replied Hannah, 'but I said no.'

'Miss Hobson?' asked Jane, puffing away on her cigarette.

'My old schoolteacher,' replied Hannah. 'The one I wrote to you about.'

'Ah . . .' replied Jane, recalling one of Hannah's letters to her. 'Of course.'

'Oh, it's not because of what Dad felt about her,' continued Hannah. 'It's just that – well, there seems to be no point really. This is where me and Louie were born, this is where we were brought up. Regardless of what's happened here over the years, it's still my home. Kinloch Street is still very special to me. I don't want to leave it for the wrong reasons.' She took a sip of her gin and turned to Jane. 'In any case,' she said, 'this place is still hiding one or two things I want to know about.'

The biggest menace now facing London were the long-range V2 rockets. Hannah's first experience of them came, ironically, on the evening of Guy Fawkes Night, when every house in Islington was shaken to its very foundations by an enormous explosion which came without any air-raid warning, a direct hit on Boothby Road near the Archway, close to the Upper Holloway Road. This latest secret weapon from the Germans created real fear and panic amongst the civilian population, not only because of its silent approach, but because there was never any time for a warning – whoosh, and it was all over. Then, just before Christmas, a rocket came down onto a Woolworth's store packed with shoppers in Deptford, south London. The death toll was horrific, and the bodies of many people, including members of the staff, were never found. This last incident deeply distressed everyone in the Holloway store where Hannah was working, and she immediately participated in the setting up of a fund to help the relations of the victims.

On the eve of Hannah's twenty-second birthday, everyday life along the streets had never been so dangerous, and when she came out of the store and saw the menacing trails of white vapour streaking across the sky, she wondered whether she would ever manage to reach her twenty-third year. Fortunately, however, she *did* survive the day, and to her astonishment and delight she and her friend Jane were invited by Dorothy Hobson and her sister Tilda to spend the evening at their home in Muswell Hill. However, the evening did not turn out to be entirely as Hannah had imagined.

The dining table in the sitting room had been set for five people, but when Hannah remarked on this, Dorothy explained that as there were so few people there to celebrate Hannah's birthday, she and Tilda had invited their next-door neighbour in to join them. Hannah thought it was a little strange to bring in a complete stranger to her party, but when Tilda assured her that the woman who was coming in was 'extremely nice' and 'very funny', she thought no more about it. However, a few minutes later, when Dorothy asked her sister and Jane if they could come and help her to carry some things from the kitchen, Hannah was a bit surprised to be told that *her* help wasn't really necessary, and that, if she didn't mind, it would be far more useful if she could put some more coke on the fire. Wondering what the hell was going on, she agreed, and once the sisters and Jane had left the room she used the coal shovel to build up the fire in the grate.

'Need any help, young lady?'

Hannah jumped, and turned with a start. Sam, in uniform, was standing behind her. 'Oh . . . oh . . .' she gasped, immediately dropping the shovel. 'Oh, Sam!' She threw her arms round him, and for several moments they stood there hugging each other.

'Happy birthday, my special girl!'

Hannah was almost in tears as he held out a tiny wrapped gift for her.

'It's not much,' said Sam, with a wide grin. 'But it's a start.'

'Sam . . . I . . . I don't know what to . . .' Hannah was struggling to find the words. 'What are you doing home? What's happening?'

'Open your present!' Sam persisted.

Her fingers weak with excitement, Hannah ripped off the brown paper from her birthday present. Inside was a ring box. Her heart missed a beat. 'Sam . . .' She was floundering like a fish out of water.

'Open it!'

Hannah opened the box, and clasped her hand to her mouth in shock. Inside was a sparkling diamond engagement ring. All she could utter was, 'Oh . . . Sam!'

'I hope the answer's yes?'

She had no more words. All she could do was throw her arms round his neck and kiss him. There were gasps of delight from the doorway, as Dorothy and her sister and Jane came back in applauding.

'Put it on, Hannah!' spluttered Jane, jumping up and down with excitement. 'Put it on!'

Sam took the box from her, then took her left hand and slipped the ring on her finger. It fitted perfectly. More gasps of delight from the others.

'I think I'm going to cry,' said Tilda.

'Please don't,' said Dorothy sternly. 'Remember you're serving the soup!'

After a delicious meal of Tilda's home-made leek soup, Marguerite Patten's Bakehouse Mutton, and Dorothy's caramel pudding speciality, everyone sat round the fire and talked about the prospects for the end of the war.

'Well, Sam,' said Tilda, trying not to show too much disappointment that Sam was irretrievably Hannah's man, 'I think it's wonderful that you're being demobbed, but with these wretched rockets coming down each day, they can hardly tell us that the war's almost over.'

'No,' replied Sam, who had his arm round Hannah on the sofa. 'But once our people have pounded away at the sites, it won't last for much longer.'

'I heard that most of the rockets they're firing are coming down in Holland,' said Jane. 'That must mean there's something wrong with the system.'

'I must say, it doesn't feel like it,' added Dorothy. 'When you think of the number of people who've been killed since the horrid things first started coming over.' She turned to Hannah. 'Hannah, my dear,' she said. 'You remember that rocket that came down on Boothby Road, near the Archway?'

'Yes I do.'

'Did you know that that young boy who was evacuated with you and Louie lived there?'

'Oh, my God!' gasped Hannah, shocked. 'You don't mean young Alfie? Alfie Grieves?'

'I'm afraid so,' replied Dorothy. 'I only found out myself quite by accident about a week ago. I met someone who lived just a few streets away – their two boys used to go to a school I used to teach at. They say the Grieves' house was quite literally blown away by the impact. The whole family were killed. It's been a terrible time for the father. He's been away in the army.'

'Oh, God,' said Hannah. 'How terrible! Louie's going to be absolutely devastated.'

'I dread to think how many more of my pupils have been lost to this vicious war,' said Dorothy. 'I don't think I'll ever know.'

'It was bad enough losing Mum,' said Hannah bravely. 'She'd have loved being here tonight.'

Dorothy looked away, got up, and checked the blackout curtains. Hannah noticed, but tried not to react.

'Oh well,' said Tilda chirpily. 'No point in being gloomy about it all – not on your birthday.'

Hannah looked across at her, and tried to smile. But it wasn't easy.

'It's well past lighting-up time,' said Dorothy. 'I'll just go and check the kitchen.'

Hannah watched Dorothy go out of the room, then got up herself, and followed her. 'Miss Hobson.'

Dorothy stopped and turned in the hall outside.

'Thank you for this wonderful party,' Hannah said. 'I can't tell you how much I appreciate it.'

'Hannah, my dear,' replied Dorothy. 'I don't think anything has given me so much pleasure for quite a long time. To see and hear you, the way you're growing up, it gives me such a warm feeling. I can still see you in my English class — that terrible cracked accent of yours.'

'And I can still hear *you* telling us all how English is such a wonderful language, and the way you wrote the letters of the alphabet on the blackboard as though they were living things.'

'The English language *is* a living thing, Hannah,' replied Dorothy. 'Remember, it's the language of Shakespeare, and that makes it rather special. I hope no one ever forgets that.' She turned to go into the kitchen.

'Miss Hobson,' said Hannah quickly. 'Do you have anything else to tell me?'

Dorothy came to an immediate halt. She turned slowly. 'I don't know what you mean.'

'Anything,' replied Hannah. 'Just anything about anything.'

Dorothy hesitated before answering. It was clearly a difficult moment for her. 'I've told you everything I know, Hannah,' she said.

'Have you?'

Dorothy found it terribly difficult to meet the enquiring look in Hannah's eyes. To her, Hannah had always been quite special. Right from the early days when Dorothy had first become a teacher, she had always been warned that it was wrong to have a 'favourite' pupil in any class, but there was no doubt in her mind that Hannah *was* a favourite — although she had never discovered why. It wasn't that Hannah had been a particularly bright pupil, but the one great asset she had was that she knew how to listen more than any other child that Dorothy had ever known. But becoming involved in Hannah's home life had proved fatal, and now Dorothy was feeling the effects. 'The only thing I can say, Hannah,' she replied, 'is that I will never lie to you.'

Amidst great uncertainty, Hannah watched her go into the kitchen, then turned back and returned to the others in the sitting room.

After they had left the Hobsons' house, Hannah and Sam strolled at a leisurely pace up towards Muswell Hill Broadway, where they wanted to see Jane off on her bus back to her temporary posting at Greenwich. It was a starry night, and very cold, but as it was a new moon there was very little light, and both girls used their torches to pick their way along the rather rickety pavement. All three of them were in a very ebullient mood, and at one time Jane even burst into song, a kind of genteel version of 'Show Me The Way To Go Home', which she later admitted she had learnt from some of her bell-bottom mates when she had been posted to a naval training centre. Hannah of course joined in, and so did Sam, who for the past few years hadn't exactly been isolated from some of his mates' more rowdy sing-songs. But whilst they were waiting for Jane's bus, Hannah learnt something from her that a few years ago she would never have dreamt possible.

'I'm going to stay in the Navy full time,' Jane announced, quite casually. 'I haven't told my dad yet, and I know it'll hurt him, but I just can't bring myself to go back and continue trying to take the place of my mother. I have to go out and live my own kind of life.'

'Are you sure you're not just running away, Jane?' asked Hannah. 'I mean, you don't have to stay in the WRNS just to be independent – do you?'

'No, I don't,' Jane replied. 'But I like life in the Navy. It's not a nine to six job, it's not just checking out stock in the back of the shop, it's a job that's changing all the time. There's no way that I can ever get in a rut.'

After Jane had got onto her bus, Hannah and Sam strolled down Muswell Hill, arms round each other's waists, bound for Hornsey Road and Kinloch Street.

'D'you think Jane's doing the right thing, Sam?' asked Hannah. 'I mean, is the Navy the answer for someone like her?'

Sam considered this for a moment before answering. 'I think if I were Jane,' he replied, 'I'd be doing exactly the same thing.'

Hannah brought them to an abrupt halt. 'You would?' she asked with some surprise.

'Hannah,' he said uneasily, 'As soon as I get my demob, I don't want us to go and shut ourselves away in Redbourne. No – don't get me wrong – I love my family, and I'll never really abandon all the things I was brought up to believe in. But, like Jane, I've got to work out my life – *our* life – in *our* way. Before I was born, my mother and father had already decided how they wanted to spend the rest of *their* lives, and I want *us* to do the same. I'm ready to make mistakes. Aren't you?'

'You've got to be joking,' said Hannah. 'My whole life's been one big mistake.'

'That's not quite true,' insisted Sam. 'You've gone through some pretty difficult times, I know, but you're quite a survivor you know.'

'Mm,' murmured Hannah. 'I'm not so sure about that.'

They strolled on. It was now well after ten o'clock, and the last call customers were just turning out of the pubs. Even though Hannah had on her headscarf, her ears still felt like ice, and she dared not touch them in case they fell off. On the other side of the road, a man and two women were having a blazing row. One of the women was clearly the man's wife, and the other woman had plainly upset things, no doubt for obvious reasons. After they had passed further down the hill, Hannah and Sam could still hear them squabbling, so much so that their language was really getting quite nasty.

'Should we try to do something?' asked Sam.

'No point.'

'But you just can't leave people like that,' he pleaded. 'Somebody might get hurt.'

'*I've* been hurt a lot of times in my life, Sam,' she said, trying to justify what she had just said. 'My mum always used to say it's better to leave people to get on with their own problems.'

'Your mum wasn't always right, Hannah,' replied Sam tenderly, but firmly.

Hannah didn't reply, but she thought about what Sam had said; she thought about it really hard. It was true. Her mum used to say an awful lot of things that just hadn't made sense. That's why things turned out the way they did. But her mum did have instinct, and it somehow managed to get her through. Nonetheless, it was only during the last few years that Hannah had realised the pain her mum had suffered, and somehow she had to find out the cause.

It was a very long walk back to Holloway, but as Hannah had once done a much longer one she took it all in her stride. By the time they got to the junction of Seven Sisters and Hornsey Road, the streets were virtually deserted. Even the perpetually busy Eaglet pub on the corner was as quiet as a mouse.

'Why don't you leave me here, Sam?' said Hannah, bringing

them to a halt. 'You've got a long journey back to the barracks. I can easily get home from here.'

Sam pulled her close to him. 'D'you really think I'm just going to dump you here all on your own in the middle of the night?' he asked sceptically.

'Don't be silly. It's only just after eleven.'

'My future wife deserves to be treated with courtesy and respect,' he said, only half joking.

Hannah laughed. 'Well it'll be the first time!'

'I hope so.'

They leant towards each other, and kissed.

'Oh, Sam,' Hannah sighed, the moment their lips had parted. 'I do wish I could get this nagging feeling off my back.'

'What d'you mean?'

'Mum, Dad,' she replied with a sigh. 'It's hanging over me like a dead weight. There's something I don't know, and nobody seems to want to tell me. What is it, Sam? What is it?'

As she spoke, the most terrible swishing sound suddenly tore the night air apart.

'Down, Hannah!'

Sam grabbed Hannah, and threw both him and her to the ground. As he quickly shielded her body with his own, there was the most almighty explosion in the distance, but enough to shake every building around them, with the sound of windows shattering, and glass tinkling everywhere onto the pavements.

'Sam . . . !'

'Don't move, Hannah!' begged Sam. 'Whatever you do – don't move!'

They lay there for several minutes, until gradually the distant clanging of bells and horns from vehicles of the emergency services reassured them that it was safe to get up again.

Sam helped to comfort Hannah, brushing her down, and hugging her. 'It's all right, darling. Everything's all right.'

Shaking from head to foot, Hannah held on to him as tight as she could. 'S-so,' she joked nervously, 'is *this* what married life's going to be like?'

Chapter 24

In March the Allies overran the last V2 rocket bases in the north of Holland. From that time onwards the war on the civilian population in the British Isles was virtually at an end. At the end of April it was announced that the Italian dictator Benito Mussolini had been executed in Italy, and a few days later the BBC broadcast the news that Adolf Hitler was also dead. It was a time of great rejoicing for the British people, and especially for Hannah, for on the very day of Hitler's death, Sam had been demobbed.

Hannah and Sam had not met since the evening of Hannah's birthday party, when both of them had been practically blown off their feet by the force of the V2 blast in Edmonton, north London. Hannah had no idea where Sam had been serving during those last few months, but when she rushed out to greet him in the middle of Kinloch Street following his demob, she was shocked by how grey in the face he looked. There was no doubt about the warmth of his reaction at seeing her, and they hugged right there in the street, kissing passionately, whilst nearly every one of the neighbours turned out to applaud him. But once they were alone inside the back parlour, he gave his first harrowing account of the last month of his time in the army, serving in Germany.

'I never thought that human beings could treat their fellow

humans in such a barbaric way, without thought, without love, without mercy.' Sam found it difficult to find the words to describe his ordeal, which took place whilst his unit was one of those involved in the liberation of the Belsen concentration camp.

Like most people at home, Hannah had already heard on the radio the reports about the dreadful atrocities the Germans had committed against the inmates of the concentration camps, so she made a special point of not trying to get Sam to talk about anything more than he wanted until he himself was ready to do so. For the time being, she decided that her main task from now on was to help him put those nightmare memories to one side, and get him rehabilitated into what she hoped would be a calm and civilised future. Before that process could start, however, Sam had some rather alarming news for Hannah.

'I met your father,' he said.

Hannah froze.

'He was on the unit ferry coming back from France last week. Did you know he's spent the last few years as a medical orderly in the RAMC?'

Hannah slowly shook her head. 'I know nothing about him,' she replied, in a daze of disbelief. 'How did you know he was . . . ?'

Sam reached for her hands across the parlour table and held them. 'It was quite absurd really,' he replied. 'We were both at the ship's rail, looking out at the sea, waiting for the moment when we could catch a glimpse of the White Cliffs. We talked about the war, and what it had done to people, all kinds of things like that. Then we shook hands, and I told him my name. But when he told me that *his* name was Len Adams, I suppose I did a kind of double-take – I mean, it all seemed too much of a coincidence. But when we got to talking more, and I told him about you and me and Louie – well, he became very emotional.'

'What exactly did he say, Sam?' asked Hannah, whose reaction was like stone.

'He didn't say anything about – about what had happened in your family,' continued Sam. 'But he did say over and over again that as long as he lived, he could never forgive himself for what he had done to both you *and* Louie. I may be wrong, Hannah, but I thought he sounded like an absolutely broken man.'

'And what about our mum?' asked Hannah bitterly. 'Did he sound absolutely broken-hearted about her too?'

Knowing only too well the bitterness Hannah felt towards the man who had disappeared from her life without a word of explanation, Sam was careful not to inflame the situation any more than necessary. 'Yes,' he replied. 'Apparently the army *had* informed him about what had happened to your mum. But he wouldn't be drawn into why he never made any effort to contact you about it.'

'He hasn't made contact with *any* of us since that one letter I received from him soon after I was evacuated to Redbourne.' Hannah got up from the table and paced the room. 'It's no use, Sam,' she said. 'After all that happened between him and Mum, I don't know how he can live with his conscience. The least he owes Lou and me is that he sits down and tells us who and what we are.'

'I think you've got a pretty good idea of that already,' replied Sam, being as practical as he possibly could. 'From what he told me, he wants to put things right, but he doesn't know how.'

'So he just ignores us?'

Sam got up and went to her. 'You know, darling,' he said,

cupping her face between his hands, 'some of us don't know *how* to put things right. I know that from my own experience. You women are so much more practical. You're not afraid to come right out and demand answers.'

'Sam, all our lives, Lou and I have been brought up to believe that this man was our father, but then quite suddenly – he isn't. Mum took on a tremendous responsibility giving him two kids by other men. Don't you think he owes us at least *some* explanation?'

'Yes, Hannah, I do. But whether he has the courage to give you that explanation, only time will tell.'

Louie was growing up faster each day. At almost fifteen years old, she had shed all those baby looks that adolescent girls are always impatient to get rid of, and every morning she was now spending rather longer than usual admiring her figure in the mirror, just to make sure that she wasn't putting on too much weight. This was clearly important, for in a few weeks from now Hannah and Sam were going to be married in the Meeting House just outside the back door of the Redbourne post office, and she wanted to look right for whichever visitors would be turning up for the wedding ceremony.

When Hannah and Sam arrived from London to attend to the legal requirements, Louie was waiting at the station to meet them, and tell them all the gossip about how the villagers were feeling about their wedding. 'They're all so excited about it,' she said, the moment Hannah and Sam got off the train. 'In fact, they can't make up their minds what's more exciting, VE Day or your wedding!'

'Well VE Day is coming faster than our wedding,' said Hannah.

'You wouldn't believe the preparations they're making back home. D'you know, Lou, as soon as it's announced, they're going to have street parties all over the place – including Kinloch Street.'

'Well *we're* havin' them too!' replied Louie grandly. 'All of us at school are busy making bunting to put outside the shops, and if the weather's fine there's going to be a *huge* party on the village green.'

'Well if I were you,' Sam advised her, 'I'd get VE Day over first, because it's going to take at least six weeks to register our wedding before we can have the ceremony.'

As they walked back to the village, Louie wrapped her arm round her sister's waist. 'Oh, I'm *so* excited about it!' she said. 'It'll be a wonderful day. Mother's making me a new dress.'

'Now, Lou,' Hannah warned her. 'Don't forget this is not going to be like a normal wedding. I mean – not like we used to see them at the Emmanuel Church back home.'

'Oh, I know all that,' replied Louie. 'Mother's told me all about it, how a lot of it is going to be just like the meetings we go to every week. But it's still going to be – wonderful!'

Sam laughed. 'Of course it is, Lou!' he said. 'And we're all going to enjoy every minute of it.'

'We certainly will,' added Hannah, turning a loving smile towards Sam, 'especially now we know you're home for good.'

'Oh, yes!' agreed Louie. 'Mother and Father have got a wonderful surprise waiting for you. They've found a cottage that's just right for you. It's only just down the road, just near Mrs Mullard's!'

Hannah immediately exchanged an uneasy look with Sam.

*   *   *

The formalities of registration for their wedding ceremony seemed, for Hannah, to take forever. It all took place at the monthly meeting of the Friends in the Meeting House behind the post office, attended not only by Hannah and Sam, but also by Louie, Sam's parents Mary and Joseph Beedle, the registering officer, and the usual small group of members. During what really turned out to be an interview, Hannah, not being a member of the Religious Society of Friends, was asked to state to those present that she was in sympathy with the nature of the marriage. In addition, she and Sam provided letters of recommendation from two other members, who were friends of Sam's parents. The only slight hitch came when Hannah was asked to provide details about her own parents. The fact that Babs was deceased posed no problem, but when it came to naming her father, the registering official had to accept Hannah's submission that he was probably missing, presumed dead. It was a short meeting, and apart from the legal requirements of registration for the wedding, it was carried out in virtual silence. When it was over, Hannah and Sam reluctantly agreed to accompany Mary and Joseph to the cottage they had found for them.

Returning to the lane where she had first visited Mrs Mullard to talk about the Bullocks, Hannah felt as though she was somehow treading back into a past that she wanted badly to forget. Nonetheless, seeing the old lady herself standing at the gate of her own cottage, smiling and waving excitedly, it was difficult not to feel at least some warmth for her.

'It's all ready!' exclaimed Mrs Mullard, holding up the key of the cottage the small group were about to inspect just a few doors away. 'I've scrubbed the place from top to bottom, so when you move in you won't have a thing to do!'

Joseph raised his soft-brimmed hat, and took the key from her. 'Thanks so much, dear lady,' he replied. 'I'll bring it straight back to you.'

'Let me know if there's anything you need,' called the old lady. 'Remember, I'm only a few doors away!'

Hannah and Sam felt the same way as each other about that remark, but managed not to react.

The cottage Joseph took them to turned out to be utterly charming. It was real picture postcard stuff, with ivy, and climbing roses waiting to burst into bloom around the front porch, and a small front garden that had clearly been worked on with great love and care.

'Dear Ivy kept the place so well,' said Mary, with great enthusiasm, whilst Joseph was opening the front door. 'She loved it all her life. That's why she called it . . .' She indicated with a smile to the sign on the front gate: IVY COTTAGE. 'It was so sad when she died a few months ago – such a nice woman. She was only eighty-seven.'

Hannah felt her stomach churn over.

The inside of the cottage was fully beamed, and all the multi-panelled windows were leaded. Mary absolutely loved both the pastel green colour of the walls in the kitchen and the shape of the small sitting room with its bow window and old world furniture. Louie raced upstairs to look at the two bedrooms, calling down to the others to join her. Hannah was first to do so, closely followed by Mary, and then Sam and his father.

'It's lovely!' yelled Louie, immediately rushing downstairs again and out into the back garden, where she started to collect a small posy of the last of the primroses and the first of the marigolds. Hannah, Mary, Sam, and Joseph watched her in silence from one of the bedroom windows. The atmosphere was clearly not as joyous as Louie undoubtedly felt.

'I'm sorry, Father, Mother,' said Sam sombrely, guiltily, without turning to look at them. In fact everyone's eyes remained focused on what Louie was doing in the garden below. The silence that followed was, to Hannah, somewhat reminiscent of the Meeting House: so much that was being thought was unspoken.

'You don't have to say anything, son,' said Mary. 'I think we already knew, didn't we, Father?'

Joseph remained stone-faced, staring down into the garden. 'All I want to know is – why?'

Sam put his arm round Hannah's waist. 'We've decided we want to choose a place for ourselves.'

'In London?' asked Joseph, with just a touch of scepticism.

'No, sir,' replied Sam.

'We're going to look for somewhere near the sea,' said Hannah, with immense trepidation.

Mary finally turned to her. There was disappointment in her smile, but it was caring. 'What a lovely idea,' she said. 'A long time ago, Father and I once talked about living near the sea. I love to hear the sound the waves make on the shore.'

'We haven't decided exactly where yet,' added Sam, 'but in the next few weeks we're going to look around the south coast, near Brighton.'

'They say the air's very bracing down there,' said Hannah, trying to sound practical.

'What sort of work will you be looking for?'

Sam turned to find his father staring at him. 'Hard to say,' he replied awkwardly. 'Once the war ends and the chaps start coming home, jobs are going to be hard to find. But I've got a feeling I'd like to get some work in a boatyard or something.'

'Sam's been reading up about sailing boats and yachts and things,' added Hannah, with great enthusiasm. 'He reckons there'll be quite a lot of money in the trade over the next few years, especially once they've removed all the mines from the beaches and out at sea.'

'Of course,' Sam continued, 'I'll probably have to go to a technical college for a bit. It's the engineering side I'm really interested in.'

'Much better than the post office, I would imagine.'

His father's remark hurt, so much so that Sam couldn't really find the right words to answer him.

'That was not a criticism, Sam,' said Joseph. 'It was merely an observation. I've spent my life selling postage stamps to people. I see no reason why I should expect a child of mine to do the same.'

Sam could hardly believe what he was hearing, and Hannah was so moved by what Joseph had just said that she threw her arms round Mary.

'I think you know,' Joseph went on rather solemnly, 'that I'm a man of few words. But I'd like to say something that I think is important for both of you.' He turned round, perched on the windowsill, and gently took off his hat. 'On the day I was born, there was a terrible thunderstorm. The clouds were grey and heavy, and it seemed as though the heavens had opened because they knew that I was going to be one of the most difficult human beings ever born.'

Hannah and Sam exchanged a smile.

'But as it turned out, I wasn't,' continued Joseph. 'In fact, my father used to tell me that there were times when he wished I'd been obstinate, because that would then leave me room to be flexible. I know all this may sound strange to you, but what I want to tell you is that the most approachable person is the one who listens. The first sound I ever heard was in the middle of that storm, the raindrops pounding away on the window, the fury of the Lord echoing across the sky in every clap of thunder. But then I learnt later, much later, that it wasn't anger I was hearing, it was a plea, a plea to do all the things that I knew to be right, even though it might not be easy at the time. All I'm asking you to do is never close the ears that the Lord God has given you. Every creature on earth has a voice, and that voice should be heard.' He got up, and put on his hat again. 'I shall be a proud man to welcome you to our family, Hannah,' he said, with a smile that quite literally lit up his face. 'And we shall pray that life by the sea with the one you love will be the start of a brave new life for you both.'

Mary, with tears welling in her eyes, exchanged that special look of silent recognition that she and Joseph had enjoyed for so many years.

Hornsey Road was bathed in the warm dark of an early summer night. Although it was almost midnight, there were still the sounds of people chatting in bed or in their front parlours, and now that the blackout restrictions had at last been lifted, the pavements reflected the light from those who were sitting up late.

Len Adams had been strolling around the back streets now for nearly an hour. After living in secret in Edmonton with his elderly mum and dad for the past few weeks, he was fascinated to take in his old haunts again, especially seeing them with bunting and flags sprouting from windows and rooftops, in preparation for the impending announcement in the next day or so that the war in Europe was finally over. He had already passed Stagnells baker's shop on the corner of Hornsey Road and Seven Sisters Road, then Dorner the butcher, where the smell of saveloys and pease pudding was still seeping beneath the shop door after a busy evening. However, it was only when he reached Anderson's fried fish and chip shop that he stopped for a moment to look at his reflection in the window there. What he saw was a very different man from the one who had been called up at the start of the war, very different from the young man who could never resist going inside to get a penn'th of chips in a sheet of newspaper. What he saw now was a pale imitation of himself, gaunt, with eyes that protruded from their sockets like marbles, and lips that had virtually dried up over the fullness of time. But he still had that thick mop of brown hair that all the girls used to go mad about, even though it was gradually becoming flecked with grey beneath his flat cap. The army had done things to him, especially those last few months dealing with the rotting bodies and skeletons in the concentration camps of Germany.

Charlie Brend's sweet shop was closed, and in darkness, but Len spared a moment to look in the window and dream of sticks of liquorice and sherbet dips, bull's eyes and toffee swirls, and fizzy lemonade. Oh, those drinks, those 'Charlie's specials'! While he was standing there, however, he had to retreat into the shadows of the shop, because he had no idea if the couple who were passing would know him, which was something he wanted to avoid. But once they had gone, he felt confident enough to take the short alley into Kinloch Street, where, apart from Ada Jackson's moggie hissing at him as he passed, everything was quiet.

Gradually, silently, he made his way to the front door of his own home, or what he used to call his own home, before he sent himself into self-imposed exile. He took the key from his jacket pocket, and eased it into the lock, breathing a sigh of relief to discover that the lock hadn't been changed.

Once inside the house, he quietly closed the front door, but for fear that someone would think a burglar had broken in, didn't switch on any lights. For a moment, he just stood there in the tiny passage in the dark, savouring in his mind that smell, that same old smell of boiled greens which Babs had cooked so many times for want of knowing what other vegetable to serve with the fried sausages, or scrag end of mutton, or cottage pie. The atmosphere gradually overwhelmed him, so he went silently into the front parlour and sat down for a spell in the old blue velvet sofa. Yes, the springs were still sticking through the upholstery, just waiting to give someone a nasty nick in the bottom. As he sat there, the memories came flooding back. Although he couldn't see the framed photos on the mantelpiece above the grate, he knew they were there: the kids, Babs, his mum and dad, and his brother Jim. Kids? That brought the faintest of smiles to his face. Hannah and Louie weren't kids any more, especially Hannah, soon to get herself married to a more worthy bloke than Len reckoned *he'd* ever been. Kids? Oh, how he loved them. Except – well, they weren't *his* kids – not any more. Now they both belonged to someone else, someone who could love them in the way that they deserved to be loved. But it should never have ended up like this, Len told himself. He should have walked through that front door on leave any time over the past five years and been greeted by his kids in the same way that millions of other fellers home on leave would have been greeted. So why didn't he long ago have the guts to tell Hannah and Louie who they were and where they came from? And why hadn't he understood Babs, understood why she did the things that on the face of it at the time seemed completely out of order. Babs! Oh, Christ! He shut his eyes and opened them up again in the dark, half expecting to see her in the room. He couldn't bear sitting there a moment longer, so he got up quickly, went out into the passage, and made his way softly upstairs.

The bedroom – *their* bedroom – was fully lit by the wily old moon that had decided to sneak out of the clouds whilst he'd been sitting downstairs in the dark. He went to the bed that he and Babs had shared for so long. It was still made up, even though Hannah had clearly never used it, for the sheets were crisp and clean. He lightly smoothed the eiderdown with one of his hands. In his mind's eye he could feel Babs's presence there. She seemed to be as alive as she ever was. Oh, God, what that woman must have gone through. If only people knew. If only people *really* knew – especially Hannah and Louie.

He moved around the room taking in all the things that he remembered from those days when he and Babs had shared it together. Her dressing table was exactly the same. Nothing had changed; even the face cream and powder and lipstick had been left there, exactly as they were on the evening before Babs died. Finally, he went to the wardrobe. Babs was there all right, there in spirit as well as in her clothes. He idly ran his hand along the dresses and coats that were hanging there, until he eventually came to the one coat that, to him, had typified Babs's entire life. He removed the hanger containing the mock leopardskin coat, and held it up to look at it. Suddenly, something inside him made him feel weak, as weak as the man he used to be. His face screwed up, and as he hugged the coat against him, tears began to streak down his cheeks. 'Oh, Christ, Babs!' he sobbed. 'What've I done? What the bleedin' 'ell 'ave I done?'

Chapter 25

Early on the morning of 8 May 1945, there was a violent thunderstorm which, to some, sounded as if the war had started all over again. But that wasn't the case, for in a broadcast at three o'clock that afternoon, Prime Minister Winston Churchill announced the surrender of the German armed forces, and the end of all hostilities. That day was therefore proclaimed 'VE Day' – Victory in Europe – and it was the signal for the whole of the British Isles to start celebrating the end of one of the most horrific and harrowing periods in modern history. Everyone everywhere felt the need to rejoice, not least in and around Kinloch Street and Hornsey Road, where streets were sealed off to allow children's parties and endless knees-up round bonfires for the adults. There were parties out in the countryside, too, where not so long ago refugees from many of the cities found safe havens from the savage air raids, and attacks by flying bombs and guided missile rockets.

In Redbourne, the village green had been spared the worst of the morning rain, and by afternoon the residents had given every child in the community the best tea party they had ever had. Even on the green itself, a bonfire burnt furiously through until the early hours of the next day, which proved a headache for Fred Winters, who later had the job of restoring the well-mown grass to its former glory. Although there was no dancing, there were patriotic songs like 'There'll Always Be An England', 'Jerusalem', and 'Land of Hope and Glory', which was sung by everyone over and over again before they all finally retired for the night at the end of a very exuberant but exhausting day. However, a few days later, at least one small part of the community had still more excitement to look forward to.

Hannah had spent the night before her wedding sharing Louie's bedroom above the post office, whilst Sam was in his old room next door to his parents on the first floor. As expected, Hannah got very little sleep that night, not because of her own anxieties about how she was going to get through the strain of the following day's ceremony, but because her young sister was delirious with excitement about all the wonderful things that would be taking place.

'Of course,' chattered Louie, from her side of the single bed, 'I wanted to wear the pink dress Mother made for me last year, but she said it was far too casual for an event like this. Anyway, it doesn't matter. The white one is far more grown up.'

'Go to sleep, Louie!' groaned Hannah, face turned away from her on what little room her sister had left for her. 'You're making me nervous!'

'Oh, don't be so grumpy, Hann!' retorted Louie, pulling Hannah over to face her. 'How can you possibly sleep on a night like this? Just think of it – termorrow you're goin' to be Mrs Sam Beedle.'

'Yes,' replied Hannah. 'And I'll still be Mrs Sam Beedle the day after that *and* the day after that, but if I don't get any sleep tonight, I shall nod off during the ceremony!'

'Are you scared?' asked Louie, hoping she would get a positive answer.

'Of what?'

'Everything!' gasped Louie. 'I mean, just think of all those people there, coming just to see you and Sam. It's going to be so exciting!'

'And I hope you're not going to chatter all through the ceremony!' Hannah warned. 'Just remember what you've been taught by your mother and father.'

Louie flopped back onto her side of the bed again. 'It's funny, isn't it?'

'What?'

'Calling them that,' replied Louie dreamily. 'Mother and Father. Kinloch Street seems such a long time ago, as though it never existed.' She went silent for a moment or so, imagining that Hannah wasn't listening. But she was. 'D'you think he really *is* dead?'

'Who?'

'Dad.'

Hannah rolled over to face her. 'I don't know, Lou,' she said. 'Does it matter to you? I mean, it's been so long now.'

'I'd still like to know,' replied Louie, who was being uncharacteristically curious. 'I mean, when Mum told you that he wasn't our dad after all, I was really upset, but when I thought about it, when he didn't bother to get in touch with us when Mum got killed, I really hated him. Now, I try not to think about him.'

'That's the way it should be, Lou. That's the way it *has* to be. You have new parents now. They're good people, who show you more love and care than you've ever had before.'

'Except from you.'

Louie's words made Hannah realise how much she loved her sister. Over the years they had not been really close, but as she grew up Louie was realising more and more the true value of their relationship. 'You must promise me something, Lou,' she said. 'You must promise me you'll never lose touch with me, never feel that I'm not there when you want me. I'm not your mum, but I'll always be the next best thing.'

Louie waited a moment before answering. 'I'm sorry, Hann,' she said eventually.

'What for?'

'For pretending not to care when you told me about Alfie Grieves,' replied Louie, the first note of sadness in her voice. 'I wish I'd been nicer to him. Despite the way he used to get on my nerves, I liked him a lot. Alfie was good fun. I miss him.'

Hannah pulled up the bedclothes and covered Louie with them. 'I think it's time we got some sleep,' she said softly. 'We've got a lot ahead of us tomorrow.'

'It'll be the best day of your life,' said Lou, snuggling up.

'I hope so, Lou,' replied Hannah. 'I hope so.'

The following morning, the Meeting House behind the post office had filled up with members and guests by ten o'clock, and in the street outside there was a small gathering of villagers who were not members of the Religious Society of Friends, but were waiting to support Hannah and Sam after they came out from the first Quaker wedding they had ever seen in their community. This special occasion was highlighted by the burning hot sun which from first light that morning had cast a golden shine all over the village green, turning the countryside into a kaleidoscope of beautifully different colours. Inside the House itself, not a sound could be heard, for there was no real departure from the traditional silence which always plays such an important part of any Quaker gathering.

Once everyone was seated, Hannah and Sam took their places at the front of the group facing everyone. Hannah looked radiant in a simple new white dress that, with the aid of her clothing coupons, Sam had bought for her at Jones Brothers department store in Holloway, and Sam himself, in a two-piece grey flannel suit and pastel grey-coloured tie, had never looked smarter. Mary and Joseph were also dressed very simply, as were most of the members and guests, the one exception being Louie, who had not been able to resist that pink-coloured dress her mother had made for her. As all the seats had been taken, quite a lot of the men were standing in a small group at the back, including one or two guests.

After a moment or two of silence, one of the Friends stood up to say a few words. He was known locally just as Uncle Harold, and was a widower who lived in an alms house on the way to Thornton. His function was merely to explain briefly the procedures of a Quaker wedding, and the moment he stood up several other members got up too, and one or two of them actually spoke a few words of support to the bride and groom, wishing them God's love and friendship throughout their lives. And then, for Hannah, came the hard part. She and Sam got up, turned towards each other, held hands, and read out some special words from a piece of paper. Sam led the way.

'*Friends. I take this my friend, Hannah, to be my wife, promising, through God's help, to be unto her a loving and faithful husband, so long as we both on earth shall live.*'

Then, shaking with nerves, Hannah took her turn: '*Friends. I take this my friend, Samuel, to be my husband, promising, through God's help, to be unto him a loving and faithful wife, so long as we both on earth shall live.'*

Sitting with heads bowed nearby, Mary fought back tears, whilst Joseph kept his hands firmly planted on his knees. Louie mischievously caught Hannah's eye, and gave her the biggest smile imaginable.

A few minutes later the couple took their vows, all of which had been agreed in advance. They then exchanged gold wedding rings, quietly, and without any form of words from anyone. After this Hannah and Sam, together with Mary and Joseph as witnesses, went to a small table at the side of the hall, where they signed the marriage certificate in the presence of one of the Elders. Once this was done, Hannah was asked the whereabouts of her surviving parent, who would also be a witness to their wedding. Under the circumstances, Hannah found it necessary to repeat that she had no surviving parent, which seemed to create some kind of confusion with the presiding officials; that is, until a man suddenly stepped forward from the shadows.

Hannah, Sam, and everyone present swung with a shocked start to see Len Adams, smartly dressed in a navy blue suit and tie, emerging quietly from the small group at the rear of the hall. With barely a look at Hannah, he said, 'I'm the farver of this woman, and I'm a witness,' then he took the pen from the official, and signed the marriage certificate, which was then read aloud to Sam's family, village friends, and members. Once a pale-faced Hannah, Sam, and everyone had sat down again, everyone prayed in silence for them, committing themselves to supporting the couple in any way they could. All that remained was for two of the Elders to shake hands, which solemnised the marriage, followed by everyone in the hall getting up and shaking hands with each other, indicating that the special meeting had come to an end. That was the cue for the congregation to file out of the Meeting House, stopping only briefly to sign their names on the wedding certificate as witnesses, and as a mark of support for the success of the marriage.

Once the hall was finally cleared, Hannah and Sam were left with Sam's parents and Len Adams. Mary and Joseph decided it was best to leave Hannah to face her father in her own way, and so after briefly taking hold of first Hannah's hands and then Sam's, with a cursory nod towards Len, they left the hall.

During the silence that followed, Len slowly made his way towards Hannah from the rear of the hall. Hannah watched him approach with disbelief and apprehension. She found him so changed in appearance that she hardly recognised him, but she struggled against despising him to the very depths of her soul.

''Allo, Hann,' he said softly, his voice barely audible. 'Congratulations.'

For a moment, Hannah stood there in front of him, with Sam at her side, finding it impossible to look into Len's eyes. Then in one swift movement she took hold of Sam's hand and strode off out of the hall, straight to the members and guests who were waiting for them at the wedding reception which was being held in the well-cultivated gardens at the back of the Meeting House.

As they arrived, everyone applauded them quietly, but when Louie came up to hug Hannah, she had lost her previous exuberance, and tears were streaming down her cheeks. 'Oh, Hann,' she sobbed. 'Why didn't you tell me? Why didn't you tell me he was here?'

Hannah shook her head. 'I didn't know, Lou,' she replied. 'I swear to God I didn't know.'

They both turned to look as Len came out of the back entrance of the Meeting House.

'You have to talk to him, Hannah,' said Sam. Hannah shook her head. 'If you don't, this shadow is going to be hanging over you for the rest of your life.'

As he spoke, one of the members started to play an accordion, and within a few moments the newly married couple found themselves engulfed by well-wishers. Then people sat around at tables that had been laid out on the lawns, all of them chatting happily and feeding on the sandwiches, cakes and biscuits made by Mary and her fellow members, while tea was served from a huge enamel teapot by Mrs Mullard. The villagers who were there were intrigued by the lack of celebration as they knew it from their own traditional wedding receptions, particularly in the way that everyone seemed to be enjoying themselves in such an unhurried, quiet way. There were no speeches, and no dancing, but a young woman whom Hannah had once seen playing her violin as a child at a meeting in the House did so again, but this time it was a Quaker song that all the members knew and they were able to join in the words.

It was not until the celebrations were over that Hannah and Sam were left alone with Len Adams. Louie couldn't face up to seeing him, so she rushed off through the back door of the post office to wait for Hannah to come in and pass on to her whatever her former father had to say.

'If I talk to him,' Hannah asked Sam, 'will you come too?'

Sam shook his head. 'No, my darling one,' he replied, hugging her. 'This is between you and him now. It's time to know the

405

things you should have been told a long time ago.' He kissed her gently on the forehead, then went in at the back door of the post office.

For a moment, Hannah simply remained where Sam had left her. Then she gradually plucked up enough courage to look across at her father, who was on the far side of the lawn, smoking a fag at a table all on his own. Finally, she walked across to him, and stood before him in absolute silence.

'Yer look lovely, Hann,' he said, getting up from his chair, his hollow eyes staring up at her with pain and affection.

'Why did you come?' Hannah asked coldly.

'It's not ev'ry day yer daughter gets married,' he replied.

'Have you forgotten?' she asked. 'You don't *have* a daughter. You don't have any children of your own.'

'Sit down an' talk wiv me, Hann,' he pleaded. 'Just fer a minute – *please.*'

Hannah wanted to turn round and walk away from him, but she resisted the urge, and sat down at the table.

Len stubbed his fag out in an ashtray on the table, and sat opposite her. 'It broke my 'eart when I 'eard about yer mum,' he said, breaking the silence.

'Then why didn't you make contact with us when she died?'

Len knew that question was coming, and, like all the other questions he was going to have to answer, he was dreading it. 'When I was called up,' he started, 'she said she never wanted ter see me again. She said no matter wot 'appened to 'er, she didn't want me ter be a part of 'er life any more. I could've got compassionate leave ter come back fer the funeral – the army said I could – but I couldn't do it, Hann, I just couldn't do it. It wouldn't've bin right. Yer mum wouldn't've wanted it.'

'And what about me and Lou?' asked Hannah. 'How d'you think *we* felt? Couldn't you have written to us, just a few words – anything?'

'Your mum wrote ter me,' he replied. 'I know wot she told you about us . . .'

'About you and Miss Hobson, you mean?'

Len felt crushed.

'You couldn't face our knowing about the way you chased after our schoolteacher.'

'It wasn't like that, Hann,' he insisted. 'I swear ter God it wasn't.'

'Mum said you were obsessed with Dorothy Hobson.'

'I loved her, Hann.'

Hannah went quite cold, and looked away.

'I loved her, because yer mum turned away from me a long time ago. There was nuffin' I could do about it. I wanted to have kids, but yer mum didn't. It was only when she found out that . . . it wasn't possible becos er me, that she . . . started looking elsewhere. And so did I. But Dorothy . . . she was just a . . . kind, sweet, loving person . . . someone who I'd dreamt about all me life. Yes, I did love 'er . . . I was mad about 'er . . . but that's as far as it went. Dorothy wanted nuffin' ter do wiv me. She was disgusted with the way I went after 'er, an' *I* was gutted that she never wanted me.'

'How *could* you?' Hannah asked, with deep recrimination. 'You knew that you and Mum didn't love each other, but you let her go off and give you two kids by other men? And worse than that, all those years you let me and Lou believe that *you* was our dad.'

Len did not respond. He lowered his eyes, got up from the

table, and turned his back on her. In the far distance he could see a man with a horse and plough tilling the earth. It was a beautiful sight, for the sun had turned them into silhouettes which made them look like hand puppets against a bright wall.

'Have you any idea the agony you've put Lou and me through all these years?' said Hannah relentlessly. 'You went away as soon as the war started. That's more than five years ago – five years! And we haven't seen you once since then. Where were you, Mr Adams? Where were you?'

'Everywhere, Hann,' he replied, without turning back to her. 'Just about everywhere. But quite a lot of the time I was wiv Grandma and Granddad.'

Hannah got up from the table and went to him. 'Grandma and Granddad?' she asked with incomprehension. 'You mean – *they* knew about this?'

Len turned round to face her. 'They knew about a lot of things, Hann. They knew that I couldn't give my wife kids, but wot they didn't know was that – *she* couldn't eivver.'

Hannah was so stunned that for a moment all she could do was stand in silence and stare at him.

'I'm sorry, Hann, but it's true,' said Len grimly. 'That's why fings fell apart between yer mum an' me. You an' Lou never belonged ter me, an' yer never belonged to 'er eivver. You was boaf adopted.'

Hannah was so outraged that she suddenly became very angry. 'You're a liar!' she snapped. 'How can you say such a thing! Mum brought us up. She didn't like kids, she didn't want them, but she did her best to bring us up.'

'Yes, Hann,' conceded Len, 'I know that. But believe me, it's a fact. It really is a fact . . .'

'How can you say such a thing,' insisted Hann. 'Everyone said how I looked like her. I even had the same colour hair.'

'When we adopted you, yer were just tiny babies,' explained Len with immense distress. 'You were chosen becos . . . becos . . .'

'Because of the colour of my hair? I don't believe it! I just *can't* believe it!'

'With Lou, it was easy,' said Len. 'I could be taken as 'er farver anywhere. People often used ter say we looked alike.'

Hannah, distraught, returned to the table and sat there. Len waited a moment, then crouched down by her side. 'All I ever wanted in my life,' he said quietly, 'was ter 'ave kids of my own. When I knew boaf yer mum *an'* me couldn't 'ave 'em, it – tore me apart. But then when you an' Lou came along, I never fawt of yer boaf as anyfin' but *our* kids, our very *own* kids. The trouble was that wasn't enuff for yer mum. She wanted the real fing – or not at all. I never wanted ter hurt you, Hann. I never wanted ter hurt you nor Lou. That's why I never came back. After wot yer mum 'ad told yer, I didn't know 'ow I could ever face yer.'

Hannah looked down slowly at him. Tears were welling up in her eyes. He took the risk of reaching out for her hand. When she let him hold it, he felt so emotional he could hardly talk. 'I went back 'ome the uvver week,' he said. 'I still 'ave me key. You wasn't there, so there was no problem. The place ain't changed much. In fact it ain't changed a bit. Yer've kept our bedroom really nice. It was funny seein' 'er fings in the wardrobe . . .' Unable to continue talking, he got up, and reached into his jacket pocket. 'Here,' he said, handing her the key to the front door of the house in Kinloch Street. 'I fink yer'd better take this. I won't be needing it any more.'

Hannah took the key. He started to go, but suddenly remembered something. 'Oh,' he said, reaching into his inside jacket pocket. 'Dorothy Hobson asked me ter give yer this. She said she was sorry she an' 'er sister couldn't come terday, but she was sure yer'd understand why.'

Dazed with emotion, Hannah took the envelope.

'I'm sorry I've mucked up your day,' he said, 'but it'll be all right termorrow.'

As he went, Hannah suddenly sprang up from her seat and rushed after him. 'Dad!' she wept, throwing her arms round him.

They stood there hugging and embracing, the early afternoon sun just breaking through what had promised to be dark grey clouds. It was clearly going to turn out to be a very special summer afternoon.

Beechers Wood was looking very different from that traumatic evening when Hannah and Sam searched for Louie and Alfie Grieves in the dark. Today, it was streaked with tiny sunbeams just bursting through every branch and gap in the trees that they could find. As it was still only early May, the leaves and foliage were bright and alive, reflecting the dawn of an invigorating new season. The woods were also humming with beautiful sounds – birds of many different species fluttering excitedly in and out of the tall oak, elm, and chestnut trees, large bullfrogs croaking loudly in the cool shade somewhere down near the river bank, and the river itself, its surface rippling calmly as it flowed out from the man-made lake.

Hannah and Sam, their great day finally behind them, were determined to make one final pilgrimage to the spot they loved so much. The tree was still there, and so were the initials H and S that Sam had carved there with his penknife five years before. 'So what d'you think of this, Mrs Beedle?' asked Sam, arm round her waist, both of them peering close at the carvings. 'Not bad for an amateur?'

'Pretty good, Mr Beedle,' replied Hannah. 'At least this old feller doesn't seem to mind what you did to it.'

'How d'you know it's a feller?' asked Sam flippantly. 'Maybe it's a girl tree.' They both laughed.

'Oh, Sam,' sighed Hannah, as they both leant their backs against their tree, 'I can't believe how much has happened since that night we were here. Everything that's happened seems like a – a strange dream. But most of all – *you*. Did I ever tell you that you're the first boyfriend I've ever had – I mean the first boyfriend that I've ever actually *loved*?'

'And so I should hope!' replied Sam.

'Oh I've had plenty of others,' she teased. 'But when I met you I was only sixteen, and somehow – I just couldn't understand what was happening to me.' She paused a moment. 'What about you? Did you have girlfriends?'

'Oh, so many,' boasted Sam airily. 'I just couldn't keep count of them all!'

'Rubbish!' spluttered Hannah, digging him playfully in the ribs, and chasing after him as he ran off.

Their teasing shouts to each other soon disturbed the peace of the woods, and it was only when they collapsed with exhaustion down by the river bank that all the creatures who lived there dared to resume their busy activities where they had left off.

After peering down at their reflection in the river for a few minutes, Hannah sat up. 'You know, seeing Dad again like that

411

has made me feel so different, as though a whole load has been shifted from my shoulders. It was the same when I told Lou. She cried a lot, but then when she thought about all Dad had told me, about not belonging to either him *or* Mum, she just seemed to take it all in her stride.'

'That's what they call "growing up",' said Sam.

'Oh, she's doing that all right,' replied Hannah. 'In fact if you ask me, she's doing it pretty quickly. It won't be long before there's a second married daughter in the family!'

'So what happens to your dad now?' Sam asked, putting his arm round Hannah's shoulders. 'Will you see him again?'

'Eventually,' she replied. 'But it'd be wrong to blame him for all that's happened. It's funny, but I have the feeling that, despite everything, he really *did* love Mum. Anyway, he says he's looking for a job in the London Hospital up in the East End. Once he's settled down and found a place of his own, I think he'll get on his feet again.'

'Does that mean he'll find someone to settle down *with*?' asked Sam pointedly.

Hannah turned to look at him. 'I hope so, Sam,' she replied. 'I really hope so. Even so . . .' she sighed and looked out towards the river, 'I wish I knew just *something* about my real parents. It's not that I want to try to make them feel guilty or anything, but I hate that I don't know the kind of people they are, whether either me or Lou look like them, whether they got married and settled down, or even whether *they* feel guilty about what they did to Lou and me. I mean, I don't even know if me and Lou are even sisters.' She turned back to Sam again. 'I don't know,' she said wistfully. 'Maybe I should try to find out who and where they are?'

'If that's what you want, Hannah,' said Sam, slipping his arm round her waist, 'I'll do everything I can to help you. But if it was me, I think I'd want to leave well alone. Let's face it, after all these years they'd be perfect strangers to you. It'd be like opening up an old wound, both for them – and for you.'

As she clung on to him, she suddenly let out a yell. 'Oh my God!' she gasped.

Sam jumped. 'What is it? What's up?'

Hannah was in a flap, digging down frenziedly into her dress pocket. 'My letter!' she cried, suddenly producing the envelope her dad had given her. 'Miss Hobson. She wrote me a letter!' She quickly ripped open the envelope, and read aloud the contents.

12 May 1945   *Muswell Hill*
                                                                N.W. 10

My dearest Hannah,

First of all, let me say how very sorry Tilda and I are for not being able to come to what we're sure will have been the happiest day of your life. I can assure you that if it hadn't been for the extraordinary circumstances that have cast a shadow over our long years of friendship, nothing in the world would have prevented us from being there to support you and your dear husband Sam.

As you may have realised, I have for some time been in regular contact with the bearer of this letter. Your father first wrote to me after the tragic death of your mother, begging me to do whatever I could to help and advise you. It wasn't necessary for him to ask me, of course, for, as I once told you, I will always be there whenever you have need of me. However, now that you're a married woman, I feel that the time has

413

come for truth, the truth about my part in the extraordinary events that have involved me with your family over the years.

You already know of the tension that developed between your mother and me over the unfortunate situation regarding the attention your father had shown me some years ago. What you don't know, however, is that during the course of the last months before her death, your mother and I had come to a form of reconciliation which ended years of unpleasantness. That reconciliation came to a peak on the actual night she was killed by that explosion, just an hour or so after we had had the most wonderful meal at a restaurant near the Archway. I know you've always been mystified by who your mother spent those last few hours with on that fatal night, and deeply regret never having told you. However, it was your mother's wish that we should say nothing of the meeting, for what we talked about were the circumstances behind her own tragic inability to bear children, and the subsequent legal adoption of both you and your sister. But I want you to know this, dear Hannah. When your mother died, in no way did your father ignore the event. In fact, despite what he may have told you, he did go to her funeral, making quite sure that no one, especially you, were able to identify him.

And so, my dear, this sorry affair has at last drawn to a conclusion, with just one last confession still to come — from me. You once asked me if I loved your father, and, as I remember, I replied that it was a question I could never answer. But I can, Hannah. I did love your father. I loved him very much. But I want you to know that nothing in the world, neither now nor then, would ever persuade me to express that love in any way whatsoever.

That's all I have to say, dear one. If you feel that what I've

*told you is more than you can accept, is enough to prevent us
from seeing each other again, then I shall perfectly understand
your decision. But be sure that my affection and admiration for
you will remain, as that small child I taught English to at
school, and as the fine young woman you are today.*

*Go well with that wonderful young man of yours, and may
your life together make up for all the hard times past.*

With fond thoughts,

Dorothy Hobson.

The evening train for King's Cross was, as usual, two minutes late.
This always infuriated Ted Sputter the stationmaster, for he took a
pride in his job, and hated the way things were changing so fast,
the trains not nearly as efficient as they used to be. However, Hannah
and Sam had received a right royal send-off from Louie, Sam's
parents, Friends, and well-wishers from the village. Several people
were in tears, not least old Mrs Mullard, whose rheumatism seemed
to be restricting her more each day. When the train pulled away
from the station, a serene and dignified silence took over the platform, which continued long after the thin trail of black smoke
from the train's engine had dissolved high up in the sky.

As they had the compartment to themselves, Hannah and Sam
snuggled up together, and it was not long before Sam fell fast asleep
like a baby in Hannah's arms. Hannah herself, however, was wide
awake, her mind throbbing with all the events of the past twenty-
four hours, and in particular that extraordinary, moving letter from
an equally extraordinary woman. In some ways, everything that had
happened seemed now more like a dream, for she was having difficulty in bringing all the events of the past few days into focus. But
as she sat there, her mind drifting miles away from the passing

countryside of Hertfordshire, the one thing she came to realise was how wrong it was for two people like her dad and Dorothy Hobson to stay apart. Whatever either of them said now made no difference to what Hannah knew was a fact – these two people loved each other, and if circumstances had only been different, they would not be spending the rest of their lives regretting something they had lost. But what, if anything, could Hannah do about it? The answer only came when she gradually drifted off to sleep, where in a dream she could see herself taking hold of her dad's hand and linking it with Dorothy Hobson's, both of them smiling lovingly at one another. When Hannah's eyes opened again, the dream remained with her, and in a moment of complete determination her mind was hastily concocting a way to make it come true.

As she and Sam set out on their great new adventure, not only to the boatyards of Brighton, but also to what she prayed would be a life of love, not only for herself and Sam, but also for her dad and Dorothy Hobson, Hannah stared out dreamily from the train window, where the lush green fields of the English countryside were bathed in dazzling gold sunlight, and a radiant blue sky was no longer cluttered with barrage balloons or doodlebugs or rockets. Hannah had come a long way from that crowded compartment full of excited snotty-nosed school kids, who were somehow convinced that they were merely being taken on a lovely school outing. Oh yes – that was all a long time ago, almost a lifetime away. But times were changing now, slowly but surely. What would life be like without war, she pondered? Would it really be better, where people would no longer want to kill each other? It was difficult to see the future, whether it was going to be good or bad. All Hannah knew was that she had come through the worst, and was about to embark on the happiest period of her life.

JUST FOR YOU

Victor Pemberton

JUST FOR YOU

Find out…
All about Victor Pemberton

Picture…
Victor's experiences as a wartime evacuee

Discover…
The stars of the Second World War silver screen

Revealed…
How Victor started writing

JUST FOR YOU

Victor Pemberton

I was born in the London borough of Islington. I won't tell you when, other than to say that on the October day I was born it was not only extremely hot, but also the irascible midwife attending my mother was very angry that I was delaying her midday meal. On top of that, I apparently bawled so loudly that my father threatened to throw me out of the window. Not a good start for one so innocent, but at least I survived. And, fortunately, up until now, I am still surviving.

For a lad from, what was called in those days, 'the working class', I had a tough time sorting out what I wanted to do. All I knew was that I wanted to write, even if it was just something I could put in a drawer and leave, before throwing away the key. I was lucky enough to win a free place at Highbury Grammar School where my headmaster was more intent on forcing me to learn about mathematics than write stories that nobody would ever read. When I left school, I was offered a job as a junior reporter on the *Daily Sketch*, but as my headmaster refused to let me attend evening classes to learn shorthand, I lost out, and ended up as a mail delivery boy for a timber magazine in Fleet Street. That was followed by a short spell in the publicity and printing department of Twentieth Century Fox in Soho Square, where I became starry-eyed every time I saw a famous Hollywood star come through the doors of the front foyer. I've been starry-eyed about such names ever since, which is why I always carried an autograph book in my back pocket. The collection became quite formidable, and is probably now worth a king's ransom – well a prince's anyway.

After less than a year there, I was whisked off to do two years' national service in the Royal Air Force, not as a pilot, as I sometimes pretended to be, but as a common or garden AC plonk airman, setting up entertainment for the men and women on the base. I even had my own record request programme called *Our Choice* and was apparently quite good at being a disc jockey, playing songs by Bing Crosby, the Ink Spots, and Mantovani and his orchestra!

How I started writing is explained later on, but funnily enough, although my parents, Letty and Oliver, knew nothing about writing, the support they gave me for whatever I wanted to do in life was quite extraordinary. My dad, who was known by everyone as 'Pop', even bought me my first typewriter. It cost £5, and I still have it to this day, sitting near alongside me whilst I use its twenty-first-century grandchild to concoct my tales. It is greatly loved and never to be deserted. *'Guess what, Pop?'* I said as I started to type. *'I'm going to be a writer.' 'Good fer you, boy,'* he replied. *'But what you goin' ter do for a livin'?'* What indeed! Heartaches, rejections, rejections, rejections. I wouldn't be a writer without rejections. In fact, I had enough of them to wallpaper my bedroom!

That's why it's rather nice that at this time in my life I can sit back and read one of the lovely things my publisher has said about me on the cover sleeve of my novels: *'Victor's heartwarming London sagas have gained him an army of fans from all over the world, who all feel that he captures the vibrancy of life in wartime London like no other saga author.'*

If that's true, then I am indeed a lucky man.

JUST FOR YOU

My memories of being evacuated...

As a young lad, the start of the Second World War brought not only the prospect of bloodshed on the fields of continental Europe, but also the first real threat of bombing raids on mainland Britain, and in particular my own beloved Holloway in North London. By the time I had got to fully understand the meaning of the word 'evacuation', it seemed that all my schoolmates, my elder brother and myself had been lined up on the pavements outside our school, clutching carrier bags bulging with sandwiches, Tizer and lemonade, cardboard gas mask boxes flung carelessly over our shoulders, and identity tags pinned to the lapels of our coats. This was the autumn of 1939, and as we climbed onto the charabancs that were to take us away from our parents and homes, none of us had any idea that we were leaving, not on a day's outing to the sea, but on a traumatic journey away from everyone and everything we had come to know in our young lives.

Over the years, many people have asked me about what it was like to be 'evacuated', and in one sense A LONG WAY HOME is my way of expressing what I really felt like at the time. I hated the experience. Dragged away to a quiet corner of Hertfordshire, my brother and I were part of a group of boys from our school who were billeted with a sadistic retired colonel and his wife and teenage son. They were a fearsome family who treated us as though we were scruffy refugees from the back-streets of London, who needed to be bathed thoroughly before they could sleep in clean sheets, and whose hair had to be inspected daily for lice. We were treated more like soldier recruits than children, our quarters inside the grand mansion house a military billet with single iron-framed beds lined up each side of the room, and tiny bedside wardrobes for our few clothes and possessions. The communal toilets were outside in the vast formal gardens, a long walk from the house, especially in the middle of a chilly autumn night. To this day I can still remember those plain wooden seats placed over what turned out to be little more than aluminium slop buckets, which, after use, had to be emptied by ourselves in a specially dug ditch. Just imagine what it was like for small kids to have to sneak out into the garden at dead of night, freezing cold, scared stiff of the dark, the strange hooting of night owls, and the sight of alien things like trees and bushes, all casting eerie, menacing shadows in the sparse moonlight, which kept popping in and out of unwel-coming night clouds. But most of all, it was the lack of warmth from the colonel and his family that I remember most of all. In their minds, we were just snotty-nosed urchins from the London backstreets, who were lucky to have such generous foster parents prepared to protect us from the threat of bombing raids – a threat that did not materialise during that early period known as the 'Phoney War'.

As I point out in the preface of this book, not all foster parents were like the dreaded colonel. In fact, some of my schoolmates were treated with such kindness that when the great flood of evacuees eventually returned home to the gritty London streets, their real parents seemed more like strangers to them. Yes, it was a traumatic time for us young refugees. For those of you who have read my first novel, OUR FAMILY, you will know what a relief it was for me and my elder brother when our mum and dad finally turned up to take us home, especially when the colonel tried to lecture them on how children should be brought up. *'Don't talk to me about kids!'* snapped my battling mum. *'I've had three of my own!'*

JUST FOR YOU

The stars of the Second World War silver screen…

During the Second World War, a lot of kids in towns across Britain had the time of their lives. Getting up at crack of dawn after the previous night's air raid, we scanned the pavements, roads and front gardens for fragments of ack-ack shrapnel, clambering up with our buckets on to the rooftops of sheds and out-houses, searching the gutters for anything left over from the fierce aerial bombardment, all of which we would deposit at the local ARP post for recycling. We were the 'Kids' Army', a great addition to the war effort. However, some of us found the whole experience of spending every night down the Anderson air-raid shelter in the back yard wearisome and unnatural. Add to that the dark grey skies of English weather, especially during the winter months, and the very real danger of sudden air raids whilst at school, there seemed little to be cheerful about – little hope that the war would ever end.

However, there *was* one real saviour to all the depression, a knight in shining armour who distracted us from the real world of bombs, who helped us kids and their mum and dads to escape to lands draped in glorious colour. The pictures! What *would* we have done without our ninepennyworth of dark in the auditorium of the local picture house? Despite Hollywood's recent attempts to get us all to call them 'movies' and despite their constant insistence that all the great heroes of the Second World War were American, during that period 'the pictures', both American and British, gave us courage, hope, and strength. Who cared that the programme might be interrupted with a flash at the bottom of the screen proclaiming: '*Will patrons please note that the air-raid alert has just sounded. We ask that all those who wish to leave the cinema do so as quietly as possible. For those patrons who wish to remain, the programme will continue*'? And, despite the cacophony of gunfire and bombs exploding outside, hardly anyone ever left their seats. Well, let's face it, it would have been inconceivable for us to desert the enchantments of Vivien Leigh as Scarlett O'Hara at Tara in my favourite film of all time, *Gone With the Wind*, or the garish Technicolor of those dazzling MGM and Twentieth Century Fox musicals such as *The Wizard of Oz*, *Down Argentine Way*, *Meet Me in St Louis* and *Hello Frisco Hello*. For me, the moment I set eyes on those famous Betty Grable legs, listened to the warmth of Alice Faye singing 'You'll Never Know', and the magnetic voice of Judy Garland belting out 'Over the Rainbow' and 'Clang, Clang, Clang Goes The Trolley', the bombing in the streets of Holloway outside the picture house just didn't exist. Having said that, however, I have to say that films made in good old black and white during the war were just as much a part of the war effort as kids scrawling rude messages about Hitler on the coping stones of many a London front garden.

I could, of course, list a whole lot of 'pictures' that inspired me during those dark days, but I cannot fail to single out first and foremost, *The First of the Few*, Leslie Howard's moving biographical story of R. J. Mitchell, who designed the Spitfire fighter aircraft, which, thanks to the RAF, became the bane of the German Luftwaffe and certainly helped to win the Battle of Britain. Leslie Howard, who was later killed in a civil airliner shot down by a renegade squadron of the Luftwaffe over the Bay of Biscay, had proved to be one of the great British pioneer filmmakers, and who returned to London from Hollywood at the start of the war to reinvigorate the British film industry by producing morale-boosting propaganda feature films. No wonder the Nazis desperately wanted to get rid of him. But then I mustn't forget that wonderful array of British film actors who were the patriotic core of Second World War films. Hollywood may have had its John Wayne, Errol Flynn and Clark Gable, but we had our own Richard Attenborough, John Mills and David Niven, not to mention the great actresses (*not* Actors as they are called today), such as Celia Johnson, Margaret Lockwood, Kathleen Harrison – all of them the absolute backbone of British cinema. To my dying day, I shall never forget Noël Coward's *In Which We Serve*, in which he himself starred as Louis Mountbatten, Commander of a ship that was attacked and sunk during enemy action. All the gang were there: Attenborough, Mills, Bernard Miles, and so many familiar faces. The picture itself became a legend around the world. No one, including myself, could have failed to feel intense emotion and pride as we left 'the picture house'.

The Way Ahead was another memorable British war film. The story of a platoon of raw recruits right up to the final battle-front featured a much-loved cast of stalwarts such as David Niven, Stanley Holloway and William Hartnell. Then there was *The Foreman Went to France*, based on a true incident, and starring that loveable icon of the music hall, Tommy Trinder, in his first dramatic role. He played a foreman who, before Dunkirk, was sent to France to bring back some secret French machinery.

Finally, I cannot halt this journey down my own cinematic memory lane without mentioning another great tribute to the RAF which came at the end of the war. *The Way To The Stars* was about an active wartime airbase as seen through the eyes of guests at a small hotel nearby. The stalwarts were there again, John Mills, Michael Redgrave, Stanley Holloway, Trevor Howard, and even a young Jean Simmons singing *'Let him go, Let him tarry.'* But I shall always remember the film for that poignant poem by John Pudney, *Johnny in the Clouds.*

So there you have it. Those are but a few of the 'pictures' that helped me to survive the war, but as we all know, there were many more, too many to mention here. I know that over the years, most of these 'pictures' have been seen on television, but I do hope that one day some enterprising film distributor will show a long season of the films that helped to keep us all going during those dark days. Of course, my older readers will no doubt remember them well, but it would also give our new generation the opportunity to know what it was that their grandmas and granddads escaped to, even if they are far removed from *Star Wars!*

Some people call me a real film buff. I don't mind that at all. In fact I quite like it. After all, I might not have lived to tell the story of A LONG WAY HOME if it hadn't been for Vivien Leigh, John Mills, Richard Attenborough, and all those glorious stars of the Second World War silver screen . . .

JUST FOR YOU

How I started writing…

When I was young, I had never thought about writing for anyone but myself. The idea that I could be egotistical enough to think that someone would want to read anything I had written had truly never occurred to me – that is, until I was challenged to do otherwise. This extraordinary turn of events came about in 1961. At the time I was a young travel clerk in the offices of Sir Henry Lunn Limited in the Edgware Road, London, sharing a flat just across the road with two actors, who both went on to become very distinguished in their own careers in acting and directing. My annual earnings were £600, which didn't really give me many opportunities to eat at the Ritz, but I did manage to get the occasional free airline ticket which I used to great advantage!

However, as I wasn't in 'the business' (meaning the business of acting or writing or directing plays), I used to spend hours listening to my two flatmates talking about this person's performance and how good or badly directed this or that was, and so I assumed quite innocently that I too could do the same. How wrong I was, for when I launched into criticism of plays I had

431

seen on television or heard on the radio, or the films I had seen, my two flatmates rounded on me with the challenge: 'Well, if you so know so much, try writing something yourself!' I swallowed hard, retired to my bedroom in a sulk, and wondered how I was going to redeem whatever dignity I had left. That was the beginning!

I spent many happy years writing on and off for radio, and was lucky and grateful enough to have a great number of plays, series and serials produced by Audrey Cameron, John Tydeman and David Spenser. I look back on my days in radio with great affection, not only because of the talented and considerate people who worked in BBC radio drama in those days, people like John Tydeman, Peter Bryant, Keith Williams, Richard Imison and, of course, my long-time friend David Spenser, but also because writing for radio taught me how to use my imagination, how to use the spoken word with no help from background sets, how to present a character to my listeners and let them decide what those characters looked like, just the same as I can now do in writing novels. Make no mistake about it, radio is a wonderful training ground for the writer, and I hope that those who have the power of commission in radio drama today will never fail to encourage the fertile minds of those who have so much to offer.

In 1990, Headline Book Publishing invited me to do a novelisation of my BBC radio drama series, *Our Family*. This was a saga, spanning the years 1917 to 1980, and based almost entirely on my own family history. I called it a love story, for that is what it was, an extraordinary union between two people from different class structures, who remained devoted to each other for nearly sixty years of married life. As on radio, the novel was well reeeived, prompting a huge public response, and Headline asked me to continue with more novels, which I have continued to set in and around the area in which I was born – North London.

To learn more about Victor Pemberton and his much-loved North London sagas, you can visit his website: www.victorpemberton.com

We'll Sing at Dawn

Victor Pemberton

Islington, October 1940.

As a German bomber pilot releases his deadly load overhead, the residents of Hornsey Road are singing their hearts out. Sheltering in a disused piano factory, men, women and children gather round Beth Shanks, who is belting out old favourites on an abandoned piano. As they lose themselves in 'Run, Rabbit, Run' and 'Knees Up, Muvver Brown', the locals can briefly forget the damage being wrought in the streets above.

But as Beth battles to keep up everyone's spirits, she herself carries a terrible burden. The police know an Irish national has been passing secrets to the Germans, and they want Beth to keep an eye on her sweetheart, Thomas Sullivan. Beth is convinced they've got the wrong man, but when evidence of Thomas's guilt mounts, she finds herself in a dangerous dilemma . . .

Praise for Victor Pemberton's well-loved sagas:

'A vivid story of a community surviving some of the darkest days in our history' *Bolton Evening News*

'Warm and entertaining . . . brimming with the atmosphere of wartime London' *Coventry Evening Telegraph*

'You can almost hear air-raid sirens as Pemberton spins another superb story of London folk during wartime' *Peterborough Evening Telegraph*

0 7553 2384 X

headline

The Chandler's Daughter

Victor Pemberton

1937: The year of the coronation of King George VI and a pivotal year for Grace Higgs. Her father's death brings not only loneliness and heartache, but also the shocking revelation that he was up to his eyes in debt.

Determined to save her father's business, Grace takes up the reins of his chandler's horse and cart to walk the bustling streets of Islington. It's not an easy job for a woman on her own, and Grace soon realises she may have to sell up.

But Gus Higgs was a man of many surprises, and there is one last discovery for his daughter to make. It's the key to a secret that will change her life for ever, and guarantee that Grace will never be lonely again . . .

Praise for Victor Pemberton's heartwarming novels:

'Warm and entertaining . . . brimming with the atmosphere of wartime London' *Coventry Evening Telegraph*

'A vivid story of a community surviving some of the darkest days in our history' *Bolton Evening News*

'Pemberton spins another superb story of London folk during wartime' *Peterborough Evening Telegraph*

0 7553 0237 0

headline

A Perfect Stranger

Victor Pemberton

The advent of the Second World War changes everything. So, when Tom, home on leave, asks Ruth to marry him, she agrees. After all, once Tom returns to the front, who knows if they'll ever see each other again? But months go by and Tom's letters dry up. Ruth is forced to get on with her life and starts to enjoy the attentions of another man. It is this temptation which will alter her life for ever. And when the war is finally over she will find the battle for her own personal freedom and safety has just begun . . .

A Perfect Stranger is a deeply emotional, evocative and gripping account of the difficult decisions facing women left on their own.

Praise for Victor Pemberton's wartime sagas

'A wonderfully detailed and involving study of a community surviving the destruction of war' Barry Forshaw, *Amazon*

'A potent mix of passion and suspense' *Evening Herald*

'A vivid story of a community surviving some of the darkest days in our history . . . warm-hearted' *Bolton Evening News*

'A real treat' *Peterborough Evening Telegraph*

'Warm and entertaining . . . brimming with the atmosphere of wartime London' *Coventry Evening Telegraph*

0 7472 6653 0

headline